Mr Toppit

CHARLES ELTON

VIKING
an imprint of
PENGUIN BOOKS

VIKING

Published by the Penguin Group

Penguin Books Ltd, 80 Strand, London WC2R ORL, England

Penguin Group (USA) Inc., 375 Hudson Street, New York, New York 10014, USA

Penguin Group (Canada), 90 Eglinton Avenue East, Suite 700, Toronto, Ontario, Canada M4P 2Y3
(a division of Pearson Penguin Canada Inc.)

Penguin Ireland, 25 St Stephen's Green, Dublin 2, Ireland (a division of Penguin Books Ltd)

Penguin Group (Australia), 250 Camberwell Road, Camberwell, Victoria 3124, Australia
(a division of Pearson Australia Group Pty Ltd)

Penguin Books India Pvt Ltd, 11 Community Centre, Panchsheel Park, New Delhi – 110 017, India

Penguin Group (NZ), 67 Apollo Drive, Rosedale, North Shore 0632, New Zealand
(a division of Pearson New Zealand Ltd)

Penguin Books (South Africa) (Pty) Ltd, 24 Sturdee Avenue,
Rosebank, Johannesburg 2196, South Africa

Penguin Books Ltd, Registered Offices: 80 Strand, London WC2R ORL, England

www.penguin.com

First published 2009

1

Copyright © Darkwood Ltd, 2009

Set in 12/15 pt Monotype Dante
Typeset by Rowland Phototypesetting Ltd, Bury St Edmunds, Suffolk
Printed in Great Britain by Clays Ltd, St Ives plc

A CIP catalogue record for this book is available from the British Library

ISBN: 978–0–670–91781–5

www.greenpenguin.co.uk

Mr Toppit

For Lotte Elton and Abraham Elton

Part One

Luke

And out of the Darkwood Mr Toppit comes, and he comes not for you, or for me, but for all of us.

It had taken Mr Toppit a very long time to arrive, and while the wait was not a problem, the brevity of his appearance clearly was for the small coven of dissenters who felt, frankly, short-changed by the fact that when he did turn up, it was only in the last sentence of what turned out to be the last book of my father's *Hayseed Chronicles*. But what I think is that the majority of the *Hayseed* faithful were secretly rather relieved not to have to face the almost certain anticlimax of a more definitive appearance by Mr Toppit. At any rate, there has never been any shortage of people telling me in numbing detail which side of this particular fence they sit, Mr Toppit-wise. In fact, I firmly believe that, throughout the world, wherever men gather to communicate and converse, from the *Kaffeeklatschen* of Vienna to the boardrooms of Wall Street to the rock churches of Ethiopia, someone somewhere will be discussing what the last sentence of the last book actually means. Personally, I have no idea.

If I could remember a time before *Hayseed*, I think it would seem so golden to me that I could only presume I had imagined it. The truth is that there is no Before. Although it was only some years after his death that my father was elected to the sainthood of children's authors, the sales of the books had always been steady, though modest, and the name of Luke Hayseed not unknown among more progressive parents, who felt their children should not be shielded from the cruelties and uncertainties of life – the very cruelties and uncertainties that were the stock-in-trade of the *Hayseed* books. But what is undeniable is that I was not, at that time, accosted by complete strangers in restaurants or pinned up against walls during cocktail parties by people telling me how I had ruined their childhood or – much, much worse – how I had been an inspiration to them.

Our mother, Martha Hayman, always maintained that anybody could have known something extraordinary was going to happen. While the efficacy of Martha's dark powers was never in question, I doubt whether even she could have predicted that Laurie's spontaneous decision to add the 'Hayseed Half-hour' to her radio broadcasts in Modesto, California, would have been the catalyst for what subsequently happened.

But by the time Laurie had graduated from radio to television – still talking about *The Hayseed Chronicles* – not only the books themselves were all over the place but also a book *about* the books. By the time *Hayseed Karma*, originally published by a small press in Modesto whose biggest seller to date had been a guide to the bicycle trails of Stanislaus County, had sat on the *New York Times* bestseller list for forty-seven weeks, it was clear that it was time for the extant members of the Hayman family to acknowledge that something extraordinary had indeed happened.

I don't keep a complete set – why would I? I was there at the beginning. I *was* the beginning – but if you trawl book shops and gift shops and computer shops and duty-free shops and mail-order catalogues, and ads in this magazine or that magazine, and special offers on the back of certain cereal packets, you will find some of the following: the original five paperbacks (of course), the boxed set of the original five paperbacks, the activity book for older readers, the hardback deluxe compendium edition with the coloured (or colourized – the originals were black-and-white) illustrations, the board game ('A throw of the dice decides which entrance you take into the Darkwood'), the PlayStation Hayseed game ('Do you dare to be Mr Toppit?'), the Royal Doulton cereal-bowl set, the eggcups, the porcelain figurines of Luke, the DayGlo rucksacks, the pencil boxes, the notepaper, the Christmas cards, the T-shirts with 'My brother went to the Darkwood and all Mr Toppit allowed him to bring back was this lousy T-shirt' emblazoned on the back (unauthorized, I suspect – I'll get the lawyers on to it), the baseball caps and the keyrings.

For me, it is a slow descent into merchandise hell, and whenever I find myself there, I think of Lila, for it was her drawings that had trapped me in it, those simple pen drawings she had done for love. The publishers had paid her a flat fee and, in signing whatever contract they had flashed before her, she had passed the copyright to them. It was a small price to pay to secure her position in the *Hayseed* Hall of Fame and, though I still find it hard to believe, she appears to feel no resentment even though so much money has been made by everyone other than her. What she feels, as she tells everyone she meets – now mostly television-repair men as she's waiting for her second hip – is simple happiness that she could be 'a small part of it all', *ein kleiner Teil des Ganzen*.

The *Hayseed* drawings and her life with the Hayman family are all the fuel she needs to keep her warm at night, to get her through the day. Her flat, which my sister Rachel and I called 'the shrine', *does* contain every piece of merchandise, jostling alongside scrapbooks of press clippings and photographs in silver frames. She should break and tear and grind into dust every single one for what the books did to her. Now I can almost forgive her for pinning me down like a fly in aspic, trapping me on the page (on the mug, on the teacup, on the pencil box), dressed in those ridiculous pantaloons, secured almost up to my armpits with the cord from Mr Toppit's dressing-gown, the gardener's boots on my feet and a battered straw hat on my head.

She only added those details later – the drawings for the first book were much simpler, before my father had really created the world of the Darkwood. At the beginning, she kept me still on the chair in the kitchen with her legendary child-skills: 'If you do not stop fidgeting, I shall draw you with only one eye and no hair, and when you wake up in the morning that is what you shall look like.' I kept still. Her pen scratched, her eyes darted back and forth from the sketchpad to me.

5

From behind me Rachel would shout, 'Is it my turn next? Is it me now?'

And Lila never let me look. When I leaned over, she cupped her hands over the paper. I only knew the next morning how she had drawn me as I stared at myself in the mirror, touching my eyes, counting my fingers.

After the first book, she needed me less and less. She had created the template and she spun Luke Hayseed off in a direction of her own, taking him away from me (taking me away from me) and creating the likeness of a boy who would stride manfully up the path to the Darkwood. He would always be eager to return to his quest to find Mr Toppit, to flush him out, even though – as Luke knew to his cost – Mr Toppit could be cruel and capricious, and never really did, despite the last sentence of the book, reveal himself, and even though the Darkwood, every leaf and branch and stone of which Mr T inhabited, was a dank, terrifying place.

You wouldn't have caught me dead doing that.

When you were young, or maybe not so long ago, not very far from where you live, or perhaps a little closer, Luke Hayseed lived in a big old house. The woods behind the house were called the Darkwood and Luke Hayseed thought he owned them, that they were his, that they were in his blood. If trees and leaves and brown earth could travel through veins, they did so through Luke's. But if he thought he was the only one to have them in his blood, he was very wrong, as wrong as it was possible to be.

Listen: there are some rules. It isn't that I object to my childhood being ransacked, my past being vandalized, my name being stolen – not only stolen but worse: diminished, scaled down – but there should be some sense of fair play.

First, the books should have sprung out of bedtime stories. Yes, that's the way it ought to be done – a story created to soothe a frightened child in a thunderstorm, say, or a fantastical tale woven round a favourite toy, or a fanciful explanation of why certain things in the world are as they are. These stories, simple but full of meaning, unstructured but truthful, quite clearly hit such a nerve in the child (the crying child, the wide-eyed child, the enchanted child) that their weaver knows that children *all round the world* will respond in the same way.

Or what about this? Some modest note at the beginning, some disingenuous foreword implying that, despite the writer's natural diffidence, his children's lusty cries for 'More, please!' impelled him, reluctantly, of course, and with no great hope of success, to offer these humble scribblings to other children in the vain hope that perhaps they, too, would find some small pleasure in them.

Second, there should be some truth in the stories, some little nugget (at least) that rings true. The fact is, Luke Hayseed, *c'est moi*, and even I do not know where it all comes from, all that stuff in the books. I'm not saying precisely that nothing is truthful. I'm saying I don't understand the connections, and it is these connections, or whatever you want to call them – the links, the adapters, the conduits, the funnels, the transformers – that constitute the lie that became *The Hayseed Chronicles*, the lie that turned Luke into Luke.

For instance: when we were children there was a particular lavender bush by the corner of the house. In the summer the flowers were covered with bees, circling and humming and landing. I spent hours watching them, and there came a moment when I realized something important.

What I knew was this: they did not want to be there and they could not help themselves. What I did was this: I moved them from the bush and put them under the shade of a tree in another part of the garden. I picked them up, I held their wings together between thumb and forefinger and I laid them on my palm and carried them through the garden to put them under the particular tree I had chosen, which I knew, with unerring certainty, the kind of certainty I would kill for today, was where they wanted to be. And I was never stung.

In the second book, *Garden Green*, in which Mr Toppit's influence begins to be felt, this is what happens:

Luke Hayseed was not sure if night was drawing to a close or if day was drawing to an open. At any rate, he sat bolt upright in bed. He knew that Mr Toppit had been in his room.

Mr Toppit had not come through the window. Luke had left the window closed – he always did, not that Mr Toppit would ever have been so obvious as to come through the window, even one so high up that Mr Toppit could have been accused of showing off had he come through it.

But he had been in the room – Luke knew that. He knew it because of the bee. On Luke's bedside table, beside the goose-necked lamp, was a dead bee with one wing off, its body curled up, its zebra-striped fur looking dull and dusty. Now, there were often dead insects lying casually around the house without a care in the world – flies or woodlice or silverfish or earwigs or sometimes even butterflies. But this particular bee did not have the air of not having a care in the world. It had a curious preciseness. Not for this insect was there the spontaneity of lying down and dying where it felt like it. This bee had been positioned for effect.

With Mr Toppit nothing was ever simple, and normally there was more than one clue to what he wanted. Luke got out of bed. The room was cold, and in his pyjamas he felt rather exposed, even though he knew that clothes alone were no particular protection against Mr Toppit.

The giveaway – not that Mr Toppit ever precisely gave anything away – lay in the doorway and Luke found it in a second. Too easy, he was already thinking, but he could not help bending down and picking up the sprig of lavender that lay on the carpet. He brought it up to his nose, and smelled what was left of its smell, which was nothing much.

It clearly purported to have been lying there for some time, as if it had dropped casually from a vase of old flowers that was being cleared out of his room. Except there were never flowers in his room – actually, there were never flowers in the house, even though the garden was full of them. The flowers did not seem to travel well, certainly not into the house. The garden was a different world, and too close – for Luke's liking – to Mr Toppit's domain of the Darkwood.

But Luke knew what he must do, for by this time he had begun to know what Mr Toppit wanted from him, even though he did not always know why. He knew what the connection between the bee and the lavender was. It came to him, as he stood in his pyjamas, as he stood in the doorway, as he stood knowing what danger he was in.

Actually, this is one of the most famous moments in the books – one that defines the warm glow of collective memory, particularly when shared between strangers on long-haul flights unfortunate enough to be hijacked by terrorists. 'Hayseed Kept Us Sane, Say Plane Hostage Survivors', one headline ran, after the plane that had languished on the runway of a disused military airstrip in the desert for three days had finally been liberated. And on the news the two survivors in question, a vet from Portsmouth and a lay preacher in a Seventh Day Adventist church, their faces shiny with relief, told the camera crew how they had coped with their ordeal.

'Christ, I thought we were done for,' the vet whoops, his face blurring as the cameraman tries to hold focus. The Seventh Day Adventist composes himself amid the airport pandemonium and just manages to check a little grimace at the use of 'Christ', although I imagine being stuck on a plane for three days alongside 280 other passengers in ninety-degree heat with four clogged lavatories would be enough to test the faith of any preacher, lay or otherwise.

'When Mustapha – that's what we called the head guy, the one with the big gun and the orange mask – took the old woman and shot her in the cockpit, we thought it was over for all of us. Everyone was screaming and Jonathan,' he nudged his new friend, so we would know who he was talking about, 'Jonathan turned to me, we hadn't talked much, nobody had talked much since . . . you know, and he said, "Do you remember Luke Hayseed and the bees?" and it kind of broke the ice and we both creased up. It was just the way he said it.'

Jonathan, anxious for his moment in the sun, cuts in here: 'Whenever I'm tested, I think of that moment when he's crossing the lawn with the bees in his hand' – the vet's head bobbing up and down, 'Yeah, yeah' – 'and somehow things don't seem so . . .' What, Jonathan, what? I need to know this, but at that very moment a stretcher, carried by a gang of medics, crashes into the frame at some speed, almost knocking the two men over.

You can't hear what the interviewer says next, even though the boom is hovering at the top of the frame like a mangy cat. The vet leaps into action: 'My family, my kids, see my mum and dad. Have a bath. And I'm going to get that video – show my kids.' Then Jonathan and the vet beam at each other, friends for life, linked by their shared recollection of brave Luke and the Bees.

I watched gobsmacked: while it was true that the bee sequence in the television series was frightening – much more so than in the book – it seems to me, as the one who did the transporting, that, in perspective terms at least, a group of terrorists strutting up and down the aisle of the stranded plane brandishing a prodigious amount of firepower, which they had not hesitated to use, both on the old lady in the cockpit and on two hapless Dutchmen whose bodies had been dispatched through the emergency doors, marginally had the edge over the bees.

But what do I know? I'm only Luke Hayseed – and it's true that when the video of the TV series was first released, there had been a brief flurry of excitement when a national newspaper had taken up a crusading teacher's campaign to ban any videos that contained sequences disturbing to children. Her blacklist included the *Hayseed* videos, at which her anger was particularly directed because her six-year-old son had apparently been stung by a bee *while actually watching that episode*. The absurd coincidence of this seemed to escape her, but the boy now screamed uncontrollably if he saw a television set because who knew what beast might come out of it next and attack him? '*This could happen to any child*,' she told an afternoon chat-show host, her voice trembling with indignation.

I loved it. Lila, our self-appointed archivist, scanned the papers daily for all references to this extraordinary debate and Xeroxed them in quadruplicate: a copy each for Martha, Rachel, me, and one – most importantly – for what Lila called 'The Big Book of Hayseed', leatherbound and stored always in her flat. I basked in a warm glow: at last, some justice in the world – years of expensive therapy for a generation of children weaned on the video, hands over their eyes, just a crack open between their pudgy fingers, screaming, 'They're going to sting him! They're going to sting him!' as the buzzing reaches a crescendo on the soundtrack, if not in the very room they are sitting in.

And on the screen, Luke 3 – let's get the pecking order right: I am Luke 1, Lila's version is Luke 2, and Toby, the boy actor whose career took such a spectacular downturn after the series ended and who now has AIDS rumours circling around him like vultures ('Gaunt Appearance of TV's Luke Hayseed – Shock Pictures'), is Luke 3 – teeters through the garden, his brave-but-frightened face intercut with closeups of superbees the size of rats, whose stings could clearly fell a giant.

Spot the difference, spot the mistake. It is this: plucky, spunky Luke 3 overcomes his natural fear (knowing what danger he is in) to perform this terrifying and thankless task for the unsatisfiable (as it turns out) Mr Toppit.

Luke 1, for whom pluck and spunk are strangers from beyond Venus, performs this task without either bravery or fear. He does it because he knows it to be right, and the very certainty of the act gives it a dignity so lacking in Luke 3 that it takes your breath away.

But the point for me is this: they were my bees and I do not remember offering them up to the world.

There was a family. There was us. My father and mother, and Rachel and Luke, the Hayman children who became the Hayseed children. Rachel handled it quite differently from me but, then, her problems were quite different from mine.

The last time I saw Rachel properly, when she was in one of the many clinics she had got to know so well, taken like a favoured diner in a restaurant to her usual table, when she was in denial or in recovery or in remission or in relapse or hovering in a place she had made uniquely her own – the cusp between all of them – she had at last reached a state of complete impasse: she had stopped doing anything at all.

What she wanted, I think, was to stay in one place in her head. Claude said once, 'Rachel has drug-dealers like other people have accountants or dentists.' He knew because he had introduced her to them. For years, she was always going down or up, taking drugs to feel good or taking drugs to stop feeling bad, conscious like a chess-player of each move, and each move beyond that, trying always to second-guess her body and altering her moves to achieve the perfect combination that would keep her in that one place. I think the permutations finally became too many for her to cope with, spinning off into space, dividing and subdividing with terrifying rapidity. Everything altered everything else – a cigarette smoked, a dress worn, a line snorted, a door opened, a preference stated, a road crossed – until the only way she could see of just *being* was to do nothing at all, to sit in a chair absolutely silent.

The nurse who took me to her room told me she was quite co-operative over feeding – would allow herself to be fed, that is – and was lifted in and out of bed with no resistance. However, she would not look at anyone, or answer a question directed at her. If forced to do something she did not want to do, she would cover her eyes and ears with her hands and curl up in a ball, but make no sound. I did not ask about the lavatory arrangements because I suspected that nappies might come into it.

It had been a long time since I had seen her. She was sitting in a straight-backed armchair staring out of the window, but when I knelt down in front of her and took her hand, I could see that her eyes were not really focusing on anything. 'Are you going to talk to me, Rach?' I asked her. 'You don't have to.'

Clearly, she was not going to, but maybe she made some small acknowledgement that I was there, a gentle squeeze of my hand. Or maybe not. It was hard to tell.

What a consummate theatrical pro, I suddenly thought. I knew and she knew. We were back playing a game – who can stare longest without smiling: a game we had often played as children. But this was clearly not to be acknowledged now she was surrounded yet again by a phalanx of shrinks trying to coax her back into some semblance of normality, paid for – to my mother's fury – by the cascade of royalties from the books, the pencil boxes and the eggcups.

'We could call this chapter of your life "Homage to Catatonia". What do you think?' I said. No response. '"Portrait of the Autist as a Young Woman"?'

Did the corners of her mouth turn up a little? I considered tickling her ribs – she had always been responsive to that as a child – but then I thought she should be allowed to keep her dignity, if that was the word for it.

Then I saw something odd. Under her chair, the corner of a book was peeping out and I recognized it instantly from the bit of the jacket I could see. It was *Darkwood*, the last of the series, with Lila's illustration of Luke's back and head bathed in a celestial yellow light, dwarfed by a huge and menacing wall of trees that was parting in front of him to reveal a strange glow in the darkness. Not difficult for anyone to guess what the book was, actually, because there was a pastiche of the illustration on the cover of . a solo album, also called *Darkwood*, by a member of Yes, whose permed locks stood in for Luke's pudding-basin haircut. Lila had sent me the album for Christmas with a yellow Post-it sticker attached to the front, saying, 'Imitation is the sincerest form of flattery – Happy Christmas to the imitatee from the flatteree!' with the dot under the exclamation mark being a tiny smiling face that looked suspiciously like Luke's. Well, she didn't get out much.

Anyway, I picked the book up and brought it to Rachel's face. 'Is this yours? Are you reading it?' She did not reply. Now, this raised an interesting question: was Rachel only in her mute and immobile state behind closed doors? The moment the shrinks and doctors had left the room, did she dive into a secret life, reliving happy *Hayseed* days, turning the pages of the book with the kind of fervour she normally reserved for her other secret lives?

Or had one of the relief nurses, not knowing Rachel's precise condition and believing she was dealing with an amnesiac, tried to surround her with familiar things to jolt her memory? If it had been somebody else, it might have been a favourite song, say, or a recording of a loved one's voice on permanent loop, like a saccharine speaking clock, a selection of family photographs placed close to the bedside so that when those unseeing eyes eventually focused, their gaze would fall on brightly coloured images of this summer or that Christmas, smiling babies or loving parents.

But Rachel did not want to wake up to her old life. The state she was in now was the good bit. She wanted, if she could, to wake up as someone else, somewhere else. Surround her with familiar things – strait-jacket her under the *Hayseed* duvet and pillowcase set, blast the excruciating 'Luke's Theme' down stereo headphones into her ears, force-feed her through a tube from the *Hayseed* cereal bowl and mug combo – and you probably couldn't kick-start her to save your life. Put her on a spaceship, people it with beings from a different solar system who speak no known language, and you might have a chance.

Up the corridor there was a kind of recreation room where I waited to see Dr Honey, Rachel's doctor. At the other end a circle of people was sitting on chairs. One of them was weeping rather noisily, and the others were staring at him in silence. I hated this place.

As I watched, a boy looked up at me from his chair. He must have been about eighteen. 'Group,' he said, with an apologetic smile.

'Sorry?'

'Therapy.'

He was staring at me and I turned away. Behind him, on the wall, was a large pinboard. I couldn't quite make out what was on it, but as I moved closer I saw that it was filled with neatly arranged rows of Polaroid mugshots.

'Rachel's there. You'll see her if you look,' he said.

I scanned them and, sure enough, there was one of Rachel. Her face was over-exposed and drained of colour. Her eyes were closed. A chill came over me: she looked like a corpse.

'Before,' the boy said. I turned back to him, unsure what he meant. 'When we come in they take one. It's the clinic version of being fingerprinted. They take an After one when you leave.

There's not always a lot of difference.' He indicated the chair next to him. 'You can wait here if you want. I'm Matthew.'

'I'm –'

'I know who you are,' he said. 'You're Rachel's brother. Luke.' He paused significantly. 'Hayseed.'

'Hayman. Actually.'

'Yeah. Cigarette?'

I shook my head.

'We all smoke like chimneys in here. Except Rachel. She's given up. Given everything up.' He chortled. 'I've been with Rachel before.'

'Oh? Where?'

'I was at Lakewood for a bit. Near Marlow. When she was there. Like youth hostels, these places. You run into the same people if you're on the circuit. No, I really liked her.' He looked away with a jerk, and started to bite the nail of his little finger with astonishing ferocity.

I began to get up. 'I'd better go back,' I said.

He put out his hand and, with surprising strength, grabbed my wrist. He leaned into me and said softly, 'I've read the books. All of them. I can quote bits, if you like.'

I wanted to go, but something about him almost riveted me there. 'What are you in here for?' I asked.

Sheepishly, he held up his hands to me, palms out, and like a concert pianist about to play, he pushed his arms towards me so that the shirt-cuffs pulled back. On his wrists there was a mass of vertical scars. 'I expect they'll start on Rachel soon,' he said.

'To do what?'

'They're not going to put up with her being like a loony for long. See, you're meant to confront yourself, change your behaviour patterns. They break you down. If you like wearing white, they make you wear black. If you like to dance, they make you sit still.'

I heard myself ask, 'And if you've stopped talking?'

'Oh, they have ways of making you talk.' He threw back his

head and laughed so loudly that the group at the other end of the room looked round briefly.

Then he stopped. 'I know Toby, too.'

I was confused. 'Toby?'

'Toby Luttrell. Who played you. In your TV series. We shared a room at that place in St Albans.'

'It wasn't my TV series,' I said.

'I fucked him,' he added conversationally.

The appropriate response to this statement eluded me for a moment. As Matthew stared at me expectantly, I managed to conjure up, 'Well, bully for you.' I tried to mould my tone into something smooth and light, although I felt anything but. I felt as if I had stepped off a cliff, but had not yet begun to fall, like a character in a cartoon film. 'I have to go,' I said.

He looked me right in the eyes. 'You see, I know who Mr Toppit is. That's something we have in common.' He smiled as if he had just worked out something rather important. 'In fact,' he said, 'that's only one of the things we have in common.'

I got up so abruptly that my chair fell over backwards. 'Actually,' I said, 'I don't give a flying fuck who Mr Toppit is.' I headed for the doors.

'Don't worry about Rachel. I'll look after her,' Matthew called to me, and then he shouted, 'She's my *friend*!'

I wanted to put my hands over my ears, but they had the grace to remain at my sides.

I found Dr Honey's office at the other end of the corridor. I knocked, and a muffled sound came from inside. He was in the middle of his lunch. On his desk everything had been arranged with mathematical precision – a plastic cup of coffee, a KitKat, a bag of crisps and a sandwich placed exactly in the centre of a square of greaseproof paper, all equidistant from each other. He was probably an expert on obsessive-compulsive disorders.

'I want to take Rachel out of here,' I said.

Dr Honey nodded slowly. He cleared his throat. 'Do you think that should be your decision,' he said, 'or hers?'

'I don't think she's capable of making that kind of decision,' I said.

'So you think you should do it for her? Impose it?'

'Don't you impose things here? In this place?'

'As a matter of fact, we impose very little. We try to . . .' he searched for the word '. . . *suggest* a structure under which a patient can confront the issues that concern them. Has something upset you?'

'I'm not upset,' I lied. 'I'm worried about Rachel.' I didn't want to talk about Matthew yet, but I knew I had to come up with something quickly. Dr Honey had the air of a theatregoer waiting for a late curtain to rise.

'I think some of the other patients are . . .' And then I paused. I didn't know how to go on and, to my amazement, the word 'horrid' limped out of my mouth, like a straggler at the end of a race.

'Horrid,' he repeated thoughtfully. He turned his head away from me briefly and looked out of the window. Then he swung back, fixing me with his eyes. 'This is not an hotel or a health farm. Our patients are not here to improve their table manners. Nor, may I remind you, is it a prison. Anyone, including your sister, may leave when they wish. She is as free to go as you are.'

I struggled on lamely, now forced to play my remaining cards. 'Matthew . . . I don't know his last name . . .'

'Sumner,' he said.

I could feel my palms sweating. 'He said some really strange things.'

'Strange?'

I tried to lighten the atmosphere. 'I don't suppose you use that as a technical term much here.'

'Not often. No.'

'He seems to be obsessed with these books, my father's books.' It sounded impossibly feeble. 'You know, they're quite –'

He cut in: 'Yes, I know all about them. Obsessed? My goodness, the books are famous. It can't be a surprise that your father's extraordinary creation of Mr Toppit might strike a chord in someone whose issues stem from an ambivalent attitude to authority figures. You know, he has an almost iconic significance: his need to be obeyed, his withholding of approval. Naturally Matthew is interested. I doubt if it's obsession. Personally, I'm a great admirer of the books. They're as dark as Grimm but not so one-note. We use them sometimes in our group sessions. They're a surprising link: everyone has such a clear memory of when they first read them.'

'You mean like where you were when Kennedy was shot?'

He smiled wearily. 'We aren't strangers here to the children of well-known figures: film stars, politicians, the corporate world. The burden of an achieving parent can seem formidable,' he said.

I shook my head. 'He wasn't an achieving parent. He just wrote some books.'

'Rachel, if I may say so, seems more comfortable with that than you do.' He arranged a patient look on his face. 'Your sister – and please do not take this the wrong way – is not a well person, is not a *functional* person, to use our jargon. She identifies very strongly with the books – perhaps too strongly – but they represent a kind of golden age to her. That's an area we touched on in many of our sessions the last time she was here. She told me then that she is writing the official biography of your father. Has that progressed? It's important that she has a project, something that will build her confidence.'

'No, she's not writing his biography,' I explained patiently. 'She went to see the publishers and told them she wanted to do it. They've made a fortune from the books so they could hardly say no. If she's written half a page I'd be surprised.'

'I sense you have a sort of ambivalence about her work. Do you feel that it might be more appropriate for you to write his biography?' He seemed genuinely puzzled.

I couldn't help laughing as if it was the most ridiculous thing in the world. Which it was. 'It isn't "her work". It isn't anything.'

He seemed hurt. 'I can't help feeling you're competing with Rachel in some way,' he said. 'Surely you can both share in the riches – I don't mean material riches – of your father's books. His extraordinary heritage, if you will.'

'It's not about sharing. That's the problem.' I stopped because I saw something now more clearly than I ever had before. 'You've read the books,' I said. He nodded. 'There's one omission from my father's heritage. The books are about me. I am Luke Hayseed. The thing is, there's no Rachel Hayseed in them. Not a walk-on part, not a guest appearance. How would that make you feel? Don't you see? She just isn't . . . there. Somewhere in that area I think you might locate her issues. That's why she's not a functional person, to use your jargon.'

When I went back to Rachel's room, she was asleep, her head tilted up against the headrest of her chair. I leaned down and kissed her forehead.

As I said, her problems were quite different from mine.

Arthur

On a spring day in 1981, with a spring in his step, Arthur Hayman, now in his sixties and lately the author of an obscure set of children's books, but when younger general factotum to the British film industry in the shape of sometime editor, sometime scriptwriter and one-time director of the 1948 film entitled *Love's Capture*, not well reviewed at the time and not remembered precisely as a milestone in the oeuvre of Phyllis Calvert – so tenuously remembered, in fact, that the title, having once been misprinted in a *Festschrift* to its star as *Love's Captive*, now tended to be referred to, when it was referred to at all, as '*Love's Captive* (a.k.a. *Love's Capture*)' – was walking through the gardens in the centre of Soho Square. It was two minutes before one o'clock on the Monday after the first hot weekend of the year and some of the men lounging on the grass eating their sandwiches had already taken off their shirts. The girls, in short-sleeved dresses or scoop-necked tops, were rubbing suntan lotion on their shoulders and arms, still red from sunbathing at the weekend.

As Arthur walked through the gate at the southern end of the gardens and crossed the road on to the top of Greek Street, a church bell struck one. The reverberation of the chime hung in the still air and he looked up, wondering which church it had come from. When he was younger he had spent most of his time in and around Soho. He still banked there – indeed, had just walked past his bank where, in the days before he had had money, the manager would proffer a cup of tea and give him and the other young men who might have promising careers in the film industry one last chance before bouncing their cheques while they waited for the accounts department at Rank or Ealing or Gainsborough to pay the money that would clear, or at least reduce, their overdrafts.

Now he rarely ran into anyone he knew in Soho. Once, in the fifties, he might run into any number of people, normally either leaving the Sphinx, heading for lunch somewhere else, or heading for the Sphinx to drink their way through lunch. He would sometimes be sucked into their wake and cram himself with them into the rickety lift, with the peculiar smell and judder, to the top floor where Jimmy the barman would greet them – the greetings somewhat more vociferous for the others than for Arthur – and they would settle down for some serious talk as lunchtime folded into teatime and the sandwiches sat untouched on the tables.

Although Arthur was included because he was – nominally at least – one of them, he knew that his major contribution was to offer news of Wally Carter, one of his oldest friends, who was now a successful director in Hollywood. Occasionally he made it up if he had not heard from him. Actually, he almost never heard from Wally, these days. It was Wally through whom he had met his wife Martha, then Martha Jordan, who had been detached from her long-gestating PhD on the Crusades to do research on a film Wally was planning about Richard the Lionheart. Terry Tringham, who had worked with Arthur and Wally in the old days, was always particularly keen to know what was happening: 'How's Wally? How's old Wally? Raking it in? *Talented* boy.'

The trouble was, once Arthur had passed on the news, he felt he was there under false pretences. He was, anyway, slightly nervous in either of the two camps that tended to congregate there. He did not feel he had the credentials to be part of the more successful – and significantly smaller – crowd who, if they hadn't moved on entirely to smarter clubs than the Sphinx, might drop in for a couple of rounds. They had the air of people just passing through for form's sake, glancing at their watches, which had become slimmer as their stature in the film business had grown, and down-ing the last half of their gin in one gulp as they murmured, 'Got a bit of a lunch,' and headed for the thinner air of Mayfair, knowing they would have walked off their drinks and be clear-headed enough by the time they reached Les A or the White Elephant to be at their best when they met the visiting dignitaries from Hollywood, who had flown over the Pole through the night but were up and running for business by lunchtime.

Nor was he witty or hard-drinking enough to fit in with the gang headed by Terry Tringham, who might pick up the odd editing job on a documentary but had generally given up all pretence of work. Sometimes as the day wore on, waiting for the moment when the conversation had one of its cyclical upswings, Arthur would get up as if to go to the lavatory and, with a glance over his shoulder, go round the corner towards the lift and simply vanish.

As chance would have it, his publishers, the Carter Press, had a ramshackle office just round the corner from what had been the club, which was why, many years later, now that he was no longer in the film business, Arthur still came to Soho.

Just after one fifteen, he turned into Meard Street. Standing outside the door of the Carter Press, he pressed the bell and lowered his face to the entryphone in preparation to speak, but the buzzer went immediately, without anyone asking who he was, and the door clicked open. The receptionist, Stephanie, was eating a sandwich and reading the paper. She looked astonished to see him, as if someone arriving in the office was the very last thing she might have expected on a working day.

He stood awkwardly for a moment, then said, 'Would Graham be in?'

She waited before speaking, as if she was deciding whether to answer yes or no. Instead, she hedged her bets: 'Is he expecting you?'

'Well, no – not exactly. I was just passing.'

She nodded slowly, as if giving herself time to think, 'And you are ... Mr ...?'

'I'm Arthur Hayman, Stephanie,' he said gently. 'I'm ...' He moved to the wall and placed his finger on the cover of *Darkwood*, which was framed on the wall below the other four books in the series.

Even though he was an author of theirs and had remembered her name when she had not remembered his, the look of suspicion remained on her face. 'If you'll just hold on for a second,' she said, tapped at the switchboard in front of her and picked up the receiver. When the other end answered, she turned on her swivel chair so that her back was facing him. Like the girls in the gardens, she had been sunbathing at the weekend, and he could see the white bikini lines running over her red back and shoulders. She spoke in a low voice, and as he was at the other end of the room, still standing by his dust-jackets on the wall, he could hear only a mumble, then his name.

She put down the receiver, and swivelled back to face him. 'Strictly speaking, he's not in,' she said. 'He's in a meeting, but he can come down for a moment.' A few minutes later, from the top of the building, there was the sound of a door slamming and the whole structure shook as a pair of feet ran down the stairs, as loudly as a crowd of children jumping them one by one.

Graham Carter, Arthur's editor and son of his friend Wally Carter, came running in like an unkempt schoolboy, his shirt coming out of his corduroy trousers. 'Arthur!' he said, then 'Arthur!' again, as he shook his hand and pulled him into a fumbling bear-hug with his other arm. Then doubt crossed his face. 'We didn't have an . . . ? No, this is a terrible day. Sales conference. Reps. Christ!'

From behind her desk, Stephanie had put down her paper and was watching Graham and Arthur with her arms folded. There was a moment's silence, and then the phone rang. 'Carter Press. Good afternoon,' Stephanie said brightly. A cloud passed over her face and she glanced at Graham. He gave a little shake of his head. 'No,' she said, 'I'm afraid not . . . Well, we were expecting him . . . Yes. I did pass your . . . And the one yesterday, yes . . . Your agent? No, I don't see a call from him here.' She ran a hand over her desk and rustled some papers. 'Well, I will. Yes. Of course.' No sooner had she put the receiver down than the telephone rang again. Graham took Arthur's arm and led him out into the corridor. As the door closed, Arthur heard Stephanie say, 'No, I'm afraid there's nobody in Accounts now. They're all at lunch. No, Mr Carter isn't here today. He's at the sales conference . . . Yes, I know.'

Graham sat on a packing case and rubbed his eyes. Arthur leaned against the wall opposite him. 'It's good of you to come, Arthur. No, it is, really,' he said. 'It's a nightmare at the moment. Most people are setting their agents on to us. And that's just the authors. Don't even ask me about the bloody printers.'

'I don't have an agent,' Arthur said.

'The advances are so high, these days. That's the problem.'

Arthur shifted uneasily. 'You've never paid me an advance.' Graham looked pained, and Arthur said quickly, 'I mean, I never really asked for one.'

'Well, that's why I feel so rotten about the royalty statements not being done. I hope we'll have them out by the end of the month,' Graham said. Arthur hadn't planned to say anything in response to this, but Graham had already put out his hand to prevent him speaking. 'I know, I know how late we are. Bloody accounts department.' Graham's long blond hair fell over his eyes, and he brushed it back over his head with his fingers. He seemed about to cry.

Arthur felt as if he had somehow got on a bus that was going in the wrong direction and could not work out how to get off. He had not even realized that the royalty statements were late, and now he felt rather embarrassed that Graham thought that was the reason he had come – embarrassed, in fact, that he could not really remember why he had come at all.

Graham glanced up at the clock on the wall. 'Christ! I've got to go, Arthur,' he said. 'Actually, it's not a sales conference. I've got the bank upstairs. I'm trying to sweet-talk them into extending our line of credit.' He got to his feet and shook Arthur's hand. 'Goodbye, Arthur,' he said, 'thank you for coming in,' and ran up the stairs two at a time.

Arthur waited, and then, as Graham had vanished from the landing up to the next flight of stairs, he called his name. Graham reappeared, his face apprehensive.

Arthur was looking down at his shoes when he spoke. 'I'm sixty-six years old, Graham,' he said. He cleared his throat, then continued: 'Your father is my oldest friend. You've published my books, all five of them. Nobody else wanted to, except you. I'm not upset about the royalties. I came because I wanted to see if you'd put the cover of *Darkwood* on your wall, like you've done with the others. So, you see, please don't worry about money and things. Not on my account.'

Arthur let himself out of the front door, stepped from the shade into a pool of warmth and walked back along Meard Street towards Dean Street. Just before two p.m., he turned the corner and headed south.

Bunny Jones was just coming out of the newsagent's on the opposite side of the road and saw Arthur. He had just looked at his watch because he knew he had to be back at work by two fifteen for a screening. He had been one of the senior projectionists at Elstree when Arthur was there and now, in his late seventies, he worked part-time at one of the post-production houses up the road. Actually, all he saw was Arthur's back, but even though he had not spoken to him for maybe thirty years he knew immediately that it was Arthur, whom they had sometimes called Artie when he was young and doing odd jobs around the studio. What he couldn't remember was his last name, and as he walked back up the street he tried to think what it was, but it was only when he read the late edition of the *Standard* on the tube home the next day that it came to him.

People had spilled out of the bars and restaurants into the heat and were standing in the street or sitting on the pavement. It was hard for Arthur to walk in a straight line, and he had to keep weaving from the centre of the pavement out to the kerb and back again. Ahead of him, bathed in sunlight, Old Compton Street cut across Dean Street, and beyond that he could see as far down as Shaftesbury Avenue, where he and Martha had once rented a flat. As he stepped off the pavement, when he saw for a brief second what was about to happen to him, a thought came into his head.

I have no idea what that thought might have been. I've imagined some of Arthur's story ('with a spring in his step') and reconstructed parts of it from what Graham Carter told me later and from the newspaper reports that Lila clipped exhaustively and stuck into The Big Book of Hayseed with the right kind of glue that didn't come through the newsprint. Laurie's part was about to begin, but at that instant she was walking up from Piccadilly Circus and it would still be five or six minutes before she reached Arthur.

So there is nothing that covers that particular moment. All I see is an old man, dressed in grey flannels, a tweed jacket and handmade shoes, stepping off the pavement on to Old Compton Street just as the girls in the park in Soho Square were putting their suntan lotion back into their handbags and dropping their sandwich wrappers into litter bins, and the men were pulling on their shirts in order to head back to work, and Bunny Jones was threading the first reel through the projector in the viewing theatre, and Stephanie was telling someone that Mr Carter was at a sales conference, while, in fact, he was in the boardroom at the top of the building in Meard Street talking about cash flow to the men from the bank on the Monday after the first hot weekend of the year.

Laurie

A strange thing had happened to Laurie Clow, recently arrived in London from Modesto, California: she had become mesmerized by the walls of her hotel room. White paper had been pasted over thousands of tiny bumps of varying shapes and sizes. It looked like an unending Arctic landscape. Laurie lay in bed, where she had spent most of her time since she had been in England, and ran her hands up and down the wall. The texture tickled her fingers, but she had been doing it for such a long time that they had become almost numb.

While she was sleeping she had had an odd dream. She had seen a man decorating the room. He had covered the walls with glue and then, from a bucket that he held in one hand, had taken little wriggling bugs one by one and stuck them on to the walls. When he had finished, he covered the walls with long rolls of thin white paper that hid the bugs. Even before the man turned round, she knew with weary certainty that he would be her father.

As a child during the war, living in Los Alamos in the hills of New Mexico, there had been bugs everywhere. Hiding from the dry heat in the daytime, they scuttled around the apartment lurking in corners and under the beds. At night, big flying things like junebugs crashed into the screens. One morning Laurie had seen a little scorpion in the kitchen. She ran to the apartment next door to find Paully, the son of another of the lab technicians who worked with her father. They played together sometimes, not as often as Laurie would have liked because Alma said he was sly. When they got back, the scorpion was still in exactly the same place, and after Paully had prodded it with a fork to ascertain that it was still alive, he told Laurie to find a rag. Then they went into the bedroom where Laurie's mother, Alma, was still asleep. They tiptoed to the wardrobe where she kept her supply of liquor and took out a bottle of gin. Back in the kitchen, they took the cap off the gin and poured it over the rag. The room filled with a heady, sweet smell and, catching each other's eye and giggling, they licked the gin off their hands.

Kneeling down, Paully placed the wet rag in a circle around the scorpion, and then, with a glance at Laurie who was standing up against the wall as far as she could get from it, he struck a match. Laurie thought that the gin would burst into flame like gasoline, but in fact Paully had to prod the rag several times with the burning match before it lit. The flame was very blue, and it crept slowly along the rag. At any minute they were expecting the scorpion to do what they had read about – lift its tail and sting itself to death – but it seemed oblivious to the fire. Then, suddenly, it twitched and lumbered groggily towards the flame. To their horror it climbed on to the rag, sat balanced there and, with an awful crackling sound, began to burn. They screamed and Alma, dressed in the blue housecoat she had slept in, appeared at the door of the bedroom. She was looking for her cigarettes, raised a hand and said, 'Wait, hold it, just wait,' when they tried to tell her the story, but by the time she'd found the pack, lit one and sat down, the moment had passed. It was left to Laurie's father to remove the scorpion when he came back from the lab to make their lunch.

He always came in for lunch exactly at midday. 'Hubba, hubba, hubba!' he called, as he pushed open the screen door, then put out his arms for Laurie. Unless he got a lift from someone, he walked home from the lab, and his shoes were always dusty from the unpaved roads. When he took his hat off, his forehead and hair were damp with sweat. Sometimes Alma was there and sometimes she wasn't. If she was there, she was normally in the bedroom. She complained a lot of the time. She hated their quarters. 'This is just a shanty town,' Alma would shout. 'I'm sick of living in The Grapes of Wrath,' but what she really hated was living next door to Paully's family because they were Jewish.

28

Her father was always cheerful. 'You Princess Tuna or Princess Chicken Salad today?' he said, as he stood in the kitchen making their sandwiches, and she giggled and said, 'I'm Princess Cookie,' or 'I'm Princess Chocolate Chip.' He had other names for her, Princess Poodle or Princess Peach, and sometimes he made up names that sounded as if they came from *Hiawatha*, like Princess Alamita.

When their first winter came, he wore a felt hat and stayed up at the lab for lunch. He said it was too cold to walk back and that his shoes would get muddy, even though duckboards had been put down over the paths. Then Laurie made lunch for herself and Alma, but Alma always left the sandwiches untouched. When spring came and the snow melted, he seemed to have lost the habit of coming home for lunch and stayed at the lab.

He was much less cheerful after they left Los Alamos and lived in Bakersfield. He taught math part-time in a high school there. Before Bakersfield they were in Fresno where he worked in a photo lab. In Fresno he was sad most of the time. For Laurie, he began to recede, to simply go out of focus, like some of the photos that had been thrown away in the shop and he brought home to show her – whole rolls where the camera had been set wrong and the figures were grey blurs or there were great moon-shaped faces staring at the lens. By the time they left Bakersfield and got to Modesto, he didn't seem to be there at all. He had vanished, like a suitcase that had fallen out of the trunk while they were bumping along the highway. Then there was just her and Alma.

Laurie couldn't remember the last time she had taken a vacation without her friend Marge, who was a Patient Care Operative at Holy Spirit Hospital where Laurie worked afternoons in the radio station after she had finished her morning show at KCIF. Marge had always planned them and booked them and organized them, had gotten a rough schedule for what she called 'the May trip' before January was through, and when they met up on Friday nights, there was always a new map for Laurie to look at or a variation on the itinerary or a list of suggestions from someone else at Holy Spirit who had visited Florence or Machu Picchu or Maui. This year, Laurie had organized everything on her own. She had not had a conversation of any length with Marge since they had got back from St Bart's the year before.

On the day that Laurie left for England, the worst thing had happened: Marge had seen her heading for the airport. She had already had a difficult goodbye with Alma at Spring Crest – difficult because Alma had pretended not to know that she was going on vacation and kept asking Laurie to take her over to the police station to check if they had more pictures for her to look at. As Laurie was trying to leave, Alma kept shouting for one of the nurses to bring her a phone – 'I need to call the police again. *This minute!*' – and then, either by accident or on purpose, she had knocked the tray of coffee on to the floor. In the end, Laurie stood up and said, 'I'll be back soon, Alma,' in a quiet, neutral voice that might have indicated nothing more than a trip to the bathroom, and got out of the day room as quickly as possible, just managing to avoid Mrs D, who was heading down the corridor.

She drove back into town and stopped off at KCIF to leave some notes for Rick Whitcomb. Laurie did a half-hour radio show of local news every morning. Rick was the programme controller and he was going to do her show in her absence. Then she drove downtown to Holy Spirit where she had arranged to leave her car. In the afternoons she organized the volunteers at Holy Spirit Hospital Radio and did an hour of requests. She carried her bag to the main entrance and left it outside while she went into the lobby to ask Maribeth, the receptionist on duty, if she would call a cab to take her to the airport.

As the driver was putting her bag in the trunk, she saw Marge heading towards her with one of the doctors. She felt herself flush, and ducked into the back seat as quickly as she could. Out of the window, she saw that Marge had stopped walking and was standing in the middle of the parking lot looking right at her, then at her vacation bags being put in the trunk. Marge had had her hair cut and coloured and the tight curls sat on her head as shiny as a new copper coin. Even when she wasn't angry, which she was most of the time because the waiter had put sour cream on her baked potato without asking or the air-conditioning in the ward was on the fritz, her small mouth and the set of her chin gave her the appearance of a cross little dog, but now she had a look of amazement on her face. Briefly Marge seemed almost young, as she must have been before all the things in her life that made her want to explode joined forces against her, leaving her battle-scarred and weary from the fight, but then the cab turned on to the street and Laurie lost sight of her.

On the flight to London she couldn't stop thinking of what had happened on the last terrible night of their vacation on St Bart's. To try to clear it from her mind she began to zing. She closed her eyes and repeated the word under her breath – 'Zingzingzingzing-zingzingzingzingzing' – until her head was pleasantly filled with white noise and the cuts through which the thoughts seeped were healing. She had a sudden sense of relief that she was going to England – she would be safe there – but by the time she arrived in London, exhausted after the long night flight, her confidence had deserted her.

When the cab deposited her in front of the hotel, she had to fight her way through a group of students sprawled across the entrance with their backpacks. They were speaking in a language she had never heard before, and when she stepped over their bags to climb the steps, they watched her strangely. The lobby had an odd, sickly smell. It was filled with other young people jostling and talking, and Laurie had to edge her way through, carrying her bags. It was what she imagined a train station in a third-world country would be like.

When she got up to the room – what they called a 'luxury double', even though it was the size of a broom closet – having carried her bags up three flights of stairs, she lay down on the bed and closed her eyes. She felt her body sink into the dip in the middle of the mattress. It was clearly not designed for someone of her weight. She knew that Marge would have been out of this hotel in a second – even if she had made the mistake of booking it in the first place – would have had her guidebooks out and been on the phone arranging alternative accommodation while Laurie sat calmly and had a cup of coffee. The room they had shared in St Bart's had had a veranda and a view of the Caribbean and smiling, silent staff, who turned down the beds in the evening and left gold-wrapped mints on the pillows.

When she woke it was late afternoon, and the air in the room was still and hot. She was hungry now, but she had already guessed that the Waverly Court did not run to room service. In her bag, she had some potato chips and a giant chocolate bar. She took off the paper wrapping and peeled away the silver foil underneath. She broke the chocolate into chunks and neatly re-formed them into the shape of the bar on the table next to the opened potato chips. Then, taking a deep breath, she began to eat the chips out of the bag. When she had finished them, she took the chunks of chocolate off the table and put them into her mouth one by one, starting at the top left-hand corner and working her way along and down. When she had had enough, she put the remnants back into her bag, then cupped one hand at the side of the table and, with the edge of the other palm, brushed the crumbs into it and closed her fingers. She went to the window and, as if she was releasing a small bird, opened her hand and shook it. Then she felt well enough to call Alma.

'Spring Crest Retirement Complex. Good morning.'

'Barb? It's Laurie.' Barbara was the senior administrator. Laurie was grateful to get her and not Mrs Detweiler, who owned the place.

'Laurie! How's the trip?'

'It's fine, it's great. How's Mom?' She only called her 'Mom' to other people.

There was a pause. 'Well . . .'

Laurie didn't want to hear what Barbara might have to say. 'Is she in the day room? Could you plug her in?'

'Actually, Mrs D needed to speak with you.'

This was what Laurie had dreaded. 'I'm in England, Barbara. Could it wait?' But Barbara had already gone and left Laurie listening to empty space. While she was thinking whether or not to hang up, Mrs Detweiler came on the line.

'Laurie, how's London? My favourite city. Great time to be there with the royal wedding and all.'

'It's beautiful.' She hurried on: 'Mrs D –'

'I love London. What have you seen today?'

'Oh ... Buckingham Palace and ...' Laurie's mind went completely blank '... Stonehenge.'

There was a pause. 'Are you with a tour?'

'No, I'm ... I rented a car.'

'Well, you have yourself a good time, you hear?' Mrs Detweiler said brightly.

'I'm just heading out. To the theatre. Could you put me through to Mom?'

'I need to schedule a meeting with you, Laurie. When are you back?' The sheen had worn off Mrs Detweiler's voice.

'I'm not sure. I've got an open return,' she lied.

'Oh,' Mrs Detweiler said gravely. Laurie was running her hand over the wall, scraping the little bumps with her fingernails.

'I need for you to think some things over, Laurie. I think we should talk to the outplacement co-ordinator. About alternative care programmes.'

Dread welled in Laurie. 'Oh, Mrs D, she just needs time to settle.'

'Laurie, she's been with us for nine months.' Mrs Detweiler was honing the edge in her voice. 'Her personal-care needs might not be within our scope. I want you to think about that. Things haven't been right since the Memory Box.'

Laurie closed her eyes. She had hoped they'd forgotten about that. In order to identify what they called 'a resident's personal area', a small lighted cabinet was hung on the wall outside the door of every bedroom at Spring Crest. Alma's neighbours' Memory Boxes were crammed to bursting with family photos, pocket

33

watches, jewellery, locks of hair and little pieces of china. All Laurie could find to put into Alma's was a photograph of herself sitting on a horse outside the schoolhouse in Los Alamos, an old postcard of Fisherman's Wharf and a ceramic Mexican salt-and-pepper set she had discovered at the back of a cupboard. After Alma had been at Spring Crest a week, she had taken the box off the wall and thrown it out of her window. It had smashed into the Japanese ornamental garden where Mrs Detweiler had been holding her callisthenics class. Laurie's story – reluctantly backed up by Alma – was that it had fallen out of the window when Alma was trying to fill it with more mementoes. Now Alma's personal area was identifiable as the only one not to have a Memory Box outside it.

Laurie decided to take pre-emptive action. 'Fact is, Mrs D, she's upset by the assault.'

'Oh, Laurie, take it from me, we're all of us most concerned about that. It's very worrying for our other residents to have the police visiting.'

'Well, I would imagine, Mrs D, that it might reassure them. It must be disturbing to know that a man – a pervert – could get into Spring Crest. Just like that.'

She heard an intake of breath. 'This is a gated community, Laurie. We've never had any problems with security before.'

'How's Mom's trauma counselling going?' Laurie asked. She felt awful doing this when she was pretty sure that Alma had made up the whole assault thing, but she was fighting for her life now. She couldn't have Alma back living with her.

'Slowly,' said Mrs Detweiler, tartly. 'You know Walter Reinheimer, don't you, Laurie? Officer Reinheimer? He called me yesterday to talk about Alma, told me some things. In fact, he's coming over this afternoon to go over the incident again with her. He wants me there too.' Laurie picked so hard at one of the bumps on the wallpaper that her nail broke and a piece of the paper came away in a curl. She put her finger into her mouth and sucked it. Yes, she did know Walter Reinheimer. This was the worst thing that could possibly have happened.

Laurie tried to keep the shake out of her voice: 'Mrs D, I've got to go. Tour bus is waiting. Can we talk about this when I get back? I just need a second with Mom.'

'Okay, Laurie, but we'll have to talk, we really will. I'll go get her for you now. You have a good time, you hear? What's the theatre?'

'Theatre?' Laurie said.

'You said you were seeing a show.'

'Oh . . . yes.' There was a momentary silence. Laurie racked her brains. 'Camelot.'

Mrs Detweiler sounded surprised. 'Camelot? Is that on again? Really? I love it.'

Was it so unlikely? 'It's a revival,' Laurie said quickly. 'Because of the royal wedding. You know, King Arthur and Queen . . .' Her mind went blank again.

'Guinevere, dear,' Mrs Detweiler said reprovingly. 'Mr D and I saw it on Broadway with Richard Burton and Julie Andrews, oh . . . twenty years ago? A while, anyhow.'

Barbara came back on the line. 'I don't know where your mom is, Laurie. She's not in her room. Or in the day room. Can you hold? I'll have someone look for her.'

It was dusk outside now, and Laurie felt sick. The chocolate was sitting at the top of her stomach like a pool of lava. She wanted to get back into bed and go to sleep. She licked her finger and tried to stick the piece of wallpaper back to the wall with spit.

Barbara was back on the line. 'I'll be damned. You know where Alma was, Laurie?' Laurie didn't want to know. 'In the poolhouse. Smoking a cigarette.'

'Does Mrs D know, Barb?'

'No, she's back in the office.'

'Listen, Barb – don't tell her. Please.' Laurie couldn't stop herself sounding desperate.

'Oh. Okay. Your mom's back in her room. I'll put you through. You enjoy yourself now. Hey, and there's the wedding!'

'Yeah – everyone's talking about it,' Laurie said half-heartedly.

The phone clicked and began to ring. It rang and rang. Finally Alma picked it up.

'Alma?' Silence. Laurie could hear wheezing. 'Alma?'

'Who's that?'

'It's me, Alma.'

'Who is this?'

Laurie wanted to scream. 'Oh, *Alma*! It's Laurie.'

'Where are you?'

'England.'

'England!'

Laurie tried to speak calmly. 'I've only got a second, Alma. I'm going to the theatre.'

'You hate the theatre.'

'I know I hate the theatre. It's on my tour schedule.'

'Someone else is doing your radio show. I heard it this morning.'

'Of *course* someone else is doing my radio show. I'm in London, on vacation. Rick Whitcomb's doing it.'

'You watch it, Miss Laurie Clow. He'll take it over.'

'Alma, Rick's the programme controller. He stands in for any-one who's away. Anyway, if he does take over my show, I'll just work full-time at Holy Spirit.' She knew that would annoy Alma.

'That's no-pay work, that's *volunteer* work.' There was no worse category in Alma's eyes. 'Like that *Grapes of Wrath* stuff you used to do.'

Once, in college, to Alma's fury, Laurie had spent a summer fund-raising for the Farm Workers' Union in Salinas. *The Grapes of Wrath* seemed to be the only book Alma had ever read. The abridged version, in an omnibus collection with *Goodbye, Mr Chips* and *The Song of Bernadette*, had been in whatever house they had lived in since Laurie was a child. She should have put it in Alma's Memory Box.

'I remember Rick Whitcomb in high school with you. Playing Curly in *Oklahoma!*. Who were you? I don't recall.' Laurie did. She had started off with a part and ended up without one. She didn't even want to think about that particular humiliation.

'He had beautiful hair,' Alma said.

He didn't now. The year before, he and his wife Jerrilee, who had also been in high school with them, had played Don Quixote and Dulcinea in *Man of La Mancha* at Townsend Opera and Rick had worn a hairpiece like a dead animal. Marge had insisted they went along to the opening night and, to Laurie's horror, cried when Rick sang 'The Impossible Dream'.

Laurie tried to move on: 'Barbara told me they found you smoking. This isn't negotiable, Alma. You can't smoke at Spring Crest. Mrs Detweiler will go crazy.'

Alma mumbled something.

'What?'

'Mrs *Rottweiler*,' Alma snapped.

'Oh, Alma, you have to stop this.'

'The police are coming again. They're bringing some more photographs to show me. They're not too smart. Last time they kept asking me who the president was. Why should I tell them if they don't know?'

'You know, I'm really worried about this, Alma.'

'Walter Reinheimer is bringing them himself. You remember him?'

Laurie closed her eyes. Alma barked, 'What did you say? I can't hear you. It sounded like you said, "Zingzingzing."'

'Alma, it's as far away as the moon here. It's a bad line.' Laurie was gazing out of the window. She felt as if she *was* on the moon. 'You mustn't do this.'

'Do what?'

'Go on with this story.'

'Laurie – he assaulted me!'

'I think technically it's not an assault. He didn't touch you.'

'Physical isn't the only kind of assault.'

'Tell them you're not sure, tell them maybe you're mistaken.'

'I've already told them what happened.'

'They'll understand, Alma. Everyone at Spring Crest has Alzheimer's. They won't know the difference.'

'He was Mexican. I can tell you that for nothing. No question.'

'Well, there's a surprise.'

'He got his diddly out – he got his *thing* out. You hear what I'm saying?'

'Yes, I hear what you're saying, Alma.'

'Well, I never know with you, Miss Laurie Clow.'

Sometimes Laurie thought Alma had been better when she was drinking. At least then the days and nights had had a more predictable arc to them. Now she was sober you just never knew. The first two attempts to dry her out had been a disaster – Laurie didn't even want to think about what had gone down at the second place, the one outside Tularosa – but on the third go, at the clinic Marge had found near Tucson, mysteriously it had worked. Laurie had driven down to pick Alma up and on the journey back Alma had never referred to the place or what had happened to her there, but she had not had a drink since. Now she was no easier to handle; she was simply difficult in a different way. Maybe twelve steps just weren't enough for her.

'Your friend Marge came to see me yesterday, asked where you were. She's packing a lot of weight.'

'What did she say?'

'Told her you were in England, told her you'd gone to the wedding. To be a bridesmaid to that Princess Lady Di.' Alma hooted with laughter.

Laurie didn't want to talk about Marge. 'You'll get into a lot of trouble, Alma, if you go on with this story. Especially if Officer Reinheimer's coming over.'

'Not as much trouble as that wetback's going to be in when they get him.'

Laurie felt her face redden with anger. She banged her fist on the wall and screamed, '*Alma! This is insane! Don't go on with it!* Walter Reinheimer knows you. He was one of the officers who came over that night you dialled nine-one-one and told the police I was trying to poison you. Remember? You remember that?'

There was a pause. When Alma spoke, she seemed to have dredged up some long-forgotten dignity and was quite calm. 'As you know, Laurie, I was a drinker then. Now I'm a recovering alcoholic.' She pronounced it like two words – 'alco holic'. 'My guess is he'll respect that.'

'Alma . . .' But the line had gone dead. Alma had hung up on her. Laurie ran to the bathroom, got down on her hands and knees and threw up a torrent of molten brown chocolate into the stained lavatory bowl.

Late the next morning, Laurie was still lying in bed. She felt as if she was on a boat that had no sail, drifting in the breeze. She thought of trying to change her flight and going straight home. If she sat around in her hotel room, she might just as well sit around back there, but the thought of a few days on a different continent from Alma and Mrs Detweiler and Officer Reinheimer decided her.

She got out of bed. She had been there such a long time that her legs felt shaky and she sat down again. Finally she got dressed. The one bit of planning she had done was to buy a whole lot of new clothes to cope with the cold English weather. Now, with the sun blazing in from outside, the best she could do was a pair of black sweatpants and the loose black shift that Marge called her wigwam dress. Round her middle she had a belt with a pouch for her money, passport and credit cards. She picked up her KCIF bag and had one last glance in the mirror. She looked like a black blimp.

Outside her room in the dark corridor, the man who had taken her passport and given her the room key when she had arrived the day before was on his hands and knees with a scrubbing brush and a bucket, trying to get a large brown stain off the threadbare carpet. She smiled at him as she passed, and then, just before she reached the stairs, she turned back to him. 'Can you help me?' she said. She was still thinking about the wallpaper. She put her palm against the corridor wall and ran it up and down. 'I know this is a weird thing to ask,' she said, 'but does it have a special name, this stuff you have on the walls? You know, the lumpy paper?' The nail she had torn on it last night was still throbbing.

He didn't seem to think this was an odd question. 'It's Greek,' he said, in a pleasant voice, 'is Greek word.' He was foreign. Maybe *he* was Greek. Then he said a word that had a beautiful sound to it, unlike any other word she had ever heard, but he said it quickly, so quickly, in fact, that by the time Laurie said, 'Thank you, thank you so much,' it had gone out of her head. She was too embarrassed to ask him to repeat it, and as she walked down the stairs it receded further and further away. She tried to get it back by holding on to other words it had sounded like – anaconda, anaphylactic, analytical – before letting them drift away, like helium balloons, when she got outside into the bright sunlight.

On the street in front of the hotel, an ice-cream van was surrounded by a crowd of kids. There was an overflowing litter bin next to it and a sickly smell lingered in the heat around it. Laurie was about to buy an ice-cream when two of the boys looked at her and nudged each other. They blew out their cheeks to make their faces fat before erupting into giggles. Laurie felt herself flush. She turned away from the van and walked down the street as purposefully as she could. She decided to head for Hyde Park, which even she had heard of. It seemed like the kind of thing a proper traveller might do in London. 'Heard so much about Hyde Park, first place I went soon as I got there,' she could imagine herself saying to someone. She would ignore the fact that she had already been in London for thirty hours, twenty-nine of which she had spent in bed.

Laurie walked around the park for some time until she found herself by the side of a big highway coming up to a roundabout, which had a huge arch-like monument in the middle with a statue of galloping horses and a woman on the top. As she squinted up at it the traffic roared past her. She felt she had come to the edge of the ocean. People were going down a flight of concrete stairs and she followed behind them. It was like entering a labyrinth.

Under an eerie white light, tunnels spun off in all directions from a central well and people, their faces unnaturally pale, criss-crossed in front of her with a blank air of purpose. She might have been in a termite nest.

Once out of the tunnel she walked along a wide street past grand old buildings and expensive shops. The sun shone hot on her face, and gradually she found she was enjoying herself. Recognizing some of the things she passed, like Piccadilly Circus, she felt herself becoming a traveller of some experience, not just a large, middle-aged stranger, wearing the wrong clothes for the time of year, wandering aimlessly through a foreign city.

She turned into a narrower street filled with cars. The traffic had stopped and must have been there for some time because people were honking their horns and a few had got out of their cars and were trying to see what the hold-up was. About twenty yards ahead, on the other side of a crossroads, a big truck with a concrete-mixer on the back had stopped in the middle of the street. Two men were getting out of its cab, silhouetted against the sun, which was shining in Laurie's eyes. The three other narrow streets that met at the crossroads were blocked with cars. There was something curious about the way everyone was standing so still. She could hear people talking, but the words were indistinct and echoey. They all looked like aliens, as if maybe they were the same pale people she had seen in the underground tunnel, meeting here to wait for their spaceship to land. Then she saw something odd: by one of the corners of the crossroads a bundle was lying on the ground a little way off the sidewalk. Laurie moved through the line of people standing in front of the cars and saw that the bundle was not a bundle at all, but a man.

She began to run, but someone grabbed her and tried to pull her back, squeezing her arm so tightly that she let out a gasp of pain. She turned and pushed the person so hard that they stumbled backwards, and then she was free. She ran across the road to where the man lay. The sun was glaring into her eyes now, and when she squatted, lowering her head, she felt as if she had gone blind. The top half of the man's body was on its side and his cheek was pressed on to the road. The lower half was at a curious angle, as if it was part of a different body carelessly attached to his by someone who had lost the instructions. His trousers were grey flannel, but they were stained black and shiny with oil. His breathing was shallow and his eyes were open. She moved closer to him, sat on the edge of the pavement and touched him. The tip of her finger grazed his skin and she found herself tracing the bones of his hand. His eyes flickered, but his field of vision was limited by the position of his head on the road. She moved so he could see her face.

'Are you okay?' she asked shakily.

He moved his mouth, then stopped. After a moment he tried again, and said, in a surprisingly clear voice, 'I'm so uncomfortable. Will they let me get up?'

She wondered who he meant by 'they'. Then she saw that the people standing in front of the cars were advancing towards her. She thought that maybe the man was frightened of them. She put up the hand that wasn't touching his to stop them. 'I work in a hospital,' she shouted. They were staring at her blankly. 'I'm a nurse!' It sounded better than saying she was a hospital disc-jockey. She looked back at the man and folded his hand into hers.

'Oh, I wouldn't move. I think you've broken your leg,' but as she was saying it, she knew he had done much more than that. She knew that his trousers were stained not with oil but with blood, so thick and dark and shiny that she could see the reflection of the sun and smell the sickly sweetness it gave off.

'Who are you?' the man said.

'I'm Laurie,' and then she repeated it, 'Laurie.'

Behind the man, someone broke through the line of people. He was young, no more than twenty and he was stumbling as if he had been injured too. He stopped just in front of Laurie. He was gasping for breath and let out a great sob. 'I didn't see him! He just walked out in front of me!' He bent down to the man lying in the road.

42

Laurie's free hand clenched itself into a fist and she was halfway off the ground. *'Don't touch him! Don't you come near him!'* she screamed. Another man came running forward and put his arm round the boy, who put his head against the man's shoulder. Laurie was on her feet now. She shouted at the two men, 'Have you called nine-one-one? *Have you?'* There was incomprehension on their faces.

Behind her, she heard a little cough and a small voice said, 'You mean nine-nine-nine?' Laurie wheeled round and saw a short woman with grey hair. The expression on Laurie's face was clearly terrifying, because the woman stuttered, 'I think – I think someone called. There's an ambulance coming.'

'When? *When?'* Laurie yelled, right in her face.

The woman flinched and whispered, 'A few minutes ago. They called a few minutes ago.'

Laurie wanted to hit her. *'No!* When is the ambulance coming?' Then, in the distance, she heard sirens and the screeching of brakes, and everyone turned round. Down the street, about a hundred yards away, she could see the flashing blue light of a police car.

She turned back to the man on the road. He hadn't moved, but he was looking at her. 'Keep back,' she shouted at the woman, who had given no indication that she had any desire to move forward. Then she shouted it again, at everyone who was staring at her as if she was a mad person. She went back, sat on the pavement and hunched over the man. She wished she could erect a tent round them so that nobody could see them. She held his hand again, and with the other she absently brushed some grime from his thick white hair.

'Are you hurting?' she asked him.

'It's a bad break,' he said.

'Yes, it is, isn't it?' she said, then realized what he meant. 'Oh, your leg, oh, no, no, it isn't. They'll be able to fix you up just fine, don't you worry.'

She moved her hand from his hair to his forehead. It was cold and damp with sweat. 'You're going to be fine,' she said, then covered his cheek with her hand. What she wanted to do was move closer to him and put his head on her lap, but she knew not to move him.

'My name is Arthur Hayman,' he said.

She could feel him trembling. 'Are you cold?' she asked.

'I'm . . . I don't know,' he said, and then he continued to talk, but his voice became so quiet she could hardly hear him and she wasn't able any more to exclude the noise that was increasing around her, the sirens, the banging car doors, the horns honking, the footsteps running, the people talking. She looked up in frustration, wanting everything to go quiet like it had been a minute ago.

Two men broke through the line of people, police or ambulance men, she wasn't sure which, and then there was pandemonium as more men came through, forcing the people watching to move aside. Someone was shouting into a walkie-talkie and she heard a squawking response to whatever was being said, and then she was pushed aside as two men got down on either side of Arthur. One took his wrist and felt his pulse. The other put an oxygen mask over his face. 'Don't hurt him,' Laurie said. 'Please.'

Another man squatted in front of her and tried gently to move her further away from Arthur. She tried to stay where she was but he moved her more forcefully and she toppled sideways, almost into his lap, and her hand was detached from Arthur's cheek. Her throat let out a little guttural cry, and she could see Arthur gazing at her with a quizzical expression in his eyes, his face almost hidden by the oxygen mask. They were now surrounded by people, some squatting and some standing. From nowhere, it seemed, something like a coatstand had appeared with an upturned bottle, clear liquid inside, attached to it. A man with white overalls was bending down, trying to attach a tube to Arthur's neck and there was blood all over him. Behind her she heard a voice say, 'Femoral artery severed,' followed by something about trauma.

There was a clang and a gurney pushed by two other men bounced off the pavement on to the road and raced towards them. The man next to her was almost physically lifting her away and then an extraordinary thing happened: someone took the oxygen mask off Arthur's face and he said to her, in the clearest voice, 'Don't go.'

The man holding her said, 'Are you family?' and she said, 'Yes, yes, I am,' and then she added, for good measure, 'I work in a hospital,' but she didn't say this time that she was a nurse. The man eased his hands away from her middle and let her move back to Arthur. She knew she didn't have long because they were unfurling a canvas stretcher and they would be using it to get him on to the gurney. She took his hand and said, 'I won't go,' but his eyes were closed now. She wished she were closer to him, that she could hold him in her arms.

'Who are you?' he whispered.

She didn't have to think about it for long: she knew who she was now and the certainty of it banished everything else from her mind. Laurie might have said it out loud or she might not. She wasn't sure because everything around her was so noisy, but she certainly said it in her head, over and over again, as she held on tightly to Arthur's hand: 'I am the Princess Anaglypta, and I have come home.'

Luke

On that Monday, after lunch, Adam finally got the magazine and let me have it first. It had acquired legendary status around the school and the pages were already scuffed and torn from overuse. I could hear Weeks thundering down the corridor shouting my name: he had been due to have it next, but he was the last person we were going to give it to. I headed straight for the butts and locked the cubicle door. I was in the one at the end by the wall, which everyone used because it had only one other cubicle next to it.

I unbuttoned my trousers and let them fall round my ankles. My prick was on the move in my underpants. They came down too, and I sat on the loo seat. I should have wiped it first because it was liberally sprayed with piss, but I was in a hurry. I had hardly opened the magazine before I was stiff.

In the showers one day, Adam had said to me conversationally, 'It's not very big, is it?' His was bigger and seemed to have an enviable weight.

'Some people develop faster than others,' I said, in an attempt at coolness. 'I'm not in any hurry.'

'Aren't you?' he said. 'I am.'

I was thirteen and I was going through a phantom puberty. Something was happening, but not much. The testosterone was there but it had run out of steam. My voice occasionally had a nice croak, and I did have a light undergrowth of pubic hair. Sometimes I put Vaseline on it and combed it, but I had no hair under my arms, and my prick stubbornly refused to grow. The worst thing was that no spunk came when I wanked.

I'd only been in the butts for about three minutes. I had taken a length of loo paper and laid it over my thigh. One hand was holding the magazine and the other was holding my prick. The spread in front of me showed a girl with long blonde hair. She was called Donna. The text was in Dutch, but her name kept cropping up in the captions. The headline at the top of the page said: 'Donna krijgt het van twee kanten.' There were two men with her. One was called Dirk and the other was called Rex. I couldn't read Dutch: I didn't know whether Donna was being fucked by Dirk while she was sucking Rex's cock or whether it was the other way round.

A crash made me jump. The door to the butts had been kicked open and banged against the wall.

'Luke?' Adam shouted.

I stood on the lavatory and peered over the cubicle wall.

Adam's face was solemn. 'The Head Man wants you.'

We knew it was only a matter of time, but I hadn't expected it so soon. 'Me? Why is it just me?'

Adam looked sheepish. It wasn't his fault the joke had backfired, but it had been his idea to play it on Weeks in the first place, although I'd had my own reasons too. Earlier in the term, Weeks had done a blown-up Xerox of one of the drawings of Luke from the books and stuck it on the noticeboard with a big felt-tip caption, saying, 'Puke Hayseed'.

Adam's plan was brilliant. He had worked out how we should do it, how we should get Weeks hooked. Two nights ago, we had gone to Weeks's room after supper. We'd been there a while when Adam winked at me to let me know he was going to start. Suddenly he gave a pained grimace and grabbed his crotch. 'Christ,' he said to me, 'I must be early. Has yours started yet?'

Weeks's eyes narrowed.

I shook my head. 'I'm not due till next week. Actually, maybe it's the week after.'

'What?' said Weeks. 'What?'

Adam looked at me as if to ask whether or not it was okay to tell Weeks. I shrugged my shoulders.

'Your . . . you know . . . your . . .' Adam said.

Weeks stood up. 'What?'

Adam appeared embarrassed.

I said, 'No, he should ask his parents.'

Weeks couldn't bear to miss out on anything, a trait common in those who always missed out on everything. He backed against the door and put his arms across it as if we were about to force our way out. 'Tell me. Now. Please.'

Adam glanced at me and I gave him a reluctant shrug. 'You've got a sister, haven't you?' he said to Weeks. 'Does she have periods yet?'

Weeks went a little pink. 'Yeah, I should think. Christ, she's sixteen.'

'You know what a period is, don't you?'

'Course,' Weeks said, with a hint of defiance.

I raised my hand. 'No, Ad, let his parents tell him.'

Weeks butted in aggressively: 'Course I know. She's always talking about it.' He had lost his bass growl and was squeaking.

'You know that boys have them too? I mean, in a different way but sort of the same,' Adam said.

Weeks's eyes flitted uncertainly between us. 'Yeah? So?'

'Yours probably haven't started yet. Mine only just have. So have Luke's. It doesn't *matter* if they haven't started. They will eventually.'

'It's not a big deal,' I said. 'You've just got to be ready.'

'You mean . . .'

'Well, you don't want it *going* everywhere, do you?' Adam said, eyeing his crotch.

There was a pause. 'Well, I'm quite careful,' Weeks said.

'Anyway, you can get them at the chemist. The pads.'

'Yeah.' Weeks nodded in agreement.

'Your parents should have told you.'

'No, no, they did. In a roundabout way.'

'Only, you know, it would be awful if you didn't know and all that blood came pouring out of your prick. Still, it's only once a month, isn't it? Twelve times a year.'

'Yeah.'

'Actually,' I interjected, 'it's really thirteen. It's lunar months, not calendar ones.'

'Yeah, full-moon stuff,' Adam said, and made the baying sound of a werewolf.

'It's only happened a bit with me so far,' Weeks said confidently. 'I mean, it gets more every month, doesn't it?'

That morning, we learned with mounting horror that Weeks had gone to the medical centre and asked the doctor if he should have hormone injections to speed up his periods. In the lunch queue everyone was talking about what was going to happen to Adam and me. He and I sat huddled in the corner of the dining room, working out what we were going to say.

In the event, it all turned out quite differently. I was back from seeing the Head Man in less than ten minutes. I ignored everyone waiting in the corridor to find out what had happened and went into Adam's room. I shut the door and let out a sigh of relief.

'What happened?' Adam said. 'Tell me.'

I smiled, savouring every second.

'Come *on*!'

'My father's broken his leg or something. I've got to go up to London.'

Adam was mystified. 'What are you talking about?'

'My old man's broken his leg. That's what it was about – my dad. Nothing about Weeks.'

Adam whooped with delight. He put his arm round my shoulder and we kicked the door open, then pushed past the crowd outside. We were roaring with laughter.

'Close call, man,' Adam said.

'Yeah, close call,' I replied. 'Close fucking call.'

When I had told Adam I had to go to London because of my father's broken leg, it wasn't strictly true. I didn't have to go at all. Martha had rung the school and said there had been an accident, a traffic accident. Someone – a passer-by, apparently – had called her and told her that Arthur had been run over in the street, had broken his leg and was being taken to hospital. 'Nothing to worry about,' the Head Man said brightly. 'Your mother's going straight to the hospital.' That defined something to worry about, but it wasn't what I was thinking of. I had seen an opportunity, and while I weighed it up, I slipped a frown on to my face to keep the Head Man occupied.

'I'm sure it'll be fine, Hayman. They're miracle workers, these days. A splint, a lick of plaster . . .'

I had had a very specific vision: on the other side of the closed door to the Head Man's study, Weeks might be lurking, waiting to tell his story. Or there was going to be an urgent call from someone at the medical centre to tell the Head Man about the cruel joke that had been played on Weeks. It didn't take me long to decide what to do. 'I think I should go, sir. Don't you?'

'Go?'

'To the hospital.'

He gave a blustery laugh. 'Oh, I wouldn't have thought there was any need for that.'

'But nobody's actually, well, *heard* what happened, have they? I mean *properly*.'

He looked confused. 'Well, your mother –'

'She's not been well, sir.'

'Hasn't she?'

'No, sir.'

I thought I might get away with leaving it like that but I could see he was waiting for me to go on. I studied my hands, as if I was embarrassed, while I tried to think of something to say. A conveyor-belt of medical conditions passed by me and I grabbed one off it. 'It's the menopause, sir.'

'I see,' he said nervously.

I was on very shaky ground now. Maybe I meant hysterectomy. I added tentatively, 'Yes, it's been . . . a tricky one.'

'Well . . .'

'So it'll be difficult if she needs to lift him . . . you know . . . on to the lavatory.'

There was a pause. 'Won't the nurses do that?'

'He's rather particular about that kind of thing, sir.'

He looked at me in astonishment. I wondered whether I was going to have to blub as well. There was a brief silence, and then he said reluctantly, 'Well, I suppose you'd better take the train up to London.'

'Thank you, sir,' I said, in a humble voice with a little crack in it. It was the least I could do.

As I was getting up, he said, 'Oh, yes – your mother asked if you would ring your sister. She hasn't been able to track her down.'

That wasn't a surprise. Although Rachel was nominally sharing a flat in Golders Green with two girls who were at the same secretarial college, there was always some reason why she was never there. When I had last spoken to her, she'd said that one of the others had found a stray dog in the street and was taking care of it until a home could be found so she was going to have to move out because her asthma had come back.

'But you've never had asthma,' I said.

'It's normally only cats I'm allergic to.'

'What about Jamie?' Jamie was the cat we used to have. 'You weren't allergic to him.'

'Jamie was a her,' Rachel said. 'Anyway, Martha had her put down. I'll just have to go and sleep on Claude's floor.' The last time we had spoken, Rachel said she had had a row with Claude, but they had been friends for years, and were always locked in a cycle of argument and reconciliation.

After the taxi had dropped me at the station, I rang Claude's number. He lived in a house of bedsits in Earls Court. The owner of the house, whom Rachel and Claude called Mr Poontang, was a middle-aged actor who had inherited it from his mother. Claude had a room next to his new friend Damian, who had just arrived from South Africa. Since his grandfather had cut off his allowance, Claude sometimes worked as a tour guide, taking Americans round London, and Damian was helping him. Rachel said that most of their work was in the evenings, so I hoped he'd be in.

I had a lot of coins in my hand because the phone in Claude's house was on the ground floor and someone had to go up three flights to get him.

'What time is it?' Claude said, when he finally got to the phone.

'Three o'clock.'

'Who is this?' he said, in an outraged tone.

'It's Luke.'

'Oh, *Luke*. I thought it might be Todd.'

'Who?'

'Todd's in my tour group –' Claude's voice was cut off as the phone began beeping. I put some more money in. He was still talking when the coins went through. '– from Chicago. A lawyer. So he says. Though he certainly doesn't seem to have much idea of what's legal and what isn't. In this country, anyhow. Damian took him off my hands last night, but now he wants some of the money Todd gave me.'

'Do you know where Rachel is?'

'Anyway, Todd's not the point. It's his *friend* who's the point.'

'Claude,' I said wearily, 'I'm in a phone box and I'm running out of money. Where's Rachel?'

'I've no idea,' he said. I knew he was lying.

'Look, if you speak to her, will you tell her that Arthur's broken his leg and's in hospital?'

'How awful. I must get Damian to organize flowers.'

The train was coming in on the opposite platform. 'Claude, I've got to go.' I gave him the name of the hospital.

'You sound husky. Is your voice breaking?'

''Bye.'

'Luke, wait,' he wailed, as I put the phone down.

In the blank little room at the hospital where I had been sent to wait, there were many things I could have been thinking about. I could have been thinking about Arthur, who was on some other floor but seemed so distant he might have been on the moon. I could have been thinking about Rachel, who probably was on the moon. I could have been thinking about Martha, who, I'd been told, was up with Arthur and was probably making everyone wish they were on the moon. What I was actually thinking about was having left Adam to face the music on his own and how long I could spin out Arthur's broken leg.

There was a certain vagueness about the messages I had been getting from the hospital people I had talked to. People had been in and out. Cups of tea were brought. Faces were crinkled with sympathy. Lately I had noticed that eyes were averted, which made me think that maybe Arthur had broken his leg quite badly and would have to stay for a while. Weeks had broken his leg playing football and had been in hospital for a fortnight. Adam and I had scrawled obscenities on his cast with a red felt-tip pen.

After half an hour, there was a knock on the door and a doctor came in. It was nice of him to knock: nobody else had.

'I'm Dr Massingbird,' he said. 'You bearing up all right?' He looked me straight in the eyes, so intently, in fact, that I lowered them.

'How do you mean?' I was feeling uneasy now.

'Have you talked to your mother yet?'

'About what?'

'She hasn't been down?'

'No, I've been waiting here.'

There was a pause. 'How old are you? Twelve?'

What did that have to do with anything? 'Thirteen,' I said. 'Actually.'

He breathed out and shook his head. 'We're trying to get him stable. Your father.'

'You mean with crutches? Because he's unsteady on his legs?'

'He's sustained severe trauma, I'm afraid. The situation is very serious.'

My voice squeaked, 'But he's just broken his leg!'

'Among other things, yes.'

I didn't know what to say. The story I had constructed was slipping through my fingers. If I could just hold it together, everything would be fine. Arthur had broken his leg. He was unsteady on his legs. He was unstable. It had been pretty traumatic but it's all right now. Well, let's be honest, it's been severely traumatic but he's on the mend. Close call. Yeah, close fucking call.

I might have kept the story in one piece, but then he said something so awful as he was leaving that I felt the blood draining out of my face, felt myself falling down and down and down, like in an awful dream. 'Well,' he said, 'you're going to have to be a *very* brave lad.'

The worst thing was that it felt like my fault. What had been a simple broken leg that would take only a lick of plaster to fix had been worked up by me into something more serious so I could get out of school. If I had stayed there to face the music with Adam everything would have been all right. As it was, I had jumped out of the story in which I belonged into another story where I was not meant to be, in the process tampering with the natural order of things, the way it had all been meant to play out.

Adam once told me about a science-fiction story he had read in which someone travelled back through time with strict instructions not to alter anything in the past. Without knowing it, he did something that seemed inconsequential, like fart or tread on an ant, and when he got back to his own time the earth was a nuclear wasteland or ruled by man-eating cats or something. I preferred to think about that because it was so absurd rather than the other example of thinking something into existence that had sprung into my mind: at the end of *Garden Growing*, the third of the Hayseed books, Luke dreams of a bird dying – *Sometimes Luke dreamed in colour and sometimes he dreamed in black: different shades of black: dark black and light black and all the blacks of the rainbow. The crow in Luke's hands was black . . .* – and when he wakes up in the morning, to a silent and deserted house, he looks out of his window and sees the field that leads to the Darkwood black with the bodies of dead crows. Mr Toppit has made his dream come true.

The panicking Luke runs through the house trying to find his parents:

Along the corridors, across the passages, up the stairs, through the rooms, Luke's feet ran so fast that they were going faster than he was. He could scarcely keep up with them. They made no sound on the carpet and they made no sound on the bare floorboards. Doors slammed silently behind them, curtains flapped noiselessly in the silent breeze. Luke could hear himself shouting, but only at a distance: he was moving so quickly that his voice was always behind him. Where were his parents?

Sometimes, deficient though they may be, they're who you want and there's nothing you can do about it. I had to find Martha. I didn't feel precisely the panic that the other Luke did, but I felt the grimmest kind of foreboding. Actually, I felt simply alone. I now realized that Martha's non-appearance was another thing to be thrown into the murky pool in which 'severe trauma' and 'trying to get him stable' and 'very serious' were swimming around hungrily like sharks searching for something to devour.

In the corner of the room there was a small basin with a mirror next to it. I splashed cold water on my face before I realized there was no towel so I had to dry it on my sleeve. Then I unzipped my trousers and peed in the basin. What was nice was that it was exactly the right height, which made me feel a little better.

When I reached the ground floor the lift doors opened with a metallic *ping* and I was back in the entrance foyer where I had started out. The sun had moved across the sky and was shining in through the big windows right into my eyes. I went over to the boxed-in office in the corner and tapped on the glass. It wasn't the same man who had been there when I had first arrived. This one looked more like a security guard: he was dressed in a blue uniform with a cap. He slid open a panel.

'I'm trying to find out about my father,' I said breathlessly. 'They told me to wait and –'

He cut in: 'You shouldn't be walking around unaccompanied. How old are you?'

'Thirteen.'

'Where are your parents?'

'That's who I'm trying to find. I'm Luke Hayman. My father's Arthur Hayman. He's the one who's ill, who's a patient. My mother's called Martha Hayman.'

He tilted his head in the direction of the far corner. 'She's been sitting over there.' I turned. There was a row of empty chairs.

'Who?'

'Your mother. The American lady.'

'No, she's –'

'Black dress?'

'Well –'

'Dark hair?'

'Sort of brownish but –'

'She's been sitting over there. She was here a second ago, asked if there was any news about Mr Hayman.'

'But my mother's in the ward with my father. And she isn't American.'

He shrugged his shoulders. 'That's her bag on the chair. Maybe she's gone to the toilet.' I was really beginning to dislike him. I went over to the chairs and looked at the bag. It was made of black canvas and it said on the front in white lettering, 'KCIF Modesto – A Smoother Sound'.

'This isn't her bag,' I said, over my shoulder, but his chair had swivelled round and he had his back to me.

I had no idea what to do next. Short of locking myself in a lavatory and screaming with frustration, I had run out of options. I sat down and stared into space. After I had been there a few minutes, my gaze tilted to the black bag on the chair next to me. The top was bulging open and, without moving, I tipped my head sideways to see inside it. Glancing to check that the man wasn't looking, I put my hand inside the bag and felt around. It was like one of those games you play in the dark when you pass along a peeled grape and say it's someone's eyeball. There was a small box near the top of the bag, rectangular with a shiny surface. My hand pushed further in, passing what felt like damp tissues, a pen and a thin book before it hit a packet of something at the bottom. It felt a bit sticky and I snatched my hand out fast. My fingertips were brown. Cautiously, I raised them to my nose and sniffed. It was chocolate.

Saliva flooded into my mouth. It seemed like hours since I'd had anything to eat. The man was turned away from me and had his feet up on a table in front of him so I felt justified in raising the bottom of the bag and shaking it so that things slid out on to the chair. The rectangular box turned out to be Tampax, and I pushed it back in as I pulled out what had been a giant bar of chocolate. At one end, the paper and silver wrapping had been torn off. I got out a couple of chunks and ate them.

Then I shoved everything back into the bag. As the chocolate went in, it pushed out the corner of what looked like a notebook. I was about to press it back when I noticed 'Hayman' written on it in blue ink. I was so amazed that I stopped breathing for a second or two. I opened the book. Page after page – line after line, down the side, in the corner, upside down – was filled with two words: Arthur Hayman.

The lettering was in different sizes and styles, sometimes in capitals, sometimes in both upper and lower case. In places, the words were surrounded by boxes with ornate curlicues and flour- ishes. I didn't even care whether the man in the glass box saw me or not. I just dumped everything from the bag on to the chair and searched through it all. Apart from the Tampax, the chocolate and the notebook, there were some pens, a nail file, a key attached to a metal ring with the number '14' on it, a map of the Underground and – I pulled away my hand – a lot of scrunched-up pieces of tissue paper stained with blood.

I picked up the notebook again. The pages before the Arthur Hayman ones were relatively normal. There were a lot of calcula- tions, which I guessed were conversions from pounds into dollars, and bits of travel information like 'Nearest subway: Lancaster Gate', the name of an hotel with a phone number, and various things ticked or crossed out, like 'Call Alma'. Turning to the Arthur Hayman pages and those after them was like going through a door and entering a different world. There were doodles and little sketches, some just scrawls and others quite carefully done, all variations on a theme: a man and a child. Oddly he seemed to be a kind of Red Indian chief with a big headdress made of feathers. The child was a little girl, and while his face was quite carefully drawn, both head on and in profile, the child was a sort of silhouette with no features. The most finished of the drawings took up nearly a whole page of the notebook and showed the man and the child standing: he was tall and thin and she was tiny, hardly taller than his knees; they were holding hands. Running alongside all the sketches were the lines of a poem. They had been crossed out and rewritten all over the place, but a little portion of it was finished and written out neatly:

> *Oh my Anaglypta calling,*
> *Princess Anaglypta calling,*
> *Calling through the forest darkness*
> *Calling over prairie mountain.*
> *'Cross the waves of Gitche Gumee,*
> *Soaring waves that brush the seabirds,*
> *Haymanito hears her calling,*
> *Hears his Anaglypta calling.*

It was like *Hiawatha*, only it wasn't. 'Haymanito hears her calling . . .' I repeated the line aloud several times, then put the notebook, along with everything else that had spilled out on to the chair, back into the black bag as quickly as I could. I felt a strange sense of revulsion and couldn't wait to get it all off my hands. Just reading that poem had made me feel embarrassed, as if I'd been caught breaking into someone's house. But it wasn't as clear-cut as that. The frightening thing – the inexplicable thing – was that it was like breaking into a house you'd never laid eyes on, in a country you'd never been to, and finding it filled with your belongings.

So, there I was, sitting on a stackable black plastic chair in the foyer of a hospital into which my father, who might or might not be in a dangerously unstable condition, appeared to have been swallowed up, along with my mother, and I was surreptitiously going through the bag of an obviously unhinged woman, who might or might not be American and whom a security guard believed might be my mother. The opportunities for confusion were endless and I wanted something to be simple. Then amazingly – for a second – it was. There was an echoey *ping* and a light went on above the lift. The doors parted and there was Martha.

For a few seconds she didn't see me. She seemed rather small and old, and was apparently having difficulty with the lift: she was peering around her in a confused way, as if going through the open doors in front of her might not be the best way of getting out, as if, in fact, there might be several other exits that she couldn't find. Then she stepped out tentatively, looked up and saw me. I could tell that whatever the news was going to be, it was not going to be good.

I got up from the chair. It seemed to take a long time. I began to walk across the foyer to where Martha was standing and, at that moment, a number of things happened: a clanging ambulance squealed to a halt outside the entrance and the man in the glass office swivelled round to look; a troupe of chattering nurses holding clipboards banged through the double doors that led from the wards, their heels clicking on the lino like tap shoes, and crossed the foyer in front of Martha. It had been silent for such a long time that the noise was deafening, as if someone had turned up the volume too loud.

As I was moving past the glass office, the man's eyes met mine and I saw something in them that made me snap. Before I knew what was happening, I had veered away from the straight line that led to Martha and I was beside the glass office banging with my fist on the sliding panel. The man was astonished. The nurses stopped in their tracks and turned towards me. I clawed the panel open and stuck my head through the gap. He drew backwards as I shouted, 'That's my mother, you silly, stupid man! There she is! That's her! She's not American!' At the same time, I shook my outstretched finger in Martha's direction – but she was obscured now by the nurses. My nose was dripping and my mouth was filled with mucus. I had a vision of myself as a squalling, purple-faced, newborn baby. I slammed the panel shut with such force that the glass cracked and half of it fell out, shattering on the floor.

The ambulance that had stopped outside had disgorged three paramedics who were helping an old woman with a bleeding face through the entrance, and the man – grateful for the distraction – leaped from his chair and ran out of the door at the back of his office to help. The nurses were watching me, and as I moved towards them, they parted silently like a curtain. They ended up flanking Martha, looking nervously at this deranged child who probably had a carving knife hidden about his person. Everything was silent again, apart from some whimpering and shuffling as the injured woman was brought into the foyer.

Martha's face was blank, her mouth slack. She seemed exhausted. Her eyes closed and she made a guttural sound in her throat. When she opened her eyes, her mouth began to tremble and her face crumpled. 'Oh, baby, where have you been?' she said, in a thin, squeaky voice. 'Where were you? Why didn't you find me?' She looked me up and down. Tears were streaming over her cheeks. I couldn't speak. A medium-size golf ball had lodged itself temporarily in my throat. Then she let out a long groan as if she was in pain. 'Why do you always dress so horribly? You look so *weak*!'

As the man from the glass office passed us, leading the way for the three paramedics who were supporting the old woman, I thought I saw a smirk spreading across his face.

Laurie

Laurie had been sitting on the john for some time before she noticed that the toilet-paper holder was empty. She hiked her pants up, holding them round her waist without tying the drawstring, shuffled into the next booth and sat down again. Not that she cared much for kings and queens, but she couldn't help thinking it was sad that a royal hospital – it was called the Royal Waterloo – wasn't cared-for better, especially when there was this big royal wedding about to happen.

There was even graffiti on the door. Someone had written 'Bev swallows!!!' next to a drawing of a pair of lips clasped round what Alma called a diddly. The litter, the smell of food in the corridors, the scarred linoleum floors, the nurses and interns in scrubs that were clearly not fresh today, might not even have been fresh yesterday – oh, it was so depressing. It made the hospital look like somewhere people came to die instead of get better.

Laurie decided to zing for a bit. What had happened today had been so extraordinary that if she didn't get the crap out of her head she wouldn't be able to make any sense of it. It was as if she had picked up an odd piece of a jigsaw puzzle. Anyone would have said it wouldn't fit. It certainly didn't look as if it did, but Laurie knew that if she held it in her hand, if she moulded it until it formed the right shape, it would slot in snugly.

The zinging helped a curious chain of events to surface. When Mrs Detweiler had put her on the spot last night, asking what show Laurie was going to see, Laurie had plucked *Camelot* out of nowhere. Ever since her experience in high school with *Oklahoma!*, a humiliation she would have long forgotten if Alma hadn't kept reminding her about it, she had never cared much for musicals, only went to them if Marge dragged her. She wasn't even sure she had ever seen *Camelot*. Yet that was the show she had come up with: a musical about someone called Arthur, who was a king. And now she – and he – were in a royal hospital, even if, in her case, she was sitting on the john with her pants round her ankles.

She thought back to the scene of the accident – the phrase had started in her head as 'the scene of the crime' but she had altered it. Well, what had happened certainly was a crime but, of course, it wasn't a *crime* even though back home you wouldn't have been able to take a truck that big down a street that narrow. You wouldn't have been allowed to.

She tried to work out exactly how long she had had with Arthur. There was the first bit, from when she had knelt down beside him to when the paramedics arrived and tried to take her away from him. Then there was the second bit, from when Arthur hadn't wanted to let her go when they had put him on the gurney. The first bit had been longer than the second. Neither had been very long, but Laurie knew that what had happened between her and Arthur had had nothing much to do with time anyway. It might have been five minutes in all, might even have been less, but it wasn't how much he had said, it was what he had said and how he said it, and that he had said it to her.

She knew how badly he was hurt. He was cold and he was uncomfortable, but he wasn't in too much pain. If he had been less badly hurt, he would have been in more pain, but every bit of adrenaline in him must have been juicing round his body. And they would have given him morphine in the IV. He would have been happier after that had kicked in, but it had made him talk so softly she'd had to strain to hear him. Still, she had no reason to doubt what he had said even if she hadn't understood it all: his mind was clearly one hundred per cent. After all, he had remembered his phone number just like that, reeled it off with no hesitation. With all that had happened to him, you wouldn't have been surprised if he'd forgotten one of the digits or reversed a couple or just couldn't remember it at all, but the number had been right first time.

She felt calmer now. She had forced herself to be calm when she was sitting with Arthur on the kerb, but as soon as the paramedics had got him on the gurney and were lifting him and trying to keep the drips level and the oxygen mask from slipping off, really the moment she was forced to take her hand from his, she had begun to tremble so badly it was as if someone was shaking her.

The worst was when the doors of the ambulance were banged shut, and she had her hands pressed on the glass knowing someone else was beside him now, leaning over him, trying to get him comfortable. She had wanted to shout his name so that he would know she was there, would know she hadn't left him, but instead she whispered it and saw her breath condense on the window. He would hear that just as well as if she had screamed it. And then she was crying, great silly sobs, as the ambulance drove off, and she was left alone in the street with a crowd of silent, staring people who were already dispersing. Up the road, she could see the truck driver in a doorway with two policemen. She had moved somewhere else in her head now, felt almost no anger towards him. She was shaky on her feet, but she needed to get to a phone and do what Arthur had asked her to do, and she hoped she could do it before she threw up.

The first two phone booths she tried were broken. In one, the receiver was hanging down and when she put it to her ear, there was no dialling tone. In another, there was no receiver, just a bit of curly black wire. When she found one that was working, she lodged herself tightly into it and took her glasses out of her bag so she could read the instructions. The phone system was different here: instead of putting a coin in right at the start, you were meant to dial the number and when the person picked up you put the coin in. She had written the number on the back of her hand, and she dialled it. It rang for a while and she began to panic: what would happen if nobody was home? She had promised Arthur she would call. He hadn't asked her to promise, but she had anyway. She hadn't wanted him to worry. But then there was a click, and a woman's voice said, 'Hello?'

Immediately the receiver beeped and Laurie pushed the coin into the slot. It was blocked. She groaned, 'Oh, no!' She tried to force it in. She put her mouth as close as she could to the receiver and shouted, 'Hi! Can you hear me? Can you hear me?' but the phone went on beeping until it was replaced by a single high-pitched note, like a cardiac monitor flat-lining. Laurie was drenched with sweat now. She tried again.

This time the woman picked up almost instantly. 'Rachel?' she said, which took Laurie aback. She was about to say, 'No, it's Laurie,' when the beeping started and she tried again to push the coin in. She screamed in frustration when it wouldn't go. She banged the receiver down. In the dirty little mirror, her face was red and blotchy. She looked like a crazy person. She searched in her purse for another kind of coin and started again. This time it worked. It went straight in when the beeping started, and then the line was quiet. Laurie realized she had no idea what to say.

'Was it you who just phoned?' the woman said.

After a moment Laurie said doubtfully, 'Yes.' She had considered saying no.

'Who's speaking?'

'Is that Mrs Hayman?'

'Yes. Who's speaking? Who's that?'

'Your husband, Mr Arthur Hayman . . .'

'Yes?'

'Oh, Mrs Hayman . . .' Laurie's voice broke.

The woman didn't sound angry, just perplexed. 'Please – who are you?'

'Your husband's had an accident.'

'What? What do you mean?'

'Yes, he's . . . broken his leg.' She didn't know what else to say.

'But when?'

'Now – just now . . . It just happened now. Here.'

'Where?'

Laurie looked at the street through the glass of the phone booth. She didn't know where she was. 'Just . . . here,' she said.

'Is he there now? Should I talk to him? Who *are* you?'

'You can't talk to him. He's gone. They've taken him to the Royal Waterloo Hospital.'

The woman said something, and then Laurie did a terrible thing: she hung up. She stumbled out of the phone booth, leaned back on it and took some deep breaths. Right next to her, a black cab was waiting by the kerb. She hadn't noticed it at first, but as she glanced up at it, a yellow light, saying 'For Hire', flashed above the windscreen. As if she had been taking cabs in London all her life, she opened the door, got in, slumped into the comfortable leather seat and said, 'The Royal Waterloo Hospital,' and added – for the second time that day, 'I'm a nurse.'

In the john she was sifting and sorting now, processing bits of information, moving things from one slot to another, then back again. The shapes and colours were random, but she could feel them acquiring form and meaning. She knew it would take a while, but eventually it would be like flying high above the earth and seeing how the shapes that seemed arbitrary on the ground were part of some greater pattern.

She was so tired. What she would really have liked was a hot shower, a real one, not the English kind that she'd had in the hotel, like a dog pissing on you. She pulled her pants up and stretched as much as the little booth would allow. She unlocked the door, came out and stood in front of a basin. She tried the hot tap, but it was jammed so she turned on the cold, splashed water on her face and tried to get her hair back to something like it had looked when she'd had it cut and styled the day before she left Modesto. She could smell herself. She pulled some paper towel out of the dispenser, put a wad of it under the tap and rubbed the sliver of discoloured soap over it. She raised both arms in turn and wiped her armpits. Then, with a glance at the door to make sure nobody was coming in, she pulled the waistband of her pants away from her body, put her hand down and wiped the damp paper between her legs.

She was just about to open the door when panic welled in her.

She touched her shoulder, looked at the ground and ran to the first booth she had been in and then the one she had moved to. Nothing. She had lost her bag. Tears of anger and frustration came into her eyes and she let out a groaning yelp. It wasn't as if she had lost her money and stuff, which was still in the belt round her middle. That wouldn't have been so bad. You could call up about credit cards, passports and driving licences, even though she wouldn't have wanted to try in England – not with that phone system. Her bag had the notebook, which was like a record, which was like *proof*, of the time she had spent with Arthur. Of course she had it in her head too, but she wanted every single last everything she could have.

She yanked open the door of the bathroom so hard that it crashed against the wall with a bang, then ran down the corridor, huffing and puffing, going red in the face and clearing everything out of her way like a runaway train. By the time she got back to the entrance where she had been sitting she was in pain and she was lopsided. Her knee had been giving her trouble for a while, another of the many reasons she was meant to be on a weight-loss programme. It was okay: at the far end, by the glass doors that led to the forecourt, she could see her bag on the chair where she had left it. She leaned against the wall and tried to get her breath back. Well, that was one difference between here and Holy Spirit. There, someone would have taken the bag soon as look at you. Marge had even had her golf clubs stolen from outside the hospital chapel while she was at the interdenominational Sunday service.

Laurie hobbled back to her seat. As she passed the glass office she almost tripped over someone on their hands and knees on the floor. They were clearing up some broken glass with a little brush. There must have been an accident. The man who had been in the office had gone and there was now a woman in his place. Laurie smiled at her. She might need her help. She checked in her bag. Everything was still there. She hadn't realized how much chocolate she'd eaten but she finished it anyway. Then she got out her notebook and pen and began to write. She was still thinking about King

Arthur and *Camelot*. She was pretty hazy about what had happened to him and Queen Guinevere, but she knew there was something about a round table.

After a while, she went back to working on her *Hiawatha* poem. When she had been there for about twenty minutes, the doors opened and a young couple came in. They were whispering in an agitated way, as if they had just had a row. The girl was tall and thin with thick brown hair that was all mussed up. The boy was several inches shorter and was wearing a floor-length purple coat, which appeared to be made of velvet, with a dirty white ruffled shirt underneath that hung over his pants. He had tiny wire-rimmed spectacles – the lenses were round, the size of quarters – perched on the end of his nose. He needed some orthodontic work: his teeth were crooked and stuck out. Laurie went back to her writing, but then she heard the girl say, in an imperious tone, 'I've come to see my father. He's broken his leg. My name's Rachel Hayman.'

Luke

Back in the little room where I had started out, Martha was sitting on a fold-up chair underneath a 'No Smoking' sign holding a cigarette between her fingers. I was standing at the other end of the room next to a poster of Prince Charles and Lady Di that had been stuck crookedly to the wall.

When Dr Massingbird had first come in and cleared his throat nervously to prepare himself for telling us what he had come to tell us, Martha had suddenly leaned down and rifled through her handbag, which was beside her on the floor. Out of courtesy he had paused, and when she resurfaced with a packet of cigarettes, her face had crumpled like a balloon with the air let out and tears were pouring down her cheeks again. She had pulled out a cigarette, put it between her lips and held the flame of the lighter to it. She drew on it, took it out of her mouth and let her hand rest on the table. Then she turned her head away from Dr Massingbird. There was an awkward silence. I saw his eyes flick up to the 'No Smoking' sign. He glanced at me and turned back to her. 'Let me get you an ashtray,' he said. Then I knew we were really in trouble.

Since we had got back to the room, many people had been in to see us. In fact, the same person never came twice. When one left, there would be a brief lull, then the door would open and a different one would come in. I was hazy about hospital etiquette, about who were the important people and who were not. Nobody introduced themselves. They came in, said their piece and left. The team had assembled, they said. Mr Hayman was just being moved out of the resuscitation room. He was being made comfortable. Dr Massingbird kept being promised: he would be with us imminently, he was on his way, he was expected out of theatre at any moment.

Why couldn't there just be a single person who came and told us everything all in one go? It would have been better for Martha: she needed one person for her magic to work. A procession of different people did not play to her strengths. It distracted her, diminished her throw. At a party, she never stayed in a group. You always found her in a room other than the one where the party was taking place with some man she had extracted. She would be deep in conversation with him in the kitchen, or upstairs in a bedroom sitting on a pile of coats, or in a study perched on the edge of the desk. By the end of the party her head bobbed gently, as if it was floating on a rippling sea, her eyes misty as she talked to whoever was the chosen one.

Even if we were ready to leave, there was always time for another cigarette or another drink. Normally, Arthur, Rachel – if she had deigned to come – and I would be standing, powerless, by the door in our coats as the guests were leaving, making awkward conversation with the wife of the person Martha was talking to. Finally, she would appear and make her way towards us, negotiating each step carefully with her small feet and elegant shoes. At the door, she would take the hand of the person she had been talking to, might hold it in both of hers and, oblivious to the rest of us, finish off her conversation while we waited. The man, having first thought she was going to shake his hand, was now unsure whether to take it back or to leave it in her grasp, so it lay there in a kind of limbo like a small, hibernating animal. Then, often in mid-sentence, she would stop talking, give the man a distracted smile and – ignoring his wife – walk out of the door without another word. Martha always had a problem with goodbyes.

As Dr Massingbird went out of the room on his ashtray hunt, Martha looked up at me. 'It was a broken leg, that's what she said, the woman on the phone, that's all she said,' sounding as irritated as if a stranger had given her the wrong directions in the street. Then she sniffed and wiped her nose on the back of her hand.

When Dr Massingbird came back, Martha appeared to have rallied a little. He had brought with him a little foil container that might once have held a cupcake. He smiled apologetically. 'I'm sorry. That's the best we can do, I'm afraid.' He cleared his throat. 'Mrs Hayman,' he began.

Martha put her head at an angle and smiled at him. 'Where are you from?' she asked. 'Where's your accent?'

He had been about to start on the matter in hand, so the question threw him off track. 'Ireland, actually,' he said, as if he was not entirely sure.

'Ireland! Whereabouts? Which part?'

'Well . . . Skibbereen. It's just near –'

'Skibbereen,' Martha repeated dreamily, exhaling a trail of cigarette smoke, as if the sound of that one word was the only way of defining a perplexing set of emotions. Then her voice hardened quizzically: 'But isn't Massingbird originally a Suffolk name?'

His hand flew up and covered the name badge on his chest, as if he had unwittingly let out a secret. 'Well . . .' he said.

'A Father Massingbird accompanied Richard Coeur de Lion on a crusade. He died before he got to Constantinople. His body was sent home to Walberswick in a butt of brandy.' She got up and, ignoring the ashtray he had brought, walked over to the sink in the corner and turned the tap on. There was a little fizz as she put the cigarette under the stream of water, then dropped it into the basin. She gave a curious little sniff. 'I think someone's urinated in this,' she said.

I gazed at the floor.

Dr Massingbird cleared his throat again. He was gearing himself up for another try. Now we were going to hear. 'Mrs Hayman,' he said. Then he glanced at me. 'And . . . ?'

'Luke,' I said.

'Luke,' he repeated, with a little nod, as if he had just needed his memory jogged. He took a deep breath and brought his hands, now clasped, up to his chin. 'What we have here is . . . not a good situation. Not good, I'm afraid,' he said, bobbing his head up and down as if he was agreeing with himself. He turned to Martha and made a little gesture towards me. 'Would you like Luke to . . .? Is it all right if . . .?'

Outrage is not good for the breaking voice. 'What am I meant to do? Go outside and read a comic?' came out as a petulant squawk, but Martha had already given a get-on-with-it flick of her hand, so Dr Massingbird continued.

'We haven't succeeded in getting your husband stable yet. There's been internal bleeding. An enormous amount, in fact.'

Martha had gone white. I don't know what colour I was. She swallowed and her throat made a rusty squeak.

'Do you have any questions you would like to ask me?' Dr Massingbird said. Suddenly I couldn't think of anything I wanted to know. In fact, I really wanted him to go away.

Martha obviously felt the same. 'I don't think so. You've been so kind. Thank you,' she said graciously. 'We'll wait here. For news.' She was dismissing him.

A flicker of panic passed across Dr Massingbird's face. He hadn't finished and he didn't know quite how to continue, so when he said, 'We'll probably have to amputate his legs,' it came out more brutally than he'd perhaps meant it to. I turned to the wall, and found myself almost kissing the faces of Charles and Di on the poster. Martha put a hand over her mouth as if she was about to be sick.

'There's been some major trauma to the lower half of his body, I'm afraid.'

'Both his legs?' I whispered. I didn't even mind that it sounded inane.

He nodded. 'We've been trying to get him stable enough to operate for the last hour.'

'And then what would happen?' Martha asked.

'We'll operate as soon as we can.'

'No. After the operation,' she snapped.

'Well, there would be a long recovery period, if we were successful. Really quite extended. Before he could come home, that is.'

Martha shook her head. 'No. I'm sorry, no.'

'I'm afraid an operation is the only chance.'

Martha looked like a wax figure that was melting in the sun. Her eyes were wide, but everything else on her face was collapsing. 'It's quite impossible,' she said flatly.

'Well . . .' Dr Massingbird said awkwardly.

'No, I'm sorry,' she said.

I walked over to her and put my arms round her, but she slipped out of my grasp, her gaze directed intently at the doctor. 'It's not possible,' she said, emphasizing each word. 'We don't have the facilities.'

Dr Massingbird glanced at me, as if to elicit my help. 'Mrs Hayman –'

'To have him at home.' Then she cried out, 'Do you know how many stairs we have? We don't live in a *bungalow*.' She slumped into the chair and put her head in her hands. '*Ohhhh*,' she moaned, 'where's Rachel? *Where is Rachel?*'

When Rachel arrived, the first thing she said was, 'Where's Martha?', her eyes darting suspiciously round the room as if she might be hiding in a cupboard. Martha had left a few minutes before: Dr Massingbird had come back to say they were getting ready to operate on Arthur, and she could have ten minutes with him.

Rachel sat on Martha's chair and she, too, pulled out a packet of cigarettes. Her hair was all over the place. 'Couldn't they have brought him somewhere closer?' she said. 'Claude drove me. Damian was in a bate and he actually had to *pay* him to take over the tour group. How's Arthur's leg?'

'It's not a broken leg, Rach, not really,' I began.

'But that's what Claude said.'

'That's what Claude said because that's what I told him. That's what I thought. Until I got here.' And then I told her.

Afterwards – for a moment – she was like she used to be, when she was part of us, when you could say something to her and her

72

response was reflexive, not like talking to someone on the phone whose voice was being routed through a succession of different exchanges before it got to you. She listened in silence and then she said, 'But what about his books? What happens if he wants to write another?' *Darkwood*, the fifth, had been published a year before.

'Has he said he's going to do another one?'

'He doesn't *normally* say anything much, does he?'

'It doesn't mean he can't do another book. They're not saying he's not going to get better.'

'How many negatives can you fit into one sentence, Luke? Of course he's not going to get better,' she shouted at me. Then she started crying. 'Mr Toppit's only just come out of the Darkwood.' She bit her lip and put her hand over her mouth as if she was trying to stop herself screaming.

I went over to where she was sitting and put my arms round her. It felt odd. I couldn't remember the last time we had hugged. She smelled of cigarettes and joss sticks and old scent. Then she pulled away. She was trembling. 'I must get Claude. I can't leave him downstairs.'

I couldn't face him. 'He'll be fine,' I said.

'He's having a horrible time.'

'Just *leave* him. This is nothing to do with him.'

She was shaking her head, her hands clasped by her mouth. Like Martha's had, her face was collapsing. 'He's the only person I've got now,' she wailed.

'Apart from me,' I said, as neutrally as I could. 'And Martha,' I added, but that didn't come out quite so neutral.

She managed to observe the civilities. 'Yes. I know that. But Claude has nobody. Nobody at all.'

'He's got a mother, hasn't he? And that grandfather who gives him money?'

'You have no idea. His grandfather's *horrible*. Oh, it's so *humiliating* for him.'

'Why are we talking about Claude?'

'What would you rather talk about? The funeral?'

That was unfair. We sat in silence.

'He's not going to die,' I said.

'I don't know anybody who's died.'

'Me neither.'

'Except . . .' Rachel's voice tailed off.

Animals have some kind of instinct to warn them of danger in the air. People like Rachel and I had it too. It's a sort of familial code, a dog-whistle signal so obscurely pitched, so far off any conventional tonal scale, that even those NASA computers monitoring sounds in space couldn't pick it up. What Rachel had said had left a residue of something chemical in the air, a kind of static that set off a chain reaction, which forced the ions in the atmosphere to flow back on themselves, like a hand brushing suede against the grain.

'Except who?' I said. I knew perfectly well. I was just trying to brush the grain back the other way as fast as I could.

She looked at me and said, 'Nothing's gone right for us since then . . . Since . . .'

I knew what she was going to say and prayed she wouldn't. What defines a secret? Is it just something that one person knows and nobody else does? If it's something that everyone knows, it can't be a secret because they all know it and it isn't secret. But we all knew it and it was still a secret. I was willing her to stay silent, but she went on.

'. . . since Jordan,' she said.

She had said it, and in a funny way I admired her for it. I thought: How brave, how fantastically brave. It had been unsaid for such a long time that I wasn't sure what would happen when the word was uttered. And, of course, nothing did. When a train roars through a station without stopping, the sound, that clacking, rushing noise, doesn't stay with you. It's gone in a second, but your ears still throb.

We held each other's gaze. 'But that's all our lives, Rachel.'

'I don't think *time*'s got anything to do with it,' she said. 'It doesn't just go away because we don't talk about it.'

I didn't know what to say. There wasn't anything *to* say unless we wanted to go on. My bravery was nil. Rachel didn't seem to have the appetite either.

'Are you cold?' she said. 'I'm freezing.'

Actually, I was rather hot but I could see her shivering. 'Why don't you go and get some coffee or something? I'll have some too.'

She looked relieved. 'Yes, shall I? Maybe something to eat as well.'

As she went out, I said, 'It's going to be all right.'

'I don't think so,' she said.

I wasn't on my own for long, although I seemed to have lost all sense of time. I could have been sitting for days in that room. Then the door opened and it was Dr Massingbird, followed by a young nurse, followed by Martha, clutching her handbag. The door stayed open until the nurse eased behind Martha and closed it.

'What's happened?' I asked. Martha was staring at the floor.

Dr Massingbird cleared his throat. 'You know how serious the situation was. While we were trying to get him stable enough for an operation his heart stopped beating three times, probably due to loss of blood.'

'So what happens now?' My voice had gone trembly.

Dr Massingbird looked back at Martha. 'Mrs Hayman?' he said gently. They all stood there rather awkwardly.

I suddenly realized. 'He's dead already, isn't he?'

Dr Massingbird put his hand on my shoulder. 'We did everything we could but we were unsuccessful. I'm so sorry.' For someone who probably had to say the same thing several times a day, I was impressed by how freshly minted he made it sound.

I wished I'd been directly involved in a death before – then I'd have known how to behave. Adam had some experience of it: his grandfather had choked on a roast potato in the middle of Sunday lunch. His father had given the old man mouth-to-mouth resuscitation but he had died anyway. 'Well, you'd probably want to die if your father stuffed his tongue down your throat,' Adam said.

Adam had this theory: it didn't matter what you did because the day of your death is fixed from the moment you're born. I said, 'You mean that if your grandfather hadn't choked on a roast potato he would have choked on something else, like a parsnip?' It wasn't the *method* of death that was preordained, Adam said, just the day. If he hadn't choked on a roast potato he might have tripped on the front step on his way home and cracked his head open. I asked what would happen if you were on a trip abroad and your preordained day was actually the day before or the day after because of the time difference. 'No, no,' Adam said, 'there's no way you can ever beat the system. Sometimes there's a malfunction and people get taken before their time: they become the undead and they're in a state of limbo until their preordained day comes round, which might not be for another twenty years.' Adam didn't think his grandfather had been one of them.

So when I turned away from Dr Massingbird and the nurse and Martha, and rested my head against the wall, I wasn't crying because Arthur was dead. In fact, I said to them, rather aggressively, 'This is nothing to do with him being dead,' in order to make the point. I just didn't want Arthur to be in limbo. I couldn't bear that. I knew there had to be a mistake. You don't break your leg and die from it. I knew he must be one of the few – so very few, according to Adam, that it's a real headache for the statisticians – who had been taken before their time.

I wiped my nose on my sleeve. Dr Massingbird and the nurse gazed at me with great moony eyes. I made a half-hearted attempt to explain: 'It just isn't the right time for him,' I said.

Dr Massingbird shook his head. 'It never is the right time, is it?' he said gently. 'Not for the people we love.' The nurse rearranged her mouth and made a moist sound with her lips to show solidarity.

'No, it can be, actually,' I said. 'That's the whole point. It can be exactly the right time.'

I saw unease in Dr Massingbird's eyes. He was about to say something when Martha clenched her fists, tilted her head back, opened her mouth and let out a baying noise. '*Ohhhh,*' she howled, '*can't we just get on?*' Then her head fell forward into her hands and she held it tightly, as if she was trying to stop it coming off her shoulders.

I wasn't precisely sure what the phrase 'get on' meant in this context, the context of a man lying dead from a broken leg on one floor of a hospital and his widow and son standing in a room on another floor with a nurse and a doctor, trying to make sense of what had happened and what was going to happen. In the event, I didn't have much time to think about it because the door opened and the context changed: there was Rachel.

I'm not quite sure what happened when Rachel began to scream, whether bleepers were bleeped or alarms sounded or whether it was simply the level of noise that was coming from Rachel, but there was some real action now, both in our room and out of it. Even before the nurse had got outside the door and was shouting down the corridor, I could hear running footsteps.

One thing you could say about Martha was that she was good in a crisis. Even before Dr Massingbird had got to Rachel, Martha had launched herself across the room and was flailing around on the floor practically on top of her. By this time Rachel was on her hands and knees making a terrifying array of noises. Actually, it might have been Martha making them. It was hard to tell. I had turned away and put my hands over my ears. I wanted to block the whole day out, not only what was happening now but what had gone before: everything, every single thing.

Time must have passed, because when I turned back to face the room, the nurse was there, and so was Dr Massingbird, with another man in a white coat. I couldn't even see Rachel. They were bending over her. Dr Massingbird held a syringe, and had obviously given her a shot of something. When they moved back, I saw Martha sitting on the floor with her back against the wall.

Rachel was lying in a foetal position with her head on Martha's lap making small whimpers while Martha stroked her hair. They looked like a deranged Madonna and Child in one of those *pietà* paintings we had studied in Art History.

Martha tried to get up. She stretched out her arm and I went over to help them up as best I could. Once on our feet, we put our arms round each other. I could feel Martha shaking slightly. There was a silence. I was the first to speak: 'What should we do now?'

'Well,' Dr Massingbird said, letting out a deep breath, 'if you would like to, you could see your father. They'll be preparing him now, and then they'll lay him out in the chapel of rest.' He turned to Martha. 'Mrs Hayman?'

I was quite surprised that this was a service a hospital offered. If you'd asked me I would have said it was more of an undertaker thing. Anyway, I took my hat off to Dr Massingbird: it was brave of him to raise the subject of death again when his natural inclination must have been to talk about almost anything else. 'You might like to have some time to gather yourselves first,' he added.

Martha was coming back to life. 'I think we've gathered enough already,' she said.

Rachel was looking down and I put my hand on her cheek to bring her head up a little. 'Rachel? Is that okay? Is that what you'd like to do?'

Her eyes were closed. She shook her head, but not to indicate that she didn't want to, just that she couldn't cope with making any decisions. I wasn't sure whether I wanted to, but I'd never seen a dead body before so it seemed silly not to take the opportunity. Anyway, Adam was sure to have a lot of questions.

I turned to Dr Massingbird and said, 'Thank you.' It was the best I could come up with. He offered his hand and I shook it.

Then he held it out to Martha. Her eyes filled with tears, and she did something really strange, even for Martha: she raised his hand to her lips and kissed it. 'Thank you for all you've done,' she said. There was a little lump in my throat. It felt like the end of an era, like the last day of the summer holidays.

The nurse was standing by the door, holding it open for us. Martha was almost out of the room when she suddenly turned back to Dr Massingbird and waved a finger at him. 'You should research your family history,' she said. 'Those Suffolk Massingbirds are more interesting than you know.' Then she followed the nurse out with halting steps.

I presume the majority of people leave hospitals alive, so I felt we were rather privileged to be seeing a side of one that few have the chance to see. Going to the chapel of rest felt like being taken backstage in a theatre. We must have seemed a bedraggled trio as we trailed the nurse along the corridor. I imagined that we looked rather like the shell-shocked survivors of a train crash.

Eventually, we found ourselves in the lift going down to the ground floor, the same lift I'd been in several decades earlier that afternoon. The doors parted and we came out into the lobby. 'Not much further,' the nurse said. 'It's just down here through the double doors.'

As we turned away from the lobby, I saw Claude at the other end, sitting where I had been sitting, by the entrance. He got to his feet slowly and came across the lobby to where we standing. Rachel was so knocked out by whatever the doctor had given her that she appeared scarcely to recognize him.

'He died, Claude,' I said. I didn't know how else to handle it. He looked horrified. I hadn't realized how embarrassing death could be. We stood there for a moment while Claude tried to think of something to say. His mouth opened, but nothing came out.

Once he did start to speak, though, he seemed unable to stop. 'This is a tragedy, oh, it's just unbelievable. I had no idea, I thought it was a broken – Damian will be so –'

Martha put a finger over her lips to indicate that she wanted him to stop talking. 'Just look after Rachel,' she said, and propelled her into Claude's arms. In order to put them round her, he had to place the black bag he was holding on the ground. On it, in white lettering, it said, 'KCIF Modesto – A Smoother Sound'.

'Claude,' I said, 'where did you get that?'

'What?' he said.

'The bag, the black bag.'

'Oh, that? Some woman I was talking to. She asked me to keep an eye on it while she went to get something to eat.'

At that moment, the double doors opened and a woman came through them. She was short, probably Rachel's height, but huge. She seemed to be wearing a black tent over her trousers. As soon as she saw us she stopped dead and stared at us warily, like a wild animal we had strayed across in the woods. Her eyes were taking everything in, darting from me to Rachel to Claude to Martha and back again. If she had really been an animal she would have been sniffing the air, too. We had been studying this in Biology but I had never seen it in action before: neural receptors passing information to the brain for it to be processed so that – according to my class book – a hypothesis can be made based on the available evidence.

Martha, Rachel and I were the available evidence, and the processing was quick: 'He's passed on, hasn't he?' the woman said. 'He's gone.'

Martha's eyes were wide with astonishment. She must have been completely confused. I wasn't – I had seen inside the black bag with the white lettering. For a second, I thought the woman was going to flee, but then her body sagged as if some pressure had been released. The blood rushed to her face and her mouth opened in a great silent cry and she rocked back and forth as tears rolled down her red cheeks.

I had seen people cry, of course I had, but not like this. Her grief seemed totally naked. When we had cried, Martha and Rachel and I, I knew we had really been crying for ourselves, everything overlaid with our own fear. This woman was crying like a child, grief so focused and concentrated it was shockingly pure. And just as you would have stopped and comforted a strange child you found weeping alone in the street, Martha, almost as a reflex, opened her arms and the woman stumbled into them.

★

When we were younger Rachel and I used to call them 'The Rhymes'. It had been our secret name, useful for talking about them in front of other people – or, indeed, in front of them – without anyone knowing. Now we were older it had fallen into disuse: too implicitly affectionate to generate the appropriate level of parental hostility required by angry adolescents. But I thought of it as we stood round Arthur's body. It would be the last time I saw him and Martha together. Now that he was gone, there was no one for her to rhyme with: we could hardly make it singular and call her 'The Rhyme' and I couldn't think of another suitable name to go with hers that would be in the realms of the possible. Adam had been trying to read this weird German book by Hermann Hesse, but she wasn't going to meet anyone called Siddhartha unless she joined an eastern cult – unlikely, although you never knew with Martha.

I don't suppose there are rules that say only the immediate family are allowed to see the body of the deceased, but you might wonder why we had brought Laurie and Claude with us to the chapel of rest. If Rachel had been capable of speech, she would have argued that Claude was the next best thing to family, and as for Laurie, well, it would have been cruel to exclude her after she had wept on Martha's shoulder and spluttered out her story.

As she told it, it did pass through my mind that Arthur's death would have been marginally easier if Laurie had not muddied the waters with the business of the so-called broken leg, but I suppose that if there was ever a time to be forgiving, this was it. In her own way she had done the best she could – and at least someone was dripping hot salt tears for Arthur Hayman on to the scuffed linoleum floor of the Royal Waterloo Hospital. Without Laurie, we would have seemed like a group of zombies. She was like our official mourner. In Anthropology, the special subject Adam and I had chosen because Mrs Farrell, the teacher, was reputed not to wear any knickers, we had learned that in ancient Tahitian culture the designated mourner would parade through the dead person's settlement, carrying a weapon edged with shark's teeth that he would use against anyone who got in his way – not an inappropriate metaphor for Laurie, as it turned out.

As we were led into the chapel, I was so nervous that I thought I was going to be sick, but as soon as I saw Arthur I felt curiously calm. He was lying on a kind of plinth, with a blanket covering all of him except his head. Under the cover, you could see the shape of his body and I wondered if those really were his legs that I could see outlined, or whether they were so crushed that they had put rolled-up blankets in their place so his body wouldn't appear damaged. The curious thing was how normal he looked, except for one thing: he was unmistakably dead. It didn't seem to me that he was in limbo. His time probably had come.

It's difficult to know what to do in these circumstances. Rachel and Martha were by his feet clinging to each other. Claude stood at his head and Laurie and I were opposite one another on either side of him. Whatever Rachel had been given by the doctor was wearing off and her eyes were brimming with tears. Martha was shaking her head. Laurie had a curious lost look on her face. The room was very silent. It was as if we were playing that game in which the first person to make a noise loses a life.

Martha was the first to break. She made a strange kind of gurgling sound in her throat, which seemed to release some of the pressure that had built up in the room. Rachel began to cry in earnest, with squeaky noises like a rusty hinge. Claude seemed slightly desperate, as if he knew he was meant to do something but wasn't sure what. I wished I could be in the room on my own: they were all cramping my style. Left to myself I would have reached out and touched Arthur, maybe to hold his hand or move the thin wisps of hair off his forehead, but I wasn't going to do it with them there.

After a while Martha caught Claude's eye and gestured with her head towards the door. Glad to have something to do, he went over and opened it. Martha propelled Rachel out, and I followed them into the waiting room reluctantly: I wasn't convinced we had done the things we were meant to do in the chapel of rest, but we were new to this, and there was nobody to give us instructions. The door shut behind us. We stood for a moment, unsure what to do next.

'What about ... What *is* her name?' Martha said, pointing towards the chapel where Laurie still was. Her voice was croaky.

'Laurie,' said Claude.

'How do you think it's spelled?'

'I don't know. With "ie" at the end? I mean, not like the lorry you drive.'

'Well, she's the size of one,' Martha said. 'Isn't that an odd name for a woman?'

Rachel suddenly gave a gulping sob and laid her head on Claude's shoulder. Martha put her arms round both of them so they made a small circle. 'The boy ...' Rachel began, but she was crying so much she couldn't get any more out. Now, in the face of Rachel's inarticulate grief, the rest of us unravelled. Even Claude's face crumpled, and he had to remove his little round spectacles so he could wipe his eyes. Rachel drew in several shuddering gasps of air, but every time she opened her mouth to speak she stumbled at the last fence. She had one last go: she moved her head from side to side as if summoning strength. 'The boy in *Little Women* is called Laurie,' she whispered.

Tears were trickling down Claude's face now. 'Isn't that one of the sisters?'

Rachel shook her head. She looked as if her heart would break. 'No, there's Amy and Meg and ...'

Now I understood how Martha had felt when she had screamed, '*Can't we just get on?*' earlier in the afternoon. Their sobs mingled and, with their arms still round each other, they began to sway in the middle of the room. I turned away from them – they looked so silly.

'I'll get Laurie,' I said, but either they couldn't hear or they weren't listening. I eased open the door of the chapel. For a moment, I thought she had vanished, but then I saw she was kneeling by the side of Arthur's plinth, her head resting on his chest, just under his chin, and her hand was stroking his cheek. She was so engrossed that she didn't see me. Finally she looked up. She wasn't crying now. 'Such a fine man,' she said. 'You could tell, you could just feel it. The goodness came off of him.' It was an epitaph from a greetings card, but it was better than nothing.

Once I had accepted that Arthur was dead nothing else could seem very surprising, so the fact that Laurie appeared to be coming home with us, was wedged into the back of Claude's grandfather's ancient Daimler between Rachel and me, felt oddly natural.

Maybe we all thought that one of the others had asked her to come. Maybe we were too exhausted to care. Apart from the hum of the engine as we drove down the motorway and the light sound of Martha snoring in the front, it was as silent as a tomb: nobody had spoken since we got into the car. I kept nodding off to sleep, then waking with a start. I could feel great waves of heat coming from Laurie's body, and she gave off a sweet, fermented smell. It had been so hot all day and now it had turned cool. I felt we were flying to the moon.

Suddenly Laurie cleared her throat. 'London's a big place,' she said.

'We're not in London,' I said, rather surprised. The fact was, we had left London behind about an hour ago and were on the way to Dorset. The flat we had in London was tiny and, besides, we had all wanted to go to Linton. Arthur would be buried there. We had discussed how we might get there in the hospital canteen while we had something to eat and a cup of tea, but I couldn't remember whether Laurie had been with us then or not. Anyway, she might have missed it: there had been a lot of distractions – nurses and doctors coming and going, people bringing forms to be signed and asking about burial arrangements, and finally, as we were leaving, the spookiest thing of all, someone handing Martha a cardboard box containing Arthur's 'effects', the stuff he had had in his pockets at the time of the accident. None of us could face opening it. Finally, Claude had offered to drive us to Linton – subject to

84

Damian, who had been due to have the car that evening, agreeing – and had spent five minutes at the pay-phone in the corner of the canteen clearly having a difficult negotiation.

'We're heading to the country,' I said to Laurie. 'Is that all right?'

'Sure.' She sounded quite calm about driving to an unknown destination with a bunch of strangers.

'That's where we live most of the time.'

'Oh.'

'In Dorset. In the West Country.'

'The West Country,' she repeated. Then she said something quite unexpected: 'Where Camelot is.' She spoke so softly I couldn't tell whether she was telling or asking me.

'Well, not exactly,' I said. 'I don't think Camelot's anywhere, really. Isn't it, like . . . mythical?'

'No, it's real. It's a real place. They had a round table. Maybe people just can't find it. It could be real close to your house and you don't know it.'

'I don't think so,' I said, and I told her the story of our house, how Arthur had grown up there and how our family had moved in after his father had died. When Arthur, Martha and the baby, Rachel, had got there, it had taken a year to do it up. The top floors were uninhabitable, so they had lived in three rooms on the ground floor, which was scarcely more inviting – Martha said that one day they had found a rat in Rachel's cot – but at least mushrooms weren't growing out of the walls like upstairs. There was no heating, other than coal fires, and in the cold winter of 1963, Martha told us, Rachel's milk froze in the bottle beside her cot.

Over the years, Martha had done quite a bit of research on the house and she believed it had been built on the site of a Roman settlement. Shards of pottery were occasionally found in the garden, but we never located the real prize: the Roman burial ground that Martha said was almost certainly located nearby. When we were children, we had imagined it would be like Pompeii and that, despite the absence of a local volcano, we would find the perfectly preserved bodies of people in the exact poses they had been caught as the lava overtook them.

The house, though not in itself that attractive, had a pretty setting, nestled at the bottom of a hill beside several hundred acres of woodland, which Arthur had inaccurately metamorphosed into the Darkwood of the *Hayseed* books. Rachel and I knew them like the backs of our hands, and they seemed to us a place full of light. In fact, we spent most of our time there. We much preferred them to the house, which seemed to us, as children, rather forbidding. I'm not going to give you architectural descriptions of everything. All you really need to know about it is this: it was big; it was old; it was rambling; it was dark. Our parents slept in one bit, and we – after we'd stopped being frightened in the night – slept in another. To get from our bit to theirs, you went down two flights of stairs, across a hall and up four flights of stairs. You could also get over to the other side via the roof, but we hadn't done that for some time. Anyway, the point is that we did not live, as Martha had pointed out to Dr Massingbird, in a bungalow.

I almost jumped when the car turned into the drive and the tyres crackled on the gravel. Up till then, the journey had seemed like a long low hum. As Claude drove up to the front of the house, the headlights passed briefly across it, then stopped in a still beam that flooded the garden with light. He turned off the engine, and the lights, and for a moment we sat in darkness and silence.

'We're here,' he said softly, and opened his door. The car was filled with the smell of new-mown grass. Rachel groaned. She must have just woken up. We all began getting out. I was stiff, my legs and back ached and I was almost unable to move. I felt like one of those Pompeiians caught in an awkward position by the lava. Laurie was last: she had to manoeuvre herself along the back seat until she got to the door and then used the frame to ease herself out.

Rachel seemed much calmer. 'I can't believe Daddy's not here,' she whispered sadly. It was a perfectly reasonable thing to say, except that she had called him 'Daddy', which she almost never did.

'This is just lovely,' Laurie said brightly, a curious remark that hung in the air because it was pitch dark and you could see only the vaguest silhouette of the house, which actually looked rather menacing.

'It's lovelier when you can see it,' Rachel said snappily.

I went round the house to the side door we always used and unlocked it. I stood in the hall as they trooped in. 'Let's have a drink. Will you get us one, baby?' Martha said tiredly. She headed into the sitting room, and Laurie followed nervously.

Rachel was still standing by the open door as if she didn't want to come in. 'I have no idea why that woman's here,' she said. 'I mean, *why* has she come with us?'

'Didn't Martha ask her?' I whispered.

'I didn't hear her.' Rachel didn't lower her voice. 'It's your fault, Claude.'

Claude was outraged. 'She was sitting by me while I was waiting for you in the hospital. I was bored.' He looked accusingly at Rachel. 'You'd been gone so long. I didn't know what was happening. I began talking to her.'

'*Drink!*' Martha shouted, from the sitting room. 'And an ashtray.'

I went into the kitchen and grabbed a bottle of vodka from the cupboard. When I came back into the hall, Claude was trying to calm Rachel. 'You can't just tell her to go. It's the middle of the night.'

'She's American, she's got credit cards – they're incapable of going anywhere without them,' Rachel said. 'Anyway, why didn't she tell you about sitting with Daddy after the accident?'

'She didn't know I was with you. She just asked if I would look after her bag while she went to get some chocolate. She said she was called Laurie and she was visiting somebody.'

'So she lied!'

'Well, I suppose she *was* visiting someone. In a way.'

'How can you visit someone you don't even know? You have to *do* something, Claude.'

'You're not being rational.'

'I don't have to be rational. My father's just died!' Rachel hissed.

'*Drink!*' Martha shouted again. Claude looked at me helplessly. I shrugged my shoulders and went into the sitting room with the vodka.

Martha and Laurie were sitting in dimly lit gloom, facing each other, on the two sofas. Martha had taken out some of her hairpins and her hair hung round her shoulders. She had her spectacles on the end of her nose. I picked up a glass and an ashtray from the cupboard by the door and took them to her; she had a cigarette in her hand waiting to be lit.

'Are you going to pour Laurie a drink?' she said crossly.

I turned to Laurie, who gave a little shake of her head, as if she was being offered poison. 'Thank you so much, no.'

Martha took a long drag on her cigarette. 'Where are you from? Where's your accent?' she asked, her head tilted to one side.

Laurie coughed. 'Northern California. A town called Modesto.'

Martha breathed out a plume of smoke. 'Modesto – what a *seemly* name for a town,' she said thoughtfully. 'Northern California is so interesting. Those early Spanish settlements, what are they called? Missions? *Pueblos?*'

Laurie gave a gay little laugh, which sounded as if it had come from someone else. 'Back home,' she said, 'there are people who say we've a lot to be modest about in Modesto.'

There was a silence. Martha turned away. The conversation had somehow taken a wrong turn, and she stubbed out her cigarette. Suddenly there was a squawk from outside, like the sound of chickens fighting, and Rachel ran wailing past the open doorway of the sitting room, her shoes clacking on the wooden floor. Claude came in, looking as if he was going to burst into tears.

Martha indicated the space next to her on the sofa. 'Sit down.' He was shivering. 'Are you cold?' Martha asked him. He nodded.

I was still standing by the sofa and Martha said, 'Baby, get Claude that rug that's in the bottom drawer of the chest.'

This was too much. 'Why can't he get it for himself?'

She patted Claude's knee. 'Because he's life's delicate child, that's why.'

With a lot of clattering, I went over and pulled the drawer practically out of the chest. I grabbed the rug and threw it at Claude. He caught it sheepishly. Martha was oblivious. She put a hand on my arm and said quietly, 'You'd better go and see that Rachel's all right. Tell her I'll be up in a while.'

I went through the hall and climbed up to the top floor where our bedrooms were. The house smelled stale and unlived-in, as if nobody had opened a window for weeks. Rachel's room was opposite mine, with a landing between them. She was lying curled up on her bed. I stood in the doorway for a moment. 'I can't wait for today to be over,' I said.

'Why? Then it'll just be tomorrow. What'll be different?' Her voice was muffled because she was talking into her pillow.

I went and sat down on her bed and laid a hand on her shoulder.

'I'm furious with Claude,' she said angrily.

'No, you're not. You're just furious with everything.'

Surprised, she turned to look at me. Then her face softened and she said grudgingly, 'Well, he did drive us down here, I suppose.'

'Actually,' I said, 'it's good that he's here.'

'Yes,' she said, in a small, contrite voice.

'And Laurie, too.'

She shot me an angry look. 'Why?'

'Arthur was dying by the side of the road . . .'

'Don't *say* that!'

'. . . and she was with him. He wasn't alone, she looked after him. She didn't . . . well, she didn't *have* to do that, did she? She's a tourist. She might have preferred going round Madame Tussaud's or something.' Rachel was five years older than me: I don't know why I had to be the grown-up one.

Rachel put her face in her hands and said something I couldn't hear properly.

'What?'

She took her hands away. 'It should have been me,' she spat. 'I should have been there.' Then she glanced up at me. 'Or you, I mean.'

I didn't mind. 'No, you'd have done it better. You were the one who put the splint on Jamie.'

'Oh, Jamie,' she said gloomily. 'I'd forgotten about Jamie.'

I got up and opened the window. A gust of clear air blew into the room, and the curtains waved and rustled as if someone was moving behind them.

'I think Mr Toppit's out there,' she said. Then she was crying and laughing at the same time. I sat down on her bed again, but this time I pulled my legs up and lay down beside her. She rested her head on my chest. 'You won't leave me, will you?' she said.

I closed my eyes. I must have slept for a couple of hours. When I woke, Rachel was snoring beside me. My neck was cricked and I ached all over. I pulled the eiderdown over Rachel, turned the light out, crossed the landing into my own room and got into bed with my clothes on. I didn't know whether Martha had been up to see Rachel or not.

I hadn't drawn the curtains so I woke as soon as it was light. The house was grey and silent. Arthur was dead. Yesterday it hadn't seemed quite so definite. Today it did. When I went downstairs, I could hear Martha talking on the phone in the sitting room. I got a bowl of cereal from the kitchen and went in to see her. As I entered the room, she shook her head and put a finger over her lips. I backed out. She was not to be disturbed.

For a while, I sat on my own in the kitchen. Before long, I heard creaking overhead. Laurie was getting up, and I could hear her moving from her bedroom to the bathroom, which was above the kitchen. There was a wheezy noise as she turned on a tap, and a shuffling of feet. Then there was a sudden, stifled cry. Her feet clattered along the bathroom floor and I could hear her rattling the handle up and down, then banging the door.

Under normal circumstances, when there wasn't a death in the family, there was a list of things that anyone who was going to spend any time at the house was warned about: the stone flagstones at the back that were like an ice-rink in the rain, the low door frame between the kitchen and the dining room that everyone banged their head on, the loose stair-carpet that had sent at least one person straight to Casualty, but most particularly the door to the bathroom on the first floor, which was never to be locked.

When I got upstairs, she was still rattling the handle. 'I can't get out,' she whimpered. Then she added: 'There's some kind of *bug* in here!'

'Laurie? The lock's broken.' I spoke slowly, as if articulating every word might help her understand what I was saying. 'You're not meant to use the key. There's something wrong with it.'

I knelt down to talk through the keyhole. 'What you've got to do is –'

'It's flying around!' she shouted.

'If you don't frighten it, it won't hurt you.'

It was like one of those films in which a pilot has a heart-attack and a stewardess has to take the controls and guide the plane down following radio instructions from the ground. That was me: I was the ground.

'Laurie? You've got to lean on the door, really push it in hard.' The handle rattled again. 'Not the door handle, that's got nothing to do with it. It's the key, it's the lock. Push!' I could hear Laurie grunting. 'Push the door, then turn the key.'

'It's not turning!'

'Push harder.'

'I can't!'

I grabbed the handle and pulled it towards me. I could hear Laurie trying to turn the key. There was a loud groan from the other side of the door, then a little click, and I heard the lock scrape as the key turned. I pushed the door open.

'I'm so sorry,' Laurie gasped, but I wasn't really listening because I was staring at her. She was covered with towels: one round the lower half of her body, one round the top half, one over her shoulders like a large shawl and one over her head like a veil. She looked like an Egyptian mummy who had taken holy orders.

I went into the bathroom and saw the thing that was flying round and round near the window. It was one of those beetles that look so heavy you can't believe it can get off the ground.

'I can't abide bugs. I'm sorry,' she said weepily, from the doorway.

A black shroud covered the bath, and it took me a moment to realize that Laurie's clothes from yesterday were draped over a drying frame. I went past it, heading towards the window. The beetle's radar must have been faulty: it almost flew into my face. I flicked my hand up, hitting it a glancing blow, and it spiralled to the floor. Laurie gasped. It had felt hard and heavy against the back of my hand.

'Don't kill it!' she said.

I rather thought she had forfeited the right to an opinion. I grabbed a toothmug from the basin, bent down and placed it over the beetle. Laurie inched back into the bathroom to see. She had taken off the headdress towel so at least I could see her face.

'It's beautiful,' she said, leaning over me. The glass magnified and distorted the beetle. It had a shell as dark and shiny as mahogany. It wasn't moving, but it wasn't dead: its feelers were twitching. 'Back home, we call these junebugs. You get them in the desert. What are you going to do?' she asked.

I hadn't thought it was exclusively my problem. 'Do you have any paper?' I asked. 'Card would be better.'

She looked down at herself, as if she thought I expected her to be hiding some under the towels.

'No – in your room,' I said.

'I didn't bring any bags with me,' she said, panicked.

I was getting exasperated. 'There should be some paperbacks by your bed. Go and get one and we can tear the cover off.'

She seemed doubtful. I spoke very slowly: 'Look, I'll slide the cover under the glass. Then I can lift it up without the thing escaping and I'll throw it out of the window.'

She nodded. 'Oh, that's a good idea, yes.'

Holding the towels in place, she scuttled back to her bedroom along the landing. She came back and breathlessly handed me a book.

I turned it over to see the front. 'Not this one, Laurie.' It was the paperback edition of *Garden Grown*. I handed it back to her. 'This is one of my father's books. I don't want to tear the cover off it.'

She was mortified. 'Oh, I'm so sorry, I didn't know.'

'Get another.'

When she came back, she was holding a book called *Seven Types of Ambiguity*. It must have been one of Martha's. I tore off the cover with a satisfying rip. In her other hand, Laurie was still holding Arthur's book.

I slipped the cover under the glass and lifted the whole con-traption. Laurie followed me to the window and opened it. I put my arm out as far as I could, then took away the glass. The beetle sat on the book cover. In the end, I flicked it off and it took flight. It hadn't come to any harm.

When I got back downstairs, Martha was peering round the sitting-room door. 'What was that about, all that banging?'

'Laurie locked herself in the bathroom.'

'I hope you told her not to put Tampax down the loo,' she said, closing the door. It was another thing that was usually on the list to warn people about.

The floorboards were creaking again: Laurie was making her descent. I waited for her at the bottom of the stairs. She was taking small delicate steps as if she might trip, wincing as each stair creaked, and looking at the pictures on the wall. She was holding *Garden Grown*. 'Everything's so old,' she said. 'Which era is it from?'

'Oh, it's very ancient,' I said vaguely. I wasn't great on history.

When she got to the bottom of the stairs, she said, 'I'm so sorry about, you know . . . the bathroom.'

'That's okay,' I said. There was a funny smell coming from her, a sort of wet-dog smell. She was dressed in her black clothes from yesterday.

'Would you like something to eat?'

'Oh, no. Well, maybe a cup of coffee. I don't want to put you to any trouble.' I led the way to the kitchen, and she sat at the table. She placed Arthur's book, face up, next to her.

Now we sat in silence, except for the little sounds she made with her mouth as she drank her coffee. It wasn't an awkward silence, exactly, but it was somehow charged. I was having a small bet with myself about how long it would take her to mention Arthur's book. I hadn't forgotten 'Haymanito hears her calling', or his name scrawled over and over again. She was tapping the cover of the book lightly with her fingers.

'I don't even know your last name,' I said.

'It's Clow.'

I tested it out. 'Laurie Clow.'

'Yeah, weird name.' She laughed.

'Why "Laurie"?'

'It was my dad's middle name – Laurence.'

That was an explanation, not a reason. There was another silence. Finally, I said, 'We should take that key out of the lock. Everybody gets confused. The thing is, Martha says that if we take it away it'll get lost.'

She seemed perplexed. 'But if it doesn't work, shouldn't you throw it away?'

'Well, it's old, the key. Like an antique.'

'You could put a tag on it. You know, a little coloured one.'

'Laurie, how did you know the phone number?' I asked, without thinking. It was something nobody had thought to ask at the hospital and I didn't know why it had jumped into my mind. Her fingers stopped drumming. 'Yesterday,' I added for clarity. 'You phoned Martha at the flat. How did you know the number to call?'

She looked up at me with a clear gaze. 'Why, he told me, your dad told me the number. He remembered it just like *that*.' She clicked her fingers. 'Isn't that wonderful, with injuries so bad? After the ambulance took him away, I went and called from a phone booth.' Then, with a little nod, she added, 'I work in a hospital.'

My stomach lurched. 'I didn't know he was . . .' I stopped. I was finding this hard to say. '. . . still alive before he died.' As I said it, I realized how silly it sounded.

'Oh, he was real messed up but he talked some, yes,' she interjected. A sad smile passed over her face.

Then I did something I really didn't want to do: I burst into tears.

'Oh, honey, I thought you knew. I thought I said . . .'

Actually, I couldn't remember exactly what she had told us at the hospital, but if she had said that Arthur had talked to her, had had some kind of conversation with her by the side of the road, I wouldn't have forgotten.

She got up from her chair, came round to my side of the table and put her arms round me. She pulled my face against her damp shoulder. 'Don't fret. He wasn't hurting. I was just holding his hand, keeping him warm. Then the paramedics came and got him hooked up to something for the pain. They looked after him really well.' She let me go.

'Did he know how badly he was hurt?'

'I don't think so. I think the body kind of compensates.'

'Are you a nurse?'

'Well, I work in a hospital.'

'But you thought it was a broken leg.'

'I'm not on the medical staff. I work at the hospital radio station.' She looked away. 'I'm so sorry. When I got through to your mother I began by telling her he had broken his leg and I was going to, you know, say it was more than that but then the phone went on the fritz, cut me off. I didn't have any more coins.'

'So what did he say exactly?'

'Well, he kept saying this one word over and over. I thought he was saying "Mother". He was talking real soft, it was hard to catch. Then he said a phone number. I thought he wanted me to call his mother – that seemed kind of odd. I wrote it on my hand. Look.'

She showed me the back of her hand on which, half washed off, was written the telephone number at the flat.

'So he made sense?'

'Oh, yes, he told me his name, said he was called Arthur Hayman.' She nodded, as if his having given his name revealed everything about his condition. There was a pause: a perceptible change of gear. 'He didn't say he wrote books, though,' she said, with a bright little laugh, indicating *Garden Grown*. 'Wow, that's something, a writer.'

'What else did he say?'

'Mmm?' She was still looking at the book.

'He must have said something else.'

'What do you mean?'

'He said his name and gave you the phone number. That was it?'

'Well, it was hard to catch, he spoke so soft. They were digging up the road. It was kind of noisy, you know. So, the books – what are they about?'

'But you heard the phone number.'

'Yes. And his name,' she said. There was a tiny edge to her voice now.

I appropriated her little laugh. 'It sounds like a war film – you know, just his name and number. No other info allowed. Like *The Great Escape*.'

She smiled. 'That was a great movie.'

'We had it at school last term.'

'You get movies at school?'

'Every other Saturday night.'

'I love movies. What else have you seen?'

I wanted to say I had seen inside her bag at the hospital. I wanted to say I had read her poem. I wanted to ask how many times she had written his name in her notebook. 'How long were you sitting with him?'

She looked up at the ceiling, then round the kitchen. She licked her lips. 'Well, let's see, it's hard to remember. So much was happening.'

I leaned across the table and picked up the book. Her eyes followed it. 'There are five of these,' I said. 'They're called *The Hayseed Chronicles*. This is the fourth.' I turned it over in my hand and tapped each side in turn on the table, as if I was straightening a pack of cards.

'Really?' She sounded only mildly interested, but her eyes were narrow and alert, like an animal's. She held out her hand for the book.

'Do you want some more coffee?' I asked. I stood up and went to the other side of the kitchen with the book. 'Kettle's still hot.'

'Thank you.'

'You put – what? One spoonful?'

'Yes, not too strong.'

'You want milk?'

'Let me,' she said. She got up and came towards me.

I moved past her round the table and sat down. We had now switched places. 'The books are like a series. You should probably start with the first. We might have some spare copies,' I said. 'I could probably find some. If you wanted.'

There was a short silence. We were making a deal. 'It must have been five minutes,' she said. 'No more than ten, anyway. So hot, that sidewalk.' She laughed. 'The traffic!'

'London's always busy,' I said.

'The traffic in San Francisco, that's really something.'

'So you might have been there for ten minutes?'

'Well, maybe five. Hard to tell.'

'And?'

'He talked about you,' she said, in a rush. 'And Rachel. Said he had great kids. He sounded really proud of you both. Talked about Martha – Mrs Hayman – too.' She came back to the table and sat down. 'You shouldn't be sad. He wasn't in any pain.' She reached over and took the book from me.

'But how did you know it was Martha he was talking about? You said he kept saying this one word over and over, which you thought was "Mother". You said you thought you were phoning his mother after the ambulance had taken him.'

'Now I know it was Martha he was talking about. I know it *now*. It was all so confused.'

I knew she wasn't telling the truth, not just about Martha but about us too. 'He said he had great kids. He sounded really proud' was as unlikely a thing for Arthur to utter, even if he was dying, as a weather report in Sanskrit.

'Laurie, you can tell me. I'm not going to fall to pieces. I'm quite grown-up.'

She smiled at me. 'I know you are.' But then she looked away.

'Please,' I said.

She was weighing something up. 'Well, there was one weird thing, but you've got to understand, it was really hard for me to pick up what he was saying.'

I was conciliatory. 'I know, Laurie.'

'Well, here's the thing. He kept saying – I thought he kept saying – "Stop it!" or "Stop it, Mister, stop it!" I didn't know what he meant. I thought maybe he was talking about wanting the pain to stop, but I don't think it was that. It was weird because he spoke so kind of precise, so, you know, *English*, and it sounded like something from a gangster movie.'

It took me a moment, and then I smiled in recognition. 'What?' she said. 'What?'

I pointed at the book in her hand. 'It's from the books,' I said. 'He's in the book.'

'Who?'

'It's really hard to explain.'

'Luke, *tell* me.' It was the first time she had used my name.

'There's this guy in the books, this man, who's called Mr Toppit. He's like an unseen presence. It's only right at the end, in the last book, you see him, but everyone talks about him. He's like a kind of *deus ex machina*.' I wasn't absolutely sure what the phrase meant, but a review had used it.

Her eyes were small and intent. She was concentrating, taking it in. 'Okay,' she said. 'Okay.'

'He's always getting Luke to do strange tasks, but Luke never gets it quite right, so Mr Toppit's always displeased.'

'Luke?'

'Luke Hayseed. He's the main character.'

'Hayseed?'

'That's why they're called *The Hayseed Chronicles*.'

She was flicking through the pages now. 'These are pictures of you!' she said, with a broad beam. 'I get it. Luke Hayman, Luke Hayseed.'

'Well . . .'

'This is amazing. You're actually in the book!'

'Laurie, they're not real, they're novels. There's magic and stuff in them.'

She was shaking her head in wonderment. 'Did he do the pictures?'

'Lila did them. She's a friend. She's German.'

'Oh.' She wasn't interested in pursuing that. 'The other books, what are they called?'

I ignored this. 'So, apart from talking about Mr Toppit, what else did he say?'

'This is tough for you, Luke. I lost my dad when I was small. He went when I was really young.'

I wasn't too interested in her father. 'What else?'

'The books must have been really important to him if he was talking about them . . . you know, *then*.'

Suddenly Martha shouted from the sitting room: 'Luke! Baby! Can you come?'

'In a sec,' I yelled back. 'What else?' I said to Laurie. 'What else?'

Then she said something quite unexpected: 'He talked about you living abroad.'

'What?'

'A couple of years back we were going to take a vacation there.'

99

'Where?'

'The Middle East.'

'*Luke!*' Martha shouted.

'*Coming!*'

'Marge, this friend of mine, wanted to go to Petra – you know, "pink city twice as old as time", or whatever. I saw the pictures.'

'What do you mean, Laurie?'

'*Luke!*' I heard the impatient scrape of Martha's chair as she got up in the other room.

'Jordan,' Laurie said. 'Something about living in Jordan.'

I stood up, but my stomach stayed sitting down. I could hear Martha coming. 'Laurie, don't say anything. Please.'

Now she was clearly confused, but Martha was coming down the hall. 'Just don't say anything to Martha, okay? Please?'

Then Martha was in the doorway. She seemed surprised to see Laurie. 'Good morning,' she said, then to me, 'Get Rachel and Claude up. They can't just sleep all morning. This funeral isn't going to happen by itself. Has Luke been looking after you?'

'He's been very kind, made me coffee,' Laurie said. She smiled at Martha. 'Said he was going to find me some copies of your husband's books, the *Hayseed* ones. He said I should read them.' She looked at me. 'Didn't you?'

'Well, why don't you get them, baby?'

'Oh, I'd love it, I really would,' Laurie said. 'You let me know if there's something I can do for you, Luke.' Her eyes were holding mine.

'Okay,' I said at last.

There's a lot of stuff that needs to be done when someone dies, much more than you'd imagine, but it's all quite dull. Martha stayed on the phone most of the day. There were people to be notified, people to be summoned. She was talking to the local paper about the obituary, then to various people in London about who might do the address at the funeral and to the undertakers about the arrangements. She had positioned herself at the desk under the window in the sitting room, cigarettes, lighter and ashtray beside her, alongside a tray with a Thermos of coffee. She was always good in a crisis.

Martha called a lot of people that day, and they had obviously told other people, so by the next day the phone was ringing constantly. Arthur's death had made it into some of the national papers – 'Children's Author In Freak Road Accident' – and there were a couple of short obituaries, too, which would have alerted the people Martha hadn't phoned. She was in a bad mood. She didn't like the way one of the obituaries had ended. 'How can they say, "He is *survived* by his wife and two children"? Everyone will think we were all run over by that bloody truck, but he was the only one who got killed.' Then she was upset that his career as a children's novelist was given more prominence than his film career – it had always been a bone of contention between them that he had turned his back on films – and was incensed that in the other obituary his name was linked, not favourably, with that of Wally Carter: 'His career as a screenwriter and director was eclipsed by that of his friend and contemporary, the Oscar-winning director Wally Carter, but in later life he secured a niche as the well-loved author of the series of children's books known as . . .'

She threw the paper on to the floor. 'Wally Carter – that puffball. I don't suppose we'll be hearing from *him*,' she said sourly. 'I don't know how Graham's turned out as well as he has. What a childhood! The women! The drinking! Wally was always so coarse, never had any intellectual rigour. He didn't even recognize his old friend Arthur Hayman when he invited us to the première of that ridiculous film about the ship.' The story of that première had been told before, but in previous tellings Martha's inflection was different. The fault then had been Arthur's: he had become such a shadow of what he had been that even his old friend Wally Carter had failed to recognize him.

When, later that day, a telegram arrived from California – REMEMBERING THE GOOD TIMES ALWAYS MARTHA DEAR STOP AFFECTIONATELY WALLY – Martha read it several times before crumpling it into a ball and throwing it into the bin. Then she went up to her room, shut the door and didn't appear again until after dinner.

It wasn't until the second day at Linton that Lila was mentioned. The weather was still hot, and after lunch Rachel, Claude and I were lying on the lawn in the sun with the remains of the wine. Laurie was having a nap.

'Are you going to sit out there all day?' Martha shouted from inside. Then her head appeared at the window. 'Has anyone rung Lila?'

We looked at each other. As Martha had either been on the phone calling people or sitting by it waiting for it to ring since we had got home, we presumed it was a rhetorical question. 'Well, have you?' she said. 'I can't do it all by myself.'

'She'll be offended if someone else rings her. She'll want to speak to you,' Rachel said.

'Will you call her, baby?'

'Why can't Rachel?' There was no answer to that because we knew why. The two or three times Rachel had called anybody about Arthur, she had hardly started talking when her face had crumpled and she had let out a series of inarticulate wails. Someone had had to take the receiver from her to complete the conversation.

'I expect she'll turn up soon enough,' Rachel said. 'Or you could ask *Laurie* to phone her.'

'Stop that right now, Rachel,' Martha said, and slammed the window.

The night before, Martha and Rachel had had a row about Laurie. Laurie had come down in the dressing-gown Martha had lent her to say she was trying to have a bath but the water didn't seem very hot: was she doing something wrong? Rachel had put down her wine glass with a loud bang and said, 'I think you'll find, Laurie, that our water is different from yours. It tends naturally towards the cold. That's how we like it over here.'

Laurie's face had gone pink and for a moment it looked like she might burst into tears. Martha glared at Rachel. 'Why don't you use the children's bathroom on the other side, Laurie?' she said. 'The tank's bigger.'

Laurie nodded. When Claude said he would show her the way, Rachel stuck out her tongue at him. Laurie and he were hardly out of the room before Rachel had slammed the door behind them and she and Martha were shouting at each other.

An hour later Laurie hadn't reappeared and I was dispatched to find her. She was in her room, sitting up in bed under the covers. She looked quite different. Her hair, which I had got used to in the most puddingy of pudding-basin cuts, was slicked away from her forehead and combed carefully back. Her skin was tighter over her face. She looked as if she might have lost some weight.

'Do you want some dinner?'

Laurie shook her head. I sat on the side of the bed. 'Don't worry about Rachel,' I said. 'She's just upset. She didn't mean it.'

'You've all been so great to me,' she said. 'You've all been so kind.' Then she gave me a little smile and put her hand under the cover and pulled out one of the *Hayseed* books I had given her earlier. She put it into my hand. I wasn't sure what I was meant to do with it. Without taking her eyes off me, she produced the other four books one by one, as if she was a magician doing a card trick. Then she gave me a hug. 'Thank you,' she said. 'Thank you for the books.'

I had almost got out of the door when she laughed. 'Luke?' she said. 'You know, I just thought of something. When that junebug was in the bathroom, you could have picked it up by the wings and taken it into the garden, like you did with the bees.'

'Laurie, it's not me in the books,' I said patiently. 'Anyway, it might have bitten me.' She thought that was hilarious. As I left the room and came downstairs I could hear her laugh tinkling behind me. While that sound receded, another was growing.

As I went into the sitting room, Rachel was shouting, 'How could they? How *could* they?' Martha and Claude were sitting on either side of her on the sofa, trying to calm her.

'It's just a mistake, that's all,' Martha said.

'At least they didn't lose anything. That would have been much worse,' Claude said.

Rachel's chin jutted up at me accusingly. 'Look what they've done, the hospital.' Her finger jabbed at the table in front of the sofa. 'Look! *Look!*'

The little box that the hospital had given us containing Arthur's effects was open. I could see his scuffed black wallet, his glasses case, some loose change, his wedding and signet rings, a tube ticket, a notebook and a couple of pens. 'What is it?'

She prodded the box, which moved to reveal something glinting behind it.

'It's a lighter,' I said.

'They've mixed his stuff up with someone else's,' she wailed. 'How *can* they be so sloppy?' Claude was patting her back as if she had choked on something.

I picked up the lighter, one of those chunky silver Zippo ones, but old and battered. It was surprisingly light. I flicked up the top. There was nothing inside. The lighter mechanism had been removed so that it was hollow.

'He didn't even *smoke*,' she said.

'He did before he gave up.'

'Well, he's dead now,' she snapped. 'We should make a formal complaint. It's so unbelievably insensitive.'

'I bet the people whose lighter it is will be a lot more upset than you,' I said.

'Exactly. That's why we should complain.'

I turned it over in my hand. On the back, there was a set of initials 'RLC' and underneath 'Los Alamos 1945'.

'Where are you going?' Rachel said.

'Nowhere.' But when I was in the hall, I shouted back, 'I'm going to put it in an envelope and send it back to the hospital.'

'*Wait!*' Rachel wailed, but I was already halfway up the stairs. This time I didn't knock, but went straight into Laurie's room. She still had the books laid out in front of her.

'Your father's middle name was Laurence, you said.'

'Yes.'

'What was his first name?'

'Rudolph – well, Rudy. That's what people called him. Why do you ask?'

I was furious. I threw the lighter on to the bed. It landed with a plop. She picked it up. 'It was my daddy's,' she said, in a little voice. Her eyes were clear and bright. She was running her fingers over the engraved lettering. 'He worked in Los Alamos during the war. That's where we lived. He helped make the atom bombs we dropped on Japan.'

I wasn't interested in all that. 'Why is it with Arthur's stuff?'

'My dad gave it to me when I was a little girl. He took out the lighter stuff inside so I couldn't get harmed. It's the only thing of his that I've got. My good-luck charm.'

I said again, 'Why is it with Arthur's stuff?'

'Just before they put him into the ambulance I slipped it into his vest pocket. I wanted him to have something of mine. I thought it might bring him luck.'

'It didn't do him much good, did it, Laurie? He died anyway.'

'Don't say that, honey.' She stretched a hand towards me, but I just stared at her. She was beginning to cry. I wasn't going to comfort her. I didn't see why I should.

Rachel had fallen out with Claude, who was looking more and more forlorn. Martha still fussed over him, but it was Rachel he wanted. After dinner, even though he had politely asked Martha if he could use the phone to call Damian, Rachel said coldly, 'Please don't be too long. There'll be people trying to get through to talk about Daddy. Anyway, if you're going to spend the entire time on the phone there's not much point in your being here, is there?' Two little blobs of red appeared on Claude's cheeks as he shuffled out to the phone in the hall.

When, after three days of Laurie wearing the same black outfit all the time, Martha suggested to Rachel that it might be a good idea for her and Claude to drive Laurie into town to get some other clothes, she refused. 'What's the point?' she said. 'He'll only ignore me. Anyway, there isn't an outsize shop.' Martha slammed down her coffee cup and marched out of the room. 'Claude!' she shouted, from the hall. 'Where's Laurie?' Footsteps came down the stairs, orders were given, and Martha led Claude and Laurie outside. Rachel watched them balefully through the window as they got into Claude's car.

'What's the matter with you, Rachel?' I said.

'Stop being so grown-up. You're as bad as them,' she said tearfully. 'Everybody seems to have forgotten that Daddy's dead.' She was still calling Arthur 'Daddy'. It wasn't a good sign.

In the afternoon, Claude took Laurie for a walk. She was dressed in one of her new outfits, a pair of black trousers and a loose white blouse with large red roses printed on it. 'She looks ridiculous,' Rachel said, but when it was getting dark and they still hadn't returned she became fidgety. She was trying to read but every few minutes she kept getting up and going to peer out of the window. 'Why are they taking so long?' she said. Finally, when it was so dark that we had to turn the lights on in the sitting room, she said, 'Do you think something's happened to them? Will you help me look for them?'

No sooner had we gone outside than we saw them at the other end of the field, walking slowly towards the house, their laughter travelling across the evening air. As they got closer, I could see that their arms were linked. When they reached the big farm gate that divided the field from our garden, Claude got over first, then helped Laurie manoeuvre herself over the top. She gave a little shriek when she jumped to the ground and her shoe came off. She held on to Claude's arm to balance herself as she raised her leg to get it on again. She was clearly having some difficulty, because in the end she took the other shoe off and walked towards us across the lawn with bare feet.

Rachel was very still beside me. When they got to us, Laurie was still laughing. She patted Claude's shoulder. 'You've got such a true friend here,' she said to Rachel. 'He's been so dear.' It was too dark to see the expression on Rachel's face, but in a strangely bright voice she said, 'You two need a drink. Come on. It's nearly supper. Martha's been *slaving* and you know what a bad temper that puts her into.'

Rachel had been right: now it was Martha who was grumpy. After Claude had opened a bottle of wine, we sat in the sitting room waiting for supper. Laurie was asking us questions about Arthur's books. She had taken to carrying the five paperbacks around in her bag so they were with her wherever she went. Martha kept coming in and out, sitting down, lighting a cigarette, then stubbing it out and getting up to check something in the kitchen. It was an unusually over-emphatic display of domesticity, given that we were having cold chicken and potato salad, most of which had been prepared by Doreen, our daily woman, who had left it covered in cling-film in the fridge that morning.

Nothing was right. 'Why are you drinking wine out of tooth-mugs?' Martha asked.

'They're *tumblers*, actually,' Rachel said.

'Well, we do have wine glasses. Laurie might prefer her wine that way.'

'No, I'm good,' Laurie said.

'And don't drink any more of the decent wine,' she said to Rachel. 'I want it for Friday.' Friday was the funeral.

'So, are there places in the Darkwood you can find in the woods here? Like, real places?' Laurie asked.

'You'll have a headache in the morning, Rachel,' Martha said. 'There's a lot to do tomorrow.'

Rachel ignored her. 'Well, of course, Luke can never quite find Mr Toppit's lair, that's the point, but I've always thought it's beyond the bit at the top where the big path divides into two –'

'Claude, don't let that ash drop on the carpet. Doreen only hoovered this morning.' Martha got up and put an ashtray on the table in front of him, next to the ashtray that was already there, then sat down again. 'If we don't eat now, we'll never eat,' she said.

The food had hardly been served, though, when she gathered up her cigarettes, lighter and ashtray and left the dining room, her plate untouched. 'I have to phone Terry Tringham,' she said. 'He's going to give the address at the funeral.' The door slammed behind her.

'She must be hurting real bad,' Laurie said, after Martha had left. She had brought Arthur's books into the dining room with her and now she put them in a neat pile to one side of her plate.

'Open some more wine,' Rachel said to Claude, then added nastily, 'Don't be scared, I won't tell Martha. You go and help him, Luke – he'll just make a mess.'

'Do you want red or white?' Claude asked, when he returned from the kitchen.

'Ssh,' Rachel said. 'Laurie's telling us a story.'

When she was at school, when she was fifteen and the least popular girl in her class, Laurie had auditioned for the end-of-term play, which was to be *Oklahoma!*. She sang 'I Cain't Say No' at the audition and, to everyone's amazement, was given the part of Ado Annie. Shyly she sang us a snatch of the song, and I could see why: she had a wonderful voice. The problem was that she had hated being on stage when she wasn't singing: she felt lumpy and awkward and she couldn't dance and everyone was horrible to her, particularly Rick, the boy playing the lead, whom all the girls, including her, were in love with. He had beautiful blond curly hair and some of the girls he had been out with had kept locks of it. People were always trying to touch it. He took longer to have his hair and makeup done than anyone else in the cast.

When the gingham dress that had been made for her split during a dance number in the rehearsals, Laurie was demoted to the chorus and replaced by Rick's girlfriend, Jerrilee, who seemed mysteriously to know all of Ado Annie's lines already. Rick was now Laurie's boss at the radio station and he was married to Jerrilee, but he had lost most of his hair. 'He's got a wig the size of a moose pelt – but he doesn't always wear it,' Laurie said, giggling.

Rachel was almost weeping with laughter. 'Moose pelt,' she kept screaming. '*Moose pelt!*'

Claude said, 'Rach, we should tell her about us doing *Guys and Dolls* at school.'

Rachel wiped her eyes with a paper napkin and waved a hand dismissively. 'Oh, she doesn't want to hear about that. Anyway, you spent your entire time mooning over that boy who played whatever-he's-called – Nathan.' She got up, moved to the place next to Laurie and put an arm round her. 'Tell you what,' she said, 'tomorrow I'll take you into the woods and give you a proper tour. I'll show you some of the places in the books.'

Laurie's face lit up. 'Oh, I'd love it. But I need to go into town in the morning. There's something special I want to do for Martha.'

'Well, we could go at lunchtime. We could have a picnic. That would be great,' Claude said.

'Girls only,' Rachel said.

The 'something special' that Laurie wanted to do for Martha was to cook the food for the funeral. When I got up the next morning, Martha and she were in the kitchen discussing it. 'I thought chimichangas,' Laurie was saying. 'Tortillas, nachos, maybe, lots of dips, definitely guacamole, salted almonds – my mother's recipe – maybe some refried beans.'

'Ugh,' I said.

'No, you'll like them. They're really tasty.'

'But, Laurie,' Martha said, 'even if they don't all come back after the service there'll still be fifty or sixty people. You really don't have to do this. Doreen will help. We can give them lots of drink and something simple, like sandwiches.'

Laurie went over and hugged Martha. 'You've all been so kind. It would be my pleasure.'

'Do you think Arthur liked Mexican food?' I said doubtfully, to Martha, after Laurie had gone out. She waved away my objection. 'The best kind of food is the kind somebody else cooks.'

In the event, there would be one fewer at the funeral: Claude had left. When I saw that his car had gone from the front of the house, I presumed he had driven into town. Rachel was nowhere to be seen. I found her eventually in the garden, sitting on the swing Arthur had made for us as children. This was where I used to bring the bees.

She had been crying. 'Where's Claude?' I asked.

'He's left. Damian needed the car.'

'But it's Claude's car.'

She jumped off the swing. 'Oh, Luke,' she snapped, 'it's not *his* father who's died. He's got his own life to get on with. He can't just sit here cheering us up.' Then she strode back to the house.

The trip to the woods with Laurie was off. Rachel was staying in her room: she had a headache. Laurie took her some lunch on a tray, but when she went to collect it afterwards, nothing had been eaten. 'Poor munchkin,' she said, as she washed the dishes. 'I guess it's her time of the month.'

Rachel had been wrong when she said Lila would turn up soon enough. It was amazing that it was four days since Arthur had died and there had been no sign of her. When we heard the crunch of gravel that afternoon, and I looked out of the window to see a taxi drawing up, I knew our run of luck had ended.

Martha closed her eyes. 'Someone did call her, didn't they?' Her voice was doom-laden. 'Baby?'

'Don't look at me,' I said.

'Maybe Rachel did.'

The doorbell rang. 'I don't think so,' I said.

'Do you want me to get that?' Laurie called from the kitchen.

'No, we'll do it,' Martha shouted. 'Please don't let her speak German. I can take anything but that.'

Although Lila was an art teacher, she gave private German tuition and that was how Martha had first met her. Martha had wanted to read her favourite book, *Buddenbrooks*, in the original. Lila had a special technique for teaching German: she called it 'living conversation'. Her method made conversation more natural, she said, and it had the added advantage of illuminating particular aspects of German life. For each pupil, she would invent a set of German characters tailored specifically to their interests who could be discussed during lessons, as if casual conversation was being had about mutual friends. For a girl doing A levels who was keen on horses, she had invented a kind of German National Velvet who spent a lot of time show-jumping in Potsdam. For Martha, she had conjured up a bourgeois family in the 1900s, the Untermeyers of Lübeck, and they would sit and talk about Uncle Heinrich, who ran a shipping business, and his infinitely expandable set of relations, who spent their lives visiting each other for tea and organizing evenings of chamber music. Although the lessons had stopped long ago, when Martha grew bored with them, Lila went through an elaborate pretence that they still continued.

She was standing on the doorstep, leaning on her stick. In one hand she carried a large bag and in the other a bunch of flowers. She was wearing a hat. As we approached, she arranged a tragic smile on her face and put out her hands towards Martha.

'*Gnädige Frau,*' she began, '*ich muss Ihnen sagen, wie erschütternt ich bin.*' She let out a wail as she launched herself aggressively into Martha's arms. 'Oh, darling, you should have told me, you should have called. I've been waiting.'

Martha and I led her into the sitting room. She took off her hat. As always, she was wearing a hairnet decorated with coloured beads. When we were small we thought someone had sprinkled hundreds-and-thousands over her head. Martha sat her down on the sofa. A glass of brandy had to be procured. Lila produced a handkerchief out of her large bag – large, because whenever she visited friends she always carried a nightdress and change of clothing in case she was asked to stay the night, and a selection of handmade gifts to thank them for having her if they did – and sniffled tearfully into it. She looked angrily at Martha. 'My dear, I'm only a taxi ride away. You know that.'

'Oh, Lila,' Martha murmured.

'What you have gone through . . .'

'Well . . .'

'I cannot bear it. When I heard, when I saw it in the paper, I told the school to cancel my Tuesday life-drawing class. Then, naturally, people called to ask if I had heard. I said, yes, of course, but only from the paper, not from *you*. I was so embarrassed.'

Martha confronted the issue head on. 'I'm so sorry, Lila. We presumed you'd ring us. There's been so much happening.'

'My dear, I did not want to intrude. I called Graham Carter to see if they were doing a reprint because of all the mentions of the books in the obituaries. He has not had the courtesy to return my call. Actually, my calls. With an *s*.'

Whenever Graham came down to stay, Lila had to be kept away from the house: she had many suggestions as to how the books could be published better. She felt that the paper they were printed on was too thin, that the illustrations would reproduce better on thicker stock; she felt September or January or June were not good months for publication; she felt there should be more publicity; she felt it was a scandal that the books had not found an American publisher. Once she had inveigled Graham into having lunch with her when she went up to London for the January sales. After that, he had avoided taking her calls, and it was the receptionist, Stephanie, who normally had to deal with her.

'He'll be at the funeral tomorrow, I'm sure,' Martha said soothingly.

'Thank God – *thank God!* – we finished the last book when we did. Oh, if it had been only half finished . . .' I never really knew whether Arthur had wanted her to illustrate his books or whether she had simply made any other option impossible, but once she had started it was clear that, in her eyes at least, she was inextricably linked to their creation. 'But now, what happens now? Mr Toppit has only just come out of the Darkwood. Oh, poor Arthur. What you have all been through, it's unthinkable. I could have been so useful. Look!'

She dived into her bag and came up with a set of plastic folders. 'I've done them in triplicate,' she said, thrusting them at me and Martha. Inside, Xeroxes of the various newspaper pieces about Arthur's death were mounted on card. The three sets each had a different-coloured sticker. 'Green is for you, Martha, your favourite colour. Blue is to go into The Big Book of Hayseed and red is for spare. Do we need more?' Rachel and I called it the BBH. In those days, it was not big at all: a leatherbound album, only half full, with the reviews and the various bits of publicity that the publishers had done. It was only later that it overflowed into many thick volumes, and clipping became a full-time job for Lila.

'You should have *called* me,' she said. It wasn't quite a shout, but getting towards one.

'Rachel's not been at all well,' Martha said.

'Of course she hasn't. She's an adolescent. I spend my life with adolescent girls at the school,' Lila snapped. 'And poor Luke – now the little man of the family.' She looked at me pityingly. 'I could have helped, Martha, I could have helped you. All you had to do was ask.'

Martha looked desperate. 'We wanted to be alone, didn't we, baby? We thought it was best if it was just us.'

Just then there was a bang from the kitchen and a little cry of pain. Laurie clattered through the hall and appeared in the door-way, sucking the side of her hand. 'Your ovens are so hot here, I fried my hand,' she said. 'Don't hold out too much hope for my salted almonds.'

Lila turned slowly to see who it was, then back to Martha questioningly.

'This is Laurie Clow,' Martha said.

Laurie came in front of the sofa and shook Lila's hand.

There was a pause. Lila said, 'And you are . . .?'

'I'm Laurie.'

'Laurie's from America,' I said helpfully.

'You are staying here?'

'Yes. Everyone's been so kind,' Laurie said.

'You are helping in the house? In the kitchen?'

'I'm doing Mexican for after the funeral.'

'*Mexican?*'

'Well, kind of Tex-Mex.'

Lila turned to Martha. 'I don't understand,' she said.

Martha cleared her throat. 'Laurie was with Arthur when he had the accident.'

Lila put her hand over her mouth in shock. 'You are a friend of Arthur's?'

Martha laid a hand on Lila's arm and said, 'Laurie had just arrived in London. She was walking down the street when the accident happened.'

Lila seemed relieved. 'So you're not a friend of the family?'

'They've all been so kind,' Laurie said again.

'But you *are* staying here?'

Martha had had enough. 'Lila, Laurie's been good enough to help us for the last few days. We're very grateful to her.'

Laurie's face broke into a smile. 'Oh, so you're *Lila*,' she said. 'I love your little drawings. They really add some fizz to Mr Hayman's books.' Lila's mouth fell open, but before she could say anything, Laurie sat down next to her on the sofa. 'Oh, and I love how you do your hair too,' she said. She touched the hairnet. 'Those beads are so pretty.'

Lila's reaction was so extreme it was as if a bat had got tangled in her hair. She gave a little scream, jumped and shook her head wildly. Laurie's hand flew back. Lila put hers up as if to erect an invisible barrier between her and Laurie. 'I'm sorry,' she said, her voice shaking. 'I'm very sensitive.'

There was silence. The three women, Martha, Lila and Laurie, sat staring out from the sofa as if posing for a rather formal photograph. Then Lila straightened her back and elaborately patted her hair. She turned her head away from Laurie, put her lips to Martha's ear and said in a conspiratorial but audible whisper, '*Amerikaner sind doch so bizarr.* What would Uncle Heinrich say?' Then she gave a tinkling laugh, which might have been girlish except that something seemed to have been lost in the translation.

After Laurie had left the room it took some time to negotiate Lila's departure.

'Oh, Lila, it's chaos here. You must get back,' Martha said.

Lila gave a throaty chuckle. 'Chaos is what I do best, Martha, you know that. Remember what I did with your bank statements? You must rest.' She patted her bag. 'I have brought my things,' she said. 'I will be most happy in my usual room. Not to worry if the sheets aren't fresh. There's so much to do for tomorrow.'

'It's all organized. Laurie's doing the food,' Martha said.

'Martha,' she said, in an attempt at lightness, 'I'm not sure that Mexican food is entirely appropriate at a funeral. Arthur was not a *caballero* – is that the word?' She gave a little laugh.

'I think it sounds fun,' I said.

'Fun?' Lila said doubtfully. 'Well, you know me, Luke. I'm not very up-to-the-minute.' She made quotation marks with her fingers. 'And how long is Miss Clow staying, Martha? It is Miss Clow, isn't it? I can't imagine there could be a Mr Clow.'

'Laurie's been wonderful, Lila,' Martha said sharply. 'She came to see England for a week and all she's done is be stuck with us.'

'A week? How do people think they can see this country in a week? Americans – so restless, always moving on.'

'You're right. I should have a sleep,' Martha said. 'You were so kind to come, Lila.'

'Let me *help*,' she implored.

'No, Lila, you always do so much. You should keep off your feet.' Lila had trouble with her hip. 'Anyway, we'll need your help tomorrow.'

'I have a little surprise for tomorrow.'

Martha looked anxious. 'What?'

Lila gave a shy smile. 'I think you will be pleased. I know Arthur would be. My dear, let me stay. I will do supper for everyone tonight. Something simple like scrambled eggs. Unless your Miss Clow has prepared some exotic dish from one of the countries she has visited in such depth.'

Martha got up. 'Lila, you must go. Baby, will you call a taxi?'

'A taxi? I could not possibly afford a taxi. I shall take the bus. There's a seat at the stop. I have my hat.'

Martha was by the door. She made a last pre-emptive strike: 'Baby, call a taxi now. On our account. This minute.' She blew Lila a kiss, and fled. I could hear her feet rattling up the stairs.

Outside it was drizzling. Lila and I waited in the porch for the taxi to come. She was leaning on her stick. Her hat was back on, and she was clutching her bag.

'Your mother is a saint. I worry sometimes. She has so much on her plate now. You must take some of her burdens, Luke. You are the man of the family now. She will need a lot of help. Thank God she has friends. Good friends. We will rally round, all of us.'

The taxi was coming up the drive. There was a strange expression on Lila's face. She grasped my arm. 'Luke, you must be careful.' She was surprisingly strong. Her fingers were digging into me. 'That woman is a swashbuckler.'

'A what?'

'You know nothing about her, where she comes from, what she is.'

'Lila, she was with Arthur when he was run over.'

'That's what she says. That's her story. You must not leave her alone. You have so many beautiful things in the house.'

'I don't think she's going to steal anything.'

'Luke, you have no idea what people are like. One thing I know is danger. I have lived with it.'

That I didn't doubt. Her parents, her brother Thomas, who was studying to be a doctor, and her grandparents had died in a concentration camp. Her brother had looked just like her. I had seen their pictures in her other Big Book – the BBL, The Big Book of Löwenstein.

Tears were rolling down her cheeks. 'You won't let me help you. You have that woman now. I expect she is sleeping in my bed. Oh, Luke, you know how much I love you all.' She gazed up at the sky. 'Arthur was everything to me. Everything. I don't know what I shall do. The next book was going to reveal so much. Mr Toppit? We'll never know. So sad.'

★

I didn't sleep well. As soon as I got up I had a bath. I shaved, which wasn't really necessary, then rubbed Rachel's deodorant under my arms and also put a bit round my crotch, which probably wasn't necessary either. It just didn't seem to be a day to take chances.

Downstairs, the hall was being rearranged so there would be room for people to come back to the house after the funeral. Doreen had come in early to help with the flowers. She had been with us for ever and Martha spent a great deal of time complaining about her.

Jack, her son, who was a year older than me, was moving chairs against the wall so there would be more space in the centre of the hall. He glanced at me when I came in, then looked awkwardly away. As a little boy he had had a thin, feral face. He had filled out and put on some weight. He used to remind me of a rat; now he resembled a hamster storing food in his cheeks. When we were small, Doreen had always brought him with her to the house and we had to play together. The truth was that we had never liked each other much.

'Hello, Jack,' I said.

He mumbled something. It might have been 'Sorry about your dad.' His eyes were on the floor.

'Do you want a hand with the chairs?' I asked.

He shook his head. 'Got your dad's book out last night, the one he wrote in,' he said, and nodded a couple of times to confirm it.

I nodded back. 'Good,' I said, for want of anything better. He had a little walk-on part in the first book as Luke's friend Jack – another of the many inaccuracies in *The Hayseed Chronicles* – from whom Luke steals a bicycle to chase Mr Toppit. Arthur had signed a copy for him.

Martha was in the sitting room. She seemed smaller than usual, or maybe the room appeared bigger, and rather forlorn. She was smoking a cigarette in the corner by the window and her hand was trembling. She wasn't in black: she wore a grey dress that might have been silk – it had a sort of sheen. She adjusted my tie, and got the collar of my shirt to turn down properly. In the harsh sunlight, her skin was dry and papery.

She looked me up and down. 'Everybody looks better in a suit.'

'Thank you,' I said.

She sniffed. 'Are you wearing scent?'

I blushed. 'Of course not.'

'Tell Doreen you like her flowers. They're hideous.'

In the kitchen, Doreen was helping Laurie organize the food. Laurie had already made the connection between sparky little Jack from the first book and the lumpy adolescent carting furniture in the hall. 'You must be proud of him being in the books,' she said.

'He's a good lad,' Doreen said. 'No trouble. Mr Hayman was always kind to him. Gave him a signed copy.'

'He should look after it,' Laurie said.

Doreen gave a grim laugh. 'Worth a bit now, I should think, with Mr Hayman having passed away.'

'Oh, no – he mustn't let it go! It's like a little nugget of history.' Laurie sounded horrified.

'You want cling-film over the green stuff?'

'Guacamole. It's avocados.'

'Not too partial to them myself. It's the texture,' said Doreen, grumpily.

I went into the garden. It had rained in the night, but now the sun was out. It was probably the kind of day you wanted for a funeral. I could see Rachel sitting on the swing. That was a surprise: she never got up early.

'I feel so much better,' she said unexpectedly. 'I feel Arthur's like a bird and I've been able to release him.' She made a flying gesture with her hands. Her eyes were shining. 'Laurie told me everything he said to her after the accident.'

'Do you remember when we first met her?' I asked. 'Did she say anything about having talked to Arthur?'

'I think I've blotted everything out about that day.'

I tried to keep my tone neutral. 'So, what exactly did she say?'

'Did you know she worked in a hospital? Oh, he wasn't in any pain, that's the main thing. She said how proud he was of us.' She sniffed, but she didn't look unhappy. 'She told me that's how she got interested in the books, because he was telling her about Mr Toppit. Isn't that funny? Isn't that so like Arthur? Run over by a truck and still talking about *Hayseed*.' She was laughing through her tears. At least she had stopped calling him 'Daddy'.

'But he never talked about the books,' I said.

'She said he kept saying our names. Over and over, she said. Isn't that nice?'

'Nothing else?'

She sighed. 'I'm sorry I've been so stroppy. I've just felt so awful about Arthur. I mean, I still do, but I feel different.' She gave a hiccupy laugh. 'Some of it's even quite funny. Like the hospital mixing up his stuff with some other dead person's.'

'What did Laurie say about that?'

'She said, "Shit happens," and that I shouldn't blame the hospital. She's right.'

At the bottom of the drive, two big old-fashioned black cars were turning in slowly from the road and came up to park in front of the house. Both drivers got out, grown-up versions of me: dark suits, white shirts and black ties, but just so it didn't get too confusing they were wearing black peaked caps as well. Rachel and I caught each other's eye: everything was a bit unreal.

It was something of a mystery why there were two cars to drive us to the church in the first place. Even Martha seemed uncertain, and she had been the one who had made the arrangements. I offered to go in one with Laurie, but Rachel thought I should be with her and Martha. Laurie seemed quite happy for us to be in one car and for her to be on her own in the other, but Martha didn't like the sound of that. I suggested that Martha, as the widow and principal mourner, should go on her own in the first car and the rest of us should follow behind, but nobody went for that either. It was like one of those brain-teasers you find on the back of matchboxes: how to utilize both cars without dividing the family unit. In the end, we opted for the simplest solution: we all went in one car, and the other followed empty behind. The car was immaculate. It was old, but it had been polished to within an inch of its life and it smelled of air-freshener inside – there was a dangly deodorant thing hanging off the driver's mirror. Martha ignored the no-smoking sticker in the corner of the window and lit up as soon as she got in.

The hearse with the coffin inside was already waiting at the church. I thought I was going to be sick when I saw it. Everything was becoming very real. Of course I knew what pall-bearers were, I just hadn't connected them to Arthur's funeral. I didn't realize that Martha had had something so formal in mind. There were six to carry Arthur; with a lot of grunting and heaving they eased the coffin out, and then, at a prearranged signal, straightened up and raised it on to their shoulders.

I read somewhere that during a total eclipse of the sun, all the birds and insects and animals stop making any noise. That was what it felt like as we slowly trailed after the coffin up the path: it was as if the whole world had vanished. When the doors opened it was a shock to see the church filled with people – like an unwelcome surprise party.

There was a lot of subdued chattering as we came in, but as soon as the coffin was in view of the congregation, a hush came over the place and all you could hear was our echoing footsteps as we followed it up the aisle, preceded by the vicar. Although she had seemed fine during the walk up to the church, Martha turned and pulled me towards her, taking my arm so that I was walking alongside her. Lila was seated about halfway up the aisle beside Graham Carter. As we passed, she reached out to touch Martha's arm. Her face wore one of those all-purpose solemn-but-intensely-moved expressions – which transformed itself quite quickly into something else when she saw that Laurie was part of our procession.

The odd thing was that it could have been anybody's funeral. Of course, there's something quite tear-jerking about hearing a lot of people singing hymns in a sad way – the moment the first one started Rachel took up residence in Laurie's arms – but none of it felt specific to Arthur. That was why I was looking forward to Terry Tringham's address because at least that would be about him. Terry was sitting in the pew behind us. He was an old friend but I didn't know him very well. All I remembered were things Martha and Arthur had said to us about him, or things I had overheard them say to each other when they thought we weren't listening, stories that tended to start with a small crisis involving one of a set of interchangeable but consistent elements – money, drink, wives, unfeasibly large restaurant bills, troublesome children, bank managers, films that had run out of money mid-production, girls who might or might not have been under age, bailiffs – and ended with a bigger crisis that brought into play several of the other elements. Our favourite story involved one of his wives throwing his false teeth out of a porthole during a row on a Mediterranean cruise.

When Terry's moment came, there was a lot of coughing and shuffling as everybody sat down and tried to get comfortable. Terry eased himself out of his pew and headed towards the pulpit. I hadn't realized he would be climbing into it, and he handled the stairs rather awkwardly. It made me think of someone scrambling up to a tree-house. In the Rule Book for Death, someone should point out that black is not a good colour unless you're scrupulously clean: Terry's black tie had a number of milky stains on it and the shoulders of his crumpled suit were speckled with dandruff. 'I hope he's up to this,' Martha whispered portentously.

'My name is Terence Tringham,' he began confidently. 'If I were a drinking man' – he gave an ironic guffaw – 'and we were not in a holy place, I would ask everyone to charge their glasses and toast the late great Arthur Hayman. I first met Arthur when he was eighteen. You should have seen him then, fresh up from the country, shining like a flaming torch, waiting to taste everything life had to offer.' He paused. 'So different from his later years.' I wasn't absolutely sure that hit quite the right note for a funeral address, but Terry ploughed on, shuffling bits of paper and, once in a while, patting his pocket uncertainly to check if some part of his speech had gone astray.

'We were the envy of the world, those of us privileged to be part of the British film industry in the early years. A volcano of talent was erupting on our doorstep! Elstree Studios, where Arthur and I started our careers, was like Paddington station in the rush-hour. How lucky we were! Our lives intersected with those of the truly great – the Hitchcocks, the Michael Powells, the Wally Carters. Of course, our lives did not all have the same trajectory as Wally's. It was a tragedy that Arthur's magnificent little film *Love's Captive* had problems with the studio and did not get wider distribution. Made for the masses, seen by the privileged few: how painful Arthur found that. In the fifties, some of us became the forgotten men of celluloid but, happily for Arthur, he managed to use his talents in his lovely children's books. And by then, of course, he had found Martha, who was not just a wife but a woman with the strength of ten men, an ally, a friend, a fellow intellectual. It was Wally, of course, who brought her into Arthur's life when he whisked her away from the groves of academe. Silver-tongued devil that he is, he got her to interrupt her PhD to research his crusader film, and do you know what? She's still working on the PhD! It's never too late, that's what I say!' I could feel Martha stiffen beside me.

Terry was a bit tearful now. There were long pauses. He was scrunching his handkerchief in his palm and blowing his nose with increasing frequency. He wanted to 'spool back', he told us. He wanted to talk about 'the early days' when he and Arthur and Wally Carter were 'the Three Musketeers of the Elstree sound stages'. People were getting restless, but he seemed oblivious to that.

'Anyone could have guessed that if Lady Luck's light was to shine on one of us, it would be on Wally, our loyal *compadre*. What a talent! And still working! Which is why he can't be with us today. But, typically generous, he's always acknowledged the inspiration we gave him in those heady days when everything seemed possible. It wasn't enough for him to scale the Chiltern Hills of Pinewood, he had his sights set on the Everest of the film world: the Hills of Beverly.'

As Terry was rambling on, a strange thing happened: Martha stood up and moved out of the pew into the aisle. I knew, because I was sitting next to her, of course, but it took the rest of the congregation longer to realize that something was going on. Her face was expressionless, and she walked in slow, measured steps. Terry slowed to a halt and he looked around him in a panicky way, as if a fire might have broken out that he hadn't noticed. Martha headed towards the pulpit. She didn't attempt to climb into, but waited patiently, looking up at Terry. There was a moment's silence. Finally, he began to descend the stairs. When he reached the bottom, Martha whispered something in his ear, then retraced her steps back to our pew.

Terry scuttled up into the pulpit again and rustled through bits of paper on its ledge. He took several sheets off the top, stuffed them into his pocket and began to speak again, rather quicker than before. 'In later years, many of his old friends did not see him as often as we would have liked. What an extraordinary talent! What an extraordinary man! All of us here were privileged to know him and love him. Thank you. Thank you so much.'

Almost immediately, the organ began the next hymn and everybody was on their feet. Terry rattled down the aisle past our pew, his eyes firmly on the ground. When the hymn was over and everyone had fallen to their knees for a prayer, I asked Martha in a whisper what had happened.

'I told him that if he went on *spooling back* and mentioned Wally Carter *one more time* I was going to slit my throat and drink my own blood,' she said, and turned back to her prayer book.

At the end of the service, the pall-bearers reappeared to take the coffin to the graveyard behind the church where Arthur was to be buried. We followed it, Martha hanging on to me and Rachel hanging on to Laurie. The big double doors at the end had been opened and a wide shaft of sunlight streamed in. A figure was standing there, silhouetted against the light. It took me a moment to realize it was Lila.

She wore a nervous smile and was holding some pamphlets. By her feet there was a large pile. 'Please don't be cross with me, Martha,' she said. 'This is my surprise.' Printed on the front, there was a pastiche of a Victorian playbill she had drawn. In bold, blocky lettering it said: 'A SELECTION FROM MR ARTHUR HAYMAN'S FAMOUS HAYSEED BOOKS', and, in smaller lettering underneath, 'WITH THE ILLUSTRATIVE ASSISTANCE OF MISS LILA LÖWENSTEIN'. There was a bizarre little caricature of Arthur and Lila in the bottom right-hand corner: he was dressed in a cape and a top hat, taking a bow; she was next to him in a ballgown, doing a curtsy.

'I had two hundred printed,' Lila said. 'You never know how many people will turn up to a funeral.' I had rarely seen Martha lost for words. She was flicking through the pamphlet. 'I hope you approve of the selection. So many bits I could have included.'

Tears were rolling down Martha's cheeks. 'But why?' she said.

'For *you*, Martha. And for my poor Arthur,' Lila said. 'And for the children, of course.' She handed one to me and one to Rachel.

Laurie took one from her. 'Oh, this is beautiful,' she said. 'It's like a collector's item. Could I have another?'

Lila moved the pile of pamphlets under her arm. 'I'm afraid there's only a limited number.'

'But, Lila, this must have been so expensive,' Martha said.

'The only thing it cost was my time. That I was happy to give. We have a little printing press at the school. My girls helped me.'

'You shouldn't have done it.'

'It's my gift to you, Martha.'

Martha glanced over her shoulder. By now, a mass of people was in the aisle behind us, waiting to get out of the church. 'We've got to get on,' she said desperately, and almost dragged us after her in the direction the coffin had gone.

What was meant to happen was that everyone would come out of the church and go straight to the grave. Because Lila had positioned herself so that nobody could get past her without being given a pamphlet, it took them about fifteen minutes to get there. The pall-bearers stood by the hole as people straggled round the side of the church in dribs and drabs. Martha moved to the head of the grave and stood there on her own with her back to us. Finally, when everyone was there, Lila bustled round the corner and called, in a ringing tone, 'The church is empty now! I think we can start.'

Earlier, I had worried that the funeral could have been anyone's. Now, the lowering of a wooden box containing Arthur's dead body into a large hole in the ground was so terrifyingly specific to him that I longed for something more general – perhaps the funeral equivalent of a firing squad when all the rifles except one contain blanks: a mass burial in which there are twelve coffins, but only one has a body in it.

You can imagine what Rachel was like as the coffin went into the ground. The truth is, that's what I was like too, but I felt it was allowed. Only Martha and Laurie retained some gravitas. Martha's face was tilted up to the sky, and whatever she was feeling inside she managed at least to appear dignified. Laurie had a different sort of look: the tears made her eyes shine and her expression was radiant which made her seem strangely far away. She reminded me of one of those paintings of Christian martyrs whose uplifted faces are focusing on their eventual arrival in heaven, rather than the immediate inconvenience of being eaten by lions.

Terry was standing in the background, tears trailing down his cheeks. Behind me, I heard someone whisper, 'Isn't Martha remarkable? Terry's too emotional to get through his speech so – *at her own husband's funeral* – she strides up to the pulpit and tells him he doesn't have to go on with it. So generous. Amazing!'

Everyone was standing very still. Suddenly there was a rustle and some movement, as if an animal was moving along the ground through a field of wheat. Lila was heading through the rows to the front. She hobbled forward, leaning on her stick, until she reached the edge of the grave. She opened her bag and produced a bunch of white flowers, which she threw into the hole, then retreated backwards until the crowd had swallowed her again.

Unlike the drive to the funeral, Martha was quite happy for Laurie, Rachel and me to go home in the second car. Terry was looking rather forlorn on the sidelines of the crowd so she had insisted he go with her. I would have asked Lila to come in our car if I'd had to, but I could see her hanging on to Graham Carter's arm. She had obviously persuaded him to take her. In our car, although there was room in the front now, Laurie, Rachel and I still sat together in the back.

'What a perfect service,' Laurie said dreamily. 'Just beautiful.'

'I wish Claude had been here.' Rachel sniffed. 'Now I think I'd like to get really drunk.'

'Oh, I'm so dumb,' Laurie said, banging the side of her head with her hand. 'Margaritas – that's what I should have done.'

As it was, there was more than enough to drink. By the time we got back Jack had set himself up in the hall behind a makeshift bar, a long refectory table with a white cloth on it. There were glasses of red and white wine already poured, as well as bottles of gin, vodka and whisky next to a large ice-bucket.

Martha positioned herself at the door into the hall, greeting people as they came in. When Lila arrived she grasped Martha's arm. 'My dear, tell me you liked my pamphlet. I think people were pleased. I hope so.' Graham was behind Lila. He was carrying a box with more pamphlets. 'I've brought more just in case I missed anyone,' Lila said. 'Graham's been my beast of burden. So kind.'

Martha caught his eye. 'You must find a chair, Lila,' she said. Lila was leaning heavily on her stick. 'Baby, will you take Lila somewhere she can sit down?'

'Thank you, no. I will just hold on to Graham's arm for a little while and circulate.' She gave her tinkling laugh. 'He is my publisher, after all.'

Graham had an air of doom about him. He embraced Martha. 'I

talked to Wally last night. He sends his love. He wanted to come so badly, but he's starting a film next week.'

'Dear Wally,' she murmured insincerely, then turned to the people behind Graham while I took the opportunity to escape. I passed the table in the middle of the room where people were hovering round the food that had been laid out. An old woman I'd never seen before tapped my shoulder. I think she thought I was one of the bar staff. 'You couldn't get me a small gin, could you?' she said. She popped something into her mouth. 'These are delicious! What are they called?'

'Chimichangas, I think.'

'Jimmy-whats?'

'They're Mexican.'

'Well done,' she said, and handed me her empty glass to refill.

One of the surprises of the day was how successful Laurie's food turned out to be. The only problem area was the salted almonds, which were so oversalted that they made everybody drink more than they should have done. The way Jack was sloshing out the gin probably didn't help.

After a while the atmosphere in the room became looser. The acoustics seemed to have softened. At the beginning, the noise was bouncing off the hall's high ceiling. Now it had settled like a low fog just above everyone's heads. They had relaxed into themselves and I felt almost invisible: I could move around without anyone noticing.

In the kitchen, where I had gone to fill a jug with water, I came across Lila. She had been in there with the door closed. When I came in she jumped. 'Oh, it's you, Luke,' she said, her hand at her throat. 'You gave me such a fright.' She was doing something odd – easing a side of smoked salmon out of her bag. She seemed rather shifty. I was going to wait: I felt some explanation was called for.

She tried to bluff it out. 'I think it's all going well, don't you?'

'Mmm.' I was looking at the salmon.

'Of course, Arthur and Martha's friends are so interesting. So many different walks of life.'

I pointed at the salmon. 'Do you need some help, Lila?'

There was a pause. 'You know, Luke, older people find hot food, food with chilli pepper, rather indigestible,' she said.

I nodded. 'Oh.'

'Yes,' she said. 'Martha is very fond of smoked salmon.' She tapped it with her fingers. 'It's ready-sliced,' she added. She dipped into her bag and produced two loaves of bread. 'She likes this wholemeal. I often buy it for her. I thought I would do little squares of it with the salmon.' Some lemons came out. 'With a squeeze of lemon and some black pepper. Something simple. As an alternative. People might like it, don't you think?'

'There's an awful lot of food, Lila. Everyone seems to be enjoying it.'

She gave her special laugh. 'You're such a good boy, Luke. You have such a good heart.'

In the hall, everyone was making a fuss of Rachel. Each time I saw her she was in a different part of the room, being embraced by somebody and talking intently at them, waving her arms. She was quite drunk. I had knocked back a couple of glasses of wine myself so I knew how she felt. When I caught up with her, she was with Graham. Terry was slumped on a chair next to them, holding a large glass of whisky. It was possible he was asleep.

Rachel and I had always liked Graham. Even though he was in his mid-thirties, he didn't seem old. He had wild curly hair, and his clothes always seemed too small for him. Today he was wearing a rumpled corduroy suit and a shirt that was missing a number of buttons. Martha had told us he had a wife and several children, but we had never seen them.

'It's not a good time,' he was saying to Rachel. 'Publishing's had it.'

'Oh, I know it would work,' she said, grabbing his hand.

'Small publishers are dropping like flies.'

Terry's head lifted. 'If you could just send Wally the script. Don't get me wrong, I know he's a busy boy.'

Graham looked down at him. 'Sorry?'

'The below-the-line's coming from the Norwegian government. Some tax scheme for dentists. Amazing facilities up there. Money's not the problem this time.'

Rachel ignored him. 'Laurie and I were going through Daddy's study the other night. There's lots of stuff – lots of things he didn't use in the books. You know what we could call it?'

'I have a feeling it might be up Wally's street,' Terry said, taking a gulp of whisky.

'*Hayseedlings*,' Rachel said excitedly. 'Don't you think that's a great title?'

'The thing is, Rachel,' Graham grimaced, 'the fifth book didn't *do* that well, didn't hit the forecasts. We should have built up some momentum after four but it's such a tough market.'

Her eyes were shining. 'I know it would work,' she repeated. 'We have to do it for Daddy.' She was still holding Graham's hand.

'The candy-floss stuff's all right, of course,' Terry said. 'The ocean-liner film was fine, don't get me wrong, but this script is something special.'

Graham turned away from Rachel's intent gaze to Terry's moony one. 'Why don't you just send it to him?' he said grumpily.

'I did! So much for old friends, never heard a word. Of course, he's busy, these days, I know that.' Terry fumbled in his pocket, brought out a single cigarette and lit it shakily. 'He's probably still upset about what happened at the première. I did apologize, can't do more than that – but, look, Val had just left me, I was in the middle of a bloody court case. Nightmare.'

Behind Terry, Lila was heading towards us. 'Could I tempt you with one of these?' I could hear her saying. 'They're Martha's favourite. We haven't met, have we? So few of Arthur and Martha's friends I don't know.'

Graham turned his back. 'Don't let her come over here,' he said. 'She's already suggested she should take over writing the books.'

'Then do mine,' Rachel pleaded. 'I'll put it together.'

'Look, I may not even have a company in six months' time.'

Lila was getting closer. 'I'm Martha's official German teacher,' she was saying. Her laugh carried across the room. 'By appointment.'

'It's not a lot to ask.' Terry was turning aggressive. 'Just get him the bloody script.'

Rachel grabbed Graham's arm. 'Come to Arthur's study. I'll show you the stuff.'

'Now?' Graham said. A look passed between them.

'Yes,' Rachel said.

'Graham!' Lila called, but by the time she'd got to us he and Rachel were already fleeing. Lila looked down at Terry. He seemed to have slipped further down the back of his chair. 'My dear, you must eat.' She offered him the plate. 'Such a moving speech. So hard to do. I know how grateful Martha was.'

'Any more of those Mexican doo-dahs?' Terry said. He pointed at Laurie, who was at the other end of the hall. 'She made 'em. *Clever* lady. You know she was with Arthur when he died? He was still talking about the old days, apparently. Amazing.'

'I find that hard to believe,' Lila snapped. 'His injuries did not lend themselves to a cosy chat.' Her hand flew up to her mouth in horror at what she had said. 'I'm so sorry, Luke.'

She didn't need to worry about me. It was Terry whose face crumpled as the tears trickled down it once more. 'What a bugger. Everyone's dying. And Wally won't even read my fucking script.'

Within an hour, the party had thinned out, but not enough for Martha. 'Baby, can't you get everyone to go?' she said wearily. 'Stop walking round with that tray of drinks. They'll never leave.' Doreen was doing a bit of clearing up, picking up glasses and emptying ashtrays, but nobody was taking any notice. Laurie and Lila were circulating with their platters. They were like two ice-skaters gliding in concentric circles, managing never to bump into each other.

In the corner of the hall, an old man had been standing in the same place the whole time. I had noticed him come in, but had never seen him talk to anyone. He caught my eye. I turned away but it was too late: he was heading towards me. I contemplated trying to escape, but he was on me too quickly. 'Are you Arthur's boy?' he said eagerly. 'You look just like him. I expect everyone says that.'

My heart sank. 'They don't normally. They have today.'

He put his hand out. 'I'm Derek Jones, but everyone calls me Bunny. I knew your dad when he wasn't much older than you. I worked at Pinewood. I ran the projection room. We called your dad "Artie" in those days.'

I giggled: it seemed so unlikely. 'We did,' the man said. 'Promise.' Then his tone changed. 'I saw him the day he died.' He looked down at his feet. 'On Dean Street, in Soho. He was on the other side of the road. I knew it was him, the way he carried himself.'

'What happened?' I said.

The man's eyes were moist. 'Nothing. I didn't speak to him. I should have but I didn't. It had been so long, thirty years maybe. I watched him walk down the street in the sun. It was such a hot day. Then he was killed. I read it in the newspaper.' He lowered his head. 'I'm so sorry.'

Of all the strange things that had happened since Arthur died, this seemed to be one of the few that verged on reality. I thought about it for a moment and then I said, 'I think his time had come. I didn't think so at first, I couldn't believe it, but now I do. I really do. If you had talked to him, I don't think it would have made any difference.' I wasn't just saying it to make him feel better: I believed it. Nonetheless it was hard to say. I had to force the words out.

'I can tell you one thing,' he blurted out. 'Of all of those boys, he was the only one worth a hill of beans.' His face had flushed. 'Tringham?' He gestured towards Terry, who was still sitting down with his head slumped on his chest. 'He was nothing. Just an idle boy without a brain in his head. And Wally? Clever, I grant you, but not a patch on Artie. Nothing here.' He banged his chest. 'Nothing in his heart.' A bit of spittle was lurking at the corner of his mouth. 'You guard those books of his with your life, young man. I read them to my grandchildren. They're worth more than all of Mr Wallace Carter's films put together.' He was staring at me. 'Is that a deal?'

'Okay,' I said. He stuck out his hand for me to shake, then made for the door.

Only the stragglers were left now, people talking in little pockets. I found Martha on a chair in the corner of the hall. Lila was standing over her, propped on her stick. 'I have my night things,' she was saying. 'I have told the school I will not be available tomorrow.'

Martha looked old and fragile. 'No, you can't stay,' she said. 'It's time for everyone to go. I want us to be on our own now. If you really want to help, Lila, you could get everyone to leave.' She glanced round the room. 'Where's Rachel?' she said. I shrugged my shoulders.

Laurie was passing with a tray of empty glasses. 'Miss Clow,' Lila said loudly, 'Mrs Hayman would like the family to be on their own now. Do you need a taxi organized? I'm sure Luke would do that for you.'

Laurie smiled. 'Thank you. I already have one ordered.'

'Good,' Lila said.

'Crack of dawn,' Laurie said.

Lila turned back. 'Excuse me? You're staying here tonight?'

'Today's my last day.'

'Miss Clow,' Lila said, in a low voice she was attempting to control, 'the Haymans have been to hell and back. I'm sure they're grateful for your help, but do you not think they might be allowed to have just one night *en famille*?'

'Well, I –'

'They have hotels at the airport. At Heathrow. Or are you flying from Gatwick? They have hotels there too, I imagine. Luke could book one for you. Couldn't you, Luke?'

Laurie said, 'I'm taking the train to London in the morning – got to pick up my bag before I go to the airport.' She glanced at Martha.

'But you could go now,' Lila said.

Laurie was embarrassed. 'Martha said I should stay.'

The room had become silent, or maybe it just seemed so. Lila looked at Martha. I looked at Lila. Laurie was looking all over the place. Martha looked at the floor.

'Oh, Lila ...' she said, combining irritation, apology and exhaustion in those two words.

I could see the muscles in Lila's cheeks clenching and un-clenching. Finally, as purposefully as anyone could while leaning on a stick, she walked to the centre of the hall. She banged the stick three times on the wooden floor to get everyone's attention. The dozen or so people left turned to her.

'Thank you all so much for coming,' she said, her voice echoing round the hall. 'Martha and the children are most grateful for your support, but all those who have not been invited to stay the night are kindly asked to leave. Taxis can be arranged for those who need them. I will be standing by the front door in case anyone has not got a copy of my little *Hayseed* pamphlet. I have just a few left. Thank you.'

I was impressed. It was certainly an effective way to clear a room. A sense of urgency spread through the remaining guests. Cigarettes were stubbed out, glasses plonked on tables, cheeks kissed. Everyone was bustling around, except Terry, still asleep in his chair. Lila moved away from the centre of the room and, as she did so, something awful happened: her legs went up in the air and she crashed to the floor with a bang. The room shook: she was not a small woman. She gave a cry, then an awful guttural wail. There was a short silence, and the room sprang into action. I got to Lila first, and knelt on the floor next to her. Her dress had ridden up and I could see the tops of her stockings and some bloomer-like knickers. Her face was contorted, and she was letting out short, sobbing gasps.

Laurie was there straight after me. She leaned over us, but when Lila saw her she seemed to forget the pain. She raised herself slightly off the ground with one elbow and tried feebly to push

Laurie away with the stick she was still holding. 'Get her away!' she hissed. 'She's put a hex on me.' Then she began to whimper, through clenched teeth.

It seemed unfair to point the finger of blame at Laurie: Lila had slipped on a canapé that had fallen on to the floor, but it was not one of Laurie's – I could see a little triangle of pink salmon stuck to the sole of her shoe. Everyone was huddling round us, and Lila's face was almost purple. Her eyes were screwed up and she was letting out heaving sobs – but they didn't look like sobs of pain to me: they looked like sobs of anger.

I had never dialled 999 before: it was rather exciting. Martha suggested it when everyone was arguing about whether Lila should be moved to a sofa or left on the floor. There was also some discussion about whether or not she should be given a cup of tea. It took a while for everyone to calm down and Laurie took command. I heard somebody say, 'She's a nurse. She works in a hospital.'

It was she who decided that Lila should not be moved, but that a cushion should be put under her head and that a blanket laid over her to keep her warm. She found some soluble aspirin, which was dropped into warm water. Martha held up Lila's head and she took small sips until the glass was empty. She was trembling. 'I'm fine,' she kept saying. 'I'm fine.'

The ambulance arrived after about ten minutes. I don't suppose there are many emergencies in the middle of the countryside. As the men were easing Lila on to a stretcher, Graham appeared. He looked stunned by the scene in the hall. 'My God!' he said. 'What's all this?' I explained how Lila had slipped. 'Is she going to be all right?' he asked.

'They think she's broken her hip and she'll –'

'Can you do something for me?' he cut in. 'Can you find me an envelope?'

I went and got one from Martha's desk. When I gave it to him, he turned away from me and put something into it. He licked the flap and stuck it down, then produced a pen and wrote 'Rachel' on the front.

'I've got to go,' he said. 'This minute. I said I'd be home hours ago. Mel's pregnant again. It's all been quite difficult.' He patted my shoulder. 'You've got all that to come.' He slipped the envelope into my hand. 'Can you give this to Rachel? She's gone for a walk.'

Just as he was leaving, he turned back to me with a grin and said, 'This'll amuse you, Luke. Your Doreen tried to flog me a copy of *Hayseed* number one, which Arthur had inscribed to her kid. She was most put out when I told her the books weren't exactly in the signed-first-edition league. In her dreams!' He laughed. Actually, he was wrong. Five years later Jack's book lay spread open at the inscribed title page, sealed in a glass case, bolted to the wall of Graham's new office with tamper-proof brass screws.

I sat on the front steps as Lila was loaded into the ambulance. The remaining guests were getting into their cars, so when the ambulance went down the drive, there was a procession of vehicles behind it. The house felt very empty when I went back inside. I turned some lights on. It was getting dark. There was a forlorn pile of Lila's pamphlets on the table, and a great boxful near the door. Terry was asleep on the sofa. The rug that had been covering Lila was lying on the floor, so I picked it up and draped it over him. There was no sign of Martha.

I found Laurie in the sitting room. She was sitting on a chair, quite still, as if she might be in a trance. A strange sound was coming from her, a kind of sibilant hum, as if she was muttering the same word over and over again.

'Where is everybody?' I said.

She jumped. 'Sorry, I was on the moon,' she said. 'Martha's gone up to sleep.'

I sat down on the sofa.

'When are you going back to school?' she asked.

'Monday, I think.'

'Some week,' she said.

'I'm sorry you haven't had much of a holiday.'

135

She got up and came over to join me. 'You don't get it, do you?' she said. She looked happy but sad, and her eyes were glistening. 'I wouldn't have changed this trip for anything. Of course I didn't want what happened to your dad to happen, but I was proud to be with him. Oh, Luke, I knew there was something real special about him,' she said. 'I felt it here.' She tapped her chest with a fist. 'I can't explain it. That day, that hot day in London, there was something in the air hovering over him. It's in you, too. It's a part of you. You probably can't feel it like I can. Reading his books, I can see it just so clearly.'

'See what?'

'You're so lucky, Luke. You'll carry it with you wherever you go. It's like a gift.'

'What kind of gift?' I said, slightly irritated. 'A gift for what?'

Laurie seemed to be in a world of her own. 'It's like those crop circles. It just looks all mussed up when you're on the ground, but when you fly, when you're able to fly' – she made a swooping gesture with her arm – 'you can see what everything means, you can see the pattern, you can see where everything fits in. That's the gift.'

I was longing to tell Adam. He loved this sort of thing. 'This gift – do you have it?' I asked.

'It's too early to tell.' Her hand reached for mine. 'But you have it, Luke. I know that.' Then she said something really creepy: 'There's going to be a lot of people watching you.'

I'd had enough. I took my hand back. I was tired of everyone in the house behaving so oddly. 'In the hospital I saw into your bag,' I said. 'I saw what you wrote in your notebook – Arthur's name over and over again, that *Hiawatha* thing.'

She didn't ask how or why; she just nodded matter-of-factly. 'My daddy used to read me *Hiawatha* when we played. He was the Indian chief and I was a princess,' she said. 'Before I lost him.'

'But you weren't writing about him, you were writing about Arthur.'

'Meeting your dad was very special to me.'

'Why? Was it because of what he said?'

'You mean about when you lived in Jordan?' Laurie asked quietly.

'You said you wouldn't say anything.'

'I didn't, honey. I haven't.'

'What did he say exactly?'

'I told you. I thought he said something about living in Jordan. I could hardly hear him.'

I felt as if I was under water, holding my breath. 'He didn't say that. You misheard him.'

'Then what *did* he say?'

'I wasn't there.'

'But you know,' Laurie said, 'don't you?'

'It was my brother's name. He was called Jordan.'

There was wonder in her face. 'So –'

I interrupted her. 'Did he really talk about how proud he was of Rachel and me?'

'I couldn't hear. I don't know what he said any more. I tried to hold on to it all, but I've gone back over it so often I've lost it . . . everything's got so messed up in my brain,' she cried. She lowered her head and put a hand over her eyes. I could see her face trembling: she was trying to stop herself crying.

'Did he?'

'No,' she whispered. 'I'm sorry . . . I'm so sorry.'

I couldn't see her eyes: her hand was still covering them. She was sobbing now.

'I won't see you again,' I said. 'I mean tomorrow. I'll be asleep when you leave.' I kissed her cheek. Her face was wet. 'Have a good journey. I've never been on a plane.' I didn't want to sound wistful so I added, 'I've been to lots of places, but just on trains and things. I'd love to go on a plane, though.'

'Luke . . .' she said, but I kept moving towards the door. I didn't want to go back and start all over again.

As I went up to my room, I heard noises in Arthur's study. Rachel was back from her walk. I stood in the doorway and watched her. She had a bottle of wine, and a cigarette was smoking in the ashtray. Every drawer in the room was open, and there was a pile of books and papers on the table.

'I called Claude,' she said. 'He and Damian are coming down tomorrow to help me. There's so much *stuff*.'

'Are you having an attack of the busies?' I said. It was a childhood phrase of ours.

'Mmm?' She wasn't really listening. She was sorting through sheets of paper. 'You know there was originally a different ending to the second book?'

'Was there?'

'Luke doesn't follow Mr Toppit into the Darkwood, he tries to lay a trap by covering up that pit next to the top path.'

'Is Graham definitely going to do your book?'

'I think I've won him round. He says if there's enough interesting stuff he'll consider it. There's tons of Lila's left-over drawings.'

'You don't know what happened to Lila, do you? You missed it all.'

After I told her, her mouth was hanging open in amazement. I could see her lip trembling, and suddenly we began to laugh. We laughed so hard that I had a stitch and tears were rolling down Rachel's face.

'It's so awful,' she said, holding her hand over her mouth. 'Bloomers?'

I nodded. 'Sort of cream-coloured, sort of old-lady-coloured.' Another wave of laughter enveloped us. We were clinging to each other, letting out great stuttering guffaws. You could probably have heard us all the way through the house.

I had had my hand in my pocket all the time, fingering the envelope Graham had given me and the little bump it contained. The glue hadn't been very sticky, but I would probably have opened it even if it had been stuck down properly. When we drew apart, still weeping with laughter, Rachel's hair had fallen across her face. She tucked it behind her ears and I could see the pearl stud in her left ear, and the tiny dot of an empty hole in the right one. I couldn't decide whether I would give the envelope to her or not. In the end I decided I wouldn't. When I got up to my room I took the little pearl thing out, put it in my pencil box, then tore up the envelope and threw it into the waste-paper bin.

My rucksack, the one that had travelled with me from school to the hospital to Linton, was lying on the floor next to the bin. I had forgotten about it completely. I picked it up. I knew exactly what was going to be in there, and a small sense of excitement came over me. I opened the rucksack and pulled out Adam's Dutch magazine.

It's probably bad form to have a wank after your father's funeral, but I honestly felt I deserved it. I opened the magazine to the centre pages where Dirk and Rex and Donna were. They felt like old friends. I propped up two pillows against the headboard, let my trousers fall to my ankles and lay down on the bed. I didn't know how long it took other people, but I came very quickly: it was probably the stress. Then I saw something extraordinary: there was some spunk – not jets, of course, not yet, not so soon, but a fully formed white drop that sat on the end of my prick, viscous and strong enough to hold its shape. I leaned forward and moved it carefully on to the end of my finger. Against the light it was as round and perfect as a small pearl.

Laurie

'*Y de Darkwood viene el señor Toppit, y no viene para ti, ni para mí, sino para todos nosotros.*' When Rachel discovered that Laurie spoke Spanish, she had given her the Spanish translations – the only other country where the books had been published – and Laurie was flicking through them as she sat with a cup of coffee in the departure lounge at Gatwick. She was keeping all the books, the English ones as well as the Spanish, in her hand luggage, along with her notebook, partly to be able to look at them on the plane and partly to ensure their safety if there was a problem with the luggage she had checked in. You couldn't be too careful. When she and Marge had gone to the Yucatán peninsula for their year-before-last vacation, their bags had ended up in Santiago and it had taken four days for them to be rerouted to Cancún. The airline had said they would have to go back to the airport to get them when they arrived, but by the time Marge had finished with them they had agreed to transport them to the hotel and were practically offering to unpack them as well.

Laurie's Spanish was a little rusty, but it came back to her as she read. A lot of Hispanics worked at Holy Spirit – particularly the cleaning staff and the girls in the kitchens, from whom Laurie had got some of the recipes for the food at Arthur's funeral – but mostly she remembered Spanish from her childhood in Los Alamos, from the Mexicans who worked there or from the fruit-sellers at the market in Santa Fe where she had played when Alma was having a drink after one of their shopping trips. That Spanish was the only other language into which the books had been translated, and the only other language she knew, was another of the links that made Laurie question whether it was coincidence that she had come to England in the first place and had been walking down that street at the exact moment Arthur had had the accident. At first she thought her trip to England had been a voyage of discovery, but now she believed it was more like a series of reawakenings – an accumulation of events that seemed extra-ordinary and familiar at the same time.

What she did know was that it was more complicated than she had first thought. The clean line of her connection to Arthur – the chain that bound them together as strong and bright in her mind as newly forged steel – had been changed by everything she had learned about him from Martha, Luke and Rachel. The pattern had intensified, mutating and expanding like a simple image refracted through a kaleidoscope. It was harder for her to control now, but it was becoming infinitely more beautiful, larger and more solid, forming a structure so complex and volatile that its expansion was stretching the surface and making it more vulnerable to attack from people outside – like the German woman called Lila. The last addition, the discovery of the child called Jordan, a child who seemed as lost to time and history as her own father, had changed the shape again, turned it inside out, like the most intricate cat's cradle you could ever think of. Laurie had still not fully taken it in, and she was so tired that she knew no amount of zinging would clear her head enough for her to find its proper place in the structure.

A flight that had been scheduled to depart the night before had been delayed until the morning, and all around Laurie people were asleep in chairs or lying on the floor with their heads resting on cabin bags. The restaurant where she was sitting was like a war zone. There wasn't a table that didn't have several trays on it, and the floor was littered with plastic cups, bits of food and sandwich wrappings. When she brought her coffee to the table, she did nothing more than wipe the crumbs off the chair with a paper napkin and make a small space for her cup on the table. Once she would have cleared the whole thing, or stood by, trying to over-come her embarrassment, as Marge shouted at one of the waiters to do it. The truth was, she felt indifferent to it now.

When she had finished her coffee, she wandered through the departure lounge looking at the shops where you could get cheap liquor, cigarettes or perfume. She wondered about buying Alma something, then thought better of it. Alma was not someone who received gifts gracefully and, anyway, there was nothing she needed or wanted. It would be much more productive to buy a large and expensive gift to keep Mrs Detweiler sweet, but after the business with Alma's so-called assault, Laurie didn't think there could be anything in the gift shops at Gatwick that would guarantee her continuing residence at Spring Crest. She wasn't sure that even Tiffany's would stock something large or expensive enough for that. But there would be time to think about Alma when she got home: she wasn't going to waste her last hour in England worrying about her. In fact, the sharp sense of dread about Alma she always carried with her had faded almost completely.

She stood at the news-stand for a while, then went into the bookstore and glanced idly at the displays. There were detective novels and thick, glossy bestsellers, souvenir books about Charles and Diana's engagement and piles of picture books about stately homes or pretty country cottages.

'Do you have children's books?' she asked the man behind the cash register. He had a badge on his lapel, saying 'Kieran'.

Hardly looking at her, he gestured dismissively towards the far corner of the store, but when Laurie got there all she could find was a jumble of cartoon annuals and stories taken from Disney movies piled on top of each other.

She went back to the counter. 'Is that all you have?' she asked.

The man shrugged his shoulders. 'There are some comics next to the magazines.' He had a squint and the thick aviator spectacles he wore accentuated it.

'I'm not looking for comics,' Laurie said sharply. 'That's the point. What about older children? They don't want to read comics.'

'Over there. That's all we have,' he said, gesturing over his shoulder with his thumb.

The woman in the queue behind Laurie moved up and banged her book on the desk. 'Excuse me,' she said rudely. 'Do you mind? My flight's been called.' She tried to edge Laurie out of the way, but Laurie stood her ground.

'I know that. I looked over there, but there's nothing for older kids.' She was finding the man's magnified squint rather distracting. It made him look like a mutant.

'We only stock what Central Distribution gives us.'

She nodded. 'Okay. So what books can parents buy for their kids here?'

His voice was pointedly slow, as if he was dealing with a retarded person: 'They can buy what we have there.' He pointed again with his thumb. 'What Central Distribution gives us.'

Laurie forced herself to look into his eyes. 'And if there's nothing suitable?'

'I don't know. I expect children bring their own books with them.'

'Why would you expect that?' she snapped back. Actually, she had no idea what children did or didn't do. 'Anyway, if people brought books with them, there wouldn't be any call for a bookstore.'

'It's nothing to do with me, the choice of books,' he said.

'Evidently,' she said.

He folded his arms and stared at her. His face was tinged with red. 'I make sure the shelves are stocked,' he said. 'We're in daily contact with Central Distribution.'

His eyes were beginning to look quite scary. Laurie felt as if she was on a roller-coaster ride that was as exhilarating as it was frightening. The blood was coursing through her veins. 'But you don't know what they're going to send, do you?' She was almost shouting now. 'You just call them and say, "Hey, I've got five empty shelves. Fill 'em up!" I don't suppose you've even *heard* of *The Hayseed Chronicles* by Arthur Hayman?'

'The what?'

'This,' she said, taking one of the books out of her bag and banging it on the counter. He looked at it blankly. 'I want to order it,' she said.

'If you already have it,' the man said, teeth clenched, clearly trying to control his voice, 'why do you need to order it?'

It was not an unreasonable question, but Laurie had gone too far down the road now. 'Because,' she snarled, 'I want other people to enjoy it. Because I want kids to come into this God-forsaken store and find something they might like to read among all that *crap* you've got over there.' She was trembling a little as she grabbed a pen from her bag, took a paper bag from the pile on the counter and wrote on it the titles of the five books, then Arthur's name. She thrust it into the man's hand. 'Okay?' she said. 'Okay?' Then she walked away.

He said something and she turned round. 'What did you say?' she asked. She knew perfectly well what he had said: he had muttered, 'Dyke,' under his breath. Before she knew what was happening, her hand had flown up and clipped the side of his face with the *Hayseed* book she was still holding. His glasses sprang away from his face and landed on the carpet. Then she got out of the place as quickly as she could.

The phrase 'Martini, straight up, no olive' was not one Laurie could recall using for some time. Because of Alma she didn't drink much, and since St Bart's last summer she had really cut down – she didn't think she'd even had a glass of wine at Arthur's funeral – but it felt rather sophisticated now to be sitting on a bar-stool ordering a proper drink. The place was almost empty: there were just two or three tables occupied and only a few people sitting up at the bar with her. Laurie was pleased that the barman took her order without a hint of surprise that someone might ask for a martini at nine o'clock in the morning. After she had got about halfway through the drink, she understood why people drank when they were stressed. She was a little dizzy, but she felt as snug and toasty as if she was lying under an electric blanket. She was almost ridiculously happy.

Behind her, seated at one of the tables, a middle-aged woman was talking softly to an older man. Laurie had noticed them when she came in because the woman had been having some difficulty in helping the man into a chair. He was walking with two sticks and was clearly nervous about letting go of them. The woman had to guide him so that he was standing in front of the chair with his back to it, then she had pulled away the walking-sticks and gravity had let him fall safely on to the seat of the chair. Now she was leaning over the table holding his hand. Laurie couldn't hear everything she was saying, but she was obviously trying to reassure him. Laurie heard her say, 'I'll only be five minutes, I promise,' and then she pushed her chair back and got up from the table. The man's face was completely impassive, but he let out a little moan.

Laurie got down from the bar-stool. 'Excuse me,' she said. The woman turned to her. 'Would you like me to keep an eye on him?'

The woman looked surprised. 'That's very kind of you.'

'It's no trouble,' Laurie said. 'I work in a hospital.'

'He's my father. He had a stroke last year,' the woman said. 'He's fine, just a bit shaky on his legs.'

'I'll take care of him.'

'You're very kind. I'm just going to the loo. I won't be long. He can't talk, but he can understand everything.' She put her hand on the man's shoulder. 'Can't you?' The man stared blankly ahead of him.

Laurie sat down in the woman's chair and watched her leave the bar. The man looked as if he was trying to turn his head to see. He made a throaty sound. She touched his hand. 'I'll take care of you, honey,' she said, then after a second she added, 'I'm Laurie.'

The man was still looking straight ahead. His eyes were watery. On his cheek, just below the hairline, there was a little patch of shaving foam that whoever had shaved him had missed.

'Honey, you've got a . . . you know, a . . .' Laurie couldn't think what to call it, so she turned the side of her face towards him and patted her cheek '. . . shaving thing.' Now she had got used to his face, she realized it was just his eyes that showed any expression. She picked up a napkin and wiped the foam off his cheek. They sat in silence for a moment and then she said, 'I'm American, I come from northern California. A place called Modesto.' She thought she saw movement in his eyes. She smiled. 'People say we've got a lot to be modest about in Modesto.' He let out a moan, not of pain but an answering kind of moan. 'I'm heading back there,' she said. He blinked. 'Would you like me to read to you?' she asked him. She pulled the first *Hayseed* book out of her bag. 'This was written by a friend of mine,' she said. She held up the cover so he could see it, then opened it at the beginning and began: '"When you were young, or maybe not so long ago, not very far from where you live, or perhaps a little closer, Luke Hayseed lived in a big old house . . ."'

The martini seemed to have softened her voice, taken the grate out of it. As she read, the man made a light, low noise like a distant aeroplane. It was as if he was humming along to the words.

Arthur and Martha

Arthur and Martha's flat on Shaftesbury Avenue was the second place they had lived since they were married. As chance would have it, it was not much more than a hundred yards from the corner where Arthur was to be mown down by a lorry over twenty-five years later. The block was called Alleyne House and the entrance was between an off-licence and an Italian restaurant from which, when they had something to celebrate, Arthur would order dinner for them and carry it up to their flat on the first floor.

The place they used to have off Gloucester Road had been too small and too damp, and anyway, after three years there, Martha's relationship with their Polish landlord, who lived on the floor above them, had deteriorated to such an extent that their days were clearly numbered. The final acrimonious row about the state of what Martha called 'the aptly named common parts' had resulted in a trail of smelly refuse being accidentally deposited outside their front door every time Mr Bubek took his rubbish to the bins in the basement. On the day they finally left the flat, Martha had posted a representative selection of the garbage through Mr Bubek's letterbox, along with the last week's rent and the keys.

The Shaftesbury Avenue flat had been Terry Tringham's: he had had a lease on it, and it was he who suggested they might take it over. Arthur and Martha knew the flat, but not very well. When they met Terry, it tended to be at the Sphinx, or at one of his regular pub haunts in Soho. The flat seemed to be reserved for the microscopic portion of his life that revolved around his wife Eileen and their three children. When Eileen had worked she had been a script girl – they had met when they both worked on

the last film that Wally Carter had done before going to America –
and had married as soon as the divorce from Terry's first wife, Liz,
had come through because Eileen was already pregnant. Arthur
had been their best man.

Martha and Arthur had been to the flat a few times for parties,
normally drunken end-of-shoot affairs, and had had dinner there
occasionally when Terry and Eileen were having one of their
periodic attempts to pretend that their lives were not in freefall.
These awkward domestic evenings involved grubby, crying children who would not have their bath or would not go to bed, who
wanted to be read to not by the parent who was offering to read
to them but by the parent who was opening another bottle of
wine or trying to pull the disparate elements of the meal into some
kind of order.

At some point during one of these evenings, several things
might happen: Eileen might leave the table when they sat down
to eat and never return, or she might leave the table when they
finally sat down to eat and return a few minutes later with tears
on her face or a sleepy child in her arms. At some point before or
after her departure there might be a sudden electrical charge in the
air that seemed to cause a wine glass to tip over or a chair to fall
backwards.

But whatever happened during one of those evenings, the out-
come tended to be the same. At a certain point, sometimes during
the meal or sometimes after it, sometimes with Eileen in the room
or sometimes not, Terry would say, 'Fuck it! Let's go to the club.
Come on,' and stand up, groping for his cigarettes and matches
among the mess on the table.

If Martha suggested that she stay behind with Eileen while Terry
and Arthur went out, Eileen would have none of it. She was tired,
she had to do the washing, she wanted to tidy the flat, the baby
might need changing, she wanted to go to bed. She would argue
so vociferously against Martha staying that it seemed as if, out of
all the possible unsatisfactory outcomes of the evening for her, that
was the most unsatisfactory of all. Finally, as they were putting

their coats on to go out, Terry might say, 'Domestic bliss, dear,' then give what passed for a wry laugh that echoed down the gloomy stairwell as they went downstairs.

Despite, or because of, the eventual messy disentanglement of the marriage and Terry's offhand disposal of the children to various grandparents and relations when it became clear that Eileen would have to stay in what everyone euphemistically called the Nursing Home for the foreseeable future, Terry became his old self again. After a few drinks had loosened him up he would sometimes describe his wife as being a few pages short of the full script, but Eileen's story, which he dismissed so casually, had somehow lodged itself deep inside Arthur. He could not help wondering if those pages had ever been there in the first place or if they had been slowly torn out, one by one, by Terry's drinking and violence and casual infidelities.

Terry had been offered the job of production manager on a film to be shot on location in Kenya. He would be away for four months and he had decided to look for a new place when he returned. The Kenya job, which he had originally turned down because it sounded too much like hard work, had begun to seem like an attractive option: he had been receiving an increasing number of aggressive letters from the tax man questioning the earnings he had been declaring over the last couple of years; there was the potentially lethal husband of one of his girlfriends, whose anger over the affair seemed to be turning away from his wife in the direction of Terry; and, worst of all, there was a subtle but increasing emphasis from the family members on whom his children were billeted on the temporary nature of the current arrangements. Terry thought that if he went away for a few months, then didn't have a proper place to live when he returned, that particular problem would solve itself. He took the job.

Despite their long friendship, Terry drove a hard bargain: to sign over the lease to Arthur he wanted key money and he refused to budge on the amount. There was no shortage of people – Martha included – telling Arthur that it was at least twice what it ought to have been, but nobody could offer a practical way to get Terry to reduce the price. Left to himself, Arthur might have withdrawn from the whole thing, not just because of the money but because the flat seemed tainted by what had gone on there between Terry and Eileen. But Martha, despite appearing to believe that the problem lay less with Terry's intransigence than with Arthur's inability to force down the key money, seemed so keen on it, had become so uncharacteristically positive about its perceived virtues – how central it was, how easy it would be to redecorate, how it might be a new start for them – that Arthur opted for the simplest solution: he agreed to pay Terry's price.

They had already made major inroads into Arthur's savings – of the two scripts he had been working on one had been rejected, leaving him only with the fee that had been paid on signature of the contract, and the other had been through so many rewrites that he despaired of ever getting the acceptance payment. One afternoon, without telling Martha, he had taken their second-hand Ford Consul down to a garage in Vauxhall and, after a short discussion over the price that only the most generous-spirited would have called a negotiation, sold it for a great deal less than it was worth. After accepting the money with as much dignity as he could muster, he felt he had at least achieved his purpose: he was returning home with a pocketful of soiled notes that made up the deficit of the key money Terry was demanding.

Martha took the loss of the car without complaint. Anyway, there would be no shortage of public transport near the new flat: from dawn onwards, buses rattled along Shaftesbury Avenue right under the sitting-room window. The truth was, they rarely drove the car now. They used to go sometimes to Linton to see Arthur's father at the weekend, a journey that filled Arthur with dread at the thought of the gloomy, cold house and his gloomy, cold father, but curiously turned Martha into a friskier version of her usual self – pottering around in the garden, trying to make jam from the fruit on the scrawny raspberry canes, taking meals up on trays to Arthur's father, who rarely left his bed even though there appeared to be nothing specifically wrong with him – but they could take the train if they had to go.

The morning they left Gloucester Road, Arthur had arranged for a couple of the props boys from Elstree to bring a van early and move their furniture to the new flat. At Bermondsey Market, when they'd first got married, he and Martha had bought a Victorian double bed, which was taken down to the van first. A set of dining-room chairs and the desk he had had as a child went next. When they were about to leave, after the last pieces had gone into the van – the kitchen table and utensils, two armchairs and three or four packing cases filled with books – and after Martha had made her delivery through Mr Bubek's letterbox, she and Arthur stood for a moment on the kerb, gazing forlornly at the possessions they had accrued in their three years of married life, huddled together at the far end of the large, empty van.

'That it? Is that all?' said one of the lads, Barry. 'Only I could have brought the smaller van, couldn't I? Had to get the big one specially.'

'Well, there are some suitcases with our clothes,' Arthur said. He had carried them downstairs himself. They stood next to him on the pavement.

Barry gave a hollow laugh. 'Just as well we brought the big van, then.'

'We are going to pay you, you know,' Martha said pleasantly, but with a slight edge to her voice.

'Not complaining,' the other lad, Ray, added huffily. 'Easier for us, isn't it?' he said, exchanging a glance with Barry.

The day, which had begun so full of hope, had already started to lose its lustre. Martha and Arthur sat in silence in the back of a cab as they followed Barry and Ray's van along Piccadilly to the new flat. Once they were there, the day deteriorated further. As soon as Arthur opened the door – he had gone up there first after picking up the key from the caretaker – he knew there was a problem. It wasn't just the smell, sweet and sickly and overlaid with decay, but the chaos Terry had left behind. There had been no specific discussion about it, but Arthur had assumed he would leave the flat more or less ready for them to move in. He wasn't expecting spotless – he knew Terry too well for that – but he hadn't expected Terry to have simply abandoned his life on the bare floor-boards of a flat that was no longer his.

Arthur moved up the corridor, peering into the rooms that led off it – two bedrooms, a bathroom, a kitchen and a sitting room – with an increasing sense of panic. The flat looked as if it had been rather inefficiently looted. Squashed cardboard boxes and slats from wooden crates were scattered across the floor. The carpet had been taken up, but patches of it were left behind where the nails holding it had been driven too strongly into the floor. In the kitchen there were dirty pots and pans in the sink; the gas cooker was covered with black, burned-on food. It was in the kitchen, too, that the smell was strongest: the fridge appeared to have been unplugged. Arthur put his handkerchief over his nose and opened it. There were bottles of milk, which had turned yellow and solid; open cans of Spam and corned beef were going rusty. A half-eaten tin of baked beans lay on its side dripping orange gunk. In the sitting room a chair with only two legs lay alongside a broken table that might have been chopped up for firewood. On the floor an empty goldfish bowl was turned on its side, with a selection of battered children's toys and books around it. There were piles of newspapers and magazines everywhere. Spilling out of a cardboard box under the window, some white cards were crisp and bright against the stained floorboards. Arthur bent down and picked one up: they were unused invitations to Terry and Eileen's wedding ten years before.

He could hear Martha's footsteps coming into the flat. She made a breathy 'Ohh' sound, and her feet quickened as she ran up the corridor. 'Arthur!' she shouted, and then again, 'Arthur!' She came into the sitting room. She did not cry often, but Arthur always became tense when she did. A feeling of powerlessness would sweep over him like an icy wave. He tried to take her in his arms, but she manoeuvred herself out.

'It's spoiled!' she shouted, her eyes flicking round the desolate room. 'Terry's spoiled it for us!' She brushed past him and went across the corridor to the kitchen.

'We could –'

She came back, kicking a broken tricycle out of her way, her hand over her mouth and nose. 'We could what, Arthur?' she screamed, through clenched teeth. 'We could do *what*?' She banged her fist on the wall.

He was still holding one of the wedding invitations. We could call Terry, he had been going to say, but he remembered that Terry had already gone. The other night, while Martha was out, the phone had rung. It was Terry calling on a ship-to-shore line that crackled so much Arthur could only catch some of what he was saying. 'High seas, dear,' he kept shouting. 'I'm on the high seas. On my way to the Dark Continent.' There was something Terry wanted him to pick up from somewhere, and as his voice ebbed and flowed, Arthur gradually understood it was a package he wanted delivered to his girlfriend, but what the package was or where the girlfriend could be found never came down the line with any clarity. Finally, Terry disappeared and Arthur was left with the receiver transmitting a sound that mimicked the echoey sea noise of a conch shell.

Martha had turned her face to the wall and was sobbing. A clatter came from down the corridor: Barry and Ray had begun to bring in the furniture. There was a bang as they tried to get the heavy bed through the front door, then a flurry of argument as they tried to decide which way round it should go. Barry came into the sitting room. Martha turned her back so he wouldn't see her crying. 'Where's the bed going?' he said. Arthur saw a thought flit across Barry's face. 'This is Mr Tringham's flat, isn't it?'

'It's ours now,' Arthur said, more loudly than he had meant to. Martha gave a hollow laugh and went into the kitchen, slamming the door behind her. 'The bed,' Arthur said, 'on the left there. In the bedroom.'

But Barry wasn't listening: he was smiling to himself. 'Ray!' he called. 'This is Mr Tringham's old flat. You remember that wrap party, the one where he got that girl to do the funny dance?' A roar of laughter echoed up the corridor from Ray. 'What a state this place is in! When did Mr Tringham move out? Looks like there've been burglars.'

'Excuse me,' Arthur said. He crossed the corridor and opened the kitchen door.

Martha was leaning out of an open window taking great gulps of air. Her arms were tightly folded across her chest as if she was trying to hold something in. 'I don't want to stay here,' she said. 'We can go to an hotel.'

Arthur nodded. He was thinking of the key money he had paid Terry and the acceptance payment on the script that hadn't been accepted.

Then she said, 'I can't live like this any more.'

The icy wave that had engulfed Arthur when Martha started to cry closed over his head. His heart was racing. He wished she had moved her hands when she'd said the words, had gestured with them to indicate she might be talking about the state of the flat, but they had stayed folded and she had been very still as she had spoken.

He went back into the corridor and closed the kitchen door behind him. Barry and Ray were still bickering about the bed, which was half in and half out of the front door. 'How long have you two got? Are you very busy? Do you have a bit more time?' he asked them. He managed to keep the shake out of his voice.

'We said we'd be back by dinnertime.'

'Will you do me a favour?'

They looked at each other doubtfully. 'Well, what sort of thing? Only I said we'd have the van back, didn't I?' Ray said. Barry nodded.

Then Arthur said something that sounded to him as if he was speaking in a foreign language: 'I'll see you right.'

The atmosphere changed imperceptibly.

'This is what I need,' Arthur said. 'This is what I want.

Everything has to go.' He waved his arms around. 'We can't live like this.'

'Terrible,' Barry said. Ray nodded.

'I need it all out,' Arthur said, holding their gaze.

The lads exhaled in unison. Barry shook his head. 'Don't know, Mr Hayman.'

'How much did we agree on for you for you to bring our stuff over? Twenty-five, wasn't it?' Arthur put his hand into his pocket and brought out his wallet.

'It's not the money, it's the time, Mr Hayman. Really.'

Arthur opened his wallet.

'Anyway,' Ray said aggressively, 'what would we do with it, all the stuff?'

'You could sell the bits that are worth anything, keep the money.'

Ray guffawed contemptuously.

Barry touched his arm. 'Hang on a mo, Ray. There might be –'

'Firewood,' Ray interrupted. 'That's all it's good for. Look at it.'

Arthur took twenty-five pounds out of his wallet. 'Anyway, here's what I owe you for the move,' he said, and handed the money to Barry. He took out a couple more notes and held them in front of him.

'There's that dump out near Borehamwood, isn't there, Ray?' Barry said.

'We'll never be back by dinnertime.'

'No, you're right,' Arthur said. 'You'd never be back by dinner-time.' He put the notes back into his wallet, and the wallet back into his pocket. 'Well, you'd better just move the stuff in.'

Barry looked at Ray. Arthur looked at his watch. 'Come on,' he said. 'I don't want you to be late.'

'Forty,' Ray blurted out.

'Forty what?'

'Pounds,' he said uncertainly.

'You mean the twenty-five I've already given you and another fifteen?' Arthur said.

155

Ray's eyes flicked towards Barry. He cleared his throat. 'On top,' he said. 'Forty on top.'

'Oh,' Arthur said. 'I haven't got that much, Ray.' He walked up the corridor. 'Bed goes in there. Dining-room chairs up here. Try not to scuff the walls if you can help it.'

'Okay. Twenty,' Barry said. 'We'll do it for twenty.'

'I don't want you to be late,' Arthur said. 'It's getting on. You'd better make a start.'

Two hours later, the swap had been done: Arthur and Martha's furniture had been moved in, and all of Terry's junk was piled in the back of the van. Several jokes had been made about how much fuller the van was going to be leaving the new flat than coming to it. Although Barry and Ray kept talking about having to get back, they did not seem in any particular hurry to go. The dining-room chairs had been arranged in a rough circle in the sitting room and they were all drinking from a selection of chipped glasses and mugs that Arthur had discovered in one of the kitchen cupboards with a bottle of wine, which he and Martha were halfway through. The lads were drinking beer – Martha had gone down to the off-licence to get it while Arthur was cleaning the cooker with bleach. He had also cleared out the fridge and scrubbed it, and now, with the windows open, a pleasant breeze was blowing through the flat and there was only the faintest vestige of the smell that had greeted him when he had first opened the door.

Martha was laughing. Her cheeks were slightly flushed. She was telling Barry and Ray about their previous landlord, Mr Bubek, and her various rows with him. The lads had got through three bottles of beer each and were on to their fourth. When Martha got to the punchline of her story, in which she imitated Mr Bubek saying, in his thick Polish accent, 'And what is so common, please, about my parts, Mrs Hayman?' Ray, who was taking a swig from his can, laughed so violently that he inhaled the beer instead of swallowing it and it foamed out of his nose while he spluttered and coughed. Barry had to stand up and wallop him on the back.

They were laughing so much that they did not notice Arthur leave the room. He stood outside in the corridor, then leaned against the wall. Although he had only had a little wine, much less than Martha, it had taken the edge off the memory of the feeling that had risen in him as soon as he had entered the flat and had stayed, like a low hum, until Barry and Ray were moving Terry's junk out. It was like panic – on the same wavelength as panic anyway – but it didn't feel like panic about a single event or moment: it felt like something without boundaries that extended as far back as he could remember and as far forward as he could see.

Now Martha was cross-examining Barry about his accent. 'Birmingham?' she said. 'You've got those sharp vowel sounds. Newcastle? Bolton?'

Barry was giggling.

Ray was egging her on: 'Further north, to the east, little bit up, that's it – you're getting close.'

'Scotland?' she said tentatively.

'Too bloody far!' Ray said.

There was a great roar of laughter. Arthur smiled at Martha's unexpected animation. She was normally rather awkward with people on the lower rungs of the film industry. Arthur and Terry, who had worked in and out of the studios all their lives, were more attuned to the caste system that divided them from the sparks, stand-bys and props boys, and the awkward mixture of hostility and supplication they tended to give off.

After a while Arthur tuned out of their conversation to concentrate on the air blowing through the flat and the sound of traffic. He closed his eyes. He didn't know how long he was gone for, but it was as if he had left the flat and was somewhere else. Their voices brought him back: Ray seemed to be talking about a baby. 'No,' he was saying, 'she sleeps right through.'

'How old?' Martha asked.

'Nine months. And she's a big eater. Oh, she's a real sweetheart Dawn is, a little darling.'

'Dawn!' Martha said, with a laugh in her voice. 'Now, that's a lovely name for a baby girl. Whose idea was it?'

But Arthur was walking down the corridor, away from them, and Ray's answer was lost to him. He was imagining a small child with blue eyes sitting on Ray's knee. He saw Ray lift her up and hold her in the air above him. He imagined a street where Ray might live and the wife he might have, and a Sunday lunch with children and grandparents.

Arthur looked into the rooms as he passed. Now, with their furniture in place, the flat tidy and Martha laughing up the corridor, merry with too much wine, everything seemed calm. He stood in the doorway of the flat, looking out at the stairs and the lift shaft, and suddenly remembered where he had drifted off to earlier: he had been in a place where he could allow himself to think, for one brief, dangerous instant, that everything might be all right.

When the doorbell rang at seven o'clock on a bitterly cold morning in the winter of 1960, it was more than two years since they had moved into the flat on Shaftesbury Avenue. Then it had been the end of summer and for several weeks after they were first there they could leave the windows open and let the noise and heat of the city flow through the rooms. Now the inefficient central heating that had just started clanking through the pipes towards the radiators hardly took the chill off the air, and Arthur had to light the fires in the sitting room and their bedroom to bring the flat to any perceptible level of warmth.

He was up earlier than usual. He was spending his days at the studio where a film set during the French Revolution was having a problematic shoot. Arthur had been brought in to write additional dialogue for some of the crowd scenes and to beef up the tepid romance at the centre of the story. As the film continued to reel from crisis to crisis and fall further behind, the shooting of the love scenes Arthur had written kept being delayed. The bedroom set that had been built in readiness for them sat forlornly in the corner of the stage where the main Bastille set stood. Only yesterday Arthur had heard a rumour that the bedroom set was going to be struck, which meant that his scenes were definitely to be dropped and he wanted to get to the studio early to talk to the producer.

He was shaving in the unheated bathroom opposite their bedroom when the bell went. The tap was running and the noise of the Ascot was gushing in his ears so it was a moment before he heard it. He turned off the tap and the Ascot stopped. The bathroom was filled with steam. It was too early for the post, and although it was around the time the milkman usually came, he left theirs downstairs and only rang the bell once a week when the bill had to be paid, which Arthur had already done.

He had left Martha asleep when he had got up, but now he could hear her moving around their bedroom. 'I'll get it,' she called.

He peered round the bathroom door and saw her padding down the corridor in bare feet. She wore a slip and was pulling a cardigan round her shoulders. When she got to the entryphone by their front door, she picked up the receiver and said, 'Yes?' in a croaky voice. Arthur could hear a distant squawk of what sounded like static and Martha said, 'I'm sorry, I don't –' but then she stopped and the static started again. Then she said, 'Oh,' and took the receiver away from her ear. She let her hand drop so she was holding it against her leg. She stayed like that for a few seconds, her back very straight, and Arthur could see a little tear in the hem of her slip. Then she brought the receiver slowly back up to her ear. Her other hand was over her mouth and she had to take it away so she could speak. 'No,' she said. 'Wait there. I'll come down.' She tried to put the receiver back into its cradle, but it slipped out of her grasp and fell, banging against the wall and swinging by its curly wire, like a pendulum. Martha picked it up and forced it into the cradle with a cry of frustration, then unbolted the door and vanished.

There was almost no sound now, only the soft receding thud of Martha's bare feet on the carpet outside. The steam, which had hung in the bathroom like fog, was drawn out by the draught of the open front door and swirled into the corridor. Although Arthur could no longer see her, he imagined the steam trying to find her in the murky gloom outside their flat, then pursuing her down the central stairs that circled the lift shaft as she descended to the street entrance below.

Back in their bedroom, Arthur looked at his watch. It was five past seven. Martha would be back any moment. He wondered whether he should make some coffee and heat the milk. He put his dressing-gown over his pyjamas and went up the corridor. Before he got to the kitchen he stopped and waited. The flat was silent. Then, without knowing why, he retraced his steps past the bedroom and went out of the flat through the front door that Martha had left open.

He could hear talking drifting up the stairwell from downstairs. Although he could not catch the precise words, he registered Martha's voice rising and falling, his ears catching the high notes better than the low ones. Then the low notes fell away and there was the insistent high staccato of the same short word being said over and over again. He moved down the stairs to the half-landing. The word Martha was repeating was 'no'.

'No,' she said. 'No. No. No. No.' Her inflection was slightly different each time.

Through the metal grilles of the lift shaft in the centre of the stairwell, Arthur could see two pairs of legs standing against the front entrance, the bodies obscured by the lobby ceiling.

Then Martha said, 'It's simply not true.'

There was a silence. Then the other person, a woman, said, 'But I know.'

'You're wrong,' Martha said. 'You must be mistaken. You *are* mistaken.'

'There's no mistake. No mistake at all.'

'Look,' Martha said, 'I don't know how –'

'The bills. I've seen them.'

'Bills?'

'Hotel bills. For the *room*,' the woman hissed. 'In Bloomsbury. Great Russell Street. I know the hotel.'

'It's not *true*,' Martha said indignantly.

There was a pause. Arthur was thinking, Poor woman, what an embarrassing mistake to have made, what a terrible mix-up.

'Mrs Hayman,' she said wearily, and Arthur knew that this was the first time the woman had used Martha's name, 'I know about the French place, about Le Touquet.'

The woman pronounced it wrongly – she called it 'Le Tooket' – but Arthur realized what she was talking about. He knew about Le Touquet as well. A few months before Martha had gone to France for the night. She had said a friend, someone she used to work with, had won a competition in the *Daily Express*. The prize was a ferry ticket and the friend said she couldn't use it and had offered it to Martha. 'It seems a shame to waste it,' Martha had said. 'I could stock up on wine and food.' When she came back she brought with her a little tin of *foie gras* and a jar of green olives stuffed with pimentos wrapped in waxy white paper tied with a ribbon.

'And I've read the endearments,' the woman said. 'I've *seen* them. In your little notes. So please – please don't talk to me about mistakes.'

It was seven fifteen now. Arthur wondered what was going to happen, but he knew that, whatever it was, it would be better if he was dressed properly, not standing in the stairwell of a block of mansion flats in his pyjamas and dressing-gown. As he crept back up the stairs he heard the woman say, 'You're ruining us, Mrs Hayman. You have to get out of our lives. Please.' There was a catch in her voice.

The flat was still silent when he came back in, and he decided to do what he had been going to do before he had gone to see who had rung the bell: he went to the kitchen, filled the percolator and turned the gas on, then began organizing the milk. Back in the bedroom, he took a white shirt out of the chest of drawers and pulled on the grey flannel trousers that were hanging over the back of a chair. His black shoes were under Martha's dressing-table. He had polished them yesterday, but he buffed them up with a duster before slipping them on and tying the laces. He pulled his tweed jacket out of the wardrobe and, before putting it on, wrapped a dark blue patterned tie round his neck and knotted it.

The front door banged and he heard Martha come along the corridor. She stopped outside their bedroom. 'It's *cold*,' she said, shivering.

'I'll do the fires in a minute,' Arthur said. 'Who was at the door?'

'Your collar's crooked,' she said. She came over to Arthur and straightened it. Her cheek brushed his and he felt how cold her face was. 'Bloody woman doing a survey.'

'Survey?'

'From the council. Whether we're happy with the street cleaning. Writing everything down on a clipboard.'

'I've never even seen a street cleaner.'

'That's what I said.' She pulled the top drawer of the chest out, searching for something. Then she rummaged violently on the top of her dressing-table. She kept running her fingers through her hair, which looked dirty. Arthur wondered if there would be enough hot water for her to wash it.

'What are you looking for?' he asked.

'My *bracelet*,' she said angrily. 'The silver one, the African one.'

'It's on the bedside table.'

She sat on the bed, reached over and slipped it on her wrist. He thought she would stand up immediately, but she just sat there, staring ahead.

'Are you all right?' Arthur said.

'I'm just cold,' she said. 'What's the time?'

'Nearly half seven.'

'No sound?'

'Not a squeak,' Arthur said.

'He's normally like clockwork.'

'The milk's on.'

As if by magic there was an angry cry from up the corridor and Martha smiled, as if she was relieved. She got up and was out of the room in a second. 'Get the milk, will you?' she called.

When Arthur got to the baby's room, Martha was kneeling beside his cot. He was standing up, holding on to the side and stamping up and down on his blanket. He was giggling and trying to tug at Martha's hair as she moved her head back and forth towards his fat little hands.

When he saw Arthur holding the milk, his mouth widened into a lopsided grin. He reached out his hand.

'Hello, Jordan,' Arthur said. 'Hello, little pig.'

Sometimes they saw each other every week and sometimes several weeks passed with no contact. Once they had even seen each other three days in a row, but after Ray's wife had turned up on the doorstep, Martha knew it was over.

Since the doorbell had rung that cold morning, she had entered a state of what seemed to her like suspended animation. It had a curious familiarity to it and it took her some time to realize that it was how she had felt when her father was dying. But the baby needed feeding and the nappies needed washing and Arthur's sandwiches had to be made before he left in the morning for the studio, where he went every day, still waiting for his scenes in the French Revolution film to be shot.

The worst time was the afternoon, when the idiotic Spanish girl, Chita, who worked for them part-time and whom Martha was always about to sack, came in to look after Jordan so Martha could get on with her PhD, which she had been working on for more than ten years, interrupted fatally when she had gone to work for Wally Carter, researching his crusader film. She went into the bedroom, where there was a table she used as a desk, and sat moving her notes around and flipping through the books she had marked with thin pencil lines in the margins. She lit cigarettes, then put them out after a few puffs. She made cups of tea. She looked into the sitting room at Jordan and Chita playing. Sometimes she went for aimless walks through Soho, huddled up in a coat and woollen scarf against the bitter cold.

She was living in dread of something happening or something not happening. She dreaded seeing Ray and she dreaded not seeing Ray. Most of all she dreaded Ray's wife coming back and telling Arthur, but she also dreaded continuing in the state of limbo in which she and Arthur flapped slowly round the flat like dying moths.

So when the phone rang early one afternoon and it was Ray – he was conversant enough with her schedule to know that Chita turned up to look after Jordan just after lunch and therefore she would be able to talk – Martha did not know whether she was relieved or not.

'Christ,' he said chattily, 'I'd have thought Mo had enough to do with the baby not to spend her time looking through my pockets. She's been in a real state.'

'I'm sure,' Martha murmured sympathetically. She really wanted to ask why, if he was going to ring at all, he had taken so long to get round to it. She had half prepared herself never to hear from him again.

'How's Jordy?' he asked. One of the few irritating things about Ray was that he called Jordan 'Jordy'. Martha had once pointed out that that was not his name but, like a lot of what Martha said, it had clearly not sunk in.

'Jordan's fine,' she said. There was a silence so she added, 'Teething, of course.' She didn't want to return the ball and ask about Ray's daughter, Dawn, a spectacularly plain child, a new photograph of whom Ray produced nearly every time they met, but as talking about their babies was a ritual as predictable as foreplay – indeed, often was foreplay – she couldn't think of anything to say other than 'And Dawn, how's she?'

'Lovely,' Ray said, with a smack of his lips, 'Lovely. And how are you?' he asked.

'In a bit of a state too, actually,' Martha said, as crisply as she could manage.

'Yeah, well. Sorry about Mo. I could have killed her.'

'Ray, you don't think she'll come again, do you? Or maybe write to . . . my husband?' She felt awkward mentioning Arthur by name, but as she and Ray hardly ever talked about him, the problem did not arise often.

Ray let out a horse-like whinny. 'Shouldn't think so,' he said breezily. 'Hardly sends a postcard from the seaside. We've just got to be more careful, that's all.'

Until that moment, it had not occurred to her that the affair could possibly continue. '*Ray!*' she said, her voice squeaking at the madness of the idea.

'I've missed you,' he said.

'We can't –'

'Look,' he said, 'I've got a surprise. Can you meet me at Golders Green?'

'No,' Martha said indignantly. 'When?'

'Soon as you can. Now. Take the tube.'

'I can't, Ray. I can't. This is mad.'

'I'll meet you there. I'll be waiting.'

'No,' Martha said again. 'No.'

The day, which had started out sunny, had clouded over when the train rattled out of the tunnel after Hampstead and rain was pouring by the time it reached Golders Green. Martha stood holding a newspaper above her head by the taxi rank outside the station while she looked around for Ray, who was nowhere to be seen. She lit a cigarette and waited. After she had been there for a few minutes, a man came up to her and asked for a light. She handed over some book-matches and waved them away when he offered them back to her. She moved up the pavement from him and turned her back, dropped her cigarette and stubbed it out under her shoe. When she looked up the man had walked towards her. His eyes caught hers and he smiled at her. She pulled back the sleeve of her coat, squinted at her watch, then craned her neck and turned her head from side to side as if she was desperate to find someone. Her mime was so elaborate that she forgot for a moment she actually was desperate to find someone.

She began to panic. She was about to go back into the station to take the tube home when a horn honked several times and she saw Ray waving at her from inside his truck, which was just pulling into the car park opposite. She let out a cry and threw the newspaper she had been using to keep the rain off her on to the ground, startling the man next to her: he must have thought she was throwing it at him, but she didn't care about him now. All she wanted was to get across the car park as quickly as she could.

Ray flung open the passenger door of the van and put out his hand to heave her into the cab. She slumped backwards into the seat as he pulled the door shut, gunned the accelerator and tore off. She felt as if she had jumped into a getaway car after a bank raid. She thought she was going to faint. As they drove up the hill towards Hampstead, Ray changed gear, and instead of putting his hand back on the steering-wheel, he rested it on her knee, then slid it up her skirt and hooked his fingers round the top of her stocking.

He turned the truck off the main road and parked in a cul-de-sac by Hampstead Heath. He told Martha to wait, then got out and went to the back of the van. Martha could hear him opening the doors and clattering around behind her. She closed her eyes. She was having some difficulty remembering how she had come to be there in the first place.

When Ray called her, she got out of the cab. The passenger side was parked right up against the grass verge and her feet sank into the wet earth. She wished she had worn flat shoes. She made her way along the side of the van to where Ray had put a wooden crate on the ground for her to use as a step. She climbed up and peered into the dark cavern.

'What do you think?' Ray loomed out of the blackness. He was holding a lantern with a lit candle inside it. 'It's all from a picture,' he said.

Martha stepped in. He was at the far end, and she saw that he was standing next to a bed. 'It's called a *bateau lit*,' he said. 'That's what they slept in then. It's a bed like a boat.' He knelt down, lit another lantern and then a third. There were other bits of furniture lined up against the sides: ornate chairs, a dressing-table and a pair of huge gilt mirrors wedged behind a *chaise-longue*. Ray laughed. 'The guillotine was in here until this morning. They needed it back on the main stage.' He moved down the truck and pulled the doors inwards. Martha watched the dull afternoon light vanish as they banged shut. Ray secured them with a long metal pole that fitted through a slot in each door. Now there was just the shadowy light from the lanterns. 'Come on,' he said.

'This is the French Revolution film,' Martha said.

'Yes,' said Ray, surprised.

'My husband's been working on it.'

'Oh, yeah, that's right – I've seen him around.'

'Have they finished with all the props?'

'Haven't bloody used them. They're dumping the scenes. Nightmare for us. Back and forth to the prop house like a bloody yo-yo.'

'I should go, Ray. I can't do this. I'm already late.'

'You're here now. What's the point of going?'

'She's so useless, Chita, with the baby. It'll be his bedtime soon. I've got to go – I've got to give him his bath.'

The trouble was, she felt herself incapable of movement. Ray grabbed her hand and led her to the bed. The van smelled musty and damp. The floor creaked as they crossed it. 'Ray . . .' she began, but then she couldn't think what she had meant to say. She had no idea of anything. She felt she was floating.

After she had taken off her clothes, she lay back on the bed. Ray knelt between her legs holding his short, thick cock. 'Tell me how much you want it,' he said, and when she spoke it seemed to her that, in the midst of the lies and the evasions and the horror of what she was doing – had done, would go on doing – her answer was the only true thing she could almost ever remember saying.

As it turned out, it was the last time she saw Ray.

Laurie

Now it was night, the day room at Spring Crest had the air of a deserted airport transit lounge. Laurie felt that she and Alma might be trapped there for ever, waiting for a plane that would never come.

'How come you're so howdy-doody all of a sudden?' Alma said.

There were many ways to describe how she was feeling at the moment but 'howdy-doody' was not one that sprang immediately to mind. On reflection, though, Laurie thought it was as good as any. Alma's little eyes, beneath wrinkled lids, were staring at her intently and Laurie held her gaze without saying anything.

'Ever since you came back from England,' Alma snapped. 'You meet someone over there? Some man? Best thing that could happen.' She threw her head back and gave a nasty laugh. 'You're like a sack of dry leaves.'

Laurie forced herself to stay silent. She turned away from Alma and began to zing as hard as she could. She was determined not to enter this particular playground.

'You ought to come to this place. They're like dogs. Ray Tabares and Dina Nelson – Mrs D had to haul them out of the pool-house, pants round their ankles. Dina's seventy-seven. Should've poured ice water over them. Anyway, what kind of vacation could you have over there on your own? Look at you – look how pale you are.'

'I wasn't trying for a tan.'

'Weather's terrible there. Rains all the time.'

'I don't believe you've been to England, have you, Alma?' Laurie said calmly.

Alma ignored this. 'When am I going home?' she said.

'This is home, Alma. This is your home now.'

'Why can't I come home? It's my house.'

'I pay the loan on it. I have done for years.'

Alma's face creased up and she began to cry. 'You want me to die here, don't you?' she shouted.

Laurie reached into her purse and pulled out a tissue. She held it out to Alma, who brushed it away angrily. However and wherever she died, Laurie wanted Alma's death to have some kind of meaning. She dreaded what she knew would be the awful insignificance of her sidestep from life. It would be a local death, a notice in the *Modesto Bee*, maybe a few lines on the obit page, although Laurie found it hard to imagine how you could embroider the events of Alma's life into anything that approached even local note. Her homemade preserves were not legendary, her cross-stitching had not won prizes at the County Fair, she had not performed unforgettably in *Arsenic and Old Lace* with the Modesto Players. She had never even attended a PTA meeting.

Laurie saw that Alma had stopped crying and was regarding her with something that resembled astonishment. She realized that it had not occurred to her that Laurie would think about her question and not just answer it quickly and reassuringly. When Alma repeated it – 'Do you want me to die here, Laurie? Do you?' – her voice was tremulous and frightened, and Laurie saw that in extreme circumstances Alma still had the capacity to connect to something real. The fact was, Arthur's passing had spoiled Laurie. It was a hard act to follow and, in an unexpected moment of tenderness for Alma, she allowed herself to accept that when Alma died it would be unreasonable to expect her to get within a thousand miles of Arthur's grace and dignity.

Clearly Alma was not of a mind to have a rational discussion about her death. 'They all hate me here,' she said.

'Alma, you've done nothing to make anyone like you.'

'That is a lie!' she said, outraged. But it was true. At mealtimes the old people sat at assigned places, four to a table. She had lasted five days at the first table she was put on. When she had told Bea

Brooks – the oldest extant occupant of Spring Crest – it was strange she looked so Jewish, had she changed her surname from Brookstein?, Mrs Detweiler was called in and Alma was moved to another table. There, her meal companions complained that Alma would reach over and take food from their plates with her fingers. Now she sat on her own at a card table in the far corner of the dining room, sometimes muttering to herself, sometimes loudly joining in conversations at other tables.

'I'm lonely, Laurie. Nobody visits me. Even Marge Clancy doesn't come any more.' She looked quizzically at Laurie. 'You know why?'

Laurie shrugged her shoulders. She hoped her face wasn't going pink.

'It's like a morgue here,' Alma said. She was right. Even though it was only eight thirty, the place was deserted and silent. Of course, that was one of the reasons Laurie tended to visit her in the evening: she hated people veering off in another direction if she and Alma were walking in what was ambitiously called the 'Japanese Garden'; she hated the sternness of Mrs Detweiler's face when she told Laurie she needed a word. Most of all she hated the pity she saw on people's faces when they glimpsed her and Alma together. Weren't you meant to get over embarrassment about your parents when you stopped being a teenager? Weren't you meant to be able to accept and forgive your parents' faults? What baloney, Laurie thought.

'Well, where is everyone? Are they playing cards somewhere, maybe?' she asked.

'Cards!' Alma snorted. 'They wouldn't know the difference between a spade and a club.'

'They must be somewhere,' Laurie said. They couldn't all be in the poolhouse with their pants round their ankles.

'They're asleep. Or dead.'

There was a silence, then Laurie did something extraordinary: she asked Alma a question about her father. A little buzz of electricity had sparked in her brain and brought to life some long-disused circuit. If it had a sound, she thought, it would be like that zap you heard when a bug hit one of those weird ultra-violet killing boxes.

'Do you miss Dad ever? I don't even know if he's still alive, Alma. Don't you think it's right that I know?' she said. It was such a simple inquiry and it had come out so easily. She could hardly believe she had said it, but now she had, she was going to sit back and wait to see what happened.

The Exorcist was not a movie Laurie had cared much for, although she had refused to sign the petition when some of the church groups tried to get it banned locally, but it came into her mind now.

'Don't you talk to me about that cocksucker, Miss Laurie Clow. You have no idea! *You have no idea!*'

If Alma had not had arthritis of the neck, her head might have turned 360 degrees. Her body was shaking, though, and she was certainly speaking in a frightening growl. Laurie had not seen so much energy in her for years. It was like someone had put jump leads on her.

'You don't have the right to upset me,' Alma shouted. 'You don't have the right to get me all riled up.'

'I'd like to know what happened to him, that's all,' Laurie said. It was extraordinary how calm she felt.

All the fire had gone out of Alma, and she was weeping again. 'I had to protect you, Laurie. You were my only concern.'

If there was one thing worse than Alma being aggressive, it was Alma being sentimental. 'Protect me from what exactly?' Laurie asked carefully.

'He was *weak.*'

That wasn't the way Laurie remembered it. He wasn't the one who had slept in till lunchtime. He wasn't the one ensconced in that bar in Santa Fe with a row of empty martini glasses in front of him, making Laurie eat the olives off the cocktail sticks when she didn't even like olives.

'That's not true.'

'Don't tell me what's true and what isn't.' Alma's mouth and jaw had taken on the set of a pug's.

'You *drank*.'

'You don't know what my life was like with him. I lived in shame.'

'Oh, Alma . . .'

'He was practically a *Communist*,' Alma hissed. 'You take after him. You're like him.'

'Alma, I did some fund-raising once for those fruit-pickers who couldn't buy a cup of coffee with what they earned in a day.'

'Well, he believed in the redistribution of wealth, all right.' She gave a horrible laugh. 'Got us kicked out of Los Alamos – didn't know that, did you? You *loved* that place.'

It was true. The only happy time Laurie could remember of her childhood was when they had been at Los Alamos, the mountains and the desert and the sky. She had felt safe there. She had felt safe there because he was with them.

'Course we didn't know it then, but they were making that bomb, the one that fried the Japs.'

'There were two bombs, Alma. We dropped them on two cities and killed God knows how many people.'

'Good thing too.'

'Is he still alive?' Laurie had stopped feeling so calm, and her voice was shaking.

'You want to know? You pack me up and take me home and I'll tell you, Miss Laurie Clow. Otherwise I'll die here and you'll never know. You want that?' Alma folded her arms and did an aggressive zipping movement across her lips with her finger.

Laurie stood up. Sometimes the price was just too high. 'Goodbye, Alma,' she said. 'I'll see you next week.'

As she walked out of the day room, she felt a small glow of triumph that she would not have wanted Alma to observe. She had lived her life oblivious to signs and meanings, but now she had spotted a flaw in the wall that Alma had constructed to keep her from understanding, a loose stone that – with some work – might be jiggled and finally pulled free. Alma had unwittingly revealed something about Laurie's father: something had happened when they were at Los Alamos that meant they had had to leave. Laurie would keep it and nurture it, like a gift, until she could unravel it.

Anyway, it strengthened her resolve to do what she had to do next. If she didn't pull it off she would end up with Alma back home anyway. Her watch showed she was five minutes early, but that was good. Mrs Detweiler was keen on punctuality, a tall order when most of the people she came into contact with had Alzheimer's.

A framed sampler hung on Mrs Detweiler's office door. It said, 'If you aim high you can't shoot yourself in the foot.' Laurie knocked. She could hear humming from inside.

'Laurie! You look well,' Mrs Detweiler said, as she came in. 'You've lost weight.'

'You too,' Laurie said. Mrs Detweiler looked faintly surprised. She had about as much meat on her as a pretzel.

'How was it? How was the trip?'

Out of the corner of her eye, Laurie could see a file on Mrs Detweiler's desk with 'Clow' written in big black capitals on the cover. Once she would have felt terrified by what was coming, but she would ride over those old feelings like a surfer on a giant wave. She was not about to let Mrs Detweiler take control. 'We need to talk about my mother,' she said.

Mrs Detweiler was taken off-guard. Laurie could feel her brushing aside the pile of small-talk she had planned to use before getting to the point, but she recovered herself quickly. 'Yes, we do, Laurie,' she said. 'We've got ourselves in a fine mess with Alma, that's for sure. You know that the police aren't planning to investigate her intruder any further?' Mrs Detweiler smirked. 'Such an unnecessary fuss.'

'Really?' Laurie said coolly.

'Yes, Laurie,' she said, in a voice like a knife. 'Officer Reinheimer believes she invented the story, made the whole thing up. Somewhere deep down I think she wanted the attention.'

As deep as a dry riverbed, Laurie thought.

Mrs Detweiler turned the knife. 'She's got to go. Just as soon as you can arrange alternative care for her. We'll be sad to see her leave, of course we will, you know that, Laurie.'

Laurie inserted a catch in her voice. 'She's so vulnerable. I don't want to have to put her through any more. She loves it here. In her own way.'

Mrs Detweiler was implacable. 'I'm sorry, Laurie.' She closed Alma's file and lined up her pens, but Laurie was not about to be dismissed.

'Mrs D, you've got quite a few spare rooms, I couldn't help noticing.'

Mrs Detweiler corrected her: 'Suites,' she said. 'I've got a waiting list as long as your arm, Laurie.'

'Of course you have. This is such an upscale place. But you need good publicity, word of mouth.'

'I don't think our reputation is in any doubt around these parts, Laurie,' Mrs Detweiler said, with a chilly laugh. 'People know what Alma's like. I don't think her leaving will cause us a problem.'

'The thing of it is, Mrs D, Alma's confused. Something happened, maybe not in the way she thought, but I don't doubt there was an intruder of some kind. And she'll say that, she'll go on saying it. You know what she's like.'

'No one believes her. The police don't.'

Laurie had held on to her cards for long enough. Now she played them. 'They're so overstretched, aren't they? They can't follow up all the things they ought to. That's what Greg Terpstra thinks anyway.'

'Greg Terpstra?' Mrs Detweiler barked.

Now Laurie had her attention. 'He's a personal friend. You know he came to see Alma while I was away?' she said. Then she added sanctimoniously, 'He's always been so kind to us.'

Greg Terpstra was the best-known lawyer in Modesto. By no stretch of the imagination could he be called a personal friend.

Everyone said he had Mafia connections, though Laurie could not imagine what the Mafia would be doing in Modesto unless it was to take protection money from the hairdressing salons. Alma had asked him to come to Spring Crest because she wanted to change her will again. Laurie had just had his bill. As far as she knew, Alma had not mentioned the assault to him.

Laurie went on, 'Why, Greg told me that her hands wouldn't stop shaking when she was telling him about the attack, said the stress she suffered must have been enormous. In my day stress was something you just lived with. Now it's something they put a price on. You know what lawyers are like, Mrs D.'

Laurie couldn't read the expression on Mrs Detweiler's face so she decided to plough on. 'You're right, of course. It's a fine mess.' She sighed. 'I admire you so much,' she said, 'all of you who look after the seniors in our community. It's such a responsibility of care. It's not like my job. If I screw up – miss a cue or make the wrong dedication for a song – what happens? The world doesn't end. You look after these folks twenty-four hours a day, seven days a week. You can't protect them from everything.'

'We haven't screwed up,' Mrs Detweiler said coldly.

'I know that, Mrs D. You do the best you can and the world sits in judgement on you. It's just not fair.' Then she said it again: 'You know what lawyers are like.'

Something had settled in the room, something calming like a blanket of snow. She and Mrs Detweiler had evened up. 'Here's what I think we should do,' Laurie said. 'Let's put Alma in a holding pattern, like a big old jumbo jet. Nothing too hasty. You're so vigilant, Mrs D. Let's just watch the situation. Alma steps out of line again, you tell me, okay?' She grasped one of Mrs Detweiler's claw-like hands. 'Thank you.'

As she was going out of the door, Mrs Detweiler called her name. Laurie turned round. 'You must have had a good trip,' she said, with a tinge of admiration. 'You just seem . . .' She tailed off. She was struggling to find a phrase that could define how Laurie seemed to her.

Laurie gave her a little help. 'Well, it's true,' she said. 'I'm feeling just howdy-doody, Mrs D.'

Rivers and streams, gullies and inlets and creeks flowing and dividing and reconnecting: that was what had fascinated Laurie as a child. At Los Alamos, in the spring, clear streams trickled and bubbled, then dried into dusty ditches. When the winter came, the dust turned to mud and everything squelched under her feet. She wondered where the water came from and where it went.

For every river was there a spot of earth from which a little trickle came that you could pinpoint as the place where the Mississippi or the Sacramento or the Nile began? That was what she liked to think, and Laurie picked on the day after she had gone to Spring Crest to see Alma and Mrs Detweiler as the precise moment the trickle had started. She needed everything to be predetermined. Chance was too random. Chance wrote her out of the story. So she always came back to that day in 1981, as she was walking through the lobby heading towards the parking lot after she had finished her afternoon shift at Holy Spirit.

When she heard the beeping, she couldn't think what it was and looked around her to see where it was coming from. It took her a moment to realize it was inside her purse. About a year before, everyone who worked at the hospital had been issued with a pager. Marge had exploded at the extravagance of giving those she contemptuously called 'non-meds' an expensive toy and had made, as usual, a formal complaint. Although at the time Laurie had felt rather defensive, there had been a certain amount of truth in what Marge had said: she had put the pager into her purse and forgotten about it because nobody had ever paged her – until now.

'Call me – Connie' was flashing in the little window, and Laurie felt both excitement and dread. Connie Kooyman was in charge of Special Events, under which the hospital radio station came.

'Laurie, thank God, I thought you might have gone,' Connie said, when Laurie called her on the internal phone at the main desk.

'What is it?'

'The most awful thing's happened. Ed Corley's in Intensive. His wife just called.'

Laurie gasped. 'That's terrible!' She didn't much like Ed, but that wasn't the point.

'He was in an accident, I didn't get the details. Listen – can you fill in for him? I'm so sorry, Laurie. Do you have plans?'

'But he does the God slot! I wouldn't know how to do that, Connie.'

'It's non-denominational,' Connie said crisply, as if that solved the problem. 'You just need to do something inspirational. Ed reads poetry when he isn't doing one of those awful sermons. It'll only be for a couple of days – well, no more than this week anyhow. He's got a bookshelf up there. You might find something in it. Please, Laurie.'

Maybe I should read a passage from *Why Do I Say Yes When I Mean No?*, Laurie thought, as she travelled back up in the elevator. That would be inspirational. Marge – the one who really needed them – had endlessly given her self-help books, each one presented with meaningful ceremony as if to tick off yet another of the faults she perceived in Laurie.

She pushed open the soundproof door of the little studio. There was the faint smell of dope. 'Travis?' she called. There was a scuffle in the store room at the back and Travis Buckley came out, looking sheepish.

'Hey, Mrs Clow.'

'Travis, I don't care what you do in here but don't put the butt in the trash and set fire to the place.'

'Sorry, Mrs Clow.'

She had given up long ago telling him she wasn't married. He wasn't too bright, but he treated adults with the mixture of politeness and contempt most young people affected. There was always a kid helping in the studio, setting up the equipment, doing the sliders and trying to put the records back in the right place. Usually they were connected to someone at Holy Spirit – Travis was Dr Buckley's son, the professor of Oncology. The kids thought it would lead to a career as a DJ or record producer; Travis was always sitting at the turntables jiggling the discs back and forth, making an awful noise.

'You've got to help me, Travis. You heard about Ed?'

He pushed his long blond hair out of his eyes. 'Yeah, it's awful. I thought I'd have to do his show.' He gave a little snort of laughter. 'Rappin' for God!'

'What's he done the last few days?'

Travis shrugged. 'Never listen much, Mrs Clow.'

'Where does he keep his books, his reference stuff?' Laurie looked up at the big clock on the studio wall. There were twenty minutes to go.

Travis gestured casually with his thumb. 'In the back.' As they went into the store room, he said, 'Father Corley keeps his things over there,' pointing to the back wall next to the shelves that held the music library.

'Why do you call him Father Corley? You don't have to be a priest to do the God slot, Travis. He's an orthodontist.'

'Never said anything to me.'

Travis was so crestfallen at this piece of adult deception that Laurie felt sorry for him. 'Actually, he might be a lay preacher at that weird church he goes to up on Burney.'

Travis nodded several times, rallying. 'He's got a lot of faith, that guy.'

'I guess so,' Laurie said doubtfully. If Ed's reputation was anything to go by, it was all lay and no preaching. 'Okay – we need something to get through today's show, something I can just read. We'll have time tomorrow to sort out the rest of the week.'

Travis was bending down next to a pile of books. 'Hey, what about *The Prophet*? That's amazing.'

Laurie's heart sank. 'What else is there?'

Travis began reading the spines: '*Campfire Sermons, Cooking for the Soul, Having a Jesus Heart in a Judas World* . . .'

178

'Oh, Travis, I can't do all that stuff. I just wouldn't feel comfortable.' Laurie went over and knelt beside him. The first book she saw was *The Bible's Way to Weight Loss*.

'What about his backpack? Is there something in it?' Travis said, pointing.

Laurie unzipped it. There was a box of Kleenex and a small magazine called *Born-again Swingers*. 'I don't think so,' she said crisply, zipping it up again.

'Maybe you could start off with some kind of safety announcement. You know – rules for the highway, watching for traffic signals.'

Was Travis even more clueless than she'd thought? 'What are you talking about?'

'Well, the Bible says we're, like, meant to follow an example, right? So you could kind of do it the opposite way. *Not* follow Father Corley's example.' Travis looked rather pleased with himself.

'Travis . . .' Laurie's voice rose in exasperation.

'I mean, you don't want it to happen to other folks, do you?'

Suddenly Laurie felt something in the air. 'What?' she said cautiously.

'Father Corley's accident.' Laurie felt bemused. 'Yeah,' Travis went on, 'being run down like that.'

'He was run down?'

'On the corner of Paradise and Third. By a school bus. Wow! Can you imagine how those kids are feeling?'

The oddest sensation came over Laurie, a mingling of torpor and energy, as if she was being pulled in two different directions. There was a moment when she thought she might faint, but it might just have been because she'd got to her feet so quickly. She steadied herself by holding on to the record shelves. Travis wasn't the clueless one. She was. He was just the messenger.

When she told the story in years to come, in interviews and on her show, she never mentioned the thought that had come into her head at that moment: it was like that movie *The Omen* in which everyone who got in the way of Satan's master plan had some weird accident. Ed Corley had had to be taken out of the picture, and the method of his taking was a sign: run over by a bus full of kids on a street called Paradise. It couldn't have been coincidence.

The clock was ticking in the studio. 'Here's what we do, Travis,' Laurie said. 'Get everything up and running, get Ed's ident lined up. I need some time to think.' She shoved him out of the store room. 'Now!'

'But what are you going to do on the show?' he squeaked.

'Just get it ready,' she said, pulling the door shut as he went out.

In the windowless, neon-lit store room the only sound Laurie could hear was the live feed coming from the small loudspeakers on the wall. For the gaps between the shows, Connie bought music by the yard that could run unattended after Travis, or whichever kid was helping in the studio, had set it up. Now, enhanced by a light drum beat, 'Ode to Joy' was playing. Laurie was trembling a little, but not unpleasantly so. She was holding her purse tightly against her chest, and when she felt calmer she would open it and take out the book. She would have to do it soon: there were seven minutes left and she needed to get herself together.

Ed's show only lasted half an hour, but it seemed to Laurie as if it could have gone on for ever or been over in a few seconds.

She had told Travis she wouldn't need him after he had lined up the top of the show. There were no cues or music to be sorted out and she didn't want to be distracted by seeing him through the glass as she was reading. When he slipped back five minutes before the end, she didn't even notice him.

After Ed's show the station closed down for the night, so when Laurie came out of the booth the live feed had been switched off and the studio was completely silent, except for the fan, which didn't mask the smell of dope. Travis was sitting at the desk with his head in his hands. He brushed his hair off his face. 'That was awesome, Mrs Clow,' he said. 'What a great book. It was like you were reading it just to me.' His eyes were glassy and unfocused.

'Thank you, Travis.'

'That Luke, he's such a cool kid.'

Laurie cleared her throat. 'There's a real boy called Luke. I met him in England. His father wrote the books.'

'Really? Wow! That dark wood, it's spooky.'

'It's called the Darkwood. One word.'

'What's the difference?'

'That's just what it's called.'

'So what happened when Luke found the burning tree? It was Mr Toppit who did it, right? And the package on the grave – what's inside?'

'You'll have to wait till tomorrow.'

Travis laughed. 'Hey, I really want to go to England. It's so cool there.'

Quite suddenly, Laurie had had enough of him. She wasn't sure she'd wanted to share so much. It was time to be on her own and think about what had happened. 'It's a story, Travis, not a documentary,' she said coldly.

Later that evening, on her porch, she was nursing a Scotch, not the first of the evening, and feeling quite strange. Should she have called England and asked Martha or the children if it was okay to read the book on the air? What would they have said? Anyway, she had been the one with whom Arthur had shared his death – she was the one who had been chosen – and that gave her as much right as them to decide what ought to be done. Besides, she hadn't had time. She'd needed to act quickly.

But it had left her feeling empty and flat. It was not as simple as making the decision to share the books and letting them go. They were published in England, after all, anyone could read them. It was that what she held inside herself had moved somewhere else and she couldn't locate it. She had to take it on trust that it was still there.

She knew she had drunk too much, because she was missing Marge, who was already beginning to take up residence in the newly emptied space inside Laurie, bringing her anger and her clutter and her irritating habits. What would she say if they met? There would have to be some acknowledgement of why they had hardly spoken for such a long time, why Laurie found herself turning purposefully down unfamiliar corridors in the hospital if she saw Marge in the distance, why, if Marge was in the canteen, she would leave with a muffin and an apple to eat in the studio when she had planned to have lunch there.

In the check-in queue at the airport on St Bart's, Marge had tried to say something, had put her hand on Laurie's arm and said, 'Laurie, I just –' but Laurie had muttered that she needed to get something at the news-stand. They were late and the flight was full and there were only two single seats left so they ended up at opposite ends of the plane. In other circumstances Marge would have walked aggressively up and down the aisle until she had found people she could terrify into shifting so she and Laurie could sit together.

It was all too late now. Laurie stood up and went inside the house. She was going to do some work on the book. Today she had read as far as she could in half an hour, but now she was going to immerse herself in it and work out what she needed to cut in order to divide the rest into equal chunks so she could get to the end by Friday – and not have to think about Marge's rough, red hands and the awful weight of her and what Marge had told her to do, her voice a husky whisper, and Laurie's powerlessness to stop what had happened on the last night of their vacation on St Bart's.

When she got to the hospital the next afternoon after her morning show at KCIF, Travis was in a state of some excitement. 'Mrs Clow – hey, look at these!'

Laurie, slightly hung-over, was grouchy. 'What is it, Travis?'

'Look at these Double Rs!' he said, thrusting some bits of paper into her hand.

Along with their evening meal the patients at Holy Spirit were given a radio-request form to ask for dedications or make comments.

'So?' she said.

'These aren't the ones for your show,' Travis said. 'These are for Father Corley's show. He *never* gets any Double Rs.'

Mystified, Laurie looked at the pieces of paper in her hand. There were three, not that many to get excited about, she thought.

'God, thy God, is a jealous God. That Luke better watch himself and stay on the path of righteousness,' the first one read, unsigned.

The second was longer:

Dear Ms Clow,

I very much enjoyed your reading this evening. Much more stimulating than Mr Corley's fundamentalist propaganda. My name is Dr Borden Masters, now retired. I taught English literature for many years at the University of Manitoba in Winnipeg. My particular interest was, and is, children's literature. I was most intrigued by the book you read, and as you said it was part of The Hayseed Chronicles, *I presume this is one of a series. I detected some parallels with C. S. Lewis's great* Narnia *series and wondered whether the author was a contemporary of his. If it is not too great an imposition, I wonder whether I might have a brief word with you. I am recovering from a minor operation in Ralston Ward.*

Yours most sincerely,

Borden Masters

The third was written in a childish scrawl, 'I don't like Mr Toppit, I wish he would die! I hope Uncle Ed gets better,' and was signed 'Evangeline (Chicken) Little, aged 10, McHenry Ward'. McHenry was the children's cancer ward.

'So, what do you think?' Travis said eagerly.

The truth was, Laurie didn't know what to think.

The next day there were more, and more after that. The final broadcast was on Friday, and when she came in the following Monday, just for her own show now – Connie had found someone to take over Ed's slot – seventeen were waiting for her.

On Tuesday, when she had just finished *Laurie's Round-up*, the morning show she did at KCIF, her boss Rick Whitcomb strode into the studio and said, 'What's this Hayloft thing?' He glanced in the mirror and readjusted his comb-over, then sat down and put his cowboy boots on the control desk. 'My girls have gone crazy for it.' By 'my girls', he was talking about his wife Jerrilee, and their fifteen-year-old daughter Merrilee, who, thankfully, they tended to call Merry. 'Jerrilee's been in Holy Spirit, didn't I tell you? Had a hysterectomy.'

'I wish I'd known, Rick,' she lied. 'I'd have visited.' She tried to keep socializing with the Whitcombs to a minimum. She saw quite enough of Rick at work, and while Jerrilee was friendly to her now – she was always offering to take Laurie shopping to do something about her clothes – she could never quite forget how awful she had been to her when they were all at high school together.

'Crazy for it, both of 'em,' Rick repeated. 'Some book you found in England, Merry said. Deal was, she was going to keep house while Jerrilee was out of action, but she was at Holy Spirit every night listening to you.' He gave a hearty laugh. 'I've had a ton of take-out pizza.'

'Well . . .' Laurie began.

'They had a party in Jerrilee's room the night you finished. Whole ward came in and had cocktails. Jerrilee thinks you should do it on your show here. You know what she's like when she gets something in her head.'

Everything was strange now. That Jerrilee should be part of the chain made her smile.

'No, I'm serious. Never stops talking about it,' Rick said. 'Where does the thing come from?'

For what was the first time but would not be the last, Laurie told a version of what had happened in England. Later, tuning the story according to whom she was telling it required a set of more precise and intricate calibrations but now, for Rick, she had to think on her feet and trust her instincts.

'That's some story, Laurie,' he said, when she had finished. 'We could do something with this, get some publicity.'

She wanted to say, There is no 'we', but what she said was: 'Really?'

'You'd have to do it in shorter chunks, between commercials. Maybe at the top of the show. What do you think?'

Laurie cleared her throat. 'I don't want to do it like that,' she said.

'You don't?'

'It's not going to work on the *Round-up*, stuck between interviews and lists of church socials and recipes for eggnog. It's not going to work in bite-size pieces.'

'Well, what do you want to do with it?'

'It needs a separate slot.'

Rick held up his hands. 'Whoa, Laurie, hold on a minute here – I'm not having the schedule taken over by some weird kids' book from England. I've got advertisers to keep on side.'

'Ask Jerrilee what she thinks,' she said.

They called it *Hayseed Half-hour*. Rick had begun his career as a journalist on the *Modesto Bee* and still went hunting some weekends with Vern Brisby, the editor. The week before Laurie began, the paper ran an interview with her in the women's section – big photograph, strap-line saying, 'Tragic accident bears fruit for KCIF's Laurie Clow'.

Afterwards, Laurie called it 'the *Hayseed* summer'. It was the hottest year she could remember and everything seemed to move slowly. In the mornings she woke to the white noise of the sprinklers on her neighbours' lawns, and in the long evenings she listened to the hiss of barbecues and the ghostly sound of children laughing. It felt like a dream and she didn't mind whether it was or not: she had never felt more alone or more content.

She was lost in the books as she read them during her show, floating through the words as weightless as an astronaut. Never had the phrase 'on the air' seemed so pin-sharp a description. The books, the words, the letters, even the white space round the edges of the pages, lay like a haze over everything, not the dirty brown of smog but a colour both vivid and pale at the same time. She looked up at the sky and she could see it.

All the other things that were happening seemed almost peripheral: the window display in the bookstore on G Street with the photograph of her next to copies of the books that had been sent over from England; her evenings with Borden Masters and the group he had got together to discuss the meaning of the books; the interview she did on the chat show at the television station in San Francisco; the Fourth of July parade, with the *Hayseed* float that Merry Whitcomb had organized, with a little boy dressed as Luke in front of cardboard trees against a black backdrop with a pair of giant orange eyes to represent Mr Toppit.

The summer ended with a funeral, that of the little girl from the cancer ward called Evangeline Little, whose nickname was 'Chicken'. Her wish had not, in the end, come true. It was not Mr Toppit who had died but her, the white blood cells in her body multiplying out of control. She had passed away in the night and her parents had found a copy of *Garden Green* in her hands when they came to wake her in the morning. In her dying weeks when she was back at home as there was nothing more to be done for her at Holy Spirit, her parents had started raising money for a leukaemia charity, with a series of concerts, car-trunk sales and door-to-door collections. The *Bee* had publicized the fund and Laurie, who had come up with the slogan they used on the flyers – 'The Little Fund That's Getting Bigger!' – gave daily updates on her show.

Evangeline's death turned the fund committee into the funeral committee. They asked Laurie if she would talk at the service. People who were there never forgot her opening line, 'We called her Chicken but there was nobody less chicken in this town than Miss Evangeline Little,' while the passage she read about Luke Hayseed and the bees seemed so right that some people told her afterwards they had wanted to stand up and applaud.

But as Laurie had read it she had found herself strangely dis-associated from the event. When she came out of the church at the end, with the child's family, pushing her way through the people on the steps who had been unable to get in and the local TV crews who had covered the funeral, she realized she had been thinking about a different child, the enigmatic Jordan Hayman, and what that might mean. But by then she had a lot on her mind, not least of which was the offer she had received from the television station in San Francisco to do her own chat show.

Luke

Sometimes on summer afternoons, people – backpackers, families with picnic baskets, couples with cameras slung round their necks – would wander up the drive, ignoring the sign that blocked their path: PRIVATE – STRICTLY NO ACCESS. Presumably they thought it was intended not for them but for those dim enough to believe that a property immortalized in *The Hayseed Chronicles* could ever close its gates to the faithful, intended for the few people who did not assume that buying one of the million or so copies of the books sold in Britain – let alone the millions sold throughout the world – in the five years since Arthur's death entitled them to a share of the action.

Sometimes, when the spirit moved her, Martha would walk across the lawn and talk to them. We watched from the house, too far away to hear what was said but observing a scene as lively as a dumb show – a short exchange of conversation, then blankets swept up from the lawn, sandwiches put away, lens caps replaced on cameras. While Martha walked back towards us, the visitors were scurrying behind her, making for the drive with what seemed like indecent haste. What she had said to them was this: 'I'm afraid you'll have to go – there's been a death in the family.'

It was not only the gravity of the message that caused the exodus but Martha's eccentric appearance and manner. She had taken to washing her hair under the kitchen tap and putting it up herself instead of going to the village hairdresser, so it had the fragile air of a temporary structure, while her clothes, although immaculately cut and expensively made, were sometimes thirty years old and threadbare. She had the spectral presence of someone who, to a stranger, might not seem precisely grounded in the here and now, someone with whom a conversation could go in any number of unnerving ways. Her announcement that there had been a death in the family might have been a simple statement of fact, but her manner hinted at further, potentially more disturbing, revelations. Anyway, nobody was going to hang around long enough to find out. They were off.

At least there was only one entrance to the garden. The woods behind the house were more difficult. They stretched for several hundred acres to the top of the hill on which the house was built, and could be entered at various points on tracks that led from the road some distance from it. Of course there were gates, padlocked and chained, but the *Hayseed* faithful were never deterred. Who could have guessed they would be so adept with chain cutters and cans of spray paint, so strong that their boots could kick through fences, so determined to take possession of the Darkwood that no obstacle would stand in their way? They were like jungle ants that devour everything in their path, those civilized people who believed in the power of words, who read the books to their children, who listened to the audiotapes in their cars, who placed boiled eggs carefully in *Hayseed* eggcups, who politely requested autographs, who wrote to the Carter Press with their idiotic questions in such quantities that Graham had had to employ someone whose sole duty was to sort out the mass of correspondence and run what he called 'The *Hayseed* Office'.

The bonfires, the litter, the used condoms, the trees sprayed with 'Mr Toppit was here' in big white letters, or simply a giant T – the mess of the woods was clearly our problem, but for years Martha engaged in a running battle with the council over whose responsibility it was to clean the graffiti off the long wall half a mile or so from the house next to the gate that was one of the most favoured entrances to the woods. However often it was removed, one slogan kept coming back: 'THE DARKWOOD – ENTER AT YOUR PERIL.' On an official sign it might have seemed like a warning, but in three-foot-high letters painted on a wall it became the most seductive of invitations. At the summer solstice the woods seemed to hum with mysterious comings and goings. Who knew what strange rituals took place there? It was as if the Darkwood had been appropriated into some all-purpose pagan consciousness and was jockeying for position with Glastonbury, Stonehenge and those villages drowned by the sea where you could hear the church bells ringing at high tide.

We coped with the intrusions in our own way. Rachel, if you didn't keep on eye on her, might well entice – not that they needed much enticing – some of these wayfarers into the house. By the time she had been at her most intense for a couple of hours, had opened a second bottle of wine and was digging out Lila's rejected drawings or Arthur's manuscript scrawlings for their perusal, you could see that even for the faithful there might be such a thing as too much *Hayseed*.

As for me, I made myself scarce. I had enough problems with it at school, and it was too much to cope with dashed expectations on the faces of strangers. It wasn't my fault that I had grown up. I couldn't stay a seven-year-old for ever, trapped on the pages of the books. I was still just about recognizable as the boy in Lila's drawings and the comparison was not a favourable one. I came to learn the national characteristics of disappointment: the resentfulness of the English, the downright hostility of the French, who looked as if they might ask for their money back, the touching sadness on the gentle faces of the Japanese – such pain that I both was and wasn't the boy in the books. I was Dorian Gray in reverse: my attic was in every bookshop in the world.

Of the European countries, it was Germany where the sales were largest. Maybe the darkness of the books and the authoritarian nature of Mr Toppit struck some chord with its national psyche. Lila herself had supervised the German translation, had worn down Martha, Graham and the German publishers and nearly driven the hapless translator over the brink into madness. It gave her one more notch of ownership in the books – an unselfconscious *droit de seigneuse* that enabled her to ring the doorbell at almost any time with friends or relations in tow, having given them a tour of the Darkwood during which, she told us, she had cleared up litter, waved her stick and told anyone she had encountered that they were trespassing. Sometimes she threatened to call the police, and sometimes she actually did call the police, who would wearily turn up at the house only to be harangued by her for their failure to protect us properly.

Once inside the house she waited for someone to make tea for her and her guests while she handed out the *Lebkuchen* she had brought with her. By now, Martha would have excused herself to go and have a rest, Rachel, who had said she was going to put on the kettle, would have just vanished but might or might not reappear later in a state of rambling disarray, and I would be left as the sacrificial lamb. 'This is Luke,' Lila would say, as she gave her tinkling laugh and patted her beaded hairnet. 'In due course he will show us round the house. He knows all of its secrets.'

Did Lila know that her actions helped create what happened in America, all the things that later caused her such pain? Laurie would have argued that it was destined to happen anyway, that the trickles that came out of the ground were hers and hers alone, but it always seemed to me that Lila herself had set something crucial in motion.

When Laurie had phoned from California some months after Arthur's death, she had mentioned, in passing, to Rachel that she had had an idea: she thought it might be fun maybe to feature a little bit from the books on her KCIF show. Rachel was never the most reliable reporter, but it was she who had used the phrase 'in passing' and she recollected with some certainty that Laurie had not mentioned that she had already read the books on her hospital show, something we only discovered later.

That summer Martha was not to be relied on for anything rational. We dated it, Rachel and I, to after the bonfire. Walking back from town one day, we could see a great cloud of smoke rising from the garden and in a panic we broke into a run, Rachel faster, more urgent, more prescient than I. Before I came round the side of the house, I could hear Rachel screaming, 'What are you doing? *What are you doing?*' Fights in real life aren't choreographed like they are in films. They're sloppy and fumbling and disconnected; they're graceless and unfocused. Later, but not often, Rachel and I referred glancingly to the incident, but not to the awful details of it or the pained, silent aftermath that lasted for days. Martha never referred to it at all.

Late into that evening, Rachel sat by the smouldering fire, so close to the house that you could still feel its dying heat as you opened the side door, such a mad, dangerous thing for Martha to have done on her own, but maybe that was the point. Her clothes filthy, her face blackened with soot and wet from the water she had put on the fire, Rachel picked over the things she had retrieved from it, the few things of Arthur's life, all of which Martha had wanted to destroy. Upstairs we could hear her moving around, her soft footfall on the creaking floorboards. She wouldn't come down again that night.

Later, Rachel showed me some stuff she had rescued, bits and pieces of *Hayseed* stuff, and one thing that didn't appear to have any *Hayseed* connection: a charred couple of pages that seemed to be the beginning of a short story called 'A Trip To Le Touquet' about a woman who wins a ticket in a competition and goes there to meet someone.

'I didn't think Arthur wrote anything other than the books. Did you?' Rachel said, mystified.

'No. Maybe he's written whole other novels.'

'We're never going to know now she's fucking burned them all. Why did she want to destroy everything? I hate her.'

Anyway, the point of this is simply that, in other circumstances, we might have discussed Laurie's request with Martha, but Rachel, without thinking too much about it, had said, 'Fine, of course, why not?' We would have mentioned it at some point to Martha, I suppose, but more importantly, one of us must have mentioned it to Lila. What is certain, anyway, is that Lila phoned Graham Carter.

Her call had one purpose: to stop Laurie. She dressed it up in a variety of ways, the principal one being that the integrity of the books would be destroyed if they were read on the radio by an American voice. The complex rhythm of the language would be altered, the purity, the essential Englishness of the books fatally compromised – an objection, of course, that Lila did not have when it came to translating the books into German. Graham, as an editor and publisher, as an English Scholar, would surely understand, she said. 'Lila, it's not *The Canterbury Tales*,' Graham said.

Lila pleaded with him, told him that the family were paralysed with grief and could not make the right decision, reminded him that this was in his control. She was technically correct: under the original contract that Arthur had signed with the Carter Press, they essentially acted as his agent and managed all subsidiary rights: film, television, stage, translation, merchandising and – the rights in question – single voice readings. Without permission, without a fee being negotiated, KCIF would be in breach of copyright. Not that that was really the point: the contract might just have well been written in Urdu, given that the books had sold in negligible numbers in Britain and there was no money to argue over. It was only later that it became relevant, when Martha – or, to be strictly accurate, Toppit Holdings AG, a company set up in Switzerland for tax purposes – took the Carter Press to court to dispute the validity of the original contract.

What happened in America might have happened anyway, but Lila's call to Graham put him into play – but in a different way from how she had intended. Almost as soon as Lila put the phone down on him in frustration, Graham phoned Laurie to explain the copyright situation, but in a positive way. He thought it was a great idea to read the books and that there might be some money in it. He discovered that Laurie, in fact, had started her KCIF broadcasts some days before she had spoken to Rachel, and when he talked to Rick Whitcomb, Rick had no option other than to agree to pay a fee. The timing was lucky: if Rick had realized before Laurie began the readings that he would have to pay, he would almost certainly have canned the idea.

Most importantly, Lila's call alerted Graham to possibilities he had not even considered. As chance would have it, he had planned a trip to the States later that month, partly to see his father, Wally Carter, in Los Angeles, and persuade him to invest further in the business to prevent the Carter Press's chronic cash-flow problems becoming terminal, and partly for meetings with publishers in New York to try to sell US rights in his books. His list included some fiction, a series of guides to the great philosophers, a little sociology and psychology, a bit of travel writing and the five *Hayseed Chronicles*. Under normal circumstances, and indeed on any of his earlier sales trips to New York, it would not have occurred to him to try to sell the US rights in Arthur's books – not mainstream enough, too English, too niche, without even the attraction of any significant sales in their home territory.

Now, away from Meard Street and the grind of keeping his company on the rails, emboldened by Wally's agreement to stump up more cash, and enthused by the heat and buzz of New York, he talked about Arthur's books to the publishers he saw, dropping in the names Lewis and Tolkien, using the word 'franchise' and talking about the Darkwood as the new Middle Earth. It was not a bad pitch, but he had no takers. The 'phenomenon' – as Graham ambitiously described it – of Laurie's readings in Modesto did not carry as much weight as he had hoped. It seemed, to the publishers of New York, as significant as a happening in the Orkney Islands might have been to Graham.

However, Laurie's subterranean trickle began to break through the earth. The editor-in-chief at Segal-Klein, the largest and most prestigious of the publishers Graham saw, was called David Sloane, and after Graham's visit something was left lodged in his brain, nothing to be acted on then and there but a cell that would slowly multiply. He had more connection with Modesto than anyone else Graham saw: his aunt, Bea Brooks, was in a retirement home there. Six months later, when she died, he happened to be in San Francisco on business and drove to Modesto for the funeral. Afterwards, as he always did in any town he passed through, he paid a visit to the local bookstore. There, he noticed the display of Arthur's books imported from England and the photograph of Laurie beside it. He had seen her picture before: he remembered reading an article about her success in daytime television. She had been plucked from a local TV station in San Francisco and had moved to Los Angeles to front a chat show that was one of the hits of the season.

We got to know David Sloane well. Whenever he was in England he always took us and Graham out to dinner at this fancy hotel called the Connaught and he would often retell his story, which made Graham squirm: the implication was that David was the real magician in the *Hayseed* saga, the one who knew with unerring certainty which card was the Queen of Hearts.

When David returned from his trip west, he read the books and found, to his surprise, that he was intrigued by them. They resonated in his head, particularly the larger-than-life figure of Mr Toppit. He assigned a junior editor the task of doing some research on them and it was she who turned up *Hayseed Reflections*.

It was more of a pamphlet than a book, staple-bound, some forty pages long. Although it was nominally published by a local Modesto press, who did maps and guidebooks to the area, Laurie and Borden Masters had essentially paid for it themselves. They'd had a thousand copies printed, most of which sat in a pile in Laurie's garage. It had come out of the discussions they had had at their Tuesday-evening book group, when Borden, after too much wine, would become expansive and lecture them as if he was still a professor of English.

With no fuss, for almost no money, David secured the US rights to the five books from the Carter Press, then went to work on *Hayseed Reflections*. He flew to Los Angeles to see Laurie. Although the little book had really been put together by Borden Masters, he needed Laurie on the cover and he needed her behind him – hers was now one of the fastest-growing shows in syndication. He retitled it *Hayseed Karma* by Dr Borden Masters, PhD, Introduction by Laurie Clow, changed the format to make it pocket-sized, and edited Borden's text into bite-sized pieces, while retaining the essential thesis, which was that almost everything that happened in *The Hayseed Chronicles* was capable of religious or philosophic interpretation. For example, the death of the crows in *Garden Growing* was the eleventh plague of Egypt, the tasks that Mr Toppit set Luke were variations on the myth of Sisyphus, and so on. A lot of it, of course, centred round Mr Toppit, who was taken to symbolize not only the unforgiving God in the Christian faith, the Jewish Yahweh, the Hindu Vishnu, the shaman in Native American culture, various deities in Chinese religion, but also Lucifer, the Prince of Darkness, and assorted variations on the plain old Boogeyman.

David Sloane revamped the little book so that it worked on a number of levels. Borden Masters's rich prose – 'Our texts are ones of profound depth and almost infinitely extended meaning; texts that richly repay examination by the most varied and often the most contradictory techniques that modern criticism and theory can provide. These approaches, wide-ranging though they are, could still leave the Hayseed corpus open – quite wrongly – to the charge of ethnocentrism' – could be read as a kind of po-faced academic spoof, but it could also be taken seriously. Interspersed through the book were contributions from celebrities, who had written about incidents in their lives that appeared to mirror incidents in the books – Bob Woodward's piece 'And out of the Whitehouse, Mr President comes' became the best known.

Nearly eighteen months after his death, Segal-Klein published *Hayseed Karma* and Arthur's first three books. In the week before publication, Laurie interviewed on her show people who had contributed to the book. Segal-Klein's marketing thrust was towards *Hayseed Karma*, which, David Sloane guessed rightly, would lead people to the books themselves. They became word-of-mouth bestsellers, and when the last two were published nine months later, *Hayseed* was already a publishing phenomenon.

And Lila: who knows what would have happened if she had not made that phone call to Graham, if Graham had not been suddenly propelled by an inchoate sense of possibility? Maybe those copies of *Hayseed Reflections* would have stayed in Laurie's garage getting brown and faded with age in the dry California heat. Maybe Arthur's books would never have been published in America and would have come to the end of their little life in Britain, the literary equivalent of the fruit-fly's abbreviated existence, to be found occasionally with scuffed covers in Oxfam shops and car-boot sales with '10p' written in pencil on the back.

There was no doubting David Sloane's publishing savvy. He'd had a hunch the books could 'cross over' in America: he believed they could appeal to both children and adults. And just as he had revamped *Hayseed Reflections* into *Hayseed Karma*, he made one crucial change to the books to achieve this: he cut out all the illustrations. The books, as they were published in America by Segal-Klein, were Lila-less.

Most people can find some way of hiding pain. For Lila it was impossible. She wore it, she breathed it, she reeked of it. And yet, as I imagine she had done at other times in her life, when she arrived in England as an orphan during the war, her parents and brother swallowed up in Buchenwald, she fought back in her own way. She ordered fifty copies of each of the five books – negotiating with Graham to get a trade discount – and had them delivered to her tiny flat where they sat in piles in the hallway. She already had string, Jiffy-bags, stamps, air-mail stickers and return labels with her name and address printed, and she methodically sent one copy of the English edition of each book to everyone she knew, and didn't know, in America: friends, relations, acquaintances, relations of friends, friends of acquaintances, as well as the literary editors of, among others, the *New York Times*, the *Boston Globe*, the *Los Angeles Times*, the *San Francisco Chronicle*, the *Washington Post*, *Time* magazine and *Newsweek*, with a covering letter explaining that these were the authorized editions of the books and were not to be confused with any inferior versions.

Then she bought an expensive and bulky leather shoulder-bag large enough to contain the extensive contents of her older, smaller handbag and several copies of each book. Despite her bad hip, which had never fully recovered from her fall at Arthur's funeral, and the walking-stick on which she leaned heavily, she carried the bag with her wherever she went 'just in case'.

Much of Lila's life was led on the off-chance, not vicariously exactly, more with an opportunistic attention to detail – the toothbrush and nightdress always in her bag, the biscuits she baked in case someone were to drop in. Now if she heard that a friend had an American relative visiting, she would arrive on their doorstep bearing the gift of an English edition. On the train, in the street, in a shop, her hearing as fine-tuned as any animal's, she lay in wait for someone with an American accent, accosted them and thrust into their hands one or, if she liked the look of them, several English *Hayseeds*. Once, in what was possibly her finest hour, she saw a tourist reading the American edition on a bench outside Salisbury Cathedral and – a madwoman in a beaded hairnet – lurched towards them, waving her stick and shouting, '*Echt, nicht ersatz!*' like a battle cry as she grabbed the book out of their hand and threw it as far as she could.

By then, of course, the books were famous in Britain. Their success had seeped back over the Atlantic. There seemed to be endless news stories about how these obscure children's books had become a sensation in America – 'The Five Little Books That Could', as the *Daily Mail* put it – and articles with titles like 'Tragedy Behind the Bestseller List', with the story of Arthur's death and a photograph of me alongside one of Lila's drawings.

How quickly the books that had come from nowhere seemed to slot into a tradition, acquire precedents and imitators, passionate supporters and vehement detractors, correspondence in newspapers and mentions on television. The very elements that seemed so anchored to the story became detached and took on a life of their own, took flight and floated in the ether, ready to be plucked and used by people for their own ends. When Neil Kinnock, faced with Mrs Thatcher's intransigence over the miners' strike, shouted, during Prime Minister's Question Time, that she was 'in danger of becoming known as Mrs Toppit' and the headline of the next day's *Daily Mirror* read 'Thatcher Turns Toppit!' I knew we had entered a theme park from which we would never escape.

Part Two

Luke

Out of the window of the big silver car, when it seemed as if we were in the middle of nowhere, I saw a sign in the shape of an arrow with 'MT' painted on it nailed to a tree. A few hundred yards up the road we came to a T-junction, where another sign pointed right. Further on there was a third, which led us to fork left. I asked the driver what they meant. 'They're location signs so the crew can find their way to the set,' he said.

'So what does "MT" mean?'

'Well,' he said, 'when the shoot started they did signs that said "HS" for *Hayseed*, but they had problems with photographers and gawpers so they changed them to "MT" for Mr Toppit.'

'Did it work?' I asked.

'No,' he said cheerfully, 'made no difference at all.' That was a surprise – to dupe the *Hayseed* faithful it would take a code that only the Enigma machine could unravel.

I had never been to a film set before. I wasn't passionate about films, like Rachel and Claude, who spent their lives testing each other on old Hollywood movies, but who wouldn't want to go and see something being made? Of course, I would rather have gone to see almost any other one than this but I'd had only one offer. Anyway, they had sent a limo to drive us to the set. It was also my last day before going away. I had finished exams, finished school, got into university and saved up enough money to go to Los Angeles and stay with Laurie for the summer. Martha thought it was a terrible idea.

After all this time, it seemed extraordinary that the books were going to be on the screen. In the five years since Arthur's death, Martha had turned down many offers to turn them into a film. There was a pattern to the overtures: the American producers stayed in suites at expensive hotels and organized cars to take her to smart restaurants. The British ones were more low-key and expected her to get to less smart restaurants under her own steam. Wherever she was meeting them she tended to order a succession of vodkas and a small plate of smoked salmon, then eat only the slices of brown bread and butter that came with it.

The classic approaches could not always be relied on to find favour with Martha. Previous box-office successes, development deals with major studios, access to the big players, assertions that they were, in fact, the big players, guarantees that Steven always returned their calls *no problemo*, major stars who already seemed committed to the project, invitations to summer places in Santa Barbara or the Hamptons seemed to hover above the table at the restaurant without ever finding their way to Martha's side, as if an invisible forcefield lay alongside the salt and pepper shakers.

At best her responses could be construed as elliptical, a perverse concentration not on the thrust of the producer's argument but on the minutiae that hovered at the edges. Seemingly oblivious to the list of stars who had attended some producer's son's bar mitzvah, Martha wanted to know what fish, exactly, was *gefilte*. When a producer talked of how quickly he could move, how guaranteed this project was to happen, should she grant him the rights, Martha quizzed him on whether the phrase 'fast-track' had originated during the construction of the Union Pacific railroad in the 1860s or whether it had to do with the layout of metropolitan tram lines.

In her wilful obliqueness the erroneous presumption was that she must be playing a uniquely British form of hardball, a careful game designed to give her more control or to improve the terms of the deal, but whatever it was, as the expensive flowers delivered the day after the lunch wilted in the vase, so did the hopes of any number of film producers.

There were those who believed that Martha was reluctant to sell the film rights because, under the original book contract, the Carter Press were in for an unfairly large cut of the proceeds, but that was fundamentally to misunderstand what drove her. It was never about money. When she decided she was going to start litigation against the Carter Press, she ignored conventional wisdom, which was that cases like hers were unlikely to succeed. Martha's view was that the original contract had been simply 'unfair', not a term that carries much legal weight.

The nub of the case was that it went against industry 'custom and practice'. By any standards the contract was a bad one: the royalty rates were unusually low but, more than that, with the Carter Press effectively acting as both publisher and agent, they took a much higher percentage of other rights – film rights in particular – than an agent would, rights that they had no real experience in handling. On top of that, the publishers were technically in breach because they had not even adhered to the regular accounting procedures they themselves had proposed. If Arthur had chosen to employ a literary agent, the terms would have been much more favourable to him. The problem was that he had not.

Martha was on the line. Although a lot of money had already come in, she would have been liable, if she lost, not only for her own court costs but most likely for those of the Carter Press, not to speak of the embarrassment of losing the case if things went against her. But, luckily, embarrassment had never been a blip on Martha's radar. Rachel, in particular, had begged her not to go ahead with it, although it was unclear whether that had come from her or whether she had been prompted by Graham. At that time Rachel was working at the Carter Press, in what capacity nobody seemed sure, although whether it was 'designing the stand for Frankfurt', 'managing the slush pile' or 'a sort of PR thing', her job description clearly did not involve early starts or following conventional office hours: she seemed, as usual, to spend most of her time knocking around with Claude.

For Martha, none of it was personal. She always spoke warmly of Graham, behaved, indeed, as if it had nothing to do with him. Despite the lawyers' letters, they still had almost daily contact, dealing with various aspects of the *Hayseed* industry, and if he attempted to talk about the impending court case, she would simply deflect him.

Of course, there was publicity about the case and this, in the end, worked in Martha's favour. As our circumstances had changed, so had Graham's. Before *Hayseed*, the Carter Press was scarcely on the publishing map. Notorious for their non-existent advances and their late, inaccurate payments, they were at the bottom of any author's wish-list – even Wally Carter's autobiography *Hooray for Hollywood* had been published elsewhere. Now they were written up in the City pages as an extraordinary success story with little graphs showing their exponential growth. They had bought a warehouse building in Clerkenwell and had it expensively converted – 'supervising the redecoration' had been another of Rachel's nebulous tasks – and now employed forty people. Even though their list had expanded and they had found a niche as the home of the quirky and off-centre, they were always defined as the publishing house that had 'picked up' *Hayseed* and 'masterminded' one of the great publishing success stories of the 1980s.

'Squabble in the Publishing Playground' was the kind of piece written in the run-up to the court case, and it was far more embarrassing for Graham than for Martha. She, after all, did not have a business to run. Cleverly, the hearing had been timed to take place soon after the Carter Press's end-of-year results were published, in which it was revealed that the children's division was responsible for almost two-thirds of the firm's turnover. It didn't need a code-breaker to divine that there was, really, no children's division at the Carter Press – it was just the *Hayseed* books.

Graham had a clear choice: did he want his success tainted – regardless of whether he won the case or not – by the implication that it was founded on something rather dodgy, if not illegal? I think the thing Graham feared most was Martha giving evidence. With her elegant but shabby clothes, her glasses falling off the end of her nose, her hair in disarray and her peculiar way of answering a direct question, Martha, the widow-lady with her fatherless children, was always going to come out of it better than him in every way other than, maybe, financially. He backed down the week before the case was due to come to court.

In the papers it was described as an 'amicable settlement' – as amicable as lawyers fighting round a boardroom table can be – but by then Martha had grown bored with it. In the two or three days it took to hammer out the settlement, when decisions had to be made quickly, when each incremental advantage had to be signed off, she consistently forgot to return her lawyers' phone calls, ignored the faxes that spewed out of the machine, then called Graham, insisting he be dragged out of the fevered negotiation, to tell him that she didn't like the typeface used on the new jackets for the Swedish paperback edition. There was a gag clause so neither side could reveal the settlement, and a succession of photographs were taken of Martha and Graham with their arms round each other to prove there were no hard feelings. Much was made of Rachel's employment at the Carter Press as 'project co-ordinator' and 'a crucial member of the team'.

Now that the question of who got what out of the sale of rights had been resolved – the Carter Press's share was dramatically reduced – the way was clear for Martha to address the possibility of a film. The approaches she had had, and continued to get, tended not to vary much with their interchangeable but consistent set of triggers – 'passion', 'vision', 'dream', 'commitment' – and the letter she received from a junior script editor at the BBC, called Jake Cotton, was not much different except that there was a hand-written postscript that seemed to have nothing much to do with the business at hand: he mentioned he had read in a newspaper piece that Martha had done a PhD on the First Crusade and that his particular passion was the building of the crusader castles.

To his astonishment, Martha called him and, after a half-hour conversation in which the books were never mentioned, he found himself suggesting lunch because that was what everybody else seemed to do – no limos and expensive restaurants this time, but a wine bar in Shepherd's Bush. Unlike the non-alcoholic Americans who had lunched Martha in the past, Jake, for whom vodka, splash of water, hold the ice, was not his drink of choice, found himself keeping up with her out of politeness. As he stumbled back to work at four, he had the strange feeling that, although he did not recall anything specific they had said about the books, Martha seemed to have agreed that the BBC could have the rights.

That the money she received was a fraction of what she would have got from a Hollywood deal, as Graham kept pointing out to her, was immaterial. She came out of it very well: the news that the BBC would film the books was greeted by the press with the kind of patriotic fervour normally reserved for a campaign to prevent a Gainsborough masterpiece found rotting in an attic from being sold to an American museum. Everyone had forgotten that if it hadn't been for what had happened in America the books would probably have been long out of print. Personally, I wouldn't have minded if Luke had been played by some kid from a brat-pack movie with an accent like Dick van Dyke's in *Mary Poppins*. In fact, I would have welcomed it.

Rachel and Claude had an opinion, of course: they wanted the boy who was starring in *Empire of the Sun*, which wouldn't open for a while but they had already collected a sheaf of photographs and cuttings about him. They spent a lot of time compiling lists, not just of boys who could play Luke but of the actors who could have played him in the past: Jackie Coogan, Freddie Bartholomew, Mark Lester, Roddy McDowell, Mickey Rooney and – with gales of laughter – the boy with the incomprehensible accent who had played Hayley Mills's little brother in *Whistle Down the Wind*. It kept them happy, although Jake Cotton was less happy with the endless phone calls from Rachel who had elected herself consultant to the project with an opinion on every aspect, from casting to script to locations.

In the end she and Claude had no input in the choice of Luke. There was a talent search, unequalled, as the papers rather ambitiously put it, since the frenzy over who was going to play Scarlett O'Hara. The boy they eventually picked was called Toby Luttrell, a regular in *Grange Hill* who had had a small part ten years before in

Bugsy Malone. The photograph that kept appearing of him, with slicked-back hair, a trilby and his thumbs in his waistcoat pockets, did not fill me with much confidence but he had the great advantage of looking nothing like me so I was all for it.

Poor Jake: not only did he have Rachel and Claude on his back, he also had Lila. She had assumed that her illustrations would be used in the title sequence and offered her help to him. She telephoned him; she wrote to him; she threatened to 'drop in'. Would he like some special drawings for the credits? It might be a nice idea to use one on the cover of the *Radio Times* when the series was broadcast. Might it not be interesting to use the illustrations as breaks between sequences, like chapter headings, no?

No. Jake had languished at the BBC long enough, passed over for the really interesting projects, something of a laughing-stock in his department, where he was known to his colleagues as Joke Cotton. By virtue of his triumph in acquiring the rights and maintaining that 'the family' were very sensitive and only prepared to deal with him, he had elbowed himself into becoming the producer of the show and he was going to do it his way.

It was raining when we drove off the main road and up a long gravel drive, signposted by the last of the MT boards. In the distance I could see the roof of a house, but before we got there we turned off and ended up in a large field. It looked like a gypsy encampment. There were caravans and trucks all over the place and the field was churned up and brown with mud. In some places, duckboards had been put down to make walkways, along which people with parkas and heavy boots were manoeuvring themselves to avoid great pools of water.

Our driver had told us we would be there in time for lunch and already people were queuing in front of a van with an open side, out of which food was being served. At the far end of the field there was a decrepit double-decker bus to which they were heading with their plates.

'Isn't this fun?' Rachel said. 'Are we going to eat in the bus?

Claude would love this. I knew we should have asked him. Isn't it an amazing place?'

Martha stared out of the window gloomily. 'It looks like Zagreb after the war,' she said.

A girl called Roxy came to pick us up. She held open the car door with one hand, a big umbrella in the other, and helped Martha out. It seemed we weren't going to eat in the bus: Jake had organized lunch for us in his caravan. We followed Martha as she teetered along the duckboards under Roxy's umbrella.

Jake was waiting for us in his caravan doorway, arms outstretched, I had never met him before. He was small and tubby, with the rictus grin of a nervous schoolboy, quite different from how I'd imagined him – or, rather, quite different from how I'd imagined a producer to be. He was wearing a baseball cap with *Hayseed – Main Unit* embroidered on it.

'Martha!' he said, giving her an awkward kiss. 'And Rachel – everyone's really excited. Particularly to meet you, Luke,' he said with a nervous whinny, as he put out his hand to me. 'You've met Roxy? My PA?' A shadow passed over Roxy's face. 'We'll need lunch now, Rox. And weren't you going to get napkins for the table? Come on in. This is the nerve centre.'

The caravan rocked a bit as we entered. It smelled of old dog and wet socks.

Roxy, who was standing outside on the step, said, 'Are you sure you don't want lunch on the bus, Jake? It's going to be a bit crowded in there.'

It was true. We had to squeeze ourselves round a little table, Martha, Rachel and I on a padded seat against the window with Jake opposite. Next to each of our places was a *Hayseed* baseball cap in a plastic bag. Jake had his back to us, talking to Roxy, and in a rare moment of family unity, we caught each other's eye. Surely he wasn't expecting us to wear them, like putting on the paper hats out of Christmas crackers?

Roxy was reciting what was on the menu: 'Roast pork and veg, vegetarian chilli, ham salad, and then Black Forest gâteau or straw-berry cheesecake.'

'I'll have a cup of strong black coffee,' Martha said. Rachel didn't want any food either.

Jake looked disappointed, as if all the children had refused the cake at his birthday party. 'Are you sure? It's really good. Luke?'

'Okay, I'll have the pork.'

'Can you ask them to do me a cheese omelette, Rox?' Jake said. 'And chips, but not if they're flabby, and a bit of salad but can you take the beetroot out?'

'Jake, that'll take ages,' Roxy said wearily. 'They don't like doing things that aren't on the menu.'

'I think they will for me, Rox,' he said, giving a don't-mess-with-me laugh. 'And there's some wine in the fridge. Can you do that first? And I don't want those plastic things. Find some proper glasses. I'll have a Diet Coke as well.'

Roxy looked at her watch. 'I said I'd give Paul a hand with the call sheets.'

'Then you better be quick getting our lunch.' Jake turned back to us. 'They don't call me the Mr Toppit of this set for nothing.' I could see Roxy raising her eyes heavenwards.

Another place was laid next to Jake's. I hadn't thought about it because I presumed Roxy would join us but just as she had turned to leave, Jake said, 'And what about Toby?'

'I did tell him, Jake.'

'Well, will you tell him again?'

Roxy might have slammed the door, or it might just have banged shut in the wind.

'Toby Luttrell's going to have lunch with us. He's longing to meet you all. Quite a character, is our Toby. I think we've created a bit of a star.'

Roxy brought the food in, then Jake made her go back because she had brought Coke when he had asked for Diet Coke. There was no sign of Toby. In the meantime, after a second bottle of wine had been opened, Rachel had put on her *Hayseed* baseball cap and Jake was trying to tell us how well the shoot was going, how the rushes were fantastic, how happy everyone was even though the weather had been terrible and they were running several days behind schedule, Martha was on a different tack. She had brought Jake a present, a little book about a famous crusader castle called Krak des Chevaliers and was telling us a story about it. In some detail she described how the castle, the most perfectly fortified construction of the medieval age, had been brought down not by a battle but by a trick in which some enemy sultan had forged a letter from a crusader commander ordering the person in charge to surrender.

Jake was beginning to look a bit desperate, even more so when Rachel, not under the same obligation to be polite as he was, began talking over Martha to ask about Mr Toppit. Although the six half-hour episodes they were shooting mainly covered the first two books, with a bit of stuff from the third, the time would come, if they did a second series, when they would have to face up to the contentious appearance of Mr Toppit at the end. The audience would have to see someone who was never seen.

'You can't just use some actor,' Rachel said. 'I mean, *obviously* you can't show his face.'

'The sultan was called Baibars. He was a Mameluke,' Martha said.

'Claude and I had an idea –'

'The Mamelukes were slaves originally, descended from freed Turkish slaves. That's social mobility.'

'You've seen *Ben-Hur*? Claude and I thought there was something rather clever in that. There's this whole bit about Ben-Hur converting to Christianity because he sees Jesus on the way to the cross . . .'

'It's a mesmerizing place, Jake, it really is. Extraordinary. The light,' Martha said.

'. . . but you never *actually* see Jesus's face. He's wearing a kind of cowl, a hood thing, so his face is always in shadow. The only bit of him you see is his feet because Charlton Heston falls to the ground and slobbers over them. You just see a pool of darkness where his face is.'

'I'm staggered you haven't been there,' Martha said. 'Staggered. Didn't you have field trips? How do they teach things at university, these days?'

'I didn't study it at university. It's more of a hobby, really,' Jake said.

Martha looked at him in astonishment. 'But didn't you say –'

'Can we talk about your marmalade sultan some other time?' Rachel interrupted aggressively.

'Will you take that ridiculous *hat* off?' Martha hissed at her.

There was a moment of silence, then the door flew open and banged against the wall of the caravan.

I presumed it was Toby Luttrell in the doorway. He had a bag of crisps in one hand, a can of beer in the other and a *Hayseed* baseball cap, worn the wrong way round, on his head. He raised the beer in a casual greeting to us. 'You lot my family?' he said, then lay down on the window seat opposite us and burped.

Jake, who I had thought was nervous around us, was positively fizzing with anxiety now. He leaped to his feet and stood between us and Toby, either to form a conduit or to shield us from him.

The first thing to say about Toby was how extraordinary he looked. In the books Luke's age was never stated. The first was published when I was seven and the last when I was twelve, but Luke remained more or less the same in Lila's illustrations. Obviously he was a child but he often behaved with a wisdom that was not precisely that of a child, so I could understand why Jake had gone for someone older to play him. Toby was just sixteen but, like an optical illusion, you could look at him askance and he would suddenly appear much, much younger. He couldn't have been more than an inch or two over five foot. He had a husky voice but not an adult one, more like that of a kid with a bad throat, and his face was the size of a child's but with large features, like plants that had outgrown the pots they were in – huge eyes, a snub nose and full lips. His hair had obviously been dyed for the part and was a strange shade of straw blond under the baseball cap.

'Toby's been longing to meet you all,' Jake said, rather unconvincingly.

'Anyone got a light?' Toby stuck a cigarette into his mouth.

'To*beee!*' Jake said, with a nervous laugh. 'You're not meant to be smoking!'

'Mrs Hayseed is,' he said, with a child's undeniable logic.

Rachel took Martha's lighter off the table, went over and lit Toby's cigarette. 'You must be exhausted,' she said. 'Aren't you in every scene? Are you loving it?'

'I hate the mornings.' He moved his legs so Rachel could sit next to him.

'He uses the driver as an alarm clock,' Jake said, with an attempt at jovial laughter. 'Waits until he honks the horn, then gets up. We've had a few late starts, haven't we, young Toby?'

'I love your hair,' Rachel said.

'Do you? They have to keep touching up the roots to keep it like this.'

Rachel had taken off his *Hayseed* baseball cap and was picking through his hair as if she was examining it for nits. 'It's very dry. You should use conditioner.'

There was a moment's silence, then Jake said, 'Is there anything you want to ask, Toby? About the books or the character? It might be useful to have some background. These are the people who know.'

Toby shrugged. 'Not really. I just learn the scenes as I go along. Can I have some of that wine?'

Jake looked rather annoyed. 'The photographer's going to be ready for you and Luke soon, Toby. You'll have to go to Costume and Makeup in a minute.'

'Can I come with you? I'd love to see the costumes,' Rachel said.

'What photographer?' I said.

Rachel turned to Jake. 'Is that okay?'

'What photographer?' I said.

'I'm sorry about Toby,' Jake said to Martha, after Toby and Rachel had gone. 'He can be a bit offhand sometimes.'

'I like the boy's spirit,' Martha said unexpectedly, then poured herself more wine.

'What photographer?' I said, for the third time.

Jake turned to me as if he was surprised I was still there. 'We thought we'd do some stills,' he said. 'You and Toby.'

'Me and Toby doing what?'

'You know, the two Lukes.'

'You'll have to stand up straight,' Martha said. 'You always slouch.'

'I don't want to, thanks.'

'Look at your round shoulders. Just make sure he stands up straight, Jake.'

'Toby in costume with you. The press people thought it would be fun. We're getting great publicity already. We had a crew from America last week from Laurie Clow's show shooting loads of stuff.'

'And brush your hair.'

'I don't want to,' I said.

'It won't take long,' Jake said. 'Anyway, Toby's got to be back on set in half an hour. We're running late today. The rain – God, this weather!'

'I'd rather not,' I said.

'We've got it all set up,' Jake said, sounding astonished. 'He's coming specially, the photographer. He does stuff for *Vogue*.'

There was another silence, and although I had turned away, I could sense something passing between Jake and Martha. 'I've just got to talk to someone,' he said. 'I'll be back in a minute.'

Martha picked up her cigarettes and lit one. She looked out of the little window. It was still raining.

'I'm not going to. I don't want to,' I said. 'Rachel can do it.'

Martha brushed the hair away from my eyes. 'You're really a nice-looking boy,' she said. 'You should stop biting your nails, baby. No girl's going to let you touch her with hands like that. Can you believe that Jake's never been to the Krak des Chevaliers? It's absurd. He's not interested at all. What kind of scholar can he be?'

'He's a producer. He never said he was a scholar.'

'Even as a producer you need some kind of intellectual rigour. Someone was saying what a nice boy you were. Who was it? Nice and kind and thoughtful. Decent, but . . .'

'But what?'

She gazed up at the ceiling as if the word she was looking for might be found there. 'But ordinary,' she said.

I turned away.

'You need to work hard to be special, baby,' she said. 'Everyone does. Special is hard. What are your passions? You spend the holidays moving from one sofa to another.'

I was concentrating as hard as I could on a patch of damp above the window. 'Who said?'

She sighed wearily. 'Oh, baby, what does it matter? People are only trying to be helpful.'

'I don't need help.'

'We all need help.'

The damp patch had looked first like a map of Britain, but now it had become hazy and seemed more the shape of that statue of a naked man with his head resting on his fist, thinking. I was keeping my head still – held back and still – so that what was in my eyes wouldn't spill over.

'You're luckier than most,' Martha said. 'Your father gave you something, a kind of gift. These little books make people at least *think* you're special.'

I didn't want to engage with this but I couldn't help blurting out – more like a cry than I had intended, 'I don't want to be special that way!'

'Use what you've been given, baby,' Martha said. 'You don't know how many chances you're going to get.'

★

How many people does it take to do a photograph? There was the photographer, an assistant, a makeup person, a costume person, someone who called themselves a stylist, Jake and, of course, Rachel who, by the time I arrived, was fussing round Toby and seemed to have taken control of the whole thing.

'Don't you want his hair to be more tousled, more sort of *wild*? If you just –'

'He's fine,' the makeup girl said curtly, and guided Rachel away from Toby.

'This is going to be wonderful,' Jake said clapping his hands.

I thought it would be grotesque. Nobody was fussing over my hair and makeup. It seemed I was only there to add an extra colour or two to Toby's dazzling spectrum.

They had set up a backdrop in a kind of forest green, speckled and mottled with muddy brown. Hanging from the top were tendrils of real ivy, like a kind of curtain. I think it was their idea of the Darkwood. While everyone was milling around, Toby was standing in front of the backdrop, smoking, in his Luke costume and I stood next to him, self-conscious and awkward. I don't know why – he was the one who looked like an idiot.

Actually, they had been quite clever with his costume. Although, broadly speaking, Toby was dressed like the Luke in the books, they had somehow contrived to make him more contemporary or, at least, more timeless. The battered straw hat Luke sometimes wore had been replaced with a scuffed dark-brown broad-brimmed thing, like a cross between a cowboy hat and one of those Australian things with corks hanging off them. Instead of the calf-length trousers, he was wearing a baggy pair of jeans with the bottoms turned up so you could see his bare ankles above too-big-for-him boots. What they had kept, of course, was the belt holding up his trousers – the complicated machinations by which Luke stole Mr Toppit's dressing-gown cord formed a major part of the third book – but they had made it multi-coloured so it looked curiously funky, like the bright things kids sometimes use to personalize their school uniforms.

The first pictures were of me and Toby standing beside each other, not full length because Toby was standing on a box so we would be the same height. Though we were so close that we were almost touching, I felt completely disconnected from him and completely rigid. I could feel my smile freezing into a sickly grin. The photographer must have sensed something because, after the first couple of shots, he said, 'Put your arms round each other, go on, you're friends, you're old friends, go on, that's it – great! Great!' He kept snapping and the flash kept flashing. I couldn't wait for it to be over: it was like being at the dentist's. Then he said, in his horrible, jolly, hectoring voice, 'You're too stiff, Luke, loosen up. You're mates, remember, you're the same person!' My arm lay inert on Toby's shoulder like a dead snake.

I pulled away. 'Haven't we finished yet?' I said desperately.

Rachel whispered something in the photographer's ear and he said, 'Yeah, great!' and pulled the tripod with the camera on it towards us. 'We need to do some closer stuff,' he said. 'This is going to be great – don't worry, it's going to be great.' His babble seemed to be on a loop.

Leaving his tripod, he came over to the backdrop and man-handled us as if we were giant chess pieces. He twisted us round so we were facing each other. 'That's it – that's it! Hold it like that.' Toby and I were so close that our noses were almost touching, and as the photographer moved back to the camera I pulled away instinctively. But he was back in a second pushing us together again. 'Closer, Luke, closer. You could drive a truck through that gap.'

Now our noses were touching and I could smell Toby's yeasty breath. His eyes were looking straight into mine and I forced myself to hold his gaze while the flashes came in quick succession. His pupils were tiny pinpricks and he could stare without blinking. When it was finished, he winked at me and said, 'You should come to the set more often. We could have a laugh.' Before I had time to answer – not that I could think of anything to say – the makeup girl and the others had surrounded him, put a quilted anorak round his shoulders and were fussing over him. They needed him on set and people were talking into walkie-talkies about estimated times of arrival as if it was a military operation: 'Be there in five, yeah. Makeup on set, okay?'

As Toby and his entourage headed away, Rachel in their midst, he turned back to me. 'You must hate me being you,' he said.

I thought about it. 'Not at all,' I said breezily. 'I like it this way, actually.'

Martha had gone missing. As far as I was concerned this was no particular cause for alarm but Jake seemed flustered. Rachel dismissed him when he asked her if she knew where Martha could be: she was not to be disturbed. She had acquired a pair of headphones and was standing beside the director, staring into a little monitor on which you could see what the camera lens was seeing as they were shooting a scene where Toby was running out of the woods holding a huge pitchfork. She was probably giving him a few pointers on how to direct, gleaned from her and Claude's extensive knowledge of the oeuvre of Douglas Sirk.

I was standing next to a table with a giant hot-water urn on it alongside plastic trays of biscuits, cake and manky sandwiches. Jake was flapping about Martha, then got distracted by the food. 'All the Battenberg cake's gone,' he said, scrabbling in the food trays. 'God, they're like vultures. They've only just had lunch! Where do you think she can be? She was with the director – actually, she was rather rude to him, told him the house looked suburban. Then she disappeared.' There was a brown stain at the corner of his mouth from the chocolate roll he had just gobbled. I wondered if he was more worried about Martha wandering round leaving a trail of destruction than about her well-being.

'I wouldn't worry about it,' I said. 'She'll be fine, honestly.'

He clicked his fingers. 'Steve! Steve!' he called, to a burly man heading for the set. 'I need your walkie-talkie.'

The man turned. 'It's Colin,' he said.

'Sorry,' Jake said, and grabbed the thing out of his hands. 'Roxy, come in! Roxy? Where are you?' A terrible squawk came out of it.

'I'm by the set. I need you now.' Another squawk. 'No, now!' He thrust the walkie-talkie back at Colin.

Roxy arrived, flustered. 'Jake, I'm trying to –'

'Can you find Mrs Hayman? She's gone AWOL.'

'What's happened to her?'

'If I knew that, Roxy, I wouldn't be asking you, would I?'

'I'll come with you,' I said.

We left Jake searching through the cakes. Roxy was cross. 'I'm not Jake's assistant, you know,' she said, setting the record straight. 'I'm the floor runner.'

I couldn't imagine what a floor runner was. 'We don't have to look for Martha if you don't want to. She'll be fine.'

'My life won't be worth living if I don't find her.'

We walked back to the unit base where the lorries and caravans were. In the back of one of the camera trucks a group of men were playing cards. A little football game was going on behind the dining bus while one of the drivers was waxing his silver limo. In the costume truck the washing-machine was spinning and two girls were darning. There seemed to be a whole other life going on away from the set, like all the things people did at home when the men were off fighting a war.

Everybody seemed pleased to see Roxy. When she was away from Jake she had a very smiley face. We weren't getting far with the Martha mystery: nobody had seen her. Then, as we were heading back to the set, someone shouted Roxy's name.

'Were you looking for Mrs Hayman?' It was one of the unit drivers.

'Have you seen her, Lee?'

'She went off with Kenny. She asked him to drive her home.'

Roxy looked at me, as if I could explain it. I shrugged my shoulders.

'Actually, she seemed a bit upset,' Lee added.

'Upset?'

'Well, she might have been crying. Kenny had some tissues in his car.'

'I'd better go and tell Jake.' Roxy touched my arm. 'Are you okay, Luke?'

I nodded. 'Sure,' I said, although I was a bit hurt. It meant I wouldn't see Martha before I flew to America the next day. Still, goodbyes had never been her thing. 'I'll wait here,' I said. 'You go.' I didn't want everyone on the set cross-examining me about Martha. She wasn't my responsibility.

I felt a bit exposed on my own, after Roxy had left. Lee was leaning against his car having a cigarette so I went over to him.

'Sorry about all this, mate,' he said. 'Want a ciggie?' He waved the pack at me. 'Go on.'

It was such a relief to be treated like an adult that I took one, even though I didn't really like smoking. I'd had enough of them with Adam, though, not to do anything embarrassing like cough.

'Enjoying yourself?'

'It's really interesting,' I said lamely.

'You don't look anything like I thought.'

'Oh?'

'Yeah, I thought you'd be like Toby. He's a little bugger, no end of trouble. He needs Mr Toppit to keep him in order. Nice lady, your mother.'

'Really?'

'She asked where I come from. Tried to guess my accent.'

'Where do you come from?'

'Wales.'

'Was she right?'

He guffawed. 'Thought I was Turkish!'

'Why do you think she was upset?'

'I don't know. She was over there' – he waved at one of the trucks – 'having a ciggie, talking to someone, then next thing I knew she was driving off with Kenny.' He gestured with his hands to indicate that she might have vanished in a puff of smoke.

After we had stubbed out our cigarettes, I wandered over to the truck he had pointed out. It was like a furniture-removal van, filled with garden benches and tables and a lot of plants in pots and grow-bags. At the back I could see a figure moving in the dark.

I called, 'Hello!' and, out of the gloom, a woman came towards me. She was wearing dungarees and dirty gloves. Her hair was blonde and cropped short, and she would have been attractive if she hadn't been so enormous. Out of her short-sleeved T-shirt great white arms protruded, mottled pink. The tailgate of the truck groaned when she stepped on to it.

She blinked when she saw me. 'Am I having another royal visit?' she said. Then she took off her gloves, wiped her palms on her dungarees and put out her hand to shake. 'I thought you'd be spending time with the grand people on the set. We're just the oily rags down here.'

'Why have you got all that stuff in your van?'

'We've got to dress the garden for tomorrow. The people who live here, they've got a lot of poncy furniture and weird sculpture. We're making it look like the garden in the books: old benches, nice weathered wood.' She pointed to the back of the truck. 'Lot of lavender. We're putting it in the flowerbeds for the scenes with you and the bees.'

I didn't bother to correct her. 'Are you a gardener?'

She laughed. 'No, I do props. I help my dad. He's the prop master.'

'My mother's gone missing.'

She looked surprised. 'Has she?'

'The driver – Lee – said she was over here at one point.'

'She looked a bit lost. I showed her the stuff we were going to put in the garden. She liked the urns. They're Victorian. She wanted to know where we got them from. I said she'd better talk to Ray when he gets back.'

'Who's Ray?'

'Ray Parsons, my dad. He sourced all the props. I'm Dawn, by the way.'

'Then what happened?'

'It was odd. She just fled.'

*

222

Rachel's eyes were shining and she was buzzing with excitement as we were leaving. She seemed totally unconcerned about Martha's departure. She kept promising Jake she would come back as soon as she could. Maybe I had missed the moment when he had asked her to. I think he was glad to see the back of us. He was still fretting over Martha.

'I hope she's not unhappy with the filming,' he said. 'It's been a bit of a nightmare, actually.' He grimaced. 'We're over budget, but that's not unusual, not on a show this ambitious. They're not happy bunnies at Television Centre, I can tell you. Of course they love the stuff, the footage. The rushes are great. Everybody thinks so. We've got to reshoot some things, but that's quite normal. You don't think she's going to complain, do you? You don't think she'll call the BBC and say she doesn't like it?'

As the car drove away, whatever energy Rachel had had on the set dissipated and within a few minutes she was fast asleep, lying across me on the back seat, her head on my legs. In the cold afternoon light she looked pale and ill as I stroked her hair.

The plan was this: because it was my last night before I went to America, Rachel and Claude were going to have what they called a leaving dinner for me at Claude's place. He was still living at Mr Poontang's house. His name was one of Rachel and Claude's elaborate jokes – so elaborate that I never knew his real name. 'You'd recognize him on telly,' Claude said dismissively, 'He's the one who's always saying, "I now pronounce you man and wife," or "He'll be right as rain after a good night's sleep." Not what you'd call a *dazzling* career. His spell in jail rather took the lustre off that.'

Mr Poontang lived in two rooms on the ground floor and let the others. There was a shared kitchen and bathroom on each floor, but Claude's room was special because it had its own little kitchen behind a curtain. 'I can't tell you what I had to do to get it,' Claude said. 'Or, rather, what Damian had to do.' But Damian was no longer living there. He had gone to New York, and Claude became uncharacteristically vague whenever his name was mentioned.

Claude was desperate to hear about the filming.

'I've got a surprise for you. You'll find out later. You'll really like it,' Rachel said to him, then clammed up and wouldn't say any more. When she had changed, she seemed much livelier and helped Claude to get everything ready. She was wearing a kind of kaftan with a shawl round her shoulders and had put her hair up, like Martha did. Claude was wearing a green velvet jacket with a bow-tie and smoking his Turkish cigarettes from a cigarette-holder. I was just in jeans and a T-shirt, and Claude asked if I wanted to borrow some clothes. He said he liked his dinners to be formal.

Of the other guests, one was a priest, one was a driving instructor, one worked in the box office of a theatre in the West End and wore a dinner jacket, and one was a Romanian student called Rani, who had the room next door to Claude's and was in shorts and a T-shirt. His concession to formality was a souvenir Beefeater's hat from the Tower of London. Claude whispered in my ear, 'Don't bother with him. He's very dull. He's just here to make up numbers.'

Although it was summer and still light outside, the curtains were drawn and the room was lit by candles. There was a peculiar smell that Claude said was church incense. 'The best, the very best,' he said. 'I nicked it from All Saints, Margaret Street.' The priest laughed so much that he knocked over the jug that contained the special cocktail Claude had made with vodka and blue Curaçao.

While Rani mopped up the mess, Claude began to prepare a Thai meal, swapping pans like a juggler on the single burner of his little stove. He couldn't eat any of it himself because he was having work done on his teeth, which had been crooked and brown ever since I had known him. Dental work was the only way he could get money out of his grandfather. Luckily, Claude had managed to persuade him not to pay the dentist direct so he was just having the front ones done and keeping the remainder of the cash.

Claude kept asking Rachel what her surprise was, and finally she whispered in his ear. He gave a little whoop of excitement and hugged her. 'This is fantastic!' he kept saying. 'Fantastic! Poony will be creaming himself!' Then she and Claude went off somewhere

224

and didn't return for half an hour. Everyone was smoking and talking. I felt sick.

It was only towards the end of the evening – after several jugs of Claude's cocktail had been drunk and not much of the food had been eaten – that Mr Poontang joined us. I had thought the dinner was a send-off for me, but he seemed to think it was to celebrate him getting a part in a sit-com. Claude made rather a fuss of him, rudely ordering Rani off the sofa and on to the floor so Mr Poontang had somewhere to sit. He was wearing a dressing-gown with a woollen scarf round his neck because he was trying to fight off a sore throat. Claude kept tapping his watch and throwing meaningful glances at Rachel.

Mr Poontang had to be up early the next morning to get to the studio and wanted us to help him with his lines. He was playing a doctor who passes out when he has to deliver the heroine's baby and he was hoping to become a regular character in the show. We went through it several times while Mr Poontang tried out his lines in different ways. Rachel played the wife and the priest played the husband, but when we came to do it for the fifth or sixth time – after we'd had some more of Claude's cocktail and Mr Poontang had asked us in turn what we thought – the priest had fallen asleep on Claude's bed. Rani offered to take over because he thought it would help him with his English. When we started reading again, I saw that Rachel was crying, and after she and Mr Poontang had had their final exchange – 'How does it feel?' 'How do you think it feels? I must be giving birth to an elephant!' – she threw her script on to the floor and got up unsteadily. 'This is crap,' she said. 'It's just crap.'

Mr Poontang looked upset, and Claude and Rachel began arguing. 'Well, you were the one who said he was coming!' Claude shouted.

'He told me he would if he could.'

'If he could? You didn't say that. You said he *was* coming!'

To be honest, I was having some difficulty following what was going on, but I'd twigged that Rachel must have invited Toby

Luttrell. Something terrible had gone wrong with the evening. Although I had been there all the time, I felt as if I had missed the bit where it had changed from how it had begun to what it was like now, as if I was reading a book with some of the pages torn out. When I got up I headed for the loo because I knew I was going to throw up.

When I went back into the room, the man in the dinner jacket had fallen asleep too, and Rani and Mr Poontang were going through the script again, Rani reading the parts of both husband and wife. To differentiate between the two, he put on his Beefeater's hat when he was the wife and took it off when he was the husband.

Rachel wasn't there. I asked Claude where she was and he said sulkily, 'Well, I hope she's sorting herself out. I don't know what's the matter with her. She's let us all down.'

That didn't seem strictly accurate, but I wasn't in any state to argue. It was after midnight, and Mr Poontang's house was dark. There were light switches in the corridor that you pushed down and the dim lightbulbs came on for about thirty seconds, then turned off again. The ceiling had brown water stains that had made the dark red wallpaper peel away at the top. It was stuffy and there was a smell of mould and cheap air-freshener. I didn't want to call Rachel and wake the other occupants of the house, so I kept whispering her name.

I found her on the ground floor. She was sitting in the space under the stairs where the pay-phone was, her arms round her scrunched-up knees as if she was trying to make herself as small as possible. She looked awful. Her hair had come down, and there was a stain at the top of her dress.

'Are you okay?' I asked. I knelt down beside her.

'I wish you weren't going,' she said. 'I don't know what I'm going to do.' I knew she wasn't talking about what she would do while I was in America. 'Do you know that Graham Carter has five children?'

'That many?'

'So fucking fertile. Bettina, Olivia, Mary, Prudence, and you know what they call the boy? Podge. *Podge!*'

'That can't be his real name.'

There was an odd look on her face. 'You watch everything, don't you? You observe it and take it all in. What do you do with it when it's inside? It must *fester*.'

'Like in *The Addams Family*. Do you remember him?'

'What was he? I loved him. The uncle? That's right. I'm going to the loo. Don't go away.'

I had to pull her to her feet. She handed me a bottle of clear liquid. 'What is it?'

'*Grappa*. It's made from all the grape crap left behind after they've done the wine. Claude loves it. It's Italian. Don't drink it all.'

The *grappa* seemed to avoid my stomach and go straight to my head so when Rachel came back I was feeling a bit dizzy.

She was talking even before she reached the bottom of the stairs. 'I don't understand why Toby didn't come. He said he would. Well, he said he would if he could but he said it as if he meant to come. You know when people are saying things just to be polite. Claude's furious, but I didn't *absolutely* say he was going to come.'

'I'm really glad he didn't,' I said.

Her nose was dripping. 'I liked him,' she said. 'I thought he was exotic. You're just jealous.'

'Of what exactly? His size? His dyed hair?'

'I'm pregnant,' she said. 'Isn't that a bore?'

'Maybe you shouldn't be drinking.'

'I won't be pregnant for long. I hate babies. They squall and they never laugh at your jokes. What do you think Martha would say?'

We both seemed to be ignoring the fact that her eyes were brimming with tears. 'Do we care? She didn't even say goodbye today,' I said.

'Anyway, I still haven't forgiven her for burning all that stuff. All Arthur's *things*. How could she do that?'

'You saved some of it,' I said.

'Big deal. Some charred bits and pieces.'

I took another swig of *grappa*. 'I like this,' I said. She took the bottle and had some too. It was almost finished now.

'You don't have to go. Do you really have to go?' Then she groaned. '*Ohhh* . . . I don't know why everything's so . . .'

I would have liked to know what she was going to say, what she thought everything was, but from above us there were hoots of laughter, then Claude and the others clattered down the stairs. By now, I had lost the rhythm of how it had been in Claude's room so it was a shock to have them invade the little hideout Rachel and I had created by the pay-phone under the stairs.

They wanted us to go outside. God knows what time it was. Mr Poontang was flapping around, trying to keep them quiet before everyone in the house got woken up. Claude didn't care. He grabbed Rachel's arm and pulled her to her feet. My head was spinning. They might have been singing.

Outside the street was quiet and the air smelled new and fresh. Oxygen surged into me and I could feel the blood racing through my veins. Rani had his Beefeater's hat on but his trousers were round his ankles and he was making the kind of screeching noise you might make if you were skiing down a mountain. There seemed to be more of us than there had been before but I couldn't really remember how many there had been before. I tried to picture us all back in Claude's room but it seemed too long ago.

Claude was rattling the gate that led into the gardens in the middle of the square, but it must have been padlocked. It might have been him who was the first to try climbing over the railings, or it might have been Rani. Then we were in the gardens and Rani was lying on the ground holding his bare leg, which was bleeding. Rachel and Claude were trying to climb a tree. I lay down and put my cheek against the damp grass. It was hard to get the order of everything right. I don't know whether the police came then or whether I had fallen asleep and it was later. Then there was the van, and then there was the police station, and then there was filling in forms. Maybe Rani was with us or maybe he had been taken to Casualty. Everybody seemed to be talking about his leg. It seemed that we had Disturbed the Peace and although the policeman I talked to kept repeating, 'This is a serious offence, sir,' I couldn't see that what we had done was so serious. Maybe Claude felt the same. I could hear him shouting at somebody down the corridor.

I don't know what time they let us go, but it was starting to get light when we walked back to Claude's place, just me and Rachel and Claude – the others had vanished. Anyway, I didn't really care about them. I slept for an hour or two in a sleeping-bag on the floor. When I woke up, all I could hear was Rachel and Claude snoring. They still had their clothes on and were fast asleep on his bed. The room was a tip. Bottles and glasses, overflowing ashtrays and plates with the remains of Claude's Thai food were all over the place. I had to get to the airport and I collected my stuff together as quietly as I could, although I don't think a nuclear bomb would have woken them. I'd been going to leave a note, but I couldn't think of anything to say so I just let myself out.

Once I had gone through check-in and was in the departure lounge I had the strange sense that I had escaped unscathed – from what, exactly, I wasn't sure. I felt free and clear of everything: nothing could touch me. Then, as I was looking through the magazines on the news-stand, my heart jolted. Propped up next to the piles of newspapers was an *Evening Standard* placard on which was written in big black felt-tip capitals: 'HAYSEED BOY POLICE CAUTION'.

If I'd thought Martha wouldn't have heard about it yet, I was wrong. I rang her just before the flight was called and she was icy with anger. By that time I had had half an hour to let it settle, and as I talked to her on the phone, watching passengers come and go with their luggage, listening to the noise of the busy airport, the world seemed normal again. What did it matter? It was just a blip, so small as to be imperceptible in the scheme of things.

In Martha's scheme of things, however, the scale seemed to be different and I let her rant on. Then, suddenly, I was sick of everything, sick of *Hayseed*, sick of all of us being locked together. 'I never thought you'd be such a fool,' she shouted. 'How could you?'

I thought for a moment, and I said, 'Because I'm special,' and then I hung up on her.

Laurie

I had to go back to Los Alamos to do the show. I left there when I was five or six and never went back. I'd forgotten the colour everything was in those mountains. People call it red but it isn't close, not even pink. It's a kind of terracotta. A dirty colour, but it looks clean with the sky and all that air. I don't know what you'd think of it, Luke. It would look like the moon if you came from England.

I didn't recognize Los Alamos at all. No connection. Nothing came back. There's even a Starbucks there! It looks like anywhere else now. They've paved the roads, of course, and there are more of them, but I hardly even recognized Fuller Lodge, it seemed so small. Los Alamos was originally some school for rich kids but they kicked them out when the army took it over in the war, and that was the schoolhouse. There's a lake by Fuller Lodge called Ashley Pond, and when I was a kid, it seemed vast and open, like it went on for ever. Someone even told us it was bottomless, just went all the way down to the centre of the earth. Now it's surrounded by buildings and it's like a pissy little thing that wouldn't go higher than your ankles if you jumped in.

In my head Los Alamos is my dad's place. I don't remember much about it except him. And Paully a bit – the kid who lived next door to us. There's Alma, of course, but I try to siphon her out of it. She sort of spoils it for me with her moods, her drinking, and her grousing about the heat, the cold, the bugs and the Jews. Jews! The whole place was filled with Jews, all those foreign scientists who had come over from Europe to build the bomb. We couldn't have won the war without them, though I don't feel too good about it now. Most people don't. Now they think the war would have ended anyway; they just wanted to test the bomb on people. Still, it was an achievement, the bomb, an amazing piece of work done in those conditions, and I'm proud of what my dad did, not that he was much more than a technician. He wasn't high up or anything, but they couldn't have done it without guys like him.

Everybody had doubts then. First the Russians were our allies, then they weren't. What were people meant to think? And that place – Los Alamos – must have been like a hothouse of secrets and gossip. They must have talked about whether what they were doing was right, whether the bomb technology should be kept from everyone else. Work was all they did. There weren't football games or TV, and people cared then. It isn't like now when nobody gives a shit about what's happening.

They didn't want me to do the Los Alamos show. Nobody's heard of it, nobody cares, the advertisers won't like it, yada yada. That's what they said, but it was more than that – they were frightened. Anyway, I forced them into it. I can't just talk to movie stars tub-thumping some new movie. Anyhow, the show works better if I can do serious stuff sometimes. Even they know that.

There is no past in this country. It's like everyone's been programmed to forget everything. Who knows about the Rosenbergs? Ethel's brother worked at Los Alamos, passed stuff out to Julius, who passed it on to the Russians. Kind of minor stuff, but they electrocuted them, left two kids behind. Can you believe that? And people were in such a fever they applauded! 'The day they fried those Jews', that's what Alma called it, not that she's representative of people in this country. At least, I pray she isn't.

The whole civil-liberties issue is as important now as it was then. That's what the show was about. You may not get your security clearance revoked now, like they did to Oppenheimer, the man who ran Los Alamos, but the government's always watching you. If I'd lived then – I mean been grown-up then – I'd have had the government on my tail or the FBI or whatever. I was pretty involved with radical stuff when I was a student. Marched on Sacramento with César Chávez in '66. I'm proud of that. My name'll be in some dusty FBI file – 'Laurie Clow's Radical Past' probably on the cover of National Enquirer. I don't care. I don't have a security clearance to be taken away.

The weird thing is, I see pictures of Oppenheimer and get him confused with my dad. He was tall and thin too, legs like a stork. I certainly didn't inherit those genes. You always see Oppenheimer wearing a hat in pictures and my dad wore one too, so I think of him when I see Oppen-heimer. Now, I know that's crazy, but I've got nothing to connect my memories to, Alma saw to that. No photos of him, no papers, nothing. She destroyed them all. When we cleared out the house in Modesto there was zip. For such a terrible housekeeper, she was certainly thorough.

That's why I did the Alzheimer's show, got one of the biggest audience shares we've ever had. The letters we got! Thousands! It touched such a nerve in people. You know, what parents pass on to their kids is so important and that's what I was talking about, not the medical effect of Alzheimer's, though that's pretty terrible too, but how it destroys what I called the 'Legacy Gene'. I just came up with that phrase and already people are using it. There's something in people that wants to pass stuff on to the next generation – experience, wisdom, life lessons, call it what you want. And that's what Alzheimer's takes away, not just your own memories but the ability to pass them on. That's the harm it does. That's the killer.

I was kind of nervous about doing it, but I'm glad I did. Bringing on Alma, I mean. You could have heard a pin drop. Of course, we had doctors and Alzheimer's experts on the show, and I had a couple of families who talked about how they'd suffered, but I had to make it personal. That's what people love. That's why the show's so popular, I think, because I bring it all back to me.

At the end I just announced Alma, and Erica brought in the wheelchair. She'd had to be pretty heavily sedated – you never know what she's going to do. I didn't want her to launch into one of her tirades. But she was good as gold, just sat there staring into the audience with a blank face. It couldn't have worked out better. I knelt down by the wheelchair and said quietly, 'Alma, do you know where you are? You're on television.' Didn't react at all. Then I took her hand and said, 'If only you could share your past with me. I need what's in your head,' and I stroked her hair. I said, 'I know it's there, Alma, but it's like it's locked in one of those Swiss bank accounts and you've lost the combination.' By this time I was pretty cut up. You can imagine. I had to turn away from the cameras.

When we got Alma out of the studio the medication must have been wearing off because she began to shout and scream. Erica was wonderful.

Best carer we've had. The first ones when we moved to LA were terrible, couldn't cope with Alma at all. Erica was in control from day one. No nonsense. She's good with her but strong. Alma knows where she can go and where she can't. It's better now we keep the gate on the path up from the guesthouse locked. She can't fall over on the slope. You should get to know Erica. I hadn't realized how tough the Dutch were. Erica says it's from living below sea level with just those walls to stop the water flooding everywhere. Such a strong woman. That face. Like something from Mount Rushmore.

It's different for you. You've still got him, your dad. He's always there. Martha sees to that. She keeps his memory alive for you and Rachel. You wouldn't get her going around destroying things. And you've got the books. Oh, that's such a legacy for you, Luke, such a shining beacon, like those Olympic torches that the old Greeks passed from runner to runner. And you'll be able to hand them on to your children. You can hold up the books and say proudly, 'Look, this is me! I am Luke Hayseed. This was my father's legacy to me and this will be my legacy to you.'

Luke

Laurie did talk a lot but she didn't actually spew all that out in one long session. If she had, I'd have been asleep in about five minutes. I've put it together from the various conversations I had with her while I was in Los Angeles. Other people's pasts just aren't that interesting, so I've cut it down a lot to give the flavour.

With her show being on five days a week, and the never-ending planning needed for the upcoming ones, you'd think you'd want to wipe the old ones from your mind as soon as they'd gone out, but she talked about the Los Alamos show a lot. One evening she asked if I wanted to watch it. She had a VHS of it, but couldn't get her video-player to work and I thought I might be off the hook. In the end, she called through to the poolhouse and got Travis, who was living there for the summer, working as what she called her 'gofer', to come and set it up.

It was odd seeing Laurie on television. The surprise was how good she was. She was sort of just like herself but different at the same time. She certainly looked a lot better, which was probably the makeup, but she moved more fluidly too. At home she some-times limped a bit because she was having trouble with her knees, but on the set, despite her size, she seemed to glide around as if she was on castors, shoving microphones into people's faces and talking to the camera.

Actually, the show was surprisingly interesting. The first bit was some footage of Hiroshima and Nagasaki after they had been hit with those bombs. Then Laurie was in an old army truck with an open back, joggling around with a lot of old guys as they were being driven to Los Alamos where the first bombs had been built. They had all worked there and she was asking what they remembered, and then there was a lot of stuff of them walking round Los Alamos, interspersed with old photos of the place.

Then they were in the studio having a discussion about the rights and wrongs of building the bomb in the first place, and whether it was wrong to have doubts and if that made you subversive. It was all pretty theoretical. She talked about the power of the FBI to destroy people's lives, called it – of course – the 'Mr Toppit of our democratic system'. Big nervous laugh from everyone. Then she took her microphone into the audience and talked to some people who had FBI files and whether they had got access to them under the Freedom of Information Act. There was one guy, sitting in a corner with his face in shadow, who had been involved in some student revolutionary stuff and living under an assumed name for twenty years because the FBI were still after him.

Then she went back on to the stage and sat down. The lights dimmed and she was talking straight to the camera. 'Doing this show has been a journey for all of us,' she said, gesturing at the guys she had gone to Los Alamos with, 'a journey into a past that many people in this country would rather forget. I want to know and I want to remember. My father, Rudolph Laurence Clow, was one of the men who worked with Oppenheimer, and I spent some of my childhood in Los Alamos.' I realized she must have been storing this up: she hadn't mentioned it all through the show.

'My father wasn't a top guy like Oppenheimer, he was low-level, a technician, just another guy in overalls working in the lab. But they couldn't have done it without people like him. You know what? He had some doubts. Doubt isn't illegal in this country. Never was. Scepticism isn't a federal offence. I don't know what sort of trouble he got into, some kind of security issue, but they kicked him out, took away his clearance, like they did to Oppenheimer after the war. They removed my dad's right to work at what he did best. Last I remember, he was working in a photo lab developing people's vacation pictures. A man who helped in ending the war. That's not right. Can I find out what happened to him there? Can I get the FBI to show me his file? The wheels of bureaucracy grind pretty slow in Washington. What I do know is this: his life was destroyed. I don't know what pressure he was under, how ruthlessly the FBI pursued him. All I know is that he left us and I never saw him again, a man lost to time and history. One of the many, then and now. Thank you for taking this journey with me.' She stared at the camera for a moment, then bowed her head and the credits rolled.

She stopped the tape. 'I wish you could have known my dad,' she said.

'What happened to him? I mean, after.'

She shrugged her shoulders. 'Lost to time and history,' she repeated. I had a sneaking suspicion it wasn't entirely her own phrase.

'People can't just vanish.'

'This is a big country.'

'Maybe you should hire a private detective,' I said.

She threw back her head and laughed. 'You've seen too many movies.'

The buzz of the intercom made us jump. There were phones all over the place and you could call any part of the house. You could even call the garage. It was Erica, calling from the guesthouse at the other end of the garden where she lived with Alma.

Laurie picked up the phone. 'Tell her I can't come now,' she said. 'I'm with Luke. Tell her I'll see her in the morning. She should be asleep anyway.'

I glanced surreptitiously at my watch. It was only nine o'clock, but I'd already discovered in LA that people did things at strange times.

'Have you given her the diazepam? If her back's really painful try the Percodan . . . Yes, two. You coming up?' Laurie smiled. 'That would be great. See if you can find BJ and Marty.' They were Laurie's cats, two big fat long-haired Persians, who required a lot of grooming or they might drown under all their fur.

'Erica's going to come and do my knee,' Laurie said. 'She's like a healer. She approaches everything in a holistic way. You've no idea what poisons we have in our bodies, the crap doctors give you.'

Erica came in with a basket over her arm and BJ draped over her shoulders like a shawl. She was very tall and thin, her hair scraped back and held in a tight ponytail. Her face was all bone – cheekbones and jawbones and weird bones around the side of her head that moved behind her skin like ball bearings when she spoke. There was no fat on her: I had seen her play tennis and there were great cords of muscle on her legs and arms as if her body was operated by a pulley system.

As soon as Erica was in the room BJ jumped off her shoulders. 'Look!' she said. 'She needs her mother.' She spoke the kind of English that was so precise she had to be foreign, with just a tiny sibilance that pushed a word like 'needs' towards 'neadsh'. In fact, BJ didn't head anywhere near Laurie but scuttled under the sofa.

'Poor little girl,' Erica said. 'I think she might have met a coyote in the garden. Bad monsters! Marty's still out there, but she's a little toughie.' The thought was rather exciting: it seemed impossibly exotic to be somewhere where there might be proper wild animals, not just dull old squirrels or dormice, lurking around, ready to attack.

'Is Alma out for the count?' Laurie asked, and Erica did a little mime, putting her head on her shoulders, closing her eyes and letting her tongue loll out. Laurie hooted with laughter. Erica looked pleased. 'Now,' she said, putting the basket on the table, 'let us look at the patient. Your knee, please, madam.'

Laurie raised her leg on to a footstool in front of her chair and Erica knelt beside her. 'I have that nice lavender oil you're fond of, Laurie, or the bergamot. You choose. I think the skin absorbs the lavender better. It's a little lighter.' She turned to me. 'Now. What will Luke do during our little procedure?'

I could see the problem. Erica had rolled up Laurie's black trouser leg, which had hit the obstacle of her thigh where the material had bunched and come to a halt. The trousers would have to come off.

'Honey, why don't you go see what Travis is up to?' Laurie said.

'He might take you out for a drive. He's supposed to be looking after you.'

'Supposed to be looking after you' had a ring about it that I didn't entirely like, implying not only that I needed looking after but that someone had to be assigned to do it – but at Laurie's there were people to do everything.

Perhaps in England, if you were really grand, you might have butlers and chauffeurs and cooks, and gardeners to trim the edges of your lawn, but most people didn't. At Laurie's the drive was sometimes so full of the cars and trucks of those who had come to do things in the house and garden that the intercoms would be buzzing all the time because someone was needed to move their vehicle so that someone else could go out or in.

Jesus and Ronnie came every day to sort out the swimming-pool. They didn't speak much English. Lupe and her daughter, Consuela, were the housekeepers. They did the cleaning and cook-ing. They were there from about six in the morning, when Laurie was picked up by her driver, Stan, to go to the studio, and stayed until the early evening, leaving a lot of stuff in the fridge for dinner. On Fridays, when Laurie always had lots of people over for what she called 'family supper', even though none of them were family, they stayed later and served the food. They didn't speak much English either. Ruthie and Bob were a husband-and-wife gardening team, who came every morning and did the lawns, the plants and the watering, and had arguments with Jesus and Ronnie because the grass round the pool always had brown patches where they spilled the chemicals that went into the water.

Not everyone came in pairs. Angie, the cat person, managed to groom BJ and Marty on her own. She was English, doing cat stuff at the same time as trying to be an actress. I used to flee whenever she came because she was such a big fan of the books. The first time I'd met her, she'd got me to autograph a set of paperbacks, then forced Lupe to take some photos of me and her with BJ and Marty on our laps.

Kevin was Laurie's wardrobe supervisor, which meant he helped her choose her clothes. It seemed a strange job for a man. He turned up on Friday mornings in a van with lots of clothes rails and an assistant who wheeled them, clattering, into the house. Kevin seemed ageless, with an unlined face and dyed-blond hair, but he must have been quite old because he said he had been one of the dancers in the film of *West Side Story* and had once shared a house with George Chakiris, one of the stars. Laurie always seemed to dress in black so I didn't know why she needed so many clothes, but I suppose if you were on television in America it was like being in the Royal Family. You couldn't wear the same thing twice, even though it looked like the same thing. People who watched the show regularly could probably tell.

Travis was the only staff member, apart from Erica, of course, who lived in. He stayed in the poolhouse, in the small dark space behind the changing room. He had helped Laurie in the studio when she did her hospital radio show back in Modesto and she had brought him down for the summer. He did odd jobs for her and drove her around at weekends when Stan, her other driver, didn't work, but I suspect his real job was to look after me – actually rather a kind thought, given that Laurie was not there most of the time and that, because I'd failed my driving test, I would have been stuck in the house without him to take me places.

Then there were the programme people. Her show was on five days a week. She did each edition a week in advance and shot five over the first three days of the week. On Fridays, there was an all-day meeting at the house – that was when the driveway got really chaotic – to plan forthcoming shows. Probably fifteen people turned up, producers, executive producers, researchers, assistants, demographics and audience-research people, publicists and a variety of note-takers and secretaries. It was a really popular show – driving up Sunset Boulevard, I saw a giant poster for it with Laurie's face, heavily retouched, staring down. She was now so well known that she didn't even need a name: the caption simply said, 'She's the One!'

Of course, Rick Whitcomb was there too, but he was always

around. Because he was her manager, I suppose in the staff equation he was half programme and half personal. I'd thought only pop stars had managers, and Laurie laughed when I asked her why she needed one. 'Even managers have managers in this town. It goes with the territory. Martha must have endless agents and money guys and lawyers now, doesn't she?' Then she grimaced. 'I hope they're smarter than Rick.'

Despite that, she was curiously deferential to him. She seemed to enjoy letting him be man of the house. He was full of advice for everyone – advice that hovered precariously on the cliff edge of demand. 'You should think about tobacco plants under those palms, Ruthie, scent's so pretty in the evening,' or 'Tad too much chlorine in the pool today, Jesus. I'm smelling like a pharmacy,' or, after grabbing a reluctant Consuela round the waist and whispering, 'How's my best girl?' in her ear, 'Went a little heavy on the mayo in that chicken salad. Ladies got to watch their waistlines!' as he tapped his own, bulging uncomfortably over his too-tight jeans.

He was always boasting about the success of the management company he had set up since moving to LA with Laurie, but she told me that until a year before she had been his only client, and her show had opened the doors for him. It was true that he had expanded the company and taken on a few new clients, including, she laughed, a ventriloquist he was grooming for stardom. Laurie had turned down Rick's attempts to get him a spot on her show.

Erica and Laurie bitched about Rick endlessly, making fun of him, and particularly his comb-over hairdo. He had a little Mazda convertible, but their joke was that he never had the top down because it would muck up his hair. 'Top not down today, Rick? Such lovely sunny weather,' Erica would say, and catch Laurie's eye. According to Rick, Jerrilee was worried about skin cancer and didn't want him to have too much sun. Jerrilee and Merry were always over at the house as well although, unlike everyone else, they were not paid to be there. I think Jerrilee would have liked to change that. Maybe she could have been Laurie's stylist: 'Little too much blusher on the show yesterday. I'm not sure they're getting your eyes right either. More definition, I'd say. Glad to come in and talk to your makeup girls if you want.' Or her housekeeper: 'I couldn't help noticing your den, Laurie. Mine's the same. Mess, mess, mess. I'll come over on the weekend and help you clear it out if you want. No trouble.' Or maybe her clothes consultant: 'Your friend Kevin! Never understood why the gay boys think they know so much about our clothes. I saw some great stuff for fall at Barney's. I'm sure they'll let me bring it over if I say it's for you.' Behind Laurie's back she was less unctuously polite. One night in the kitchen I heard her whisper to Rick, 'For Christ's sake, talk to the producer about her clothes! She looked like a truck-driver in drag on the show the other day.'

The vice-like grip of Rick and Jerrilee together was hard to resist at the 'family supper' on Friday. He put himself at the head of the table while Jerrilee organized where everyone else sat. He opened the wine while Jerrilee liaised with Consuela and Lupe over serving the food. He said grace, or delegated it as if it were a special prize. I'd never been in a house where grace was said before a meal – we certainly never did it at home. At the first Friday supper I was at, I was already sitting down before I heard Rick give a little cough and realized they were all still on their feet.

'Thank you, Luke. Erica, perhaps you would like to say grace,' he said. They looked very solemn.

Erica cleared her throat and put her hands together. 'Creator, Earth Mother, we thank you for our lives and this beautiful day. Thank you for the bright sun we received today and the warm rain we received last night. Thank you for the opportunity to be together under your watchful care and for bringing the gift of Luke to us.' Everyone turned towards me and clapped. Laurie leaned over and kissed my cheek.

'That was really pretty, Erica,' Jerrilee said. 'Some kind of Dutch thing? Lutheran?'

'It's Hopi Indian,' Erica said curtly.

'Not sure about "Earth Mother",' Rick said. 'Dutch-woman-talk-with-forked-tongue.'

Jerrilee gave a little tinkle of laughter to indicate how charmingly curmudgeonly he was. 'Oh, *Ricky*!'

'I think it's neat,' Merry said.

'Did it rain last night?' said Travis, dreamily.

'It's a prayer, Travis, not a weather report,' Laurie said.

What did we talk about at those Friday-night suppers? A lot of stuff about the show, of course. It seemed to bear endless analysis from Laurie and Rick – the audience share, how many stations it was syndicated to, ideas for future shows. Rick would hold forth about his career plans for Laurie. 'You shouldn't dismiss endorsements. What you got to realize is that you're a brand. Now, that's a good thing, don't get me wrong, but a brand's got to *move*. It's a living thing, it's an animal, it's like a shark. Keep moving, dodge the bullets. That's line one, page one.'

'I don't think a shark is an animal, Rick,' Travis said. 'Isn't it, like, a mammal?'

I wasn't immune from his career advice either. 'Listen, I know those books have sold millions of copies. I mean, you're in the record books, son. You're a phenomenon. But what next? That's one thing I've learned – there's always got to be a next. Your brand needs some savvy management. You should put me in touch with your mother. She sounds like a smart lady. You know *Gone With the Wind*? The estate of Margaret Mitchell is going to commission a sequel. Maybe you should do that. You got a load of people wondering what happens when Mr Toppit comes out of that forest. More when the TV show airs. That's a lot of people with money to spend. Don't turn your back on them.'

Luckily, there was someone round the table who felt they could rise to the task of extending the *Hayseed* brand, improving it, even. Merry clapped her hands like a child given the present she had waited for all her life. 'Oh, I could do that! I know so much about the books.'

'Everybody knows a lot about the books, Merry,' Laurie said sharply.

'Merry's doing an English major,' Jerrilee informed us, with a little smile of pride.

'Merry, the books are what they are,' Laurie said firmly. 'Luke's dad was a very special person. Nobody could follow him.'

'Don't get me wrong. I have, like, total respect for his genius. But that's what I'd want to do – bring out his genius.'

'It's in the books already,' Laurie said coldly.

'But he died! He might have written more. Was he going to write more, Luke?'

'I don't know,' I said truthfully.

'Don't you want to know what happened next?'

'There's always got to be a next,' Rick said, nodding sagely, as if his statement of five minutes earlier had become a famous phrase or saying in the interim.

'And how would you do that, Merry, bring out his genius?' Laurie could hardly keep the contempt out of her voice.

'I've seen things in the books, hidden things.'

'Like what?'

Merry turned to me. 'You know that bit in the fourth book, *Garden Grown*, when you think Mr Toppit is chasing you through the Darkwood? When you get back to the house, you see that you've been cut all down your body by thorns and falling over and stuff? They're down your front, those wounds, aren't they?'

'It's not me, Merry,' I said.

'Do you think your dad ever did chakra healing?'

'I don't know what that is.'

'Well, I'm studying with this guy up in Topanga. It's a kind of healing energy. You use crystals and stones.'

Laurie sniggered. 'I don't think chakra healing has reached England yet.'

Merry ignored her. 'Those wounds sort of correspond with the seven chakras – um, the crown, the brow, the throat, the heart, the solar plexus . . . I can't remember the other two. You know, maybe Mr Toppit is a kind of healer with a split personality that makes him bad sometimes. Like Lucifer being an angel before he became Satan. There's so much you could bring out if there were more books.'

Travis cleared his throat. 'Well, the lady who wrote *Gone With the Wind*, she ended it with Scarlett O'Hara saying that tomorrow-always-comes-around thing. Maybe she wrote it like that because she wanted everyone to wonder what happened the next day. That's why they're doing a sequel.'

'It's a different book, Travis,' Laurie said crossly. '*The Hayseed Chronicles* do not end with Mr Toppit saying, "Tomorrow is another day."'

'I love *Gone With the Wind*,' Jerrilee said, to nobody in particular. 'Always makes me cry.'

'But wouldn't that be cool?' Travis said. 'To know what happens to Mr Toppit? Wow! Imagine him in the real world. Maybe he has superpowers.'

Then Laurie did something quite mean: she shunted her anger at Merry on to the hapless Travis. Her voice was trembling. 'Travis, just think for once before opening your mouth. This is really difficult for Luke. His dad passed away not so long ago. Can you imagine how he feels, you discussing it round the table?' She probably felt she could be rude to him because he was staff but five years seemed quite a lot more than 'not so long ago' and, any-way, we weren't really discussing Arthur's death. Nonetheless, her eyes brimming with tears, Laurie put out her hand and squeezed my arm. Everyone looked at me.

'It must still be so raw,' Erica said.

Rick nodded. 'Big thing to deal with.'

'Hard, seeing him everywhere in bookshops,' Jerrilee added.

Thank you, Laurie. Now the entire table was waiting for me to say something.

'Is there any more meatloaf?' was the best I could come up with. In unison a sickly how-can-he-be-so-brave? expression settled on their faces.

'Yes, life goes on, doesn't it, son? That's painful too,' Rick said.

★

Because of jet-lag I woke up early, sometimes early enough to say goodbye to Laurie when her driver came to pick her up at six o'clock. She would have some high-energy drink thing that Consuela had left in the fridge for her to blend, and I would have a bowl of cereal. BJ and Marty would slink round our legs as we sat at the breakfast bar in the kitchen. Sometimes, if Alma had woken early too, there would be a squawk through the intercom as she shouted for Laurie angrily and, with a graceful little movement as if she was wiping away a speck of dust, Laurie would flick the speaker switch off and continue what she had been saying.

Laurie was gentler in the mornings before she had to put on the tough show persona that lasted well into the evenings. Fresh from sleep she was rather sentimental and would say things to me that sounded like country-and-western song titles, the ones that have brackets in them: 'Without You (I Don't Know Where I'd Be Today)' or 'If I'd Known That This Was Home (I'd Have Come Here Long Ago)'.

Often she would hold my hand, which made eating my cereal rather awkward – often by the time I got to it it had gone soggy. Then Stan, her driver, would be ringing the doorbell and there would be a flurry of picking up pieces of paper and research stuff, looking for her reading glasses, and then she would be off, dressed in black, in her shiny black limo with Stan, who happened to be black, too.

Then I was on my own for a while before the day got going for everyone else. I liked the silence or, rather, the sounds that broke it: the hoses in the garden, which were set on timers, the tropical birdsong and the whir of the giant fridge in the kitchen. It would be a couple of hours before Travis was up. I would know because I could hear him practising his guitar – mostly the chords from 'Layla', reverb-y and distorted through the primitive speaker system he had set up. When I got to the poolhouse, Merry was sometimes there – she could get to it through the garden without coming into the house – and we would do a ritual of bear-hugs and hand-slapping as if we hadn't seen each other for decades.

Merry had lived in Modesto all her life so she was almost as much of a stranger in Los Angeles as I was. Travis had spent some of his childhood there before his father had moved to the hospital in Modesto so that made him the expert, even though he seemed incapable of going anywhere without getting lost. He kept saying he wanted to show us what he called 'secret LA'. Actually, I wouldn't have minded doing some of the touristy things, like the Universal Studios tour or Disneyland, but they did not seem to be on Travis's agenda. We spent most of one afternoon trying to get to the Hollywood sign – not exactly what I would call secret as there was almost nowhere in LA that you couldn't see it from – but it proved elusive: streets that seemed to be heading towards it petered out into dirt tracks, while others twisted and turned with the sign above us vanishing and reappearing behind the hills leaving us far over to the right or left of it as if the sign itself had moved instead of us.

In fact, many things proved elusive for Travis. The house where the Charles Manson murders had taken place, way up on a street called Cielo Drive, was lost to us as well: Travis couldn't remember the number but thought he would recognize it from a photograph he had once seen. That wasn't the only confusion: he seemed unsure whether it was Sharon Tate or Sharon Stone who had been among the victims, until Merry corrected him. After we had driven high up into the hills for several hours, peeking unsuccessfully into driveways, he decided it had probably been demolished out of respect to the people who had died.

Several times a week, Merry went to have her chakra healing lessons. Travis went with her but I couldn't tell whether he was just driving her there or having the lessons too. Her teacher was called Wade and he lived at the top of Topanga Canyon. Apparently Wade was longing to meet me, thought the books were the 'most awesome things' he'd ever read and had 'total respect for their philosophy', but he also seemed rather shy so it was always the next time that I would be taken to visit him.

When they came back they were fired up with excitement and – after the usual bear-hugs and hand-slapping – we sometimes drove up the coast to a place called Paradise Cove where there was an old-fashioned shack-like restaurant. There, we had beer and hamburgers, then walked up the beach to go swimming. If you went far enough it was almost deserted, and if there was absolutely nobody around, Travis and Merry would skinny-dip. I tried hard to avoid having to do it too. Showers at school were bad enough but it was just about okay there because everyone felt embarrassed. A beach in California, well, that was different.

Merry and Travis seemed totally casual about it and they had brown, easy bodies, as if they'd been hewn from a single piece of wood that had been carved and sanded and oiled to smooth perfection. I had to pretend that I didn't feel like swimming – I couldn't go in wearing trunks when they weren't. I had a stomach ache, I didn't like swimming after a meal, I was worried about cramp, I didn't want to get sunburned. How many excuses could you come up with? Finally, after we'd been to Paradise Cove three or four times, Travis said, 'Hey, bro, you're not shy, are you? Nothing to be frightened of,' and Merry giggled, and so, as if I didn't have a care in the world, I peeled off my trunks and ran, with my white, uneasy body, which had been bolted together from various scrawny bits of driftwood, as fast as I could into the surf, hoping that nothing shrank in the cold water.

What we did in the days and evenings when Laurie wasn't around remained between us, became a secret for no particular reason other than maybe it was more fun that way. When Laurie asked what I had been up to, the cover-up you do when talking to a parent kicked in like a reflex: 'Oh, you know, we drove to the beach, then went to Century City and had Thai in the food mall.' If Travis was with us when she asked, there might be the tiniest eye-contact between us, a telepathic agreement not to mention skinny-dipping or the margaritas Travis had made in the poolhouse with the limes and tequila we had taken from the store cupboard, or that either the little baby monster from *Alien* had been burrowing in Travis's jeans when we went to see *Big* at Grauman's Chinese Theater or Merry's hand was.

On Friday nights, a different Merry would arrive with her parents, more of a high-school cheer-leader, wearing a little light makeup, her long blonde hair tied demurely into a ponytail, and a short, powder-blue dress that made her look about fourteen. She would give Travis and me a sophisticated both-sides peck on the cheek and was ready to discuss with bright-eyed eagerness the shows Laurie had done that week or how the rehearsals were going for the amateur musical Rick and Jerrilee were starting rehearsals for.

'You're going to come to the opening, aren't you, Laurie?' Rick said. 'You know how much it would mean to us.'

They had obviously been through this before. 'Oh, Rick, you don't want me there,' she said disingenuously. 'It'll turn into a circus. It's about you two, you and Jerrilee, and the show.'

'You should invite your ventriloquist to the opening,' Erica said. 'That would get you some publicity. What is he – Puerto Rican?' A little flicker of eye movement passed between Erica and Laurie.

'You're making fun of me, Erica. You maybe don't have ventriloquists in Europe but they're part of our vaudeville tradition over here. He's called Johnny Del Guardo, and he's going to be big. You wait.'

'What play are you doing?' I asked.

'Last year we did *Hello Dolly*,' Jerrilee said. 'Back in Modesto we did everything – *Finian's Rainbow*, *Oliver*, *Man of La Mancha*, *Grease* . . .'

'You name it,' Rick said.

'You were so great as Sandy,' Merry said.

'Isn't Sandy, like, a teenager?' Travis said.

'We tend to cast by voice,' Jerrilee said primly. 'It's about the music. We're doing *Camelot* this year.'

'But it must be so time-consuming,' Erica said. 'How do you fit it all in with the management company, the clients?'

'You always find time for your passions, don't you, Erica? Like your tennis,' Jerrilee said. 'Actually, it's been tough this year. In Modesto, people stood in line to be in the shows. They don't seem to get it here. Still haven't cast some of the parts.'

'I expect people who work hard just don't have the time,' Erica said.

Rick gave a manly chortle. 'If only we could get Mr Jerry Herman to do us a musical version of *The Diary of Anne Frank* we might even get you on stage, Erica.'

Erica ignored this. 'It's what I like about LA,' she said. 'People have such a strong work ethic here. It reminds me of home.'

Jerrilee gave her tinkling laugh and put her hand on Erica's arm. 'Oh, Erica, only you would get the similarity between LA and – where is it you're from? Utrecht?'

'What's the show about?' Travis asked.

'It's the love story of King Arthur and Queen Guinevere.'

Travis looked blank. 'Like Charles and Diana?'

'Not exactly, Travis,' Jerrilee said. 'It's set in medieval times, like in the Dark Ages.'

'And who will you be playing, Jerrilee?' Erica asked innocently.

'Look at her!' Rick said. 'Doesn't she look like a queen?'

'Will you be wearing a wimple?' Erica said.

Jerrilee was momentarily shocked. 'A *what*?' She seemed to think it was a dirty word.

'You know, it's a kind of hood. The women wore them on their heads then,' Erica said.

'Actually, we're keeping the costumes real simple,' Rick said. 'Everyone's going to wear a canvas shift with a leather belt round the middle. They didn't have fancy clothes in those days. Jerrilee and I'll have crowns to make us stand out from the rest because we're royal.'

Jerrilee had been helping Consuela take the plates off the table and shouted from the kitchen, 'You ever acted, Luke?'

'Only in school plays. I was one of the witches in *Macbeth* and I was Reverend Parris in *The Crucible*.'

'I bet you were good,' Laurie said. 'So tall.'

Suddenly Jerrilee was back in the room, a dishcloth in her hand, her eyes shining. 'Rick! He should do the show!'

Rick seemed confused.

'Mordred!' Jerrilee squealed. 'Mordred!'

There was a silence while this sank in. 'You can sing, can't you?' Rick said.

'Not really,' I said. 'I can't –'

'That's okay,' Jerrilee butted in. She turned to Rick. 'He's only got one song. He could speak it, like Rex Harrison.'

'Hold on, Luke doesn't want to be in a play. This is his vacation,' Laurie said.

'No, no, no,' Rick said, cutting across her. 'This is so great. We haven't cast Mordred yet.'

'Who's Mordred?' Travis asked.

'The story's kind of complicated,' Rick said. 'King Arthur has this weird sister called Morgan Le Fay. She might be his half-sister or step-sister or something, but that's not the point. Way before the story starts Morgan Le Fay casts some kind of spell on him and they have a baby together called Mordred.'

'This is absurd, Rick,' Laurie said. 'You can't be serious.'

'He sleeps with his sister?' Travis said.

'It's incest,' Erica said.

'This was before they had laws,' Rick said. 'That's why King Arthur invented the round table. Anyway, this Mordred stirs everything up. He gets Morgan Le Fay to put King Arthur behind an invisible wall, so Queen Guinevere and Lancelot think they're alone and get discovered in bed together.'

'You're putting this show on in Sherman Oaks?' Erica said incredulously.

'It's a famous show. It's a great part for you, Luke.'

'I want you to stop this,' Laurie said.

'I think it sounds cool,' Travis said.

'Will you shut up?' Laurie snapped at him.

'This is a big chance for Luke,' Rick said.

'A big chance? He's not looking for a big chance,' Laurie hissed.

'For God's sake! Some amateur show in a dump on Ventura Boulevard?'

'The Whiteside Theater is quite an upscale place,' Rick said, wounded.

'He doesn't want to be an *actor*,' Laurie snarled. 'He's going to be a writer.'

That was the first I'd heard of it.

'What do you think, Luke?' Jerrilee asked.

'Don't ask him,' Laurie almost shouted. 'He doesn't want to do it.'

'If we can get Jerrilee's hair-colourist to do Lancelot – he sings in a gay men's choir, great voice – we've got everyone cast. We're rehearsing next week. "Luke Hayseed as Mordred" – might even get a TV crew at the opening.'

'It's like it's meant to be,' Merry said excitedly. 'Your dad was called Arthur and you'd be playing King Arthur's son.'

'You're royal blood, you're the king's son. You could wear a crown, too. Just you and Rick and me. The others won't have them,' Jerrilee said.

'Yeah, you'd be playing my son,' Rick said.

It happened very slowly or very fast, I couldn't tell which. I think the first thing was the bottle going over and the wine chugging out across the tablecloth. Normally somebody would have righted it and put a napkin, or maybe salt, on the stain, but before that could happen Laurie was on her feet. There were blotches on her face and her eyes had constricted into little slits. She looked like a Halloween pumpkin.

Rick was on the other side of the table but she seemed to be there in a second. It was as if she was trying to clamber on to him, like she wanted a piggy-back. *'Don't you dare! Don't you dare!'* she kept shouting. Marty and BJ, who had been sitting under the table, scuttled out of the room.

'Laurie! Be careful of your knee!' Erica screamed, and she was on her feet, too.

'You don't know what you're talking about,' Laurie was

shouting at Rick. 'Luke has a father – he's got a father you couldn't even imagine with your small-town mind!'

Jerrilee's mouth was hanging open. Merry had begun to cry. I was amazed by Erica's strength. She was about a quarter of Laurie's size but she was holding her round the middle and dragging her backwards.

'Luke has something inside him you wouldn't be able to understand if it was spelled out for you on a billboard in Times Square! You could no more be his father than build an atomic bomb!'

The last we saw of Laurie was her feet as Erica dragged her round the corner into the kitchen. Then a door slammed and it was quiet.

'She's kind of upset,' Travis said, to nobody in particular.

'She can't talk to you like that, Rick,' Jerrilee said. 'I won't put up with it. Not after what you've done for her.'

Rick was smoothing his hair back into place. He looked a bit shaken but was philosophic. 'It's been a tough week. The ratings aren't so great. Lot of pressure.'

'It's her,' Jerrilee said. 'It's Erica. She's poisoned Laurie. Never been the same since she arrived. She's just the help. She shouldn't even be eating with us.'

'So, are you going to do the show?' Travis asked me.

'I don't think so, Travis. Anyway I'd be really bad.'

Travis turned to Rick. 'Maybe I could play the part. I sing. You've heard me sing.'

'Wrong kind of voice, son,' Rick said.

Maybe we'd all had a lot to drink. My head was spinning by the time I got to bed. I think I fell asleep really quickly but I seemed to be awake again in minutes. It was two o'clock. Through the window I could see a dim light on in the poolhouse. I walked through the garden in bare feet and knocked on the door. 'Travis? Are you still up?'

There was a scuffling from behind the door, then Travis was peering out. 'Hey, bro, what's happening?'

'I can't sleep.'

Merry's voice came from inside the room. 'Let him in, Travis.' That was surprising because I'd said goodbye to Rick, Jerrilee and Merry hours ago. 'I came back,' she said, then pulled me into the room and, as usual, we all had to hug. I felt a bit awkward. I was still in the boxer shorts and T-shirt I had gone to bed in.

There was only a desk light on so the room was filled with shadows. A bottle of tequila stood on the table.

'Some night,' Travis said.

'We were saying maybe she's going crazy, like that weird mother of hers. Like it's in her genes. You want a drink?'

'Why not?' I said. It had been such a strange evening that it seemed like quite a good idea.

She showed me how they had been drinking the tequila. You put some salt on the back of your hand, licked it off, took a big swig, then sucked a lime quarter. Its sharpness made me shiver as the tequila went down.

'She was so mean to my dad,' Merry said. 'She wouldn't have a career if it wasn't for him. And us, I guess. When she was reading the books on the hospital radio, my mom was having surgery and we really got into them. It was us that got Dad to let her read them on KCIF. She should be grateful.'

'I helped her at Holy Spirit. That first time she read them I was the one who told her how great they were,' Travis said.

'Nobody *heard* them at the hospital, Trav.'

'Your mom did. You did.'

'Yes, but it was just a few people. Half of them are probably dead. It's a hospital. It needed someone to give it a proper audience, like a national audience. Dad did that.'

'KCIF isn't national. It's a local station.'

'Well, I organized that *Hayseed* float on the Fourth of July. Everyone saw it.'

'Everyone in Modesto. That doesn't make it national.'

Travis and Merry went on like this for a while, neither listening to what the other was saying. Then, without any apparent pause for breath, they seemed to be talking about which was the best Beatles song.

'"A Day In The Life",' Travis said. 'Obviously.'

'You're full of shit!'

'I mean technically. Those chord changes.'

'What do you know about technical?'

'Okay – so what's better than that? "Octopus's Garden"?' Travis said disdainfully. 'Please!'

'"Hey Jude".'

'Oh, come on!'

'I organized a candlelight vigil in the school gym when John Lennon was shot and we sang it.'

'Lennon didn't even write it! He didn't have anything to do with it! That was McCartney. Everyone knows that. There's some contractual thing . . . they both get credited but –'

'He did too!'

'They weren't even speaking by then. He was with Yoko.'

'Ask Luke.' They turned to me.

'I like "Norwegian Wood".'

'That's cool,' Travis said. 'I mean, it's kind of an early song but it is pretty good.'

'We need some more chakra,' Merry said, and they burst out laughing.

'You need some healing, bro,' Travis said.

'You've done this before?' Merry asked, as Travis undid the package and began chopping up the white powder with a razor blade.

'Yes,' I said, lying without a moment's hesitation. 'My sister and I do it all the time.'

Travis's tongue was curled up round his lip, like a child concentrating. 'Ladies first,' he said, when he had finished, and three lines were ready on the table. I was glad I didn't have to go first so I had some kind of guide, but I soon realized that all those movie jokes about people sneezing were just silly. It wasn't difficult at all.

'You're going to love Wade,' Merry said, for about the hundredth time since I'd been in Los Angeles. 'He's so spiritual. Dealing's just a sideline. He's not even that into drugs but he needs the money. He only teaches a few people, just people he can see into. He could be a really famous teacher, but he's just not into the fame thing.'

I wasn't listening to what she was saying. I was trying to concentrate. Of course, nothing happened instantly. I'd had quite a lot of wine at dinner and then there had been the tequila so I knew I was a bit drunk, but the odd thing was that gradually my head cleared. When you're drunk you get a bit sluggish but suddenly the blood was moving round my body more efficiently. In a while I could feel every pulse inside me working in unison, like those oilfields you see with the pumps going up and down like crazy.

The next time round we combined it with tequila. Slug of drink, lick of salt, suck lime, snort line. Merry did it quickest. I don't know who suggested going into the pool then, but it seemed such an obvious thing to do. It was pretty dark outside and we thought it best not to turn on the lights because the house wasn't that far away. There was a light mist coming off the water, not because it was cold but because it was actually warmer than the air. It felt amazing, getting in. I didn't worry for a second about not having any trunks. I had just slipped off my boxer shorts without thinking, as if it was the most natural thing in the world. Anyway, it was dark and nobody could really see.

Merry and Travis swam silently under water, and because it was dark I couldn't tell where they were. They brushed past me, against my legs and body, the feel of them rough compared to the smoothness of the water. I lay on my back and watched the stars. I knew they were beneath me even though there was no noise except when one broke the surface of the water. Nobody would have known we were there. It was another of our secrets. It was only when I got out of the pool that I saw we hadn't been completely unobserved. Marty and BJ were sitting by the door of the poolhouse, watching us. They had probably been there all the time.

Merry might have been crying when she came out of the water or it might have been when we got inside while Travis was sorting out the lines and cutting up another lime for the tequila but she kept saying it was only because she was so happy. Of course, it was colder when we got out of the pool but we wrapped ourselves in towels and sat on Travis's bed. What she was so happy about, she kept saying while she was crying, was that she had read the books and had realized that while they were about me they were also about her. Travis was there for some of what she was saying but then he didn't seem to be. She knew who Mr Toppit was, she was saying, not who he was, like being a person you could recognize if you saw him in the street, but who he was if he was in your family. I wasn't really concentrating because I was trying to sort out the things I needed to tell her. To be honest, I wasn't feeling so clear-headed now. The pulses that had been pounding in unison now seemed out of synch, operating at different levels and frequencies.

What she was crying about was that she knew Mr Toppit was Rick, and reading the books reminded her of when she was a child and of what he had been like with her then. She forgave him, she kept saying. She loved him, she would always love him, but he shouldn't have been like that. He shouldn't have lost his temper. He shouldn't have shouted all the time. She remembered the bruises on her arm. It had been worse for Jerrilee. She remembered Jerrilee screaming in a corner with blood on her face. She could forgive him now. That was why she was happy, even though she was crying. Wade had helped her. The chakra healing had made it come to the surface. That was the cool thing about it: it revealed things but it made them heal too.

Then she wasn't crying any more, which I was quite glad about, but the vital thing I wanted to tell her seemed to have gone from my mind, but by then she had cupped my balls in her hand and was licking the end of my prick and when I was putting it inside her it felt like getting into the swimming-pool all over again, not her wetness but the incredible warmth, not just of her cunt but her whole body. The pulses seemed to have sorted themselves out and were now back in unison. Everything was working. It wasn't difficult at all.

'Go on,' she kept saying, 'go on,' and there was a moment when I thought she wasn't talking to me but to Travis, who was sitting on the floor in the far corner of the room moving his hand up and down his prick, his tongue curling up round his lip, the same grim concentration on his face as when he was chopping the drug. Maybe he had been there all the time, or maybe he had just sneaked in. Anyway, what did it matter who she was talking to? I was the one inside her.

'Go on, go on, go on,' she repeated, over and over again, but this time she was whispering it, her face right up against mine, her mouth by my ear, and I thought she was probably talking to herself by this stage, but I knew she was talking to me when she was kissing me and she was saying, 'Go on, go on, go on, fill me with your hayseed.'

Rachel

Dear Luke,

*I'm missing you. Claude is, too. We imagine you sitting by the pool
(I presume she has one) at Laurie's swanky house, drinking neon-coloured
cocktails with little parasols in them. Claude says that the last great
contribution to culture made by America was the martini and it's been
downhill all the way. I hope you're not wearing a Hawaiian shirt, and if
you are, make sure it isn't turquoise. Not a good colour with our porridgy
Hayman complexions.*

*You left a lot of chaos behind when you flew off! Let's not even talk
about the hangovers. There was a horrible (sorry!) photograph of you in
the Daily Mail. Where do they find these things? Don't worry, it was only
on page five. You looked like someone on day release from a loony-bin.
Like Martha says about you, 'Neck like a chicken, arms like a gorilla.'
Why are we so unphotogenic? You look much better in real life now your
spots have cleared up. Ha ha.*

*We were all quite jealous. It wasn't just you who got the police
caution! Claude would have loved his photo in the papers, even with his
bad teeth. So would Mr Poontang. Actors like any kind of publicity.
Anyway, the good thing is that Martha is furious, so that's a result. What
a fuss! It's only a caution. We're not going to be hauled in front of some
hanging judge and publicly flogged, which, of course, is what Martha
would like. Not that I've spoken to her for the simple reason that she isn't
speaking to me. Tant pis. I've had – and I expect you will find it waiting
when you get back – a letter from Fräulein Löwenstein. Apoplectic, or
whatever it is in German. Apoplechtische? What an old bag. Why
doesn't she mind her own business? 'I hope you won't mind me being
honest with you, my dear, but I look on you and Luke as family . . . blah,
blah.' We have let Martha down. She who has been so loving and kind.
She who has proudly been the figurehead of the good ship Hayseed. She,*

who has taught us standards we have chosen to ignore. For fuck's sake! I feel like writing back and telling her we're talking about the she who cleared out Arthur's stuff and put it on a fucking bonfire, probably destroying in the process many original Lilagraphs that could have found their way on to the walls of what the Krauts call a Kunst Museum, with the emphasis on Kunst.

I miss you. Did I say that already? Claude isn't much fun at the moment. Endless rows with his grandfather over money. The old man twigged he'd only had his front teeth done and not used the money to repair all of them so he's cut off Claude's allowance. Apparently he practically had his hand in Claude's mouth examining his teeth as if he was a horse! I'm broke too. No point asking Martha for money. I talked to Graham about writing a biography of Arthur and he said he'd think about it. Then he said he thought it was a good idea but maybe someone 'more academic' should do it! We had a row because I said he was just stealing my idea. Anyway, I'm going to work on him and shame him into letting me do it (and giving me a fat advance).

Claude and I are meant to be meeting Toby Luttrell tonight after they finish shooting. Claude is slavering with excitement. That producer, Jake, was on the phone asking if he could come as well, but Toby said under no circumstances. Apparently they all hate him and think he's completely useless. Got to change now, though it'll take much longer to help Claude sort out his outfit. I'll go on with this later.

I wouldn't put much on today being a great filming day on the Hayseed set. Toby's just left, called his driver and told him to pick him up here instead of at home. Late night. Claude's just gone to bed and is snoring for England. Toby turned up with his makeup still on, which is one way of dealing with spots. Claude cooked one of his Thai things (again) and then sulked because nobody was very hungry. Now I can't sleep. I expect Jake will accuse us of leading Toby astray. No leading needed, believe me. He's got very bad breath. The difference between us and them is that we look after our teeth. Oh, my God! That wasn't me talking, it was Martha! Don't you find that? She's so ingrained in me that I find myself thinking her thoughts even when I know they're complete bollocks. All those ridiculous life lessons of hers keep invading my head. Only the intellectually inferior have 'amusing' books next to the loo. It's vulgar to serve a choice of puddings at dinner. 'Silent Night' is not a proper carol and must never be sung at Christmas. Only idle minds have time to listen to the radio. And the real killer – that thing she's always quoting from Goethe or Rilke or whoever it is, 'Everything serious is difficult . . .' and then she gives that awful pause and says, like it's a punchline: '. . . and nearly everything is serious.' God! No wonder we're so fucked up.

I wish you were here even though I know I wouldn't get much out of you. I wish you were here now so I could talk to you and not have to listen to Claude snoring. I was hoping Toby would be like you, like a better version of you. Sorry, not better, but more sort of lifelike, like one of those super-real oil paintings – except he doesn't look anything like you. That hair. That yellow – like a colour that doesn't exist in nature. Give me your mouse shade any day. And, of course, he's the size of a toothpick. He kept nipping off to what he called 'the toilet' (sorry! Martha again) as if we didn't know what he was doing. Anyway, what did we care? Claude had got us a little party-bag (I know you disapprove but, honestly, we needed to cheer ourselves up) so we had some every time he went to the loo, which seemed to be most of the time. In the end, like the good hosts we are, we came clean and pooled it. Then Claude made a bit of an idiot of himself. Why can't he keep his mouth shut? Even though Toby is clearly game for anything, it was a bit much even for him. A little goes a long way – and luckily he is little.

Why doesn't Arthur invade our heads? Why is it just Martha? What happened to his life lessons? I can't even think what they could be. Can you? Spend as little time with your family as possible? Lock yourself away in your study? Was he so unhappy? Did we make him unhappy? Do you remember sitting with Martha and Arthur years ago in their bedroom one summer and the window was open and there was a loud bang, some noise from the woods, and Martha said, 'What was that?' and Arthur said gloomily, 'Maybe someone's shot themselves'? Even Martha was amazed.

Sometimes I think he threw himself in front of that concrete truck, like Anna Karenina. Just thought he couldn't go on. Maybe that gloomy, withdrawn thing is his life lesson. Maybe that's what's inside us and we dwell on Martha's ridiculous ones because it's easier. Wouldn't you like to be a cat or dog and not feel much, just respond to simple physical stuff, like it's either hot or cold or you're hungry or not hungry? I don't understand you. I never know what you're reacting to, what's going on in your head. You're like Arthur. You hold it all in. I suppose that's a defence, but I don't know against what. What happens to people? There aren't any cigarettes. I'm going out to see if one of those early-bird paper shops is open. I wish you were here. I might post this. Or I might not.

    Love, Rachel xxxx

Luke

Travis didn't really want to go and, to be honest, neither did I, but Laurie had organized it and presented it to us like a big treat so we had to try to look enthusiastic. I couldn't get there unless Travis drove so he had to come. Anyway, we didn't have anything else to do. Merry seemed to have stopped coming over so Travis spent a lot of time in the poolhouse working on his songs, or just moping.

Laurie had seen a piece about it in the listings section of the *LA Times* and had got tickets for us: 'Film Legend's 75th Birthday – BAFTA Tribute'. BAFTA was some British film organization and they were going to show a movie called *The House on the Hill*, which Wally Carter had made in 1946, with him doing a Q and A session afterwards. They called him Wallace Carter, of course. Rachel and Claude would have loved it, except they would have probably seen it already. 'It's going to be in black-and-white,' Travis said gloomily as we were driving there. 'I hate that. Why did they make films in black-and-white? You can't believe something if it isn't in colour.'

Even though Wally Carter was quite a famous director – he had won a couple of Oscars – you wouldn't have thought many people would turn out on a Sunday night to see an obscure film he had made years ago but, in fact, the place was pretty crowded. As we were heading towards the bar I realized, not surprisingly, that a lot of people were British and most of them fairly ancient. I sometimes felt out of place in LA and it was odd now to see Travis looking as if he'd come from another planet with his pink T-shirt saying, *You Know You Want It – You Just Don't Know How To Ask*, cargo shorts and long blond hair tied back in a ponytail. We must have been the youngest people there by about twenty years. While we were waiting to get a drink, I listened to two men next to us talking.

'It's going straight to video. Big market now. Huge. What happened to your thing?'

'Amblin said they were really keen. Never heard from them since.'

'Didn't you have something at Disney?'

'They're cunts at Disney.'

'You know Puttnam gave Wally a deal at Columbia?'

'Unbelievable. He falls out with Ray Stark but he wants a film from Wally?'

'The last one was so bad I'm amazed they released it.'

'Was that after his stroke?'

'He has a stroke and he *still* goes on working.'

'Didn't his girlfriend write it?'

'I hear she's good with her hands.' They roared with laughter.

'What happened to his wife?'

'Which wife?'

'Wasn't she a lezzer?'

'What was that awful ocean-liner film of his? Talking of going down.'

'*Neptune.*'

'Made a fortune, of course.'

'Lucky bastard. I never liked him.'

Travis and I headed into the auditorium so we could get a seat near the front. It filled up really quickly and then the lights dimmed a little. There was a microphone on stage and a middle-aged woman climbed the steps to a lot of clapping. She was rather nervous and, with her plummy English accent, might have been happier announcing the winner of the best chutney at the village fête.

'Our honouree tonight can honestly be described as a legend. He sometimes jokes that he's the oldest working film director in Hollywood, and he's about to enter his sixth decade in the industry with many projects in development. Today we celebrate his seventy-fifth birthday and we're proud to show his first feature, *The House on the Hill*, which he made in 1946. It's based on Dickens's novel *Bleak House*, but the distributors, Rank, insisted on a title change because, for a depressed post-war Britain, the original title sounded too, well, *bleak*.' She was pleased with her joke and a titter ran through the audience.

'Actors always queued up to work with Wally. Margaret Lockwood stars as Lady Dedlock with the young Jean Simmons as Esther Summerson, and the extraordinary Alastair Sim as John Jarndyce. As an interesting footnote, you might notice a small credit for Additional Dialogue going to Arthur Hayman who, many years later, became famous as the author of the *Hayseed* books.'

Travis gave a great surfer's whoop. 'You didn't tell me, bro!'

Everyone turned to see where the noise had come from.

'I didn't know,' I whispered, and sank down in my seat. Luckily she had finished her speech and the film began. I had done the book for A-level English so I knew the story pretty well, even though they had cut masses out and changed lots of things. Travis had difficulty following it and talked almost from the opening frames.

'That looks so fake,' he whispered, when we first saw Bleak House. 'It's got to be a model.' Then, 'Why's she got such bad skin?' when Esther Summerson appeared.

'She had smallpox,' I whispered.

'What's that? Like an acne thing?'

'It's a disease.'

'Why has that lady got a big black spot on her face?'

'It's a beauty spot.'

Travis went on and on. 'The old guy with the bad teeth, he's, like, a lawyer, right?' and 'I don't get whose daughter she is' and 'Are they, like, suing them? Why don't they settle out of court?'

Finally, the man in the row in front of us turned round and said loudly, 'Will you please shut up?' For the last half-hour Travis stayed silent even though he did a lot of shifting in his seat.

When the lights came up at the end there was a big round of applause.

Travis said, 'Man, that was the worst movie I've ever seen,' then added hastily, 'I mean, I'm sure your dad did great work.'

The woman was back on stage now and someone was bringing some chairs on. 'Where are you, Wally?' she called.

A spotlight ranged round the audience in a random way, then came to rest in the front row. A cheer went up as a small, balding old man got rather hesitantly to his feet. He looked nothing like Graham. Dressed in a tweed jacket with a Viyella shirt and a knitted tie, he was more like a retired bank manager than a famous Hollywood director, except for the huge pair of square black spectacles that dwarfed his face. Then, to more cheers, he did a creaky *Rocky*-style victory punch with his arms over his head.

A young Japanese girl, who was sitting next to him, helped him to the stage with an arm through his while he leaned on a stick with the other. It seemed to take a very long time. There were three chairs on stage now, and the woman who had introduced him gave him a big hug, then helped him to sit down and adjusted a microphone in front of him. The Japanese girl sat next to him and held his hand.

The woman said, 'Many happy returns, Wally. Tell us how you came to make *The House on the Hill*.'

He said something incomprehensible, and the woman moved the microphone closer to him. He cleared his throat and started again, in a rather hesitant, slurred voice. 'They said, "The British are coming," but I was here before the lot of them.' Round of applause.

The woman looked rather confused, but decided to move on. 'What's next for you, Wally?'

I think his stroke must have been quite bad, because he appeared to have drifted off somewhere and the woman had to ask him the question again.

'A little *Candide* story, which Ryoko and I are writing about . . .' He stopped. He appeared to be out of breath. The girl next to him – Ryoko, presumably – whispered in his ear.

'Fish out of water,' he said, then stopped. There was a long pause.

The woman waited. Then she attempted a little joke. 'Another sea story, like *Neptune*?' she said, a little too brightly.

'No, not *Neptune*, that was a picture about an ocean liner,' Wally said. 'Made me more money than anything else I ever did.' He chortled. 'FU money.'

'But your new film?'

'A little *Candide* story,' he said. 'No guns.'

At this point, Ryoko got up and whispered in the woman's ear, then sat down again.

'Ah,' she said, happy to be back on track. 'Ryoko tells me it's about the adventures of a Japanese girl who arrives in Beverly Hills with no money and speaking no English. What fun!'

'No guns,' Wally said again. He took off his glasses and began cleaning them with the end of his tie.

'Shall we take some questions from the audience?' the woman said desperately.

A hand went up. 'I'm studying film at UCLA and I wondered, Mr Carter, if you thought there were some thematic links between your early British work and your later movies in Hollywood.'

'Too much cutting, these days. Everything's cut-cut-cut.' He made a chopping movement with his hand.

'Yes, but would you say that –'

'Where are the characters? That's what I always ask.'

'Next,' the woman said, a little too hastily. 'We've got to wind up in a minute. Third row, the lady in the middle.'

'I was fascinated to hear that Arthur Hayman worked on your film. What are your memories of working with him? Did you see then how talented he was? Did you think he would become so famous?'

'Arthur,' Wally said. 'Arthur. Arthur. Arthur.' Maybe he was trying to jog his own memory. I hadn't known you could give a word so many different inflections. He looked down at his shoes and said something quietly that the microphone didn't quite pick up. I thought I understood what he had said but I was hoping I was wrong. I wasn't. He repeated it, closer to the microphone now so that everyone heard: 'Sad boy,' he said.

I wanted the next question to come very, very quickly.

'What does he mean?' Travis whispered.

I hadn't cried for a long time, but if ever I was going to it would have been then.

After a few more questions, the woman – obviously relieved that the evening had finally come to an end – thanked Wally again and everybody clapped. Even before the lights had come up I was scrambling out of my seat and barging past people to get out. I could hear Travis behind me, saying, 'Hey! Luke! Hold on!'

I waited for him outside the building. It had been air-conditioned inside and it was lovely to be back out in the hot night air with the cars rushing by. It was like getting into the swimming-pool the other night.

Travis looked a bit hurt when he found me. 'Hey, bro, what happened?'

'Sorry,' I said, 'I felt a bit sick. I'm fine now.'

'Let's call Merry. We could go to that bar on Melrose. She loves that place.'

There was a phone booth on the other side of the road and Travis headed off to it. Most of the people had come out by now and were dispersing down the street. I was leaning on the wall by the entrance, watching Travis make his call, when I heard the distinctive English voice of the woman who had been on stage. She was a few yards away, standing next to Wally Carter, who was leaning on his stick beside Ryoko.

'The car should be here in a minute,' she was saying. 'I'm so sorry. They're normally awfully reliable. I can't tell you how grateful we are, Wally. Just a marvellous evening. And you too, Ryoko, of course.'

Wally seemed to be staring into the middle distance. 'Would you like me to get you a chair?' the woman said.

'I think he's okay,' Ryoko said. 'Maybe glass of water.'

It's probably best to think about things before you do them. As the woman headed inside, I walked over to Wally and Ryoko. I felt like I was on wheels. I wasn't really sure what I was doing.

'Excuse me,' I said. I didn't know what to call him so I opted for 'Mr Carter'. 'I really enjoyed the film.'

I seemed to tower over them. They were both quite small. His head didn't move, but his eyes swivelled up to look at me. 'Nice little picture,' he said. 'It's all guns now.'

I put out my hand. 'I'm Arthur Hayman's son.'

'Mmm?' he said. My hand stayed there between us – he couldn't shake it because he was leaning on his stick and Ryoko was grasping his other hand.

'I'm Arthur's son,' I said again.

'Martha's son?'

'Well, hers too. I mean, they're both my parents.'

'Martha. Now she was quite something,' he said.

'She's my mother.'

'Quite something. Yes.'

That seemed to be all he was planning to say. His eyes swivelled down again, like those headlights you get on sports cars.

'I know Graham,' I said. 'Your son.'

'Graham,' he said dismissively. 'All those silly books.'

His eyes came up again and they seemed much clearer this time. It was as if he was seeing me properly.

'Are you the boy?' he said. 'Are you Jordan?'

I didn't know what to say. If I could have I would have turned and run, but he put out his hand and grasped my arm. 'I'm sorry,' he said, 'I'm so sorry,' and then he began to talk.

When we got home, Travis said he was going to bed. Unusually for him, he had been silent on the drive back. Merry either couldn't come to meet us or didn't want to. 'See you in the morning, bro.' He gave me a rather sad hug and shook my hand.

Laurie was on the phone in the den when I got in. She waved at me, gesturing for me to stay.

'Some guy,' she was saying. 'He's called Paul Schiller. No, I

269

don't know who he is. I thought maybe he was someone from Modesto. I thought you might know him. I don't want another thing like the last one. Okay, Rick. Thanks.'

I don't know whether an apology had been made behind the scenes, but she and Rick seemed to be speaking. He had been over at the house a couple of times since that evening but the last family supper had been just Laurie and Erica, Travis and me.

'This guy keeps phoning,' Laurie said, when she'd hung up. 'He's called about twenty times a day for the last couple of weeks at the studio, says he knows me. He won't leave a message. He says he'll only talk to me. You've got to be careful. This town's like Stalker Central. We had a real problem with this woman last year. She hung around here, tried to get in once. Police came, we had to have security patrols. In the end we went to court and got a restraining order. Hey, how was the movie?'

'Something really strange happened,' I said. 'After the film . . .'

'Do you want a soda?'

'No, I'm fine. After the movie I talked to Wally Carter and . . .'

She was brushing cat hairs off the sofa, then got up and put a great clump in the wastepaper bin. I waited for her to come back. I could tell she had something on her mind.

'It's been so great having you here,' she said. 'I wish I could have done more stuff with you but the show just takes everything over.'

'I've had a really good time,' I said, which was more or less true.

'You're going back when? Week after next?'

'A week on Tuesday.'

'I need you to do something for me.' I waited. 'You know we sent a crew over to England? To cover the filming?'

'Yes. They said, when we went to the set.'

'We've got some great stuff. That kid. What's he called?'

'Toby Luttrell.'

'He's good. Strange-looking.'

'At least he's nothing like me.'

She laughed. 'You're much better-looking. We've cut it together.

It's really good. Great interviews. I've got the show set up. We could shoot it the Monday before you go. We won't air it yet. I want to hold it until September when the ratings will be up.' She looked me up and down. 'I'll get Kevin to take you shopping, find you some nice clothes. Do you want to get your hair cut?'

'Laurie . . .' I said.

'I try to do a *Hayseed* show every six months or so, sometimes just a segment. Audiences love it. We've had some great people on. Larry Hagman, Sally Field – Robin Williams did one. He was hilarious. Did a great improv on what he thought Mr Toppit's voice would be like. I should show you some clips.'

I felt really awkward. 'You want me to be on the show?'

She squeezed my hand. 'We'll rehearse it, go through the questions first. It's easy.'

'I'd rather not, Laurie.'

'Look, you don't need to be nervous. I know it seems like a big thing, with the audience and all, but I don't do it like other people. I make it really intimate. It'll just be like you and me talking now. That's not difficult, is it?'

Actually it was. 'I don't want to.'

'Come on, it'll be fun. You can take a VHS back to England, show everyone. National television, think of that. Martha'll enjoy it.'

I doubted that. 'I really don't want to do it.'

Her voice became harder. 'Look, I've got the footage we shot in England. I've got to build it round something.'

'Why don't you get Robin Williams again?'

'Listen, these guys' schedules are really complicated. You can't just snap your fingers and get them on the show. They like to do it when they've got a movie to publicize at the same time.'

'Isn't there someone else who's got a movie coming out?'

'Luke, I've lived and breathed these books for five years. You are the books. This is probably the most important show I've ever done. I need you to do this for me. Everyone's already working on it, been working on it for most of the summer. Don't you want to

271

do it for your father? Make him proud? What would he think if you were too nervous to do it?'

It was such a ridiculous notion wondering what Arthur would have thought about me being on a television show that I couldn't help laughing. Laurie didn't like that. She tried to add something honeyed to her voice. 'It's a nightmare being your age. I remember. You feel so self-conscious. This could be your entrance to the adult world.'

In fact, I felt like I'd done that already with Merry. I wanted to say, as a child would, 'Please don't make me.' Instead I shook my head.

'Oh, Luke, it'll be fine. I promise you. There's a book my friend Marge gave me: *Making Fear Your Friend*. Isn't that a great title?'

'I'm not frightened, Laurie. I just don't want to do it.'

'Why not? It's not a lot to ask.'

It's really difficult saying no to people, and this was like a double negative because I also didn't want to explain why I wouldn't do it.

'Why are you turning your back on everything your father did?' she said.

You can tell when everything gets stripped from a voice: the layers that have been added, the warm colours. We were down to bare walls now. 'Haven't you had a good time here, Luke? Lots of kids would love to have a summer in LA. Swimming-pool, sun, people driving you around, everyone making a fuss of you. Is that it? You want more? You have a pretty good life, Luke. I've worked all my life, had to. You're going to be a wealthy young man. You've got to give something back. What your dad did for you is what everybody dreams of. You've got to pay your dues. Respect him.'

'I'm sorry,' I said.

'I'm asking this one thing of you.'

'I can't. I won't. I'd rather ...' I was trying to think of all the terrible things that I would rather do. Martha would have said, 'I'd rather slit my throat and drink my own blood,' but I didn't want to copy her. Instead, what slipped out was 'I'd rather act in *Camelot*.' I wish I hadn't said it, but she'd pushed me.

She was shaking with anger. I'd seen what she was like when she lost her temper. So had Marty and BJ. They jumped off the sofa and scuttled out of the room. She managed to hold it back while she pulled herself up to her feet. Her face was turning into that pumpkin again. 'You couldn't play the son of a king, Luke. You wouldn't know how. You don't have it in you,' she hissed, then left the room.

Maybe the summer had lasted too long. It felt like that the next morning. It felt like everything had turned sour. By the time I got up Laurie had gone. Actually, I'd made sure of that. I had waited until I heard Stan's car pulling out of the drive taking her to the studio. If I could have, I would have flown home then. As it was I was stuck, not only in Los Angeles but in that house. Laurie lived in what were called 'the flats', the area just south of Beverly Hills before it became hills, and there was nowhere even to walk to unless you liked very long walks.

Travis seemed as gloomy as I was. I told him what had happened with Laurie and he, of course, thought it was extraordinary not to want to be on television. He put it down to English eccentricity and I didn't bother to correct him.

'I wish she'd ask me,' he said. 'I could do some of my songs. It'd be like a showcase. I might even get a record deal. You think I should ask her? I mean, now she's got an empty space.'

I laughed. 'It's either you or that ventriloquist of Rick's.'

'You think so?' he said earnestly.

'No, Travis, I don't.'

'You think Merry might come over today?'

I didn't see any reason why she would as she hadn't been over for a week or more. 'I don't know, Travis.'

'I know she's got some heavy shit to get through, but we could help her,' he said.

'Maybe she needs to do it on her own. I'm not sure taking all that . . . chakra's helping much.'

It was never a good idea to use metaphors with Travis. 'No,' he said, shaking his head, 'it's really healing. It's like an entire healing system. I mean, for the whole body. Wade's been great. He's been to India and everything. He's like a guru. You should meet him, you'd really like him.'

I'd have to take Travis's word for that. 'Let's go out,' I said. 'I'm feeling claustrophobic.'

He looked around the poolhouse. 'Yeah, this is kind of a small room.'

'In general, Travis, not just here.'

'Okay, where do you want to go?'

We went to Paradise Cove. We sneaked into the store room behind the kitchen and took a six-pack of beer to keep us going, as we usually did when we went swimming. Travis brought his surfboard with him, although I'd never seen him do any surfing without falling off. As if by an unspoken agreement we took our swimming trunks: like the best of the summer, the days of skinny-dipping had come and gone.

When we got back, I could hear the regular thwack of tennis balls being hit. It was like a metronome. Erica had a weird machine that automatically threw balls at her so she could practise on her own. I was surprised to see her heading towards the house. She didn't come up often if Laurie wasn't there.

'Ah, Luke,' she said. 'I wondered when you'd be back.'

'Hi, Erica. We've been swimming. I'm just going to change.'

She ignored this. 'You've upset Laurie,' she said bluntly.

She was so tall that she always hunched over a little. With her long, thin legs she reminded me of a heron.

I couldn't think what to say, so I tried, 'I'm sorry.'

'Yes,' she said, 'I'm sure you are. It's not too late to apologize.'

'Apologize for what?'

'I don't know, Luke. You were the one who said you were sorry.'

'I didn't mean to upset Laurie.'

Erica was taking no prisoners. 'But you did. It's done now.'

'Well, that's what I'm sorry for.'

'You must rectify it. It's not hard.'

'You mean go on the show?'

'It's up to you, Luke. You got yourself into this situation and now you must get yourself out of it.'

'I didn't get myself into this situation, Erica. I didn't ask to go on the show.'

'What are you? Eighteen?'

'Yes.'

'Well, then, you should be more grown-up. You think being on the TV is so frightening? What? Like Red Indians, you think it will steal your soul?'

The truth is, I had been wavering. I was thinking that maybe it would be easier if I just did the show. This was all too agonizing, but Erica saying that pushed me in the opposite direction. It was so ridiculous I just wanted to laugh.

I tried to sound calm and in control. 'I wish people would stop saying I'm frightened. It's not that at all. I just don't want to do it. Honestly, Erica, I'd feel happier talking about this with Laurie. It's really between her and me.'

'Is that because I'm only the nurse? The staff? I know what you English are like, all upstairs-downstairs.'

This was turning into a nightmare. 'That's not what I meant.'

'I'm sure it would have been nice to keep it between you and Laurie but she chose to talk to me, Luke. It was her who elected to open it into a wider arena, not me.'

'I should go and change,' I said, holding out my wet towel as evidence.

She looked at it with contempt. 'Is there something more Laurie could have done for you? You use this house as your own.'

'Is that wrong? Laurie invited me. She stayed with us in England.'

'I don't suppose she was stealing things.'

'What?'

'It's an unusual way to repay hospitality.'

'I haven't stolen anything.' This was so outrageous that my voice squeaked.

'Consuela mentioned it. She was very embarrassed, poor thing.'

'Mentioned what?'

'Oh, Luke, people aren't blind. Even if they're just servants. The beer, Luke, there seems to be a shortage of beer in the store room. I know how refreshing it can be on these hot days, but to steal it?'

I stumbled through the next bit. This was awful. I knew my face had gone bright red. 'I didn't steal it.'

'Oh, I see. You asked if you could have it. Fine. Who was it you asked?'

'Laurie said I should make myself at home,' I said feebly.

'So everything is fair game, is it? Are there some books you would like to take? Some jewellery? Perhaps some hi-fi equipment?'

'It was only beer.'

'Oh, fine. And what about the tequila? Do you often drink hard liquor? How old did you say you were?'

I felt sick. Let's stick to the clichés: I wanted the ground to swallow me. 'I told you.'

'Yes, you did, Luke. You know what a puritanical country this is. The legal drinking age is twenty-one in California. Did you know that?'

'Laurie offers me wine at dinner.'

'What Laurie does in her own house is up to her, Luke.' I wished she would stop using my name. 'And, of course, you haven't taken any of this alcohol outside the house, have you? In a car maybe?'

'I haven't driven anywhere. I haven't passed my test.'

'But your friend Travis – he's your designated driver as they say here, isn't he? How old is he?'

I didn't say anything.

'Mmm?'

'Twenty.' It came out as a whisper.

'You'd expect Travis to be foolish. He's not so bright. But you, Luke, with that expensive English education? This is a very litigious country. You and Travis on some joy-ride. You run over a child. You're both under age. Oh, the lawyers would love that. They're thirsty for blood here. Who gets sued? Not you two, no. The person who supplied you with the alcohol, the person who has done no wrong other than to invite you into her house and asked you to treat it like your own. And you've done that, Luke, you've done that with great style, if I may say so.'

I hated her. I hated her more than anyone I had ever met in my whole life. No exceptions.

'I won't tell Laurie any of this. She has so much on her plate. She would be so disappointed. You have much to set right, Luke. I would start as soon as you can. You know what you must do?'

'Yes,' I whispered.

She looked at her watch. 'I must go now. It's my night off and I'm going to the movies.' Then she turned and left the room.

I felt as if the skin had been stripped very slowly off my body. I didn't know what to do with myself. I thought of going to talk to Travis but I didn't want to lay it on him. It wasn't his fault. I went out into the garden. It was dusk and the light was slanting through the trees – beautiful, but I wished it had been raining. I would have preferred the weather to be more like I felt.

I had never been to the other end of the garden, beyond the manicured bit. You couldn't see it from the house because it sloped downwards behind the palm trees. It seemed a good place to be because nobody would find me there and I could think, even though that was the last thing I really wanted to do.

Ruthie and Bob didn't bother to do much watering there. It was dry and hot and airless, and everything crackled under my feet. At the end of the path, there was a long fence, and as I got closer I saw a little low wooden house behind it. It was rather dilapidated and so hidden away that it had the air of a Hansel-and-Gretel cottage in the woods. I peeked through the slats and could just about see a little overgrown garden with some rickety chairs and an old wooden table. There was a tall metal gate at the other end of the fence and I headed towards it so I could get a better view, but before I got there, a voice barked, 'Hey! You! What are you doing?' I jumped. When I got to the gate I saw a very old woman on the other side. If it was possible to lean aggressively on a Zimmer frame, that was what she was doing.

'I've got a shotgun so you'd better watch out,' she shouted.

I found that hard to believe, but in Los Angeles, who knew? I guessed it must be Alma. There had been a lot of promises from Laurie about meeting her but, like the meetings with Wade, they had never materialized. Laurie kept saying Alma was too infirm to leave the guesthouse. I didn't ask her how she had managed to get her to the studio to do the Alzheimer's show.

Ridiculously, I put my hands up – I was terrified of doing something else wrong. If Alma shot me, Erica would somehow make it into my fault. 'I'm Luke Hayman,' I gabbled. 'I'm staying with Laurie. I'm a friend of hers, just walking in the garden. Is that all right?'

'You're that boy from England.'

'Yes.'

'I've heard about you.' She managed to give the words a faintly sinister ring.

'Hello,' I said.

'Hello yourself. You coming in?'

'I'd better not.'

'I want to get a closer look at you.'

'Are you sure?' I would have liked her to sign a legal document saying she had invited me in of her own free will to appease Erica.

She beckoned me closer. 'You got to unlock the gate.'

'Do you really have a gun?'

'Wouldn't you like to know?'

There was a big metal bolt on my side and I pulled it across. The gate creaked open and I went through.

'Now lock it again,' she said. 'I don't trust those pool boys.'

You had to wiggle your hand through the bars of the gate and contort your wrist to pull the bolt back. 'You mean Jesus and Ronnie?'

'I hear them coming over the fence at night, them and their wetback friends. They'll do anything to get into this country.'

My heart sank. I was stuck with a madwoman who thought her garden fence was the Mexican border.

'Sit down,' she said. 'I want to look at you.'

I sat by the table and she slowly turned herself round with the Zimmer frame and eased herself down opposite me.

'I don't see so well. They call it macular degeneration.'

I was quite impressed. She might have been mad but she had a sense of detail. Then she said something that really threw me: 'You a Jew?'

I couldn't think how to answer.

'I'm not saying you are and I'm not saying you're not. I'm just asking,' she said.

'I don't think so. I wouldn't mind if I was,' I said, rather primly.

She made a humph noise in her throat. 'My husband said he wasn't a Jew but I think he was. He said a lot of things. His family came from Poland. Lot of Jews there. They rounded them up and put them in that Warsaw grotto.'

'I should go,' I said, looking ostentatiously at my watch.

'You've only just got here,' she said aggressively. 'You worried about the ditch?'

I looked round. Maybe they had built a little moat as an extra precaution to stop her getting out.

'Erica,' she said. She drew out the word, saying each syllable very slowly as if I was very stupid. 'Dutch bitch. You get it?'

I got it. That did make me laugh. Then I thought of something and I couldn't help saying it under my breath to find out what it sounded like.

'What? I can't hear you.'

I shook my head. 'Nothing.'

'Don't "nothing" me, boy,' she said angrily.

'I can't.'

'I'm old. You can tell me anything.'

Okay, she had asked. 'Dunt,' I said.

There was a moment's silence, then she threw back her head and roared with laughter. It might have gone on longer if the laugh hadn't turned into a rasping cough. 'I like you,' she said, emphasizing the 'you' as if she was singling me out from a group of people. 'You want a drink? You'll have to get it yourself.'

'No, thank you,' I said very quickly, even though she probably meant just water. I wasn't going to take any chances.

'Why does Laurie talk about you as if you're the kid in those books?'

'Everybody does.'

'Why?' she said. 'Nothing like him. She made me listen to them on tape. Made me fall asleep.' I was beginning to like her. 'Who's that guy anyway, that Mr Tiptop? I don't get it.'

It wasn't that I disagreed with her, but out of family loyalty I thought I should stand up for them a little. 'They're really popular. Lots of people have bought them.'

'Lots of people buy sanitary napkins,' she said dismissively. Then she added, 'I'm eighty-three, how about that?'

'That's quite something.'

'I don't want to die here,' she said.

'Where do you want to die?' It sounded like a heartless thing to say, but she had started it and she was right: I did feel I could say anything to her.

'New Mexico. The mountains.'

'Los Alamos?' I said. She looked surprised. 'Laurie told me about it. I saw the show she did.'

'Didn't much like it when I was there, but I dream about it. I dream a lot. Too much sleeping. All the pills they give me.'

'Why didn't you like it? It looks beautiful.'

'Too many Jews,' she said. 'Still, you got to run them up a flagpole and cheer. They built that bomb, got us out of the war. Nobody said they weren't smart. My husband was a Communist, thought he was anyway. Lot of them there, too.'

'What happened to him?'

'I hope he's dead, what he did to us. You should have seen Laurie then. So pretty. Fat little thing. I did her hair in braids. She had a tough time. She loved that place. *She* didn't want to leave.

You know I was an alcoholic?' I shook my head. 'Well, that's what you're meant to call it. In the place I went they said it's a disease. I just liked to drink. That's not a disease. You like peaches, it's not a disease.'

'My father's dead,' I said.

'Some people need their parents. You don't, you're okay. Laurie never comes down here. She doesn't like me much.'

'She talks about you a lot.'

'Big deal. Why doesn't she come and talk about me down here? She made me sell my house. It was mine, not hers. We should have stayed in Modesto. That show of hers, it's not going to make her happy. She was better on the radio. She doesn't have the face for TV. They're all so skinny.'

'Isn't that why people like her? She's different.'

Alma made her humph noise. 'You want different, you should put Erica on TV. And she's skinny enough. Like a potato chip.' Then she laughed. 'That Dunt.'

Now I felt nervous. 'Don't say I said it, will you?'

'I'm good at secrets. You got to keep secrets. The Jews next door, they couldn't keep a secret. I begged them, but they told on him. I said I'd repay them soon as I could.'

'What?'

'The money. Only a couple hundred dollars, but that was a lot then. You know what Los Alamos means in Spanish?'

I was getting lost. 'What?'

'Poplars. Trees. Never saw any there, though.'

'Where?'

'In Los Alamos. My husband – Rudy – stole the money from them. The Jews in the next apartment. Laurie played with their kid. Paully. Mean little boy with little pig eyes. Paully had seen him in their apartment, then the money was missing. I'll say that for him, he 'fessed up straight away. Lost money playing cards. We could have repaid it, but they went all high and mighty. That's Jews for you. Always better than you. They said we'd betrayed a code of honour. Well, I never signed up for it. Then they said I was drunk, wasn't fit to look after a child. Okay, I shouldn't have shouted at them but they shouldn't have gone to the MPs.'

'The what?'

'Military Police. They kicked us out. The Jews watched us when we left. I could see them smiling. That little Paully. Mean kid.'

'So where did you go?'

'Back to California. He got a job. I don't know, one of those towns. Never stuck to anything. We moved around. Bakersfield, Fresno. Wasn't hard to get a job – all the men were overseas fighting. He was four F, something wrong with his feet. He was always lazy. Always playing cards – poker, blackjack, anything he could put a couple of bucks on. We weren't much by then. Maybe we never were. Laurie cried when we left Los Alamos. Broke my heart.'

It was dark by now. Beyond the palms at the top of the slope I could see the lights of the main house. I still hadn't got used to the way the temperature didn't drop much at night. It was balmy and airless. All I could see was Alma's profile and the light reflecting in her beady little eyes when she tilted her head towards me.

'He was no good, I knew that, but she was crazy about him, Laurie. Snappy dresser, nice-looking too, but you get sick of all that. You wait. We could have gone on, I guess, but then he got that job teaching. Then there was the girl.' She stopped. 'Why are you interested in all this?' she said aggressively.

I thought that was a bit unfair. I hadn't asked her to tell me anything. She'd wanted to. 'I don't know,' I said. 'It's like a jigsaw.'

She humphed. 'You got better things to do than jigsaws.'

'Maybe I should go.'

'Go if you want. It's nothing to me. You're a strange kid. You don't say much. What you got to hide?'

'I had a brother who died.'

There was a pause. 'That's tough,' she said. She waited for me to go on.

It took me a moment to get started again. 'He was called Jordan. He died a long time before I was born. My parents never talked about him. My mother still doesn't. Ever. My sister and I don't know anything about him, just his name. There's nothing stopping us asking about him, but we don't. It's like a spell's been cast on us.'

She nodded. 'Sometimes it's better not to ask,' she said. 'Some things, you better be sure you really want to know.'

'I never knew what happened to him and I just found out. The other night, here, I met this man, this friend of my parents. He's pretty ancient. He was confused, his memory's kind of gone. He thought I was Jordan. He knew Jordan was dead, but he thought for a moment I was him. Like a ghost. Then he was embarrassed. He told me what happened to Jordan. I think I'd built it up in my mind to be something really complicated, but it was simple. They had some nanny, my parents, some au pair, and my mother was late back from somewhere and the nanny was bathing the baby and she left the room for a moment or something and when she came back the baby was dead. The baby had drowned. That was it.'

I was crying now. I was sitting with an old woman and crying at her. She might have been mad, but she was tactful. She didn't do anything awful like hug me. I wouldn't have wanted anyone to do that.

'Better to know,' she said. 'Not always, but you want to know, if it's your brother. Your parents, hard to get over that. You don't want to fail your children. You want to protect them. I tried to do that for Miss Laurie. Lot of thanks I got for it.'

'I'd better get back.'

'You don't have to go,' she said.

'It's late.'

She put out her arm, fragile as a chicken's wing, to stop me getting up. 'This girl,' she said. 'This girl. Nine or ten, I guess. In the class he taught. She was "slow", you called it back then. Sweet-natured. Pretty. Her parents always put flowers in her hair. Nicely dressed, little blonde thing. Didn't look at you when you spoke to her. The parents weren't too bright either, else they'd have spotted it earlier. He pumped gas in a filling station, the father. Drifters, a lot of them around then. Rudy made her put his thing in her mouth.'

I didn't know what to say, and I didn't want to ask her any questions so I stayed silent. She didn't like it. 'You still there? You gone to sleep?'

'No, I was thinking about it.'

'Too much thinking'll kill you. You watch out. The parents wanted money or else they were going to the police. I knew they wouldn't, they weren't the kind of people who went to the police, probably in trouble themselves. Rudy knew that, counted on it, I guess. But I would. He didn't count on that.' She gave a grim laugh. 'I told him if I ever saw him again, the police would be round faster than I could cut his balls off. I had Laurie. She was eight or nine, she loved him. Never had much time for me but she loved him. I gave him the savings we had, not much but enough to get him out of town. Never saw him again. He might have gone to Oregon. He sent cards from there for a while, but I never gave them to Laurie. Best that way. Then we moved up to Modesto so he didn't know where we were. I hope he died in jail taking it up the ass from some stinking Mexican.'

'I'm sorry,' I said.

'What's to be sorry for? It's not your doing.'

'You protected her, though.'

She gave another humph. I bent to kiss her goodbye. There was a little tremor in her cheek. She smelled musty and powdery. 'I'll come back again, shall I? When the Dunt's not around.'

She shrugged. 'You could,' she said. 'I don't mind if you do and I don't mind if you don't.' She was holding her hand to her cheek where I had kissed her.

I was trying to unbolt the gate when she said, 'Funny thing, the kid kept the secret. The little girl. She didn't mean to tell on him.'

I turned back to her. 'So how did the parents find out?'

'She thought it was a game. He'd made it into a game. That's how they found out. The kid tried to do it to her father, tried to get him to play the game. Some game.'

I'd got the gate open and was on the other side, pushing the bolt back. 'Goodbye, Alma. Sleep well.'

'It was like a Red Indian thing,' she said, 'the game Rudy played with the kid. She was a princess and he was Hiawatha. I never dream about him. I dream about the mountains.'

By the next day I had decided I would do the show. I was feeling bad about a lot of things, about Laurie really, about what Alma had told me, and I wanted to make things as right as I could. What I couldn't bear was it seeming like Erica had had anything to do with it, because while my position about Laurie and the show had shifted, nothing about Erica had.

What I'd been thinking was this: maybe some of what Laurie had said to me was true – the stuff about giving something back and honouring Arthur's legacy. My life wasn't that much of a hard-luck story, after all, and I could just about entertain the possibility that maybe I was being a bit self-indulgent. I even came round to thinking that being on the show might be fun.

The odd thing was that before dinner the next night, the first time I had seen Laurie since that awful conversation, it seemed like she was the one who was apologizing to me.

'I need to talk to you,' she said, but not in a heavy way. In fact, she put her arm round me when she took me into the den. 'I thought it would be fun to go out for dinner tonight. We'll go to Dan Tana's. It's real old-style LA. You'll like it.' Then she put her hand on mine. 'I feel just awful that I said those things. The show really takes it out of me, makes me kind of grouchy sometimes.' She sighed. 'Everyone has an opinion. The ratings could be higher, the advertisers are worried, we didn't think Tuesday's show worked, the guests aren't right. It just goes on and on and I get so tired of it sometimes. It would really help me if you did the show.

Of course, I can sort it out in some other way if you want.' She didn't sound totally convincing.

I was just about to say, 'Yes, I'll do it. I really don't mind,' when she said, 'And Erica, you mustn't worry about her. When I said treat this place like your own, I meant it. When I think how good you all were to me in England – you want beer, you have it. Anything you like.' She gave a little laugh. 'I'd watch the tequila, though. You know they dissolve worms in it?'

My mind stopped in its tracks. One of two things had happened: either Erica had lied to me – she'd said she wouldn't say anything to Laurie about the booze until I had sorted things out with her – or, worse, Laurie had known about it from the start and they'd cooked it up together to shame me into doing the show. My instinct was that it was the latter. Whichever, it made me dig in my heels and I didn't say what I'd been going to say. Instead, I said, 'I'm glad there's some other way you can do the show. That's great, Laurie. Thank you.'

Clearly it wasn't what she had expected, and there was a moment's silence. 'Fine,' she said, 'fine. It's your choice,' but the lightness had vanished from her voice. 'I'll make other plans. Now, we ought to get going.'

There were just the four of us, Laurie and Erica, me and Travis. Travis had to drive. Erica and I were sitting in the back. Nobody said anything in the car. My guess was that Laurie and Erica had planned the dinner as a celebration to thank me for agreeing to do the show, so now we were all there under false pretences. I kept close to the window. I didn't want to be near Erica.

The restaurant was rather quaint, with red leather and booths and checked tablecloths. A lot of fuss was made of Laurie as we went in, kisses from the head-waiter and warm handshakes for the rest of us. She was very gracious, saying things like, 'You know I get withdrawal symptoms if I don't have your Eggplant Parmigiana at least once a week, Jimmy.' As we walked through to our table, people stared. 'This is so cool,' Travis kept saying. 'This is like a real celebrity place.'

Erica wore a fixed smile. She was sitting opposite me so I had plenty of opportunity to see it. Before we'd even had a chance to order anything, a waiter brought us a bottle of champagne on the house. He poured Laurie's and Erica's glasses first, then turned to me.

I had just opened my mouth and was saying, 'No, thank –' when Erica put her hand out and said, 'He'd better not. He's only eighteen.'

I could tell I was going bright red. 'You should be flattered, Luke. They think you're grown-up,' she said, with a light but discernible emphasis on 'think'.

I didn't know how I was going to get through the meal. Thank God for Travis, who was completely oblivious. 'I don't like champagne too much,' he said. 'It gives me gas.'

'Oh, Travis, really, spare us,' Erica said teasingly. 'That's too much information. You must keep your gastric arrangements to yourself.' She and Laurie gave an awful phoney laugh, and Travis glowed with pleasure at the unexpected attention.

Laurie didn't say much all the way through dinner. I kept glancing at her, but she was keeping her gaze well away from me and looking at Travis, who began telling us about his song-writing. Erica watched him, wide-eyed, as if he was the most fascinating person in the world. He was working on a song about Merry, he said.

'Don't you need to be a very special person to be immortalized in a song? Like "Lili Marlene"?' Erica said.

Travis looked confused. 'Who?'

'Oh, Travis, before your time. One of the great songs. Or "Eleanor Rigby". You'll know that one, I expect.'

'Or Ruby,' he said, warming to it.

'Ruby?'

'You know, like "Ruby, Don't Take Your Love To Town".'

Laurie snorted, and Erica's eyes flicked in her direction. 'I don't think I'm familiar with that one,' she said.

'Or "Mrs Robinson".'

'Yes, all quite special people.'

'Merry's special,' he said.

'She's very attractive, of course.'

'No, she's got like an aura.'

'An aura. My goodness.'

'No, she is. She is special.'

'I'm sure she is. You're clever to have spotted something in her that has eluded the rest of us.'

Travis took that as a compliment. 'I'm still working on the song,' he said. 'I've got the chorus and some of the words.'

'And how does it go? Your song.'

'Well, the chorus is "I watch you through my eyes, Until" . . .'

'"I watch you through my eyes,"' Erica repeated quizzically.

'Yes.'

'But who else's eyes could you watch her through?'

'I'm, like, seeing her through my eyes.'

'Yes, I understand that. But it wouldn't be possible for you to see her through anybody else's. Unless you have special powers.' She gave a gay little laugh.

'But.'

'No, go on. I'm sorry, I don't really understand song construction.'

He cleared his throat and started again. '"I watch you through my eyes, Until the summer ends. I know how hard you try, To force the pain to mend."'

'Oh, it's a sad song,' she said. 'That's nice. That's a good rhyme: end/mend – it's clever, Travis. Cole Porter better watch out.'

'I find the rhyming stuff really hard,' he said.

She laughed again. 'If it was easy, we'd all be doing it. It's obviously a special gift of yours.' Travis looked pleased. 'But it's so sad,' she said, with a little catch in her throat, 'forcing the pain to mend. How could such a golden creature as Merry have pain?'

'She's quite a deep person,' Travis said.

'Deep? You do surprise me.'

'She's the deepest person I know.'

'Really? In what way, Travis? You are perceptive.'

It was going to go on and get worse. 'Don't do this,' I said. I hadn't even begun to eat. My Clam Linguini was still sitting on the plate. It was meant to be one of their specialities, but it didn't look very nice. I hadn't known the clams would still be in their shells.

Erica turned to me slowly. 'I'm sorry, Luke?'

'You don't have to do this.' My voice was trembling.

'Do what? Travis is just telling us about his songs.'

'Yeah, bro, what's up?'

They all looked at me. I couldn't explain it in front of Travis and I didn't want to hurt him. He was the only innocent one at the table. I didn't say anything.

'You seem upset, Luke,' Erica observed coldly.

I turned to Laurie. She was the closest thing I had there to a parent and, ridiculously, I wanted her to protect us, but I knew it was too late for that. She was staring straight in front of her, as if she was somewhere else. I was on my own.

'It's just mean,' I said, in a voice so clear that even I was surprised. 'It's mean and cruel, Erica. Like pulling the wings off a butterfly.'

She wiped her mouth and put down her napkin. There was silence for a moment. 'I'm delighted to think you know me well enough to talk so frankly,' she said, then got up and left the table. The look on Laurie's face: I thought she might hit me, but she pushed her chair back and hurried after Erica across the restaurant.

The day before I left to fly home, I wanted to see Alma again to say goodbye. After lunch I could hear Erica doing her tennis practice with the ball-throwing machine and knew that would keep her occupied for a while. I sneaked through the garden to Alma's little house. I had to call her name several times through the gate before she heard me.

'Who's that?' she shouted from inside.

'It's me. Luke.'

The screen door opened and she manoeuvred herself out on to the porch with her Zimmer frame.

'Hi, Alma.'

'I've got a shotgun,' she said.

'It's okay,' I said. 'It's me. Can I come in?'

'I've got a shotgun,' she said again. 'You tell those Mexican friends of yours I'll blow their brains out if they come here one more time.'

'It's Luke. I was here the other day.'

'Luke who?'

'I'm from England. The boy from the books. Laurie's friend.'

'What's she got to do with it? Did Erica send you?'

'The Dunt. You remember that?'

'The what?'

'The Dunt!'

'You're going to be in big trouble if you don't get off my property. You and your friends. You think I don't know how to use a shotgun? Think again, sonny.'

Just then, I heard Travis shouting for me: 'Hey, Luke! Get up here! Where are you?'

I turned round and saw him gesturing wildly by the palm trees at the top of the bank. When I turned back, Alma had gone inside and the screen door was swinging on its hinges.

When I got to him Travis was breathless with excitement. 'What is it?' I said.

'You've got to see this! It's like a surprise. Come on!'

He put his arm round my shoulder and practically dragged me back to the house. We went through and out to the front. In the driveway, Stan was opening the rear door of his big black BMW. Out of it, her eyes squinting in the bright sunlight, came Rachel.

'Oh, this is so fabulous,' she said. 'I've been itching to call you but Laurie made me promise not to say anything so it would be a big surprise for you. She's flown me over to be on her show! First class! Free champagne all the way! And now you're about to go home. I can't bear it.'

'I don't like champagne too much,' Travis said. 'It gives me gas.'

Laurie

Several houses away, which meant – being Beverly Hills – that you practically needed a cab to get there, an enormous blue plastic sheet enveloped the whole building: there was an infestation of termites, which was not an uncommon occurrence. You had to move yourself and your possessions out while the house was tented and some toxic gas pumped in to kill the bugs. A baseball player and his family lived in this particular house, not that Laurie had met them. She hadn't met anybody in the area. It wasn't neighbourly like Modesto – standing in the heat with a welcoming casserole dish in front of someone's security gates while CCTV cameras swivelled to get you in their sights took away a little of the spontaneity.

Laurie had had a dream: the termites were heading, with some determination, up the street from the baseball player's house towards hers in battle formation. Only – being a dream – they were sometimes termites and sometimes people: the dispossessed wearily on the move again, with their patched clothes and scruffy suitcases. It was the Joad family from *The Grapes of Wrath* or the people you saw in scratchy wartime documentaries scrabbling to find the remains of Grandmother's china in the rubble of their bombed house. But whatever they appeared to be on the surface they were termites underneath, no question, and they weren't coming to her house: she was going to make sure of that, even if she had to nuke them off the sidewalk.

She was tired. It was four in the morning now. She hadn't slept well for the last week, ever since that awful dinner at Dan Tana's. She wished she could have seen the look on the boy's face when his sister arrived. He wasn't indispensable. Nobody was. She was under no illusions that it would have been better to use him on the *Hayseed* show next week, but she wasn't going to let him hold her to ransom. The girl would do. Anyway, she was much more interested in the books than he was. She knew them backwards, and was a better talker.

The boy kept saying prissily that he wasn't the boy in the books. He was right there. It was a pity Arthur hadn't used some other name for the main character. Then there would have been no confusion and the boy could have had the life of obscurity he appeared to want. How could anyone turn down the gift Arthur had given him? He didn't deserve it anyway: he was quite a dull boy. No spark. He just watched everything with those cold blue eyes. She had given him everything and he had flung it back in her face.

Ungrateful: it was one of the irritating words Alma had thrown at Laurie since she was a child, but her situation was quite different from Luke's. What was she meant to be grateful for? A mother like Alma? A father who had found his wife so awful he had had no option other than to leave, abandoning his only child? Not that she blamed him. Anyway, she knew he was inside her. He had given her what he could: his beliefs, his knowledge of what was right and wrong. And she knew he loved her, though it was sometimes hard to hold on to that, to take it as much for granted as she would have liked. Still, through it all, through Arthur, she had found a strength that was entirely her own and she was proud of that.

And look at her now! That was the proof. Five years ago the fixed points of her life had been KCIF, the hospital, Spring Crest and her house, all joined in a circle that surrounded the nothingness at the centre. Her days then were filled simply with coping: with Rick at work, with Alma, with Marge. Keeping everybody happy was like one of those tasks from the Greek myths that never ended however hard you tried, rolling a stone up a hill only to have it roll down before it reached the top. Now it was different. Now she had wrested back control of her life.

And yet ... What she needed was to sleep better. Maybe she

should get some sleeping pills: it was only in the middle of the night that these unwelcome thoughts arrived. She should take some of Alma's. Her bathroom cupboard was like a pharmacy store. But what had really changed? That was the question that kept sliding in. She was still spending her days coping, only now she worked all the time on the show and was exhausted as well. Rick hadn't gone away. Alma hadn't gone away. The only person who had gone away was Marge, but now Laurie had Erica to cope with instead. Not that she wasn't great, but she was pretty high-maintenance, always grousing about everyone else and forcing Laurie to cope on her behalf, too.

Of course she had money now, but even that needed coping with. Rick seemed to be in charge of her investments, which was one of the many things Erica groused about. Left to herself, she would have kept it in the bank. 'You're a corporation now,' Rick kept saying. 'You've got to *grow*, Laurie.' She'd grown enough already. Did she want to invest in an Olde English Tea Room in Carmel that Clint Eastwood had already put money into? Did she want to buy a chunk of some forest in Oregon? Did she want to develop a condominium in Maui? Maybe she did, but what did she know? Trouble was, what did Rick know? Her contract for the show was up in a year's time and would need renegotiating. The original terms had been on the low side, but she'd just been starting out. Anyway, it had seemed like a fortune to her. 'Big pay-day coming up. You got to get a bigger chunk of those residuals. Time to make 'em bleed, baby!' Rick was already saying. She didn't really want him going on the warpath with the programme people on her behalf. She didn't want them to bleed. They'd been good to her.

It was time for Rick to go. Weren't managers meant to dress in suits and work in buildings designed by fancy European architects, with assistants who organized expensive leather goods to be sent to you at Christmas? Weren't they meant to be grateful that you were their client? They certainly weren't meant to dress in jeans and too-tight T-shirts that scarcely covered their belly, worry about their comb-over all the time and have wives who considered themselves smarter than you.

She'd never asked him to be her manager anyway, but she had needed help with her contract and he had offered. She'd certainly never asked him to move down to LA. Maybe that ventriloquist of his would take off and then she wouldn't feel so guilty. Jerrilee could help him with his outfits and makeup instead of bothering her all the time. Weren't relationships meant to alter with circumstances? At high school she had spent her life trying to please Rick, or at least be noticed by him. She had tried to please him at KCIF, and she was still doing it now. But he hadn't created any of this: it was her. She had done it all and it still felt like he was the grown-up in the front seat of the car and she was the child in the back being told to keep quiet, squeezed between the luggage and the dog.

She would have to get up in a while. Stan would be here soon. She tried to keep thinking about Rick, for her thoughts to go round and round. That was preferable to the other thing that sometimes happened: discovering a little nick in the unbroken line of the circle and being pulled outside it into uncharted territory. That was when she thought about the source: the stream that had once bubbled through the earth pure and untouched, as clear as anything you could ever imagine. She had never thought much about what would happen after that moment. She had never considered how the rivulet would change as it ran down the hillside.

What had happened? Was it her fault, or was it just a fact of life that nothing stays untouched? She had done a show about pollution not so long ago: she had interviewed environmentalists with their grim warnings and foreboding statistics and had shown footage of rivers in places like Alaska which – even there, miles from human habitation – had that discoloured soapsuddy stuff clinging to the banks. Everything gets destroyed. It couldn't just be that people didn't recycle enough, it wasn't what people did or didn't do, it was the people themselves, emitting some kind of toxic gas that seeped into everything and rearranged the DNA.

She was losing Arthur: that was what she didn't want to think about. Maybe she should just acknowledge it, *Making Fear Your Friend* like Marge's book said. Then she could take steps to reclaim him before he became lost to time and history, like her father.

She heard a car door slam outside: Stan was here. She was already late. They would just have to do her hair and makeup quicker when she got to the studio. As she pulled herself out of bed her hand brushed the smooth wall and she remembered the hotel room in London. Anaglypta: she rolled the word round in her head, exploring it this way and that, and a surge of hope flooded in, like crystal-clear water. Maybe she could make it all right. With Rachel there, she had the perfect opportunity. The girl loved the books, she loved her father, and together they could repair the damage the boy had done, like repainting a room, bringing up the dull colours so they were vivid and bright and clear again. *I am the Princess Anaglypta and I have come home.*

As she went outside into the dawn light, Stan was waiting by the car, holding open the back door for her. Suddenly she felt so buoyant that she kissed him before she got in. As they drove away, she could almost see the line of termites on the sidewalk drawing to a halt in front of her house, their wiggling antennae sensing that things were changing here, that there might be danger for them if they tried an assault. Any minute now they would admit defeat and wearily continue their journey to some other house further up the street where the defences were less impregnable, where the people were more careless with their property, some other house where cracks and fissures were left unrepaired in the fabric of the building, perfect little entry-points that would allow the termites to start their voracious destruction.

Luke

I had left LA, of course, when all the stuff happened, although calling it 'stuff' is to undersell it in quite a major way. There's not really a coherent narrative, but over the years I pieced it together from what Rachel – never the most reliable source – said, and from what Graham Carter told me, and I've guessed some, not hard with the personalities involved.

Like the bomb that Laurie's father either did or didn't help to build in Los Alamos, certain events needed to take place for the required explosion to happen. In the case of the bomb, two sub-critical masses of fissionable material would have to come together to form a supercritical mass. On top of that, they have to come together in a precise manner and at high speed. That's what I learned in physics, anyway.

In the case of Laurie, there were two separate but unrelated news stories – I think even hardened conspiracy theorists would find collusion between the *National Enquirer* and the *LA Times* unlikely – that appeared just after I left and Rachel had arrived. Graham brought the *Enquirer* back to England with him so I eventually saw it: the front cover with a huge picture of Laurie and a giant headline, '*Laurie Gay Scandal*', and underneath '*This Woman's Shocking Charge*', with a little inset photo of a dumpy middle-aged woman in a nurse's uniform.

The piece began, 'Laurie Clow has become tangled in a messy gay scandal triggered by shocking allegations that she plied her vacation companion, Marge Clancy, 54, a care worker from Laurie's home town of Modesto, Calif., with alcohol and then forced her into sordid sexual acts on the exclusive Caribbean island of St Bart's.' Marge Clancy was described as an 'angel' by her patients, and much was made of her good works with terminal-cancer sufferers, as if that somehow proved she must be the innocent party. Co-workers called them 'thick as thieves', unnamed friends had noticed 'something odd' about their relationship and said they were 'constantly' planning vacations together, as if there was some correlation between sex and holidays. Marge Clancy, who had thought they were 'just friends', felt 'betrayed by Laurie's sordid actions'.

But there was more: Laurie had recently been 'linked with Dutch care worker, Erica Hauer, 43, employed by the star to tend to her mother, Alma Clow, 84, an Alzheimer's sufferer', and there was a blurry photograph of Erica playing tennis. Unnamed staff 'in her spacious Beverly Hills mansion' were quoted as saying that Laurie and Erica were 'constantly together' and that Erica seemed 'to rule the household'. What they clearly considered the most damning piece of evidence, produced near the end of the piece, like the vital clue in the final minutes of *Kojak*, which proves the obviously innocent person to be obviously guilty, was this: Laurie's 'prized pedigree Persian cats, Marty and BJ, are named after lesbian tennis legends Martina Navratilova and Billie-Jean King'.

There was a coda: the magazine intimated that Laurie's championing of the 'best-selling *Hayseed* books, with their celebration of family values' was some kind of smokescreen to mask her 'unconventional lifestyle'. That was the only bit that made me laugh. While the books could be interpreted in many different ways, putting them in the same category as, say, *The Little House on the Prairie* or *The Waltons* seemed an outrageous slur.

I don't really know what happened next, what the immediate fallout was for Laurie. I imagined the house to be like an ants' nest that had been disturbed – suddenly they were swarming all over the place, particularly at the Friday programme meeting. I should think the driveway was like a sardine can full of cars that day, with extra PR people drafted in to sort out the crisis. My guess is that Laurie would have put a good face on whatever she felt like inside. It was probably worse for Erica. I certainly hope so.

They probably tried to spin it in the most positive way possible:

nobody believed anything in the *National Enquirer* anyway – the story might just as well have been 'Chat Show Star Abducted By Flying Saucer'. Whether the story was true or not, there was nothing illegal about being gay. The show tended to skew towards a more liberal demographic, it attracted a sizeable gay audience and so on.

The day probably ended calmer than it had begun, and what I do know is that Laurie talked about the article on her show a few days later. I wasn't there so I didn't see it, but I imagine she did a piece to camera right at the end, like the one she'd done about her father on the Los Alamos show: lights dimmed, one to one, direct but intimate. Something like 'I'm as interested in gossip as the next person. I didn't realize I'd be the next person. If I were gay, you could rely on me not to be quiet about it. I'd be so proud I'd be shouting it – proud of the battles gay people have fought in this country, proud of the fight to push through changes in legislation, the fight for the dignity of expressing your sexuality with no fear. But sometimes you realize that the upward climb still has a way to go. Magazine covers are a great attention-grabber. Why waste one on some untrue story that they think is "scandalous"? You want a scandalous cover story? I'll give you one: medical care in this country. You want sleazy? The treatment of immigrant labour in this country. You want sordid? This government's arms programme. You want downright disgusting? The homophobia that still exists all over this country.' Et cetera, et cetera.

Back at the house, Laurie's liberal credentials were not enough to stop her doing a cull of staff. Somebody inside must have leaked the Erica bit of the story and taken that blurry photograph of her playing tennis. Consuela and Lupe, Jesus and Ronnie were exonerated because it was felt they didn't speak enough English to be able to leak a story. Anyway, I think even Laurie would have balked at sacking Mexican labour. The axe fell on the garden people, Ruthie and Bob, who were paid off. That was just to be on the safe side.

The general consensus was that the leaker was probably Angie, the cat person. Being English didn't quite count as immigrant labour, and Erica had never liked her much. She thought that Angie skimped on the arduous process of combing out the cats' long hair and left too many knots. The evidence against her was circumstantial but damning: she knew the cats' full names, she had been seen with a camera at the house the day she asked Lupe to take a picture of her and me together, and she needed the money the magazine was presumed to have paid – there was no better definition of 'desperate' than an unknown English actress trying to get work in LA with no green card. She went, too, protesting her innocence, but Rick gave her cash, made her sign a gag clause and threatened to go to the authorities about her working illegally if there was any comeback.

They must have slept easier once they thought they had contained the *National Enquirer* story but, like the second bomb on Nagasaki a few days after Hiroshima, there was more to come. The story wasn't a big one in the *LA Times*, only second page, no picture, but it hit them where it really hurt because it was about the show.

The Paul Schiller who had been calling Laurie after he had seen the Los Alamos show had obviously got sick of never being put through to her and had contacted the *Times*. In a previous life he had been Paully, the little boy who had played with Laurie, the son of 'the Jews next door', and what he told them was essentially what Alma had told me: far from being a fellow traveller who had had security problems in Los Alamos because of his political beliefs, Laurie's father had been kicked out for stealing money. More than that, which Alma hadn't told me, he wasn't even working in the labs but was an accounts clerk doing invoicing.

The lucky thing for Laurie was that it had all happened a long time ago and was so small-scale compared to everything else going on in Los Alamos that the records of her father's life there appeared to have been destroyed, if they had ever existed. However, no records could work the other way, too: there was no FBI file on him – according to the *LA Times*, the FBI was known for its punctilious record-keeping – which meant there was no evidence that he had either had security clearance or that it had been withdrawn. After Los Alamos, the trail was cold. Who knows what had happened to him? He might have changed his name and been run over by a concrete truck. In the absence of any paper trail it was essentially Paul Schiller's word against Laurie's.

Because the *LA Times* had contacted the people who made the show the day before the story ran for their comments, they had time to issue a flat denial to cover the wound until they could get their act together. The TV news picked it up and it flowed into other newspapers, not headline stuff but enough to be very uncomfortable indeed. It was a difficult story to handle and, I imagine, brought forth even more ants to scurry around. Stories about people's private lives were one thing, but this entered the arena of broadcasting standards and ethics: the implication of the story was that Laurie had lied on a national television show that travelled on the integrity ticket.

At the several crisis meetings the production team had, they went through the various denial scenarios that might play. According to Erica, who told Graham later, it was she who came up with the Alma defence. On Laurie's part, it required a certain amount of lateral thinking to regard her mother as any kind of trump card but it was all they had.

The first pass at how they would play the Alma card was that she and Laurie should appear at a press conference to deny Paul Schiller's story. Old person, wheelchair, maybe a few tears, how could it not work? Alma had been an adult when the Clows left Los Alamos; Paul Schiller, like Laurie, had been five or six. How accurate could his memory be?

There were two problems with this, one of which only Laurie knew about: Alma had simply turned her face to the wall and refused point-blank to discuss her father. The other, pointed out by a junior PR assistant as they were practically fixing the time and location of the press conference, was that either Alma had Alzheimer's or she didn't. The Alzheimer's show had aired six months before and it was still fresh in everyone's mind, particularly

Laurie's 'personal' ending with the mute Alma being wheeled on stage. If Alma was produced, like a rabbit out of a hat, articulate enough to corroborate Laurie's story, it would cast doubt on the validity of the earlier show and might make people think Laurie had no qualms about using her mother and father in ways that came perilously close to dishonest to make her show more sensational. The girl didn't put it that bluntly, but everyone knew what she meant and the press conference was canned.

In the end, they used Alma in an equally dishonest way in an interview in *People* magazine, but she wasn't going to know:

Chat-show host, Laurie Clow, 54, grew visibly tearful at the effect recent stories were having on her mother, Mrs Laurence Clow, 84, who suffers from Alzheimer's. 'My mom's been everything to me. Since my father left, she's been a single parent and she brought me up to be proud of him. Doing what I do, I know that you're fair game for anyone to take pot-shots at. I don't mind people telling lies about me – but my dad! Smear stories have always been part of our political tradition but it's sad that he, like many people who were caught up in the post-war witch hunts, is still having his reputation questioned. For my mom's sake I'm not going to involve lawyers and put her through more pain. She has precious few memories left as the Alzheimer's has progressed and I want to leave those memories untroubled. I don't even remember Paul Schiller. I'm glad he has such a detailed memory of what happened when he was five. Lucky guy. I hope he feels proud of what he's done to a remarkable and courageous lady.'

Poor Laurie. The end of my trip to LA was horrible, but she was somehow part of our lives and I wouldn't have wished all that on her. I don't know what she must have been feeling, what the stress levels were like in the house. I wondered how BJ and Marty were being groomed in the absence of Angie – with all this going on and still having to do five shows a week, I don't suppose finding a new cat person was high on Laurie's list of priorities.

There was something else I worried about. There was a specific scenario I imagined: in northern California, in Bakersfield or

Fresno, 'one of those towns', there might be a couple who had once run, maybe still did, a gas station. They had one daughter with some kind of learning difficulties, always something of a problem to them. As she hit adolescence, the problems increased, maybe drugs, maybe drink, maybe teenage pregnancy, maybe all of them. I imagined her being killed in a road accident on the back of some boyfriend's motorbike, leaving her parents years to mull over where it had all gone wrong. Then, in a newspaper, they see a reference to a name they had tried never to think of again, Rudolph Laurence Clow, some kind of supply teacher who gave their little daughter extra math tuition, a man who liked to play *Hiawatha* games, a man who turns out to have a famous daughter who seems to have all the advantages their child didn't, so they begin to weigh up their options: lawyers, newspapers, money. But maybe Laurie would be lucky: only two bombs were made at Los Alamos, and they had both been detonated.

The strand in the story I've left out, in order to keep one side of the narrative relatively clear, is Rachel. Now she has to be factored into the mix. All the events I've described happened in the days after she arrived in Los Angeles and while, in one sense, she wasn't involved, I knew that she couldn't be in a house, let alone a room, without affecting the flow of ions. It was not in her personality to be detached, simply to watch. That was me.

Most of this is speculation – at least until Graham enters the story when it becomes fact – but remember that I had spent six weeks in that house: I knew where the bodies were buried. While I was there, I didn't see much of Laurie. She worked really hard, was out of the house from early until late, but we often ate together in the evenings and sometimes went places at weekends until it all went wrong. And, of course, there were the Friday-night suppers. More than that she wasn't under any particular stress, or at least no more than the usual stress of doing the show. Now, just after Rachel arrived the mood was very different. The ants were scurrying, the staff were departing, the phone was ringing: the people who would, under any other circumstances, have made a great deal of fuss of Rachel had their minds on other things. That didn't play to Rachel's strengths.

The show was scheduled for the week after Rachel arrived. Not a high priority for the programme team: they were used to doing a catch-up *Hayseed* show a couple of times a year – it was like Laurie's signature tune – and this time they had the footage that had been shot in England while the BBC series was being filmed so they had only half the slot to fill. Rachel spent most of a day with the researchers, going over the questions they had prepared for Laurie to ask her, then saw the costume and makeup people, who worked out what she would wear and how they would do her hair. That was it. The rest of the time was hers.

Although a stranger wouldn't necessarily have known it, Rachel had been going through her own kind of crisis – that was obvious from the time I'd spent with her and Claude before flying to Los Angeles – and in a crisis Rachel had a way of drawing in everyone around her. She had to be right at the centre, to elbow the crowd out of the way to get there. Because of what was happening she wasn't going to get to the centre of Laurie's world so she had to look elsewhere – and elsewhere, in this context, was Travis.

He was kind to me and he liked me, but I wasn't exotic like she was: in fact, because he knew the books, I was probably something of a disappointment to him. But Rachel, who – much more than I – seemed to come from a different planet, must have been fascinating to him. Anyway, she was a girl. Though she was naturally inquisitive, I don't suppose he held the same fascination for her, but she was always good at working with what she had, with the materials to hand.

How much Merry was around I don't know, but she must have been there for some of it because she was certainly implicated in the fallout, certainly apportioned some of the blame. I know that she and Rachel would not have made a great combination. I don't suppose there was too much skinny-dipping for the three of them at Paradise Cove.

Although, in our own way, Rachel and I were close, we were

very different characters, and nothing shows up that difference more than the one crucial fact of what happened in LA: she got to meet Wade, and I have no idea how she managed it. I was mildly intrigued by Merry and Travis's stories about him, but I didn't care one way or the other about him, and given their resistance to producing him, I would have had to find a compelling reason to persuade them to do so.

Now, if she knew that he was rather more than someone who was just giving Merry lessons in chakra healing, I know what her reason might have been. For Rachel, meeting a drug-dealer with healing powers would have been like a double jackpot, but my guess is that she knew none of it at that point. After all, the revelations about Wade had come piecemeal to me over the six weeks I was there. She had been there only a matter of days before he came into play. Either she had a sense about him before she met him, or it was much simpler: she hated being left out. That was another difference between us.

The three or four days before the *Hayseed* show was scheduled to be shot were Laurie's firestorm. That was when the second story – the *LA Times* one – was published, so her concentration on what Rachel was up to must have been non-existent. It was then that Rachel – somehow – got included in a trip to see Wade. Maybe Travis drove her, maybe Travis and Merry together. I wasn't clear enough about the relationships to know whether or not access to Wade had to be through Merry.

But I know Rachel. During that meeting, something must have passed between her and Wade, a signal, some Freemasons' handshake, some acknowledgement of something shared: a secret deal that, from now on, was going to exclude Travis and Merry. Rachel had a credit card and a driving licence, and at some point after that first meeting she hired a car. I know this because there was endless hassle from Hertz later on, which we had to sort out when the car was found, weeks later, abandoned in the San Fernando valley with the windows smashed and the tyres stolen. With the comings and goings around the house, nobody would have noticed, or cared, about another car in the driveway. Now Rachel had no encumbrances. She was free.

Here it gets murky. I imagine that Rachel was never around much and nobody, except Travis, noticed. But he wasn't her keeper and, anyway, there was no reason for him to think that anything untoward was going on. Did anyone notice her bed hadn't been slept in? Maybe Consuela and Lupe did – if they knew Travis and I had been taking drink earlier in the summer, they would have clocked that. But they didn't speak much English and, for all they knew, she might have been using Laurie's house as a base while she toured around. Travis must eventually have realized that she wasn't just not around much, she wasn't there at all. What was he meant to do? Maybe he guessed she was with Wade. Maybe not. I think he just kept quiet.

Now Graham Carter joins the story. He was in New York on a business trip and he had planned to come to LA while Rachel was there and stay with Wally. He was keen to see Laurie, too. He normally saw her whenever he was in the States: he had a lot to thank her for, after all. Maybe he began telephoning and leaving messages about when he might be coming. Maybe he spoke to Laurie because Rachel wasn't returning his calls. Perhaps, anyway, Laurie needed to see Rachel to talk about the show, which was now only a day or two away. I think there must have been a moment when everybody converged, when everyone swapped notes, and realized that no one had seen Rachel for days.

I think by this time Travis would have guessed that Rachel might be with Wade, but he still probably didn't say anything. He didn't want to implicate himself or Merry. I know that at some point he drove up to Wade's place in Topanga, found Rachel's car there and the house empty – not just empty but seemingly abandoned. Maybe after that he came clean with Laurie, but tried to play down the drugs angle. But, of course, Erica was there. She would have got it out of him, no problem, with or without electrodes to his genitals.

Now, in a normal situation the police would have been called, but this was not a normal situation. Imagine: in a week when the two news stories are published and while they're still working out how to deflect them, a girl – not famous in herself, but related enough to fame for it to be another gift of a story – staying in Laurie's house goes missing under circumstances that almost certainly relate to drugs. Would you have called the police?

So: it's the evening and they're all at the house – Laurie, Erica, an ashen-faced Travis, fiddling with his long hair as he always did when he was nervous, Merry in tears, Rick and Jerrilee, who had been ordered by Erica to bring their golden creature over to the house. Laurie's publicist and a couple of press people from the show are there as well. They go through the possibilities: the police are out, at least for the time being. No question. They decide not to call Martha. She's in England – what can she do? Maybe they even consider calling me to get me to fly back, but the consensus is that I'm probably too young to handle it. The only solution is Graham, who is in New York. If he takes the early flight the next morning, he'll be there by lunchtime. That will sort out another problem: the *Hayseed* show is the day after tomorrow and their guest has just gone AWOL. If she doesn't turn up, he can do it. Not the world's most exciting solution, but he is, after all, the man who discovered the books. Anyway, they weren't going to get Robin Williams to do his hilarious riff on Mr Toppit's voice at such short notice.

So that's what happens. Stan picks Graham up from the airport. Laurie's at the studio doing her show so Erica briefs him when he gets to the house.

He told me he managed to extricate Travis from Erica's clutches and talk to him on his own, when Travis was a great deal more frank about his and Merry's relationship with Wade. They tried calling him again but, as it had for the last few days, it went straight to answerphone. Travis then drove Graham up to Wade's house. This time Rachel's car was gone. Graham had always had a bit of Boy Scout gung-ho about him and decided that extreme measures were called for: they broke into the house. 'House' was a generous description, he said. It was more of a single-storey shack, way up a gravel track off the Topanga Canyon road, perched on the edge of a hill and almost hidden by overgrown foliage. It seemed to me that 'break-in' was also a pretty generous description: nothing was locked and they walked in through the door.

Clearly, Wade was not much of a housekeeper at the best of times, but Travis was shocked by the state of the place compared to when he had last been there. It seemed to have been ransacked. They didn't, of course, know what they were looking for, but thought they might find something like the phone number of a friend, some way of contacting Wade. Maybe they thought they would come across his Christmas-card list. They didn't. There was nothing. But Rachel had been there, and Travis recognized her sunglasses lying broken on the floor.

As they were leaving, Travis had an uncharacteristically bright idea. He saw the light of the answerphone flashing and pressed 'play'. It turned out that half the messages were from him, sounding increasingly desperate, but there were others as well. Several were hang-ups: thirty seconds of static, background noise and a bit of breathing before the click. One was a voice shouting, over music, 'Wade – you better get your ass down here right now', one was from a woman complaining that Wade hadn't been there when she turned up for her chakra lesson, and one was from Rachel. Graham said it sounded as if she was calling from another planet, not just far away in terms of distance but far away from any kind of Rachel he'd thought he knew. 'I'm in a phone box,' she said. 'Do they call them that here? Oh, Wade – are you there? Wade? Where are you? I thought you were going to be here at eleven. I'm in the parking lot by the bar on the corner. That's where you said, isn't it? I want to come home.' Graham said she was crying now. 'Please. Please. Please come. They're not here yet, but you've got to come. I'm trying to do what you said. I'm trying to focus on the base of my spine. What's the energy called? I can't remember. Is it the *prana* thing? I haven't got any more coins. I need –' The message cut off.

Graham said that he and Travis drove back to Laurie's house in silence. He told me he had had almost a physical fight with Erica when they got there as he tried to get to the phone to call the police and she blocked him. He was now really worried about Rachel, but Erica was adamant. I could just imagine.

'She is an extraordinarily foolish girl, Graham. She's how old? Twenty-four? Twenty-five? Are you saying she's been kidnapped by this person? No, you're not. Is she being held by force? No. Is she mentally retarded? No. She is simply thoughtless and stupid. She and her brother before her, not to speak of the clueless Travis and Merry, who started this whole thing. I will not have any of them jeopardize Laurie. She is the only blameless one in this grotesque situation. There must be no more lies in the newspaper about her. Those kids – kids! – have abused her generosity and hospitality. They have used her unmercifully and I will not, I repeat *not*, have Laurie suffer because of it. Rachel left this house of her own free will. She got herself into this and she must get herself out of it. Whatever it is.'

Just then Laurie arrived back from the studio and promptly burst into tears at the sight of Graham and Erica shouting at each other. She had to be taken off and comforted by Erica. After they had calmed down, Graham sat with Laurie and went through how they were going to do the *Hayseed* show the next day.

Even if Graham had called the police, I don't suppose it would have made much difference. Rachel was missing, but she wasn't exactly what you would call, in police terms, 'a missing person'. Anyway, how would they possibly locate her and Wade in the whole of Los Angeles? Nobody even knew his last name. In the event, the day after Laurie and Graham did the show, Rachel and Wade were found.

That day was the first time I knew any of this, and the person I heard it from, surprisingly, was Martha. She called to tell me that Rachel had been involved in a car accident. The police had found her bag, with her driving licence and address, and telephoned Martha. She had possibly broken her leg but she was all right and in hospital. Martha sounded completely unruffled by the news, in fact seemed rather irritated by the inconvenience. Would I call Laurie to get the details? Martha was always good at getting other people to do things for her.

You read about people breaking into a cold sweat but until then I hadn't known it actually happened or what it felt like. Martha, always oblivious to irony, appeared to have missed something obvious to me. It was Arthur all over again: the phone call, the broken leg, the hospital. Rachel was going to die, if she wasn't dead already.

Erica picked up the phone, and before I had the chance to say anything more than 'It's Luke,' she said, quite calmly, 'Oh, Luke – I'll hand you straight over to Graham.' I hadn't even known he was there.

When I told him about Martha's phone call he sounded stunned, and I could hear his voice trembling. I gave him the number the police had left and made him swear he would ring me as soon as he had spoken to them. In fifteen minutes he was back. He told me he had talked to the police and the hospital and that, apparently, she wasn't in any danger. He was going straight there. I thought I'd go mad waiting and by the time he called me, a couple of hours later from the hospital, I had already found out about flights to LA. 'There's absolutely nothing to worry about,' he said. 'She's fine. Just in a bit of pain.' I think that defines 'understatement'. I was gabbling about going straight to the airport and getting on to a plane, but Graham said, 'Honestly, Luke, there's no need for that. I'm going to stay until she's out of hospital, until she's absolutely fine, I promise you. And then she can be at Laurie's, recuperate, sit in the sun. Anyway, Erica can look after her – she's a nurse.' That was the most terrifying scenario of all. What he seemed most insistent on was that Martha must not come. I didn't tell him there was no need to worry about that: it was the least likely thing to happen.

Afterwards, Rachel never talked about it so nobody knows exactly what happened, but at some point in the night, after Wade had picked her up, his car had come off the road halfway up

Mulholland Drive. It might have been what the police called 'a chase situation' – something to do with the tyre tracks and the speed of the car. Another driver, not at the time but at dawn, saw the car turned over and had called them. Rachel, like the well-brought-up girl she was, was wearing a seat-belt. Wade wasn't. He had been killed instantly. As the car turned over, the bonnet had caved in and had crushed Rachel's left leg. She was 'stable' but unconscious, although that might have had more to do with the alcohol and drug levels in her body than the injury itself. In the boot there were several crack pipes, a bag of cocaine and a large amount of crystal meth, cash-and-carry amounts, not personal use.

The fixers moved into action. Laurie's lawyer and the press people from the show convened at the house to work out a plan, not so much for Rachel but to distance Laurie from any potential fallout. Graham was the one on Rachel's side, although I don't suppose he was immune from self-interest either – none of this, if it got out, would be great publicity for the books or the BBC series that was due to air at Christmas.

You can do anything with money in America and there was no shortage of that, either from Laurie or from the inflated coffers of the Carter Press. The first thing was to sort out medical care. Graham called his office and had Rachel put on the company insurance policy that would routinely cover employees on business trips. Then, on the lawyer's advice, she was moved out of Glendale, the hospital in the valley that she and Wade had been taken to, and transported to Cedars-Sinai in Beverly Hills. The imperative was to distance her, as best they could, from Wade and the drugs. Anyway, Cedars-Sinai was much closer to Laurie's house.

It all seemed to be about distance, to make sure Rachel was as weightless as a balloon, floating above the earth with no connections, no cord attaching her to anything. In the forms that needed to be filled in by the hospital and insurance company, there had to be an address she was staying at in Los Angeles. On the lawyer's orders, it could not be Laurie's house so they put her down as care of Wallace Carter at his house in Brentwood. More than that, nobody even connected to Laurie was to telephone the hospital or to visit Rachel. No flowers, letters or gifts were to be sent. Her stuff was packed up, put into her suitcase and delivered to the hospital, the luggage label, with Laurie's address on it, removed and substituted with another that bore Wally's. Only the faithful Travis ignored the directives and spent most of the days after the accident hanging around the waiting area of Cedars-Sinai in case he could see her.

She was in hospital for ten days and had two operations on her leg. She would always walk with a limp. When she was released from hospital, she was installed in Wally and Ryoko's guesthouse, with a nurse to look after her. The final hurdle of distance to be vaulted was the inquest into the accident. Laurie's lawyer pulled every trick out of the bag. Because of Rachel's 'extensive and life-threatening injuries alleged to have been caused by the deceased', she was allowed not to testify in person but to give a written deposition. Her statement, prepared by Laurie's lawyer, stated that she was a publishing executive on business in Los Angeles, she had met Wade for the first time at a party that evening and he had offered her a lift. Because of her jet-lag, she had fallen asleep in his car and had no recollection or knowledge of the accident. She also had no knowledge that he was 'alleged to be a habitual and known drug user', or that the boot of the car contained any illegal substances.

After two weeks at Wally's house, when she could walk unassisted, she was taken to Cottonwood, a drug-rehab centre in Arizona, where she stayed for a month, the reason for her sojourn there stated as 'depression'. The twenty-five-thousand-dollar fee was paid by the Carter Press and deducted from the *Hayseed* royalty account without making much of a dent. Travis quietly packed his guitar, amp and surfboard, left Laurie's house without saying goodbye to anyone, drove to Tucson, where Cottonwood was, and booked into a motel for the duration.

The one detail of her 'extensive and life-threatening injuries' that I didn't know until years later was this: the accident had caused her to lose the baby she was carrying, the one she had told me about, the one she was going to get rid of.

Rick

CHRISTMAS GREETINGS 1990

It's that special time of year again when we write to our friends and loved ones. And with some guilt as we missed last year. Somehow it just snuck up on us and before we knew it, it was too late to send the letter. Where have I heard that one before???

We are both well, and Merry, too. That indeed is always a great blessing, and particularly appreciated as one hears of the problems with old friends and colleagues. The past eighteen months have brought quite a change in our lives, mostly for the good, with lots of goings-on and anticipation for the year to come.

1989 was not a great year. Someone once said that all a man's troubles begin when he leaves his village. I think the Whitcomb family are the living proof of that statement! But the great thing is you can go back to your village, and when we decided to leave the so-called City of Angels and return to Modesto back in May, I think we made the right decision. Don't worry – that party I've promised is going to happen as soon as I get the garden fixed up and Merry is more like her old self.

I'm only working part-time at KCIF, but they seem delighted to have me back. These are difficult times in broadcasting and I should know! My experience running my management company, which had many successful clients in LA, is going to come in very useful as advertising revenue drops and it becomes harder to keep those listeners loyal.

Jerrilee is working full-time as the office manager at Spring Crest Retirement Complex. She is a natural and popular leader, forever fussing about the needs of her staff and patients and working with Ros Detweiler to keep everything running smoothly. This is no small task in the world of managed care and all the problems generated from same.

The great regret here is that she has not had time to exercise her recognized talents in her favourite arts and crafts situations. Alas, even

*her marvellous yearly photo albums are two years behind entry. She
complains of being overburdened, and rightfully so.*

*The Chinese are wrong: 1990 wasn't the Year of the Horse, it was the
Year of the Lawyer – for the Whitcomb family anyway! Happily, we've
had Greg Terpstra in our corner, one of the few gentlemen in that
profession, manners being something that those lawyers in LA might
learn something about! The case is still continuing so I'm not permitted
to talk about it and I'm certainly not going to give a certain person any
more publicity than she – drat! I've given something away already! –
has anyway and not all of it good, if any of you read the* National
Enquirer.

*Our argument with that lady is professional. All I will say is this: in
my book, a management contract is a legally binding document – that's
why it's called a contract, dummy! – and you can't just decide to tear it
up with three years more to run on it. Sadly, in the world of show-
business, certain high-profile people feel they can do anything they like
just because they have the resources, but the Whitcombs are fighters –
make no mistake about that! – and one thing we're not going to put up
with is the untruths that have been circulated about my abilities in the
management field. That lady has already proved she is not totally
reliable as regards the truth, if recent stories in the press are anything
to go by.*

*All I will say is that in a short space of time I built up an enviable
management company in a city that has more management companies
than the Napa valley has wineries! Many famous people became personal
friends of Jerrilee and me and I'd gathered a lot of respect as 'the new kid
on the block'. There was nobody who wouldn't take my calls – and I'm
talking people like Les Moonves and David Geffen. These are busy guys!*

*I'm not denying that a certain person was my major client, but people
in the industry had begun to sit up and take notice of some of my other
clients, like Johnny Del Guardo, a ventriloquist/comedian who is getting
a lot of exposure on the comedy circuit. Watch out for him! Since I had to
stop managing him, CAA, one of the biggest talent agencies in the world,
has been sniffing around him and may soon take him on. That says
something about my 'abilities'.*

My theory is that Los Angeles is a very corrupting place and I'm thankful that Jerrilee and I got out before we were 'changed'. Certain people haven't been so lucky. Modesto is where our heart lies and we're delighted to be back. Our old friends have been very welcoming.

Our trip to Yosemite in the summer was one of the high points of the year. The scenery there is as magnificent as any you will see in this country and our senses were refreshed. We spent a lot of time loafing and reading and generally recharging the life batteries. Our only sadness was that Merry was unable to join us.

The one thing I'm going to say about that particular situation is that Jerrilee supports me one hundred per cent. If you're stuck between a rock and a hard place, stick with the rock! That's what that lady's been. One of our plans when all this stuff with Merry is over is to renew our marriage vows. I know that's kind of corny but, as they say, it's for better or worse and we've had 'worse' for too long. We want to celebrate the 'better' when it comes along. What we want more than anything is Merry as a bridesmaid, and back to the girl we know as a loving daughter. It'll be some party!

Sadly, Merry picked up some of that Los Angeles 'darkness', associating with the wrong people who did not have her best interests at heart, and here I do take some blame. When you work as hard as I was doing you can take your eye off the ball. It's easy to do, and we just didn't see the spiral that Merry was going into and that's a source of regret, I can tell you. You've got to protect your children and maybe we failed there a little.

Now, I'm not one to diss the various 'psychos' – analysis and therapy and so forth. I just think the family therapist we saw was not the right one for us. You know, it isn't only kids who have reason to grouse: the old parents have a few complaints too, and I felt we were sidelined. Now, of course I don't blame the therapist for reporting some of the allegations – she has codes of conduct in her chosen profession, like we all do – but Jerrilee and I felt it could have been handled in a more contained and private way. After all, a therapist doesn't know automatically what is true and what isn't. We all know how terrible domestic violence is, but it never happened in our house. I might have a short fuse, but not that short!

I would never harm anyone in my family. Ask Jerrilee. She'll tell you loud and clear.

One thing I will say is that the Modesto police could not have been more courteous, particularly Walter Reinheimer who I was at high school with. And the reporting in the Bee was very fair. I've been in news reporting myself so I understand how important accurate journalism is. All I will say is that there never were, still aren't and probably won't be any formal charges. It is simply 'under investigation' and my lawyer, Greg Terpstra, tells me everything is proceeding according to plan.

You've probably read about this thing called 'recovered-memory syndrome'. (Jerrilee thinks there are enough 'syndromes' in our lives already without another one being added!) All I'll say is this: if you're a kid playing baseball and the ball goes over the fence into your neighbour's yard just at the moment the phone rings and you have to go inside to answer it, you might have forgotten what happened to the ball when you get back outside. You think, Hmm . . . where's the ball? And then you remember. Of course! It went over the fence! That's a 'recovered memory'. Why? BECAUSE IT ACTUALLY HAPPENED! *That's what I want to say to the so-called 'experts' – how can you 'recover' a 'memory' that wasn't there in the first place? It's what I call 'invented-memory syndrome'. There – that's a new syndrome to add to the textbooks!*

None of this is a critique of Merry who, as you know, is the dearest soul in the world to Jerrilee and me. She came late in our lives and we've always regarded her as a miracle from God as it was so unexpected after so many years of the stork not arriving. She's never given us a moment's trouble – beautiful, straight-A student, a real help to her mother and me, and one of the most popular girls at Downey High. All the problems happened when we left our 'village' and went to what I call the City of Devils. You won't find that place in the index of your guidebooks!

Life's confusing enough for a girl on the fringe of womanhood. And so are memories. And, anyway, this violence she says she remembers from when she was a child, what does that mean? Is a little smack when a kid is naughty domestic violence? How many parents can put their hand on their heart and say they haven't ever touched their child?

Anyway, our message to Merry is this: we will give you all the love we have in our hearts, we respect you as a person and we want you back to that girl who baked forty separate muffins and put a candle in each one for Jerrilee's fortieth birthday. What a day that was! Many of you will remember the party we had – and the hangovers the next day! Mmm . . . must remember the recipe for that punch!

The great sadness is that Greg Terpstra has advised that I should have no contact with Merry until this situation is resolved. She has a little apartment downtown and Jerrilee visits her twice a week. She had to postpone her college plans while this was going on, and she's keeping herself busy by working part-time at Avian Accessories on J Street. She's always been great with animals and Jerrilee tells me that the shop is gaining recognition in the bird world as a producer of quality customized perches. They are more and more into the bird-breeding situation; indeed, a better solution for endangered species and the despicable practice of illegally importing exotic birds under intolerable and deadly circumstances. Say 'hi' if you're passing by. She needs a lot of support.

Not everything is bad news! Our big press release is that we're going to do Mame at the Townsend Opera this coming March. I'd get booking now – it's going to sell out fast! Jerrilee and I have wanted to do this for years, ever since we saw Angela Lansbury do it on Broadway. We think it's Mr Jerry Herman's finest show by a long stretch and we can't wait to get back on that stage. No prizes for guessing which role Jerrilee is going to do! She was born to play the madcap, eccentric Mame Dennis and I'll be playing Beauregard Burnside, her Southern beau. I'll have to do a little work on that accent, though! The title song is a hymn of love to Mame and I'm going to end this by quoting some of it. It sums up what I feel about Jerrilee, my rock, my wife, my bridge over troubled waters. Here's to you!

> You coax the blues right out of the horn, Mame,
> You charm the husk right off of the corn, Mame,
> You've got that banjo's strummin'
> And plunkin' out a tune to beat the band . . .

You've made us feel alive again,
You've given us the drive again,
To make the South revive again, Mame.
Mame! Mame! Mame! Mame!

We're looking forward to a good 1991, and thinking how fast it will be that we are entering into a new century. A time for all of us to reflect on the past and the future that is coming toward us with multiple problems and opportunity.

We wish that all of you are well, and also very much wish you and yours the best for the holiday season.

Love and best wishes to all,

Rick and Jerrilee Whitcomb

Luke

It was a song that always seemed to be around that summer, one of those infectious tunes with jangling acoustic guitars and harmonies, and a slight reggae beat. You heard it in the background, on transistor radios and ghetto-blasters in the park, and it was somehow already inside your head without you ever being conscious of how it had got there.

At university I hadn't listened to much music and wasn't part of the crowd who swapped records, went to gigs and had posters of very cool singers on their walls, so my receptors were pretty unresponsive, and it was a while before I concentrated on it enough to register the words. Even then, only half listening, I didn't make the connections. I even sort of knew that the song was by Travis Buckley but I still hadn't put two and two together. First, I'm not sure I even knew his last name, and second, LA was a long time ago and I'd done enough thinking about it at the time.

Still, there must have been a moment when I suddenly saw it – heard it – clearly, like one of those optical illusions that look like two profiles in silhouette until you see them again and realize they're actually a vase or something. What I do remember is going to HMV in Oxford Street on the way back from work and looking under B in Rock/Pop. There were two albums by him and the sleeves both had the same idea: the first was a photograph of a road sign, which gave the album its name, *Slow – Children*, and the second, a different road sign, *Ped X-ing*. His next album would probably be called *Beware – Landslides*. There were photographs of Travis on the back and they made me smile for no other reason than that they were unmistakably like him, even five years since I'd last seen him.

When I got back to the flat I shared with Adam and listened to the second album properly, the one with the song on it, I realized he had changed two things. He had tinkered with the chorus, and instead of 'I watch you through my eyes/Until the summer ends', it was now 'I'm dazzled by your eyes/Until the summer ends/ I know how hard you've tried/To force the pain to mend'. It made me laugh to think he had taken on board Erica's point about who else's eyes he could be seeing her through. I don't suppose there are many other hit songs with a lyrical contribution from Erica Hauer. And, of course, she was wrong: it had been better as it was before.

The other thing was the title: while he never actually told us the title when he was talking about it that evening in Los Angeles, he had said he was writing a song about Merry. Now it was called 'Song For Rachel'. Maybe he felt she fitted more naturally into Erica's 'special person' category, or maybe it was simply that he was trying to write a song about a girl in some kind of pain, and when he met Rachel he had realized Merry was an amateur in comparison.

After Los Angeles, after Wade, there were the years of drift. People thought that that was when she started to unravel, but that wasn't how I saw it. People talked of her as being 'different' but I don't know what she was meant to be different from. She was always the same to me, or maybe it was simply that I knew the unravelling had started much earlier and was used to it. I knew, in Laurie's incredibly irritating stream-to-river analogy, where and when the first bubbling trickle had broken through the soil.

She had money, which was either the problem or not, depending on how you looked at it. Because of some tax-planning thing, the benefit of a portion of the copyrights had been passed to Rachel and me, not by Martha – I should think she did everything she could to prevent it – but by Toppit Holdings AG, the Swiss corporation created to hold and exploit the copyright in Arthur's books in order to minimize capital-gains liability. Don't ask me. I didn't use any of it.

What she did with the money was to travel, with Claude at the beginning, but later, always on her own. When he died, when the Aids became full-blown, she was in Nova Scotia. It was often islands she went to. She liked Cozumel. She liked Sri Lanka. She liked Mount Desert Island off the coast of Maine. She quite liked Menorca, but only in the winter. She had a bad experience on the Florida Keys so she only went there once. You don't have to be Dr Freud to see the attraction of islands: contained, womb-like, elemental, safer somehow. Maybe she felt that, on an island, the access points to threat or danger might be more clearly identifiable. Or maybe she just liked the sea.

Of course she wasn't away all the time. Of course she came home sometimes, either to Linton or to the flat Martha kept in London. Her visits were often preceded by a variable but consistent set of signals that were as unmistakable to me as the equivalent signals (the dog off his food, unusual activity in the wasps' nest, a certain cloud formation at sunset) would be to an earthquake diviner. There would be a postcard from an unlikely place. Although cryptic and characteristically vague, it would contain one unequivocal statement, which was that, sad though it would be for both of us, there was no possibility of a reunion in the foreseeable future. 'Because of the palaver over the boat, it doesn't look as if I'll be able to extract myself until the New Year. Damn and blast!' ran one such postcard from Crete. Or from Cuba: 'Talk about voodoo! I had my cards read and the old girl said that home was full of dark forces, so I'm staying put for the time being.'

They were always relentlessly breezy and littered with exclamation marks. As only one card ever came from each place, I guessed they were sent when the time had come for her to go, when her bluff had been called or the game was up or some disaster had happened, and the sending of a card indicating such a firm plan to stay made her feel her departure was a sudden whim rather than the necessity it had clearly become.

Of course, she did not always head for home. It was the postcards allied to certain other significant portents that indicated an early return.

Usually, until he became too ill, there was contact from Claude, as if he could sense her getting close. It might be a phone call that didn't appear to be about Rachel at all: 'Luke?' He was the only person who could turn 'Luke' into a two-syllable word. 'That restaurant we all went to last summer, the Thai one where they did that noodle thing, you can't remember the name, can you? I'm looking for somewhere to take Justin tomorrow. It's his birthday.'

He always got round to Rachel eventually. He was lost without her. She had begun to cut him off, as she had all of us. 'Have you heard from Madam?'

'I had a postcard.'

'When is she coming back?'

'I'm not sure, Claude.'

'Will you tell her to call me?'

He was sometimes 'just in the area'. He was sometimes 'passing through on the off-chance'. The last time I saw him was in the coffee bar at the supermarket in Linton. He was wearing aviator sunglasses and sharing a doughnut with a boy who was young even by Claude's standards. He looked terrible. He had always been thin, but not like he was now.

As I walked towards him, he rose from the orange plastic chair with a papal gesture of the arms. 'This *is* a surprise,' he said.

'Why? I live here.'

'Yes, but *I'm* just passing through. Isn't this extraordinary?' He turned to his friend. '*This* is who I was talking about,' he said, in a what-a-coincidence voice. 'Rachel's little brother. *Luke*. You know.' They exchanged a glance that had a certain conspiratorial content. He turned back to me. 'We're ploughing our way through Pevsner.' The idea that the medieval churches of Dorset were on, or even part of, his silent friend's agenda required a certain suspension of disbelief. 'Is your . . .' he mouthed 'mother' '. . . in residence? The thing is, I'm still trying to find all that crusader stuff she asked me to look up so I'm *far* too embarrassed to speak to her.' And then, in a down-to-business voice, 'Now. Have you heard from Rachel?'

The other thing that tended to happen was an influx of packages delivered for Rachel. They tended to arrive within a few days of each other, so presumably they had been ordered in one go with some cumulative purpose that was hard to fathom from their diverse contents.

A catalogue from an outsize women's wear wholesaler was curious enough for someone who had flirted with anorexia while other girls were going through their pony phase, but when it arrived in the same post as the brochure from a company that manufactured prosthetic limbs, even Martha raised an eyebrow. There was the Hot-As-Hell Creole Spice catalogue, the Hans Christian Andersen Museum in Copenhagen's Christmas gift catalogue, a list of Bob Dylan bootlegs that could be ordered from a PO box number in Germany, the Philadelphia cream cheese cookbook, a bibliography of large-print books and their publishers, issued by some society for the blind with a special supplement of books-on-tape.

I suspect, although I don't know for certain, that on what was to be her last day in wherever she was, when whoever she was with had dumped her or when her credit card had been snipped in half or swallowed whole by the machine because she hadn't bothered to pay the bills, she was filled with a sense of purpose and would begin telephoning. 'I wonder if you can help me,' she would say, when she got through, or 'Would it be possible for me to speak to the person who deals with . . .' She would certainly want to explain to someone the precise reason for her request, to get them to understand her rather unusual need for the heavy-duty fish kettle as soon as possible or why it was essential that the strimmer be delivered by Friday or why she had to see the handbook of registered children's entertainers so urgently.

Then, because children had suddenly come into her mind, she might get on to the firm that made children's clothes from natural undyed fabrics, and a whole host of possibilities would spin in front of her like a roulette wheel. Leaving might not be such a bad thing. In fact, there was now an actual reason to leave. She could set up an office or a second-hand-clothes shop or a consultancy business and ... And what? Something good would come of all this, even though Julian or Pascal or Pietro had been such a shit. Yes, she would go home.

A taxi would come up the drive a day later, or a week later. Rachel would be pale and tired, but buzzy with enthusiasm for her new scheme. Martha tended to keep out of her way as much as possible, and for the first few days Rachel would spend a lot of time on the telephone, dropping her voice if anyone came into the room. She would only talk about her project in the most general terms. She had spotted 'a niche in the market', or she had realized that 'There's one service you can't get for love or money outside London.' The idea had come to her 'on a *bateau-mouche* going under the Pont Neuf' or 'when I found this extraordinary shop *literally* in the middle of nowhere'. But what the idea was, precisely, was not to be divulged until she had done more research.

But then things began to change: she spent less time on the phone; her morning appearances became later and later until sometimes she didn't appear at all; she didn't want any lunch, she was going to have a sandwich on the run; Claude was arriving any minute and there was so much to do before he came. And then, most telling of all, she began to spend all day in Arthur's study, with only an espresso machine, which had arrived by special delivery from Rome, for company.

Like a child trying to run away from home, she had reached the garden gate and then, too frightened to go on, had returned to what she was trying to leave: all her schemes, which had once seemed so fertile and full of promise, finally evolved, by some strange Darwinian process only understandable to her, into *Hayseed* projects. What had begun during one particular stay as a business plan for opening a chain of sandwich shops, to be financed by someone she had met on Long Island, morphed into a catalogue of plant references in the *Hayseed* books, which she was going to sell in garden centres – only half finished, anyway, by the time Claude appeared in his new reconditioned MG Sprite to whisk her off to the villas of the Veneto or a boat on the Marne. I would run into people in London who knew her, and I would politely answer their questions about the annotated manuscripts Rachel was preparing for the University of Texas, or the limited edition of Lila's unused drawings she was working on, or the *Hayseed* board game she was devising 'with the people who invented Trivial Pursuit'.

All the while she travelled, and even after she came home for the last time and the travelling stopped, there was one thing she never lost, one thing she always managed to keep with her when she was mugged in Cyprus or held up at gunpoint in Costa Rica or her luggage was lost by the airline or stolen from her hotel room: a stone, worn round her neck on a silver chain, with a chakra mandala symbol painted on it in red, the symbol that indicates grounding, balance of physical body and clearing of fear.

Mr Toppit has come and gone. These were the enigmatic words that were found scrawled on the wall in Rachel's room after she had gone. Some of the newspaper stories talked about her 'escape', but I remembered Dr Honey's sanctimonious statement that Broadmeadow was not a prison and I preferred to believe that she had simply checked out.

In the days that followed, I found a strange fascination in seeing our lives spread across the papers. Unlike Laurie, we didn't have fleets of lawyers and press people to hush up the story. Anyway, as Dr Honey had said to me, they weren't strangers to the children of well-known figures at Broadmeadow and so many members of staff were probably getting backhanders from newspapers and clicking away with secret cameras that even Laurie's crack team would have had difficulty in plugging the holes.

Without the graffito the story might have faded away quite quickly but it brought another element into play: the mysterious words were just enough to shift the narrative up a gear and give the papers the opportunity to rehash the old stories about the phenomenon of the books but with a quirky twist of mystery. '*Hayseed* Girl's Cryptic Message – Clue To Disappearance?' The question mark in the *Daily Mail* story was appropriate because nobody had any real idea whether Rachel's words meant anything or were just one of the many unanswerable – or, at any rate, unanswered – enigmas that were such a major factor in the success of the *Hayseed* saga.

The other element of the story that intrigued people was that Rachel was not on her own, which added a kind of Bonnie and Clyde spin to it: she had decamped with Matthew Sumner, the strange boy I had met at Broadmeadow, the one who had told me he knew who Mr Toppit was. He should have talked to Merry: they could have compared notes. My guess is that it was him who had scrawled the graffito. For one thing, it didn't look like Rachel's handwriting, though I admit it's hard to recognize anyone's handwriting when the writing implement is a paintbrush. It was too crude a gesture for Rachel, cheap and on-the-nose, too obvious, really.

The stories – for once – were less about me than about Martha and Rachel. Of course, I was described, as usual, as 'eponymous' in some of the more upmarket papers, not strictly accurate because my name is Luke Hayman, not Luke Hayseed, and, also as usual, many of the pieces printed a childhood photograph of me alongside one of Lila's drawings of Luke. But luckily I led a life 'away from the limelight', as one newspaper put it, so apart from retelling the story of my 'arrest' the night before I had left for Los Angeles five years before, there wasn't much to add about me.

There had been articles about us in the past, but now the tone of the pieces was quite different. The *Hayseed* story had been shoehorned into that particular arena where journalists drop lottery winners whose lives are destroyed by money, and movie stars who crash and burn: we were a living illustration of the Price of Success. The problem was that Rachel had not ignored whatever limelight the *Hayseed* phenomenon had shone on our lives. She would always speak to journalists, much to Martha's fury, so there were many old quotes by her that now found their way into the newspaper pieces, and many references were made to a particularly shambolic interview she had done on television when the series aired. Even at the time it had caused comment, although the most pejorative adjective used had been 'rambling'. Now, 'sources close to the family' were quoted as 'alleging' she had been 'drunk' or 'under the influence of drugs'. It was reported that her disastrous interview had caused her family to insist on her going into rehab for the first time. Untrue: she had already done that stint at Cottonwood after Wade.

In the piece entitled 'Troubled Legacy of a Publishing Phenomenon', Rachel and I were described as 'heirs to a pot of literary gold'. From time to time, Martha had been labelled 'eccentric', but now the tone of the pieces was less kind: she had become 'reclusive and bitter' and, in one article, 'viciously protective of her late husband's heritage'. She was 'estranged from her children' and 'at loggerheads with the publishers'. While the first statement could be construed as relatively accurate, in Rachel's case at least, the second was not: the court case with the Carter Press had been resolved some years before and her relationship with Graham was reasonably calm.

As the days wore on, what had seemed like a minor blip in Rachel's chaotic life acquired a more worrying dimension. There had been many times when we didn't know precisely where she was, but somebody would hear from her: me, or Claude when he was alive, sometimes Martha. Even Lila got the odd postcard. This time there were enough unusual elements to make it different. The graffito, for one thing – even if she hadn't done it herself, she must have been party to it. Then there was Matthew Sumner: not her style, I would have thought, from my one meeting with him – too young, too needy, too insubstantial. As it turned out, I was wrong. Then there was the most worrying thing of all, which only I knew about: how she had been the last time I saw her, when I had visited her at Broadmeadow.

It was like LA all over again: although she was missing, she wasn't a missing person – she was an adult and had presumably left Broadmeadow of her own volition – and while the police were helpful, they were clearly not going to instigate a full-scale man-hunt for an over-privileged girl with a history of unreliability and drug issues.

There wasn't enough oxygen to keep the story burning for long, but just when it seemed exhausted, Matthew Sumner turned up. '*Hayseed* Boy Found' was the irritatingly imprecise way it was described. I didn't often feel proprietorial but I did have a moment of outrage that he had stolen my crown. He was spotted early in the morning by someone he had been at school with just a few miles from his home in Weybridge. Rather pathetically, he was buying a Crunchie for breakfast.

He was 'unharmed', as the papers had it, though I couldn't imagine what harm was meant to come to him: he and Rachel appeared to have travelled rather slowly from one end of Surrey to the other, not crossed the Gobi Desert. They had been staying in a bed-and-breakfast – another troublingly uncharacteristic element for Rachel – outside Weybridge, but by the time the police got there she was gone. Some days later Matthew was shipped back to Broadmeadow to continue his treatment for what the papers called 'a nervous disorder'.

Then there was an interview with his parents entitled 'Every Parent's Nightmare'. The piece had one of those cute photographs of Matthew aged about twelve, smiling and gap-toothed in his school uniform, so perfect in its depiction of innocence that it can only tempt fate and end up one day in a newspaper as an icon of what the subject was like in the good years, the years before God had told him to stab his classmates during school assembly or whip out a Kalashnikov in a Burger King or end up, in Matthew's case, incarcerated in Broadmeadow with borderline schizophrenia caused, in his parents' view, by smoking marijuana.

Matthew had been a perfect child – weren't they always? – a keen footballer and a grade-six flautist, popular at school, plucky but caring, top of the class. It was a 'loving family', churchgoing, of course, in which an unspecified but definite set of values had been instilled in Matthew and his younger sister. So far, so numbingly predictable: such an obvious set-up for the fall that, inevitably, would come.

And so it did: bad influences, peer-group drug-taking, trouble with the police, behaviour and control issues, eating disorder, self-harming, unhealthy obsessions. It was at this point that a degree of blame crept into the interview. There was a reference to the 'malign influence' of the *Hayseed* books, how Matthew seemed fixated on the 'terrifying' Mr Toppit. I was sick of everyone behaving as if he was real: if Matthew was of an obsessive bent, he could just as well have become fixated on Saruman in *The Lord of the Rings* or somebody from *Struwwelpeter* or one of the truly unpleasant characters in the Bible, whom he might have heard about when he sang in the church choir. God, for example.

It was 'a regrettable coincidence' with 'unfortunate consequences' that Rachel had been at Broadmeadow at the same time as Matthew: she 'fed his obsession'; he had become 'withdrawn'. It was here that the paper's lawyers had clearly got out their pencils: a sexual relationship was 'alleged' to have started between them, instigated, of course, by her. I would have liked to tell the parents that he should have been so lucky. He was probably gay. He had, after all, told me he had fucked Toby Luttrell. Anyway, they were praying for him, praying for a return to the boy whose ambition, once upon a time, was to be a fireman, who was happiest when he was flying his kite, the boy who might once have baked forty separate muffins for his mother's birthday and put a candle on each. That was what I loved about Rachel: she would never have done that in a million years.

By then, the police had been in touch with us. They couldn't have behaved more courteously: they telephoned Martha to say they had interviewed Matthew Sumner and he had made a statement she might care to see. Would she be able to present herself at the main police station in Guildford? No, she wouldn't. Why couldn't they put it in the post? Politely, they informed her that it was not 'policy' to release confidential statements. Grumpily, she told them that I would have to do it.

They were very nice at the police station. They gave me tea and biscuits and put me in a little room with a table and chair. A file was waiting for me with the statement in it, ready for me to read.

INTERVIEW BETWEEN DC JANE CLARK AND MATTHEW SUMNER. ALSO PRESENT: DR DAVID FORD (SUBJECT'S GP).

INTERVIEW COMMENCED 3.05 P.M., 24 AUGUST 1995

DC JANE CLARK: *What were your intentions in leaving Broadmeadow Clinic?*
MATTHEW SUMNER: [inaudible]
CLARK: *I'm sorry, Matthew. Could you please speak up?*
SUMNER: *To find him.*
CLARK: *To find who?*
SUMNER: *Why do you want to know?*
CLARK: *We are trying to establish the circumstances of your and Miss Hayman's leaving Broadmeadow Clinic.*
SUMNER: *We were going to find him.*
CLARK: *To find who?*
SUMNER: *Someone.*
CLARK: *Were you on medication?*
SUMNER: *I stopped taking the pills. They made me sleepy.*
CLARK: *Are you on medication now?*
DR DAVID FORD: [interrupting] *Yes, he is.*
CLARK: *Was Miss Hayman on medication?*
SUMNER: *She tried to score in Croydon.*
CLARK: *Is that the person you were trying to find? A drug-dealer?*
SUMNER: [laughs]
CLARK: *Then who was it?*
SUMNER: *I don't want to say his name.*

CLARK: *Will you write it down?*

RECORDING PAUSED 3.12 P.M.

RECORDING RESTARTED 3.15 P.M.

CLARK: *May I say his name?*

SUMNER: *If you want to.*

CLARK: *Why did you want to find Mr Toppit?*

SUMNER: *He came to Broadmeadow. I think I saw him. I think he had been there.*

CLARK: *Did Miss Hayman see him?*

SUMNER: *No. I told her, though. I told her we had to find him. He had gone.*

CLARK: *Where had he gone?*

SUMNER: *I can't tell you. He'll be angry.*

CLARK: *Did Miss Hayman want to find him?*

SUMNER: *She had to. I told her she had to.*

CLARK: *Was that when you decided to leave?*

SUMNER: *She wasn't talking then. She didn't talk to people, but she talked to me. She knew she had to come.*

CLARK: *Why did you want her to come with you?*

SUMNER: *I wanted us to be like blood brothers. I wanted us to cut ourselves and mix our blood. I've cut myself before. [*Holds up arms and shows scars.*] She was my best friend.*

CLARK: *Were you having sexual relations?*

SUMNER: *[inaudible]*

CLARK: *Was she your girlfriend?*

SUMNER: *She wanted to. I think she wanted to. She was intense. She frightened me. I didn't like it when she didn't talk.*

CLARK: *Where do you think Miss Hayman is now?*

SUMNER: *I need to find her.*

CLARK: *Do you know where she might be?*

SUMNER: *She wanted to go to Lindisfarne. She said we would be safe because of the causeway and the tides.*

CLARK: *Is that where you think Mr Toppit is?*

SUMNER: *[*becomes visibly upset*] No. No. I said we had to find him.*

He wouldn't be there. I tried to make her understand. She [inaudible]

FORD: *I think we'd better stop now.*

INTERVIEW TERMINATED 3.34 P.M.

It was a long way to go for something so short. Within five minutes I had finished. I hadn't even touched the tea. I spoke to Jane Clark on the way out. She said they had alerted the Northumbria Police about Lindisfarne. I knew Rachel wouldn't go there, but I didn't tell her that. Then, delving into her handbag, she asked if I would autograph one of the books for her children. On the train back from Guildford, I locked myself into the lavatory and cried. It was just a one-off thing. I wouldn't be doing it again.

Two days later, despite being under what they called 'increased surveillance', Matthew Sumner vanished once again from Broad-meadow. Well, it wasn't a prison. His parents were reported to be considering legal action.

I had some holiday left. The publishing house where I worked – not the Carter Press – offered to put it down as compassionate leave. I said no. It wasn't time for that yet. I called Martha and said I would come to Linton for a few days.

'Are you sure?' she said, as if it was the most extraordinary notion.

'You might like the company.'

'I wouldn't if I were you. It's so hot here. You'll be bored.'

'I'd like to.'

'You'll have to look after yourself. I can't do any cooking.'

She was right. It was hot. It had been hot all summer. The garden was parched and tired and there were great brown patches on the lawn. The woods behind were a dull green, as if they'd been covered with a fine layer of dust. Inside the house it was dry and musty. All the windows were closed and most of the curtains, as usual, were drawn. Martha didn't want the sunlight to fade the pictures. It was silent when I let myself in. I called Martha, but there was no answer. When I went into the sitting room, I could see her in the far corner on her hands and knees.

'One of our ashtrays is missing,' she said. 'You've got to be careful. It's dry as a tinderbox here.'

I wasn't the one who took sleeping pills and smoked in bed. 'There's one,' I said, pointing at the table.

'I know that's there. There's another. I might have knocked it on to the floor. Help me look.'

I hadn't seen Martha for a while, although I'd talked to her quite a lot recently because of the Rachel stuff. She seemed older. Her hair had been pinned up but it was collapsing.

'I told the TV people no,' she said. 'You didn't want to do it, did you?'

'Not really.' They had done an item on the local news about Rachel going missing and had asked Martha if she wanted to make an appeal for people who might have seen her to come forward.

'I suppose it's August,' she said, lighting a cigarette. 'Nothing happens in August. Your clothes, baby – don't you have to dress properly for work? Your hair's too short.'

'I'm not *at* work.'

'Just because they haven't got enough to fill the news I don't know why they expect us to sort it out for them.'

'I went to Guildford.'

'Oh, those awful suburbs. Mile after mile of ribbon development.'

'There wasn't much in the boy's statement.' There didn't seem any point in telling her about it.

'Who are those people, those Sumners? Why can't they mind their own business? Not everybody's longing to be in the newspapers. Have you eaten?'

'I had something on the train.'

'Because there's nothing here. You might have to go into town. Take the car.'

'I think I'll go for a walk.'

'A *walk*? You'll burn up.'

'Not for long. It's shady in the woods.'

'I'll be resting when you come back. Don't let me sleep too long, will you?'

That was day one: a short walk just to acclimatize myself. It was on day two that I began to stake them out properly, the woods. I took a rucksack with me, some food and drink. I didn't know how long I'd be – whether they were there already or whether they had yet to arrive. Although it was early quite a few people were around, cheerily saying, 'Good morning!' to me, as if there was some bond that had to be acknowledged between strangers who happened to be sharing the same woodland path.

In the books, the Darkwood is always deserted. Our woods weren't. People from the town walked their dogs, and kids rode mountain bikes along the paths. And, of course, there were the *Hayseed* faithful, fewer than there used to be but still a significant presence at weekends, as if the woods were a free *Hayseed* theme park.

The difference between us – Rachel and me – and the faithful was this: we really knew the woods; they didn't. They tended to stick to the paths. They were amateurs. They didn't want to get their shoes muddy. There were something like three hundred acres of woodland and Martha kept the main tracks cleared but the rest of it had become even more overgrown and jungle-like than it was when we were children. I shouldn't think I'd set foot in them for five years and certainly hadn't spent longer than half an hour there for much more than that, but all the markers we knew when we were young that led us to our places were still there, if you knew how to see them. We didn't invent the folklore of the woods. It was passed on to us by Arthur: he had grown up there too.

There was the holm oak a few minutes up the main track that had split and grown up like a giant V and hid a little path that went up the hill to what we called Foxhole, a low cave that you could squeeze yourself into, which we believed, had it not been blocked by boulders, led to a secret tunnel that took you to the house. In the books, it was one of the ways Mr Toppit travelled unseen.

There was the little hut that when we were children had still had a wooden roof. Now it was completely collapsed, but it still had its floor made of pine-cones set into the earth. About thirty yards above it, through tangled undergrowth, was our tree-house – actually a large piece of metal railing that had been winched into a tree and laid on its side on the upper branches to make a flat platform.

For the time being I wasn't going to any of those places. I had decided to head straight for what we called the Clearing: a strange formation of oak trees planted in an uneven circle, with a rough piece of limestone jutting up from the earth in the middle that we thought was an altar. That was where I was going to wait for a while.

At lunchtime I decided to move on. The woods were planted on a hill and I headed upwards to the part that flattened out on the top. We called it the Village. When the woods were planted, maybe two hundred years before, a series of ornamental paths had been laid out there at different levels so they criss-crossed each other with little brick bridges taking the higher ones over the lower. Most of the bridges had collapsed but there were still one or two that you could use. It was so overgrown now that foliage covered some of the lower paths, making them almost into tunnels. In the books, Luke Hayseed believed that the area was the remains of a medieval plague village and there were bodies buried everywhere. It was the epicentre of Toppit activity.

I slept for a while in the shade, my head resting on my backpack, and when I woke, the sun was lower and light was slanting through the trees. Slowly I circled back towards the house, taking a different route but ending up at the Clearing. As I was leaving, something caught my eye – the sun glinted on a shiny object under one of the trees. It was a little pile of five chocolate wrappers. This wasn't unusual in the woods, but I was far off the beaten track, away from the main paths where you would find all manner of junk strewn around. I bent down and picked them up. As clues go, it wasn't much – Matthew wasn't the only person to eat Crunchies – but my guess was that they were his binge of choice. They had arrived. It was getting dark and I wouldn't be able to find them now, but I would come back early the next day.

When I got home Martha was already eating her supper and smoking a cigarette. Doreen had left her some little ramekins of broccoli in cheese sauce, covered with silver foil in the fridge, which she had heated. I made myself scrambled eggs and joined her.

'Where have you been?' she asked, only mildly interested.

'In the woods. Walking.'

'You can't have been all this time. The whole day.'

I shrugged. 'It's good to take some exercise. I sit in an office every day.' With my abysmal track record in sport at school, becoming the kind of person who took exercise would have required a change of personality so extreme that even Martha might have noticed, but she tended to take things at face value.

'Get me another drink, will you? A small one. Vodka, no ice.' I don't know why she bothered to tell me: her drinks order had been set in stone since I was a child.

When it was time for bed and she was going round switching off the lights – it never occurred to her that other people might want to stay up later than she did – I said, 'You remember when I was in America?'

'Have you counted the ashtrays?'

'Staying with Laurie? When Rachel came out?'

'Was there one in the kitchen? Do you ever hear from Laurie?'

'Not since I was in LA.' I did know that Laurie had weathered her storms. Her show was now on Channel 4 in the mornings. I sometimes watched it.

'I never liked her much,' Martha said.

'I met Wally Carter when I was there.'

'Wally,' she said, with an expression of distaste on her face. 'Didn't he die?'

'Yes. A couple of years ago. Graham told me. He was pretty doddery when I met him. He told me something. He told me about

Jordan, what happened to him.' I wasn't going to go into any detail. I just wanted her to know that I knew, for the record.

It needed an action replay, really. If you'd slowed down the film you might have seen something pass across her face. Otherwise you wouldn't have noticed. It was just too fleeting.

'Don't put the butts in the rubbish,' she said. 'There's a lot of paper in there. If you're going to do that, put water in the ashtray first. It's like a tinderbox in here.' Then she picked up her various bits and pieces, her book, cigarettes and spectacles, took a last look round the room and went out, leaving one light for me to turn off. I could hear the stairs creaking as she went up to her bedroom.

Day three did not get off to the start I had planned. For one thing I overslept. I had meant to get up at dawn. The other thing that happened, which I could not have foreseen, was that Lila turned up. In fact, that was what woke me: the sound of car doors slamming. When I got downstairs, Martha was at the front door and Lila was being manoeuvred through it in her wheelchair by the taxi driver. This was the last thing I needed. I was late already.

Martha threw a helpless look at me. 'Lila, this is insane!'

'No, Martha. What is insane is that you never call me back. I've left message after message for you. I know you don't want to burden other people with your worries, but you don't have to suffer alone. What you are going through, my darling! Oh, poor Rachel. I know she'll be all right. She'll turn up, of course she will.'

'We're fine, Lila. Anyway, Luke's here. He's helping. He's been marvellous,' Martha said desperately.

'I'm glad you've woken up to your responsibilities, Luke. Martha told me how seldom you come to see her. Did you get my birthday card? Perhaps it was lost in the post.'

'No, I did get it. Thank you.'

'It does not take much to send a little acknowledgement, you know. Just a stamp. And a little lick.'

'Lila, you really mustn't stay,' Martha said firmly. Then she produced her trump card. 'You won't be able to go to the lavatory. You know there isn't one on the ground floor.'

338

'No, it is all arranged. Trevor is coming back to pick me up after lunch. I have made smoked-salmon sandwiches on brown bread for us. The wholemeal one you like. And don't worry about the lavatory arrangements, my dear. I have a little bag. It was changed this morning so I will be fine. It's very discreet. Perhaps you could wheel me through to the sitting room, Luke. I must let poor Trevor go.'

I felt like a trapped animal. The wheelchair was much lighter than I'd thought it would be. Lila seemed to have shrunk since I'd last seen her. You could almost have fitted someone else into the chair with her: maybe her doctor had ordered one several sizes too large by mistake. As I pushed it, a terrible gurgling noise came from somewhere underneath her.

'What I didn't bring was The Big Book of Hayseed. So heavy! We're up to volume six,' Lila said proudly. 'I've just finished clipping the pieces about Rachel departing from her clinic. What an unpleasant tone some of them have. So unnecessary.'

'Oh, Lila,' Martha said, exasperated now, 'you don't have to include everything.'

'You know me, Martha. I'm a completist.'

I deposited them in the sitting room. I had to get out to the woods. 'Will you make us some coffee?' Martha said. She looked so frantic that I couldn't refuse. It wouldn't take long.

From the kitchen, I could hear Lila talking. 'We should go back to our German lessons,' she said. 'We haven't talked about our dear relations for, oh, so many years. Such a long time.'

It was going back more than a decade, to the days when they had sat talking about the family Lila had invented to help Martha with her German conversation, the prosperous Untermeyers in turn-of-the-century Lübeck, with their sick relatives and thriving shipping business.

'Oh, really, I can't,' Martha said. 'I'm too rusty.'

'It will relax you. It will take your mind off things.'

When I took the tray through, Lila had already started. I had done enough German at school to be able to understand.

'We're all so worried about Uncle Heinrich's leg,' she was saying. 'He's a martyr to illness.' I almost laughed. I remembered Rachel and me being hauled over the coals for asking Lila how Uncle Heinrich's treatment for syphilis was coming along. 'Cousin Liesl is distraught, particularly with Christmas so close.'

Martha was staring directly ahead. She wasn't saying anything.

Lila went on, 'Since he returned from Bremerhaven it's got much worse. Such a long journey! Liesl said the twins missed him so much they cried themselves to sleep every night.' Silence. 'Martha?' Lila pronounced it in the German way, 'Marta'.

With nothing from Martha she continued, 'The dear man! He's only recently got over influenza. And their little Fritzi – I hope he's not going to catch it. He's so smart in his sailor suit. Such a bundle of energy, that child! So looking forward to Christmas! The decorations Mutti ordered from Hamburg have just arrived. The tree will be spectacular!'

There was a long pause. Martha's head was bowed and tears were running down her face. Finally, in halting German, she whispered, 'The poor little boy. I hope no harm comes to him.'

I would have stayed, I really would. I wanted to, but I couldn't wait any longer. I had to go. I should have gone hours ago. I put the coffee tray down and crept out of the room as unobtrusively as I could. As I reached the door to get outside Martha called my name, but by then it was too late. I was out. I had gone.

My heart was beating fast when I reached the woods. The sun was higher now, rising above the trees. There must have been a lot of dew in the night because everything smelled so fresh. I was running, not fast, more like a trot. I wasn't sure where I was heading but it would come to me, like an instinct. There would be a sign. There were always signs if you knew how to see them.

I turned off the main path at the big V and headed upwards towards the tree-house. I thought that was where they might have slept. I climbed up – rather harder to do than I remembered – but there was nothing up there. I considered shouting for them, but thought better of it: I absolutely didn't want to frighten them off.

I wanted to go to the quarry next, but it was more difficult to find than I'd thought because the noose appeared to have been taken down – a piece of frayed rope that had always hung from a huge oak behind which was the track that led there. Without it I was travelling blind, not helped by the fact that the woods were so much more overgrown than they'd used to be that you couldn't tell what was a path and what wasn't.

When I finally reached it I found something. The quarry was a great bowl-like crater that had been excavated out of the hill. Arthur told us that the stone from which our house was built had come from there. One side was more or less sheer, too steep to climb although we had tried enough times, and at the bottom, where it was sheltered, there was the remains of a fire. It was still warm, and peeking out of the ashes were more chocolate wrappers. I wasn't some kind of Red Indian tracker like you see in movies so I had no idea how long ago they had left, but I knew I was getting close.

In the end, it wasn't difficult. They were at the Clearing. Rachel was lying on the ground and Matthew was next to her, leaning against one of the trees. He was whimpering like a child. You'd have thought, with eating all that chocolate, he would have been spotty, but his skin was extraordinarily clear: pale, almost blue, particularly under his eyes.

I think he thought I was going to hit him: he cowered as I knelt down by them.

'She wanted me to,' he said. 'She asked me to.'

His arms were cut and bleeding. He held them up to show me, as if that proved something. All it proved was that he lacked the nerve to carry it through for himself. All it proved was that he would never be the person she was. He didn't have it in him.

'Fuck off,' I said. I didn't have time for him. He was irrelevant.

Her blood would go all over me but I didn't care. I lifted her head and laid it in my lap. She was cold, but damp: clammy, I think you'd call it. Her hair smelled of the earth and leaves. I licked my fingers and tried to wipe some of the dirt off her face. I undid the chakra pendant from round her neck and put it into my pocket. I didn't want it to go missing.

I said it was the only thing Rachel always kept with her through her years of drift. In fact, that wasn't true, but I would not discover the other thing she had kept until some days later, when sorting out her things could be construed less as an intrusion than an attempt to be systematic. It was in her handbag, behind a little flap that you might easily have missed in a cursory rummage. She had always told me that the only significant thing she recovered from the bonfire Martha had had after Arthur's death was the scrap of a story called 'The Trip to Le Touquet', but there had been something else. From the moment she found it, her plan must have been to destroy it but the act of doing so became a curiously drawn-out process, a characteristically long work-in-progress. I doubt she would ever have done it. And, anyway, it wouldn't have mattered as long as she managed to prevent me seeing it. That was what she was trying to do – to protect me. She'd thought I would be upset.

What was in her handbag, behind the little flap that you could easily have missed in a cursory rummage, was a couple of stained and charred bits of paper written on in Arthur's hand: the first pages of the first *Hayseed* book. I suppose you might call it a first draft:

When you were young, or maybe not so long ago, not very far from where you live, or perhaps a little closer, Jordan Hayseed lived in a big old house. The woods behind the house were called the Darkwood and Jordan Hayseed thought he owned them, that they were his, that they were in his blood. If trees and leaves and brown earth could travel through veins, they did so through Jordan's. But if he thought he was the only one to have them in his blood, he was very wrong, as wrong as it was possible to be.

I had to read it twice to spot the mistake: *Jordan Hayseed lived in a big old house.* Or not the mistake, depending on how you looked at it. Maybe I was the mistake. What had made Arthur change the main character? He had begun the first book after Jordan had died, had written it about his first son, the one lost to time and history. And he had imagined the kind of child he might have grown up to be, so unlike me. Years later, before the first one was published, maybe when Lila offered to do the illustrations, he had simply altered the name from 'Jordan' to 'Luke', an act as simple as stealing down to the tree on Christmas morning while the children are still asleep and changing the name on a present. And that was what they were, the books – a present, a gift, to me: unwanted, unasked-for maybe, but nonetheless valuable for that. The one thing I found hard to forgive Arthur for – and it's odd to use the words 'forgive' and 'Arthur' in the same sentence: this was a man who had nothing to atone for, the one person with true dignity in this whole story – was that he didn't give the present to both of us. It would have been so easy: *When you were young, or maybe not so long ago, not very far from where you live, or perhaps a little closer, Rachel and Luke Hayseed lived in a big old house* . . . There was enough to go round. I wouldn't have minded at all.

But, as I say, I wouldn't discover all this until later. Now I'm sitting in the woods. It's getting hot, not as hot as it will be by midday, but still warm enough to sit and feel the sun on our faces. Her head is a comfortable weight on me, like a heavy blanket. I don't know how long I'll be able to stay there before I have to start doing all the stuff that needs doing, but I'm not going to be hurried. All I want to think about is Rachel, but Martha and Lila keep straying in with their stories of Christmas in Lübeck, candles flickering on the tree, the carriage wheels making tracks on the fresh snow as they take their presents to Uncle Heinrich's father, the Judge, while the little twins, Anna-Elisabeth and Elisabeth-Anna, are shouting with excitement after decorating the tree with the new ornaments that Mutti ordered specially from Hamburg and Fritzi, that bundle of energy, looking quite the little man in his new sailor suit.